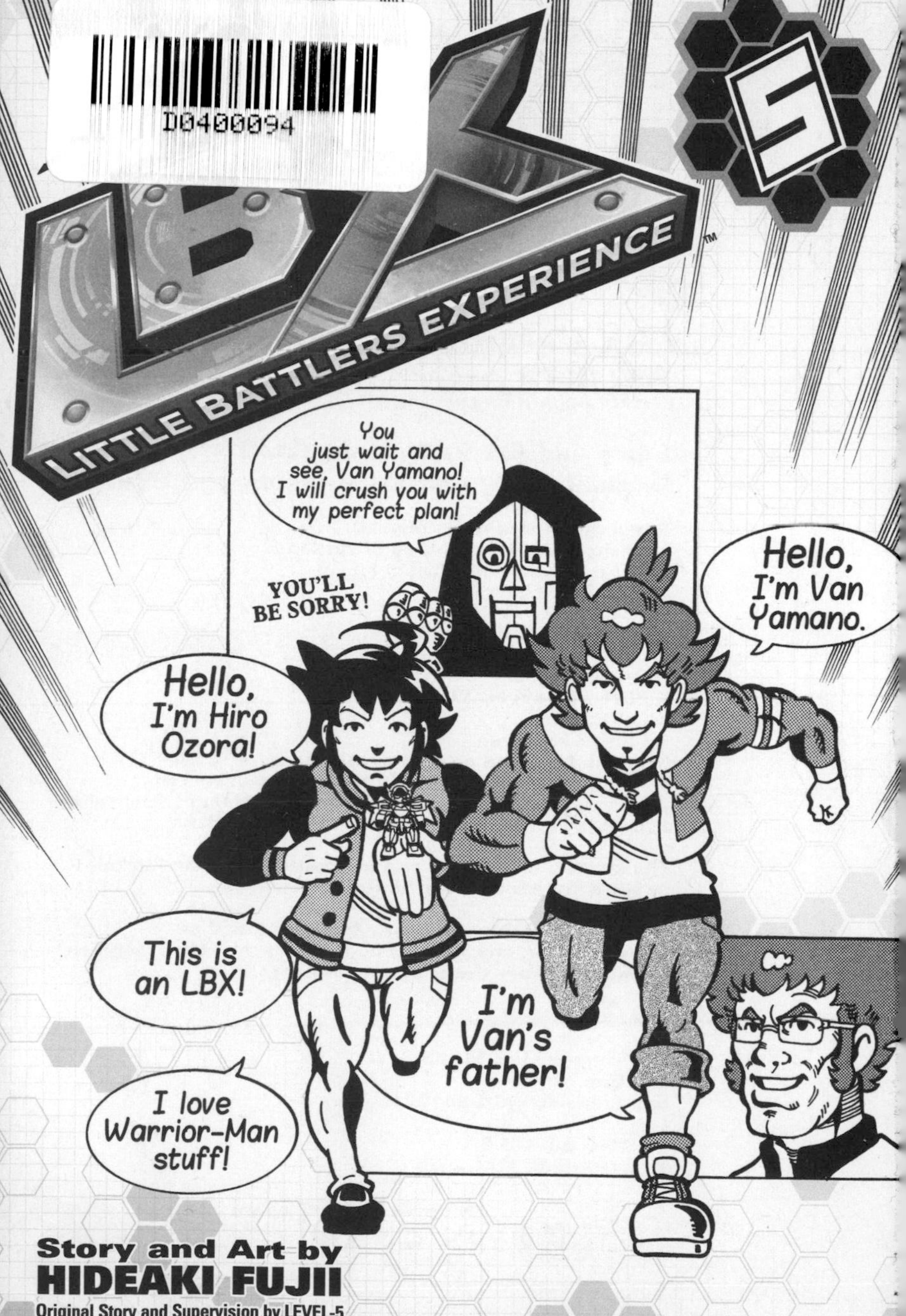
LBX
LITTLE BATTLERS EXPERIENCE™
5
You just wait and see, Van Yamano! I will crush you with my perfect plan!
YOU'LL BE SORRY!
Hello, I'm Van Yamano.
Hello, I'm Hiro Ozora!
I'm Van's father!
This is an LBX!
I love Warrior-Man stuff!

Story and Art by
HIDEAKI FUJII
Original Story and Supervision by LEVEL-5

LBX Volume 5
NEW HOPE
Perfect Square Edition

Story and Art by Hideaki FUJII
Original Story and Supervision by LEVEL-5

Translation/Tetsuichiro Miyaki
English Adaptation/Aubrey Sitterson
Lettering/Annaliese Christman
Design/Izumi Evers
Editor/Joel Enos

DANBALL SENKI Vol.5
by Hideaki FUJII
© 2011 Hideaki FUJII
© LEVEL-5 Inc.
All rights reserved.
Original Japanese edition published by SHOGAKUKAN.
English translation rights in the United States of
America, Canada, the United Kingdom, Ireland, Australia
and New Zealand arranged with SHOGAKUKAN.

Printed in the U.S.A.

Published by VIZ Media, LLC
P.O. Box 77010
San Francisco, CA 94107

10 9 8 7 6 5 4 3 2 1
First printing, May 2015

www.perfectsquare.com

www.viz.com

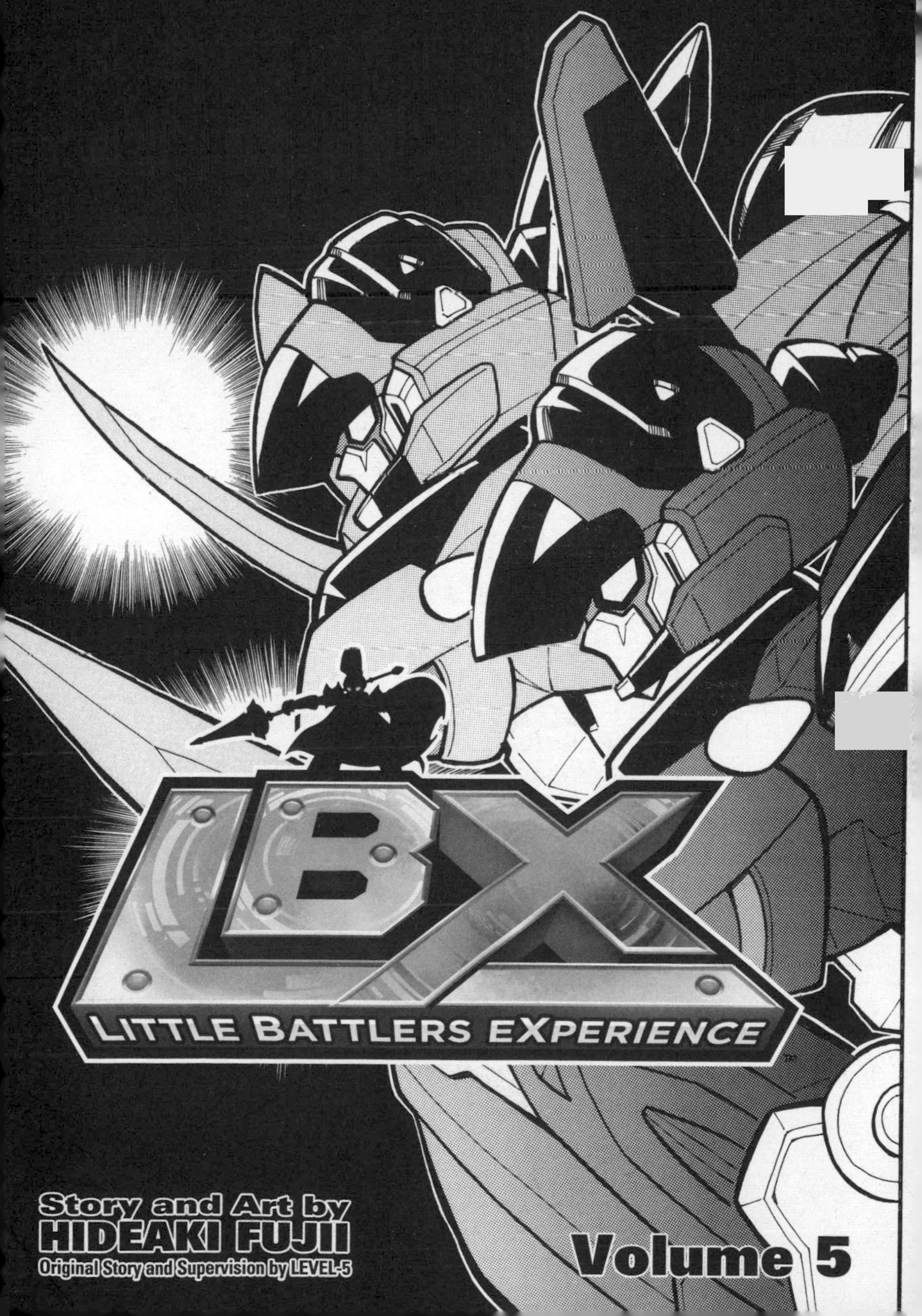

LBX
LITTLE BATTLERS eXPERIENCE

Story and Art by
HIDEAKI FUJII
Original Story and Supervision by LEVEL-5

Volume 5

INTRODUCING THE CAST

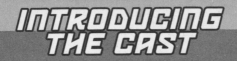

VAN YAMANO

A TOTALLY OBSESSED LBX FANATIC! A YEAR AGO, HE SAVED THE WORLD FROM THE TERRORIST GROUP THE NEW DAWN RAISERS AND NOW FACES HIS ENEMIES WITH HIS NEW LBX ELYSIAN!

LBX ELYSIAN

HIRO HUGHES

A YOUNG GEEK WHO DREAMS OF BECOMING A HERO. HE IS A SKILLED GAMER, AND EVEN THOUGH HE'S A ROOKIE, HIS LBX BATTLE SKILLS ARE IMPROVING QUICKLY. HIS LBX ODYSSEUS WAS CREATED BY DR. YAMANO HIMSELF.

LBX ODYSSEUS

LAURA HANASAKI

THE CHAMPION OF SHIBUYA TOWN'S MARTIAL ARTS TOURNAMENT, SHE'S A TOUGH NEW MEMBER OF VAN AND HIRO'S CREW. SHE CONTROLS LBX MINERVA.

LBX MINERVA

COBRA

THE FASHIONABLE PILOT OF THE "DUCK SHUTTLE," HE WAS SENT BY DR. YAMANO TO HELP VAN AND HIRO.

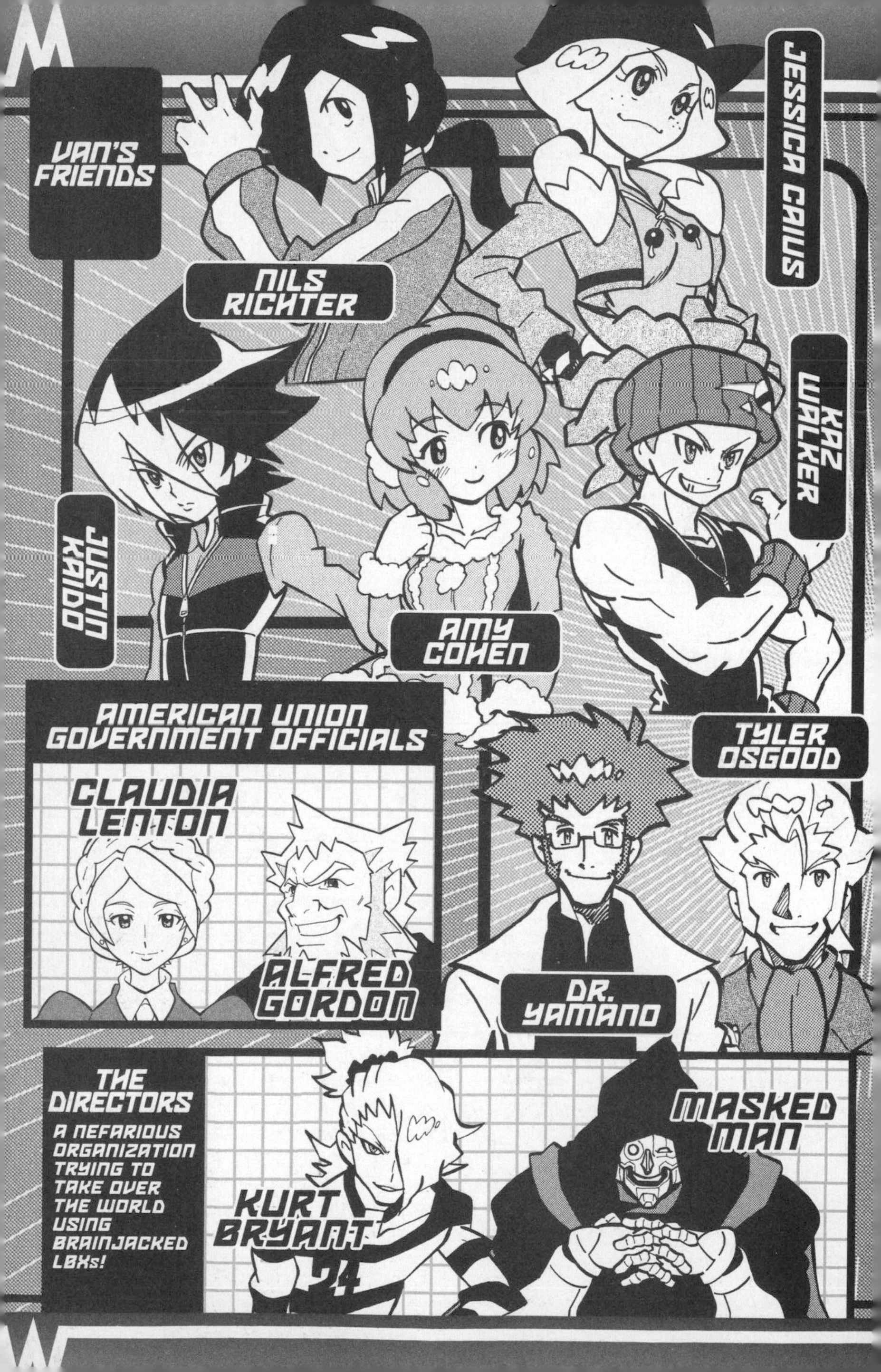
VAN'S FRIENDS
JESSICA CAIUS
NILS RICHTER
KAZ WALKER
JUSTIN KAIDO
AMY COHEN
AMERICAN UNION GOVERNMENT OFFICIALS
TYLER OSGOOD
CLAUDIA LENTON
ALFRED GORDON
DR. YAMANO
THE DIRECTORS
A NEFARIOUS ORGANIZATION TRYING TO TAKE OVER THE WORLD USING BRAINJACKED LBXs!
MASKED MAN
KURT BRYANT

TABLE OF CONTENTS

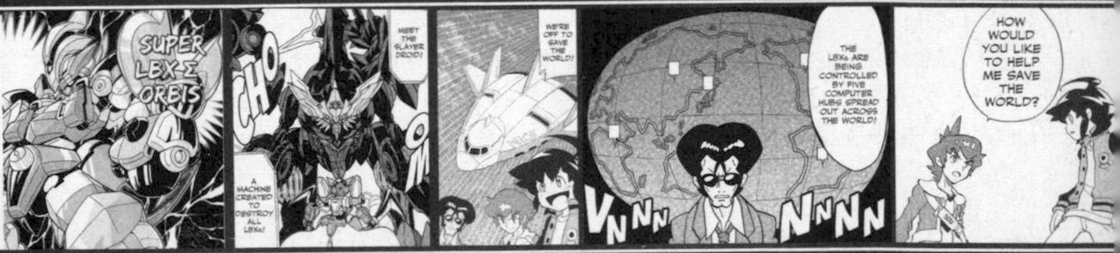

HOW WOULD YOU LIKE TO HELP ME SAVE THE WORLD?
THE LBXs ARE BEING CONTROLLED BY FIVE COMPUTER HUBS SPREAD OUT ACROSS THE WORLD!
VNNN
NNNN
WE'RE OFF TO SAVE THE WORLD!
MEET THE SLAYER DROID!
CHO
OM
A MACHINE CREATED TO DESTROY ALL LBXs!
SUPER LBX-Σ ORBIS

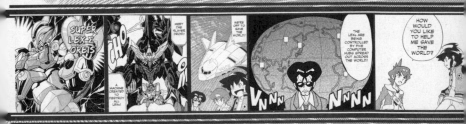

STORY SO FAR...

A YEAR HAS PASSED SINCE VAN YAMANO'S BATTLE AGAINST THE NEW DAWN RAISERS, BUT A NEW ENEMY HAS THROWN THE WORLD INTO CHAOS: THE DIRECTORS. VAN AND HIS NEW FRIEND HIRO TAKE OFF ON A JOURNEY AROUND THE WORLD TO DESTROY THE FIVE COMPUTERS THAT HAVE CAUSED LBXs EVERYWHERE TO REVOLT. BUT WHEN HIRO ARRIVES IN ENGLAND, SEARCHING FOR A COMPUTER HUB, HE IS CONFRONTED BY THE SLAYER DROID, A MACHINE CREATED TO DESTROY ALL LBXs. THE SLAYER DROID OVERWHELMS HIRO, BUT VAN AND LAURA ARRIVE JUST IN TIME TO UTILIZE THE TRIPLE UNITY MODE, COMBINING THEIR LBXs INTO THE SUPER LBX, SIGMA ORBIS!

CHAPTER 18: SHOWDOWN: SUPER LBX SIGMA ORBIS VS. SLAYER DROID!

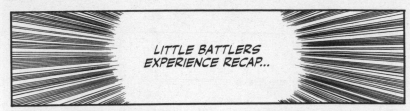

LITTLE BATTLERS EXPERIENCE RECAP...
HIRO WENT TO ENGLAND ON HIS OWN, BUT HE WAS CONFRONT-ED BY THE DIRECTORS ...
THE DIRECTORS REVEALED THEIR SECRET WEAPON, THE SLAYER DROID, AND COMPLETELY DOMINATED HIRO'S LBX ODYSSEUS.
KA-
TANG!
HIRO'S IN TROUBLE!
BUT HIRO KEPT FIGHT-ING...
...AND REFUSED TO GIVE UP!
JUST IN THE NICK OF TIME, VAN AND LAURA ARRIVED FROM JAPAN, READY TO JOIN HIRO IN BATTLE!

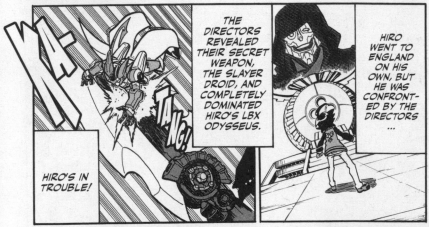

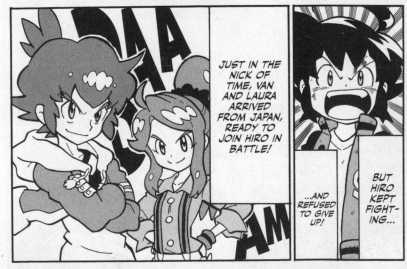

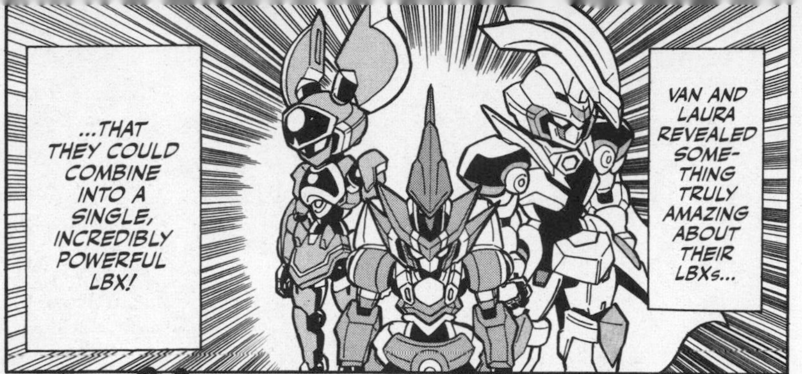
VAN AND LAURA REVEALED SOMETHING TRULY AMAZING ABOUT THEIR LBXs...
...THAT THEY COULD COMBINE INTO A SINGLE, INCREDIBLY POWERFUL LBX!
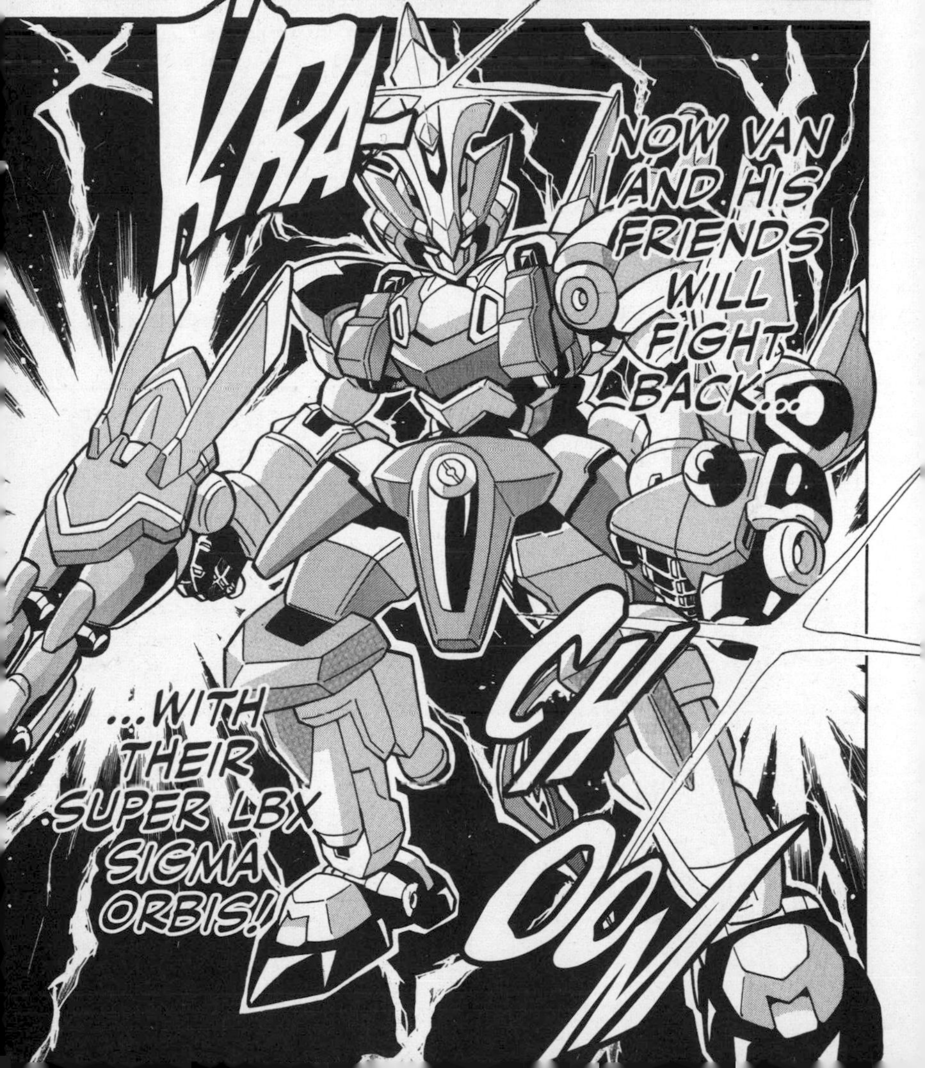
KIRA
NOW VAN AND HIS FRIENDS WILL FIGHT BACK...
...WITH THEIR SUPER LBX SIGMA ORBIS!

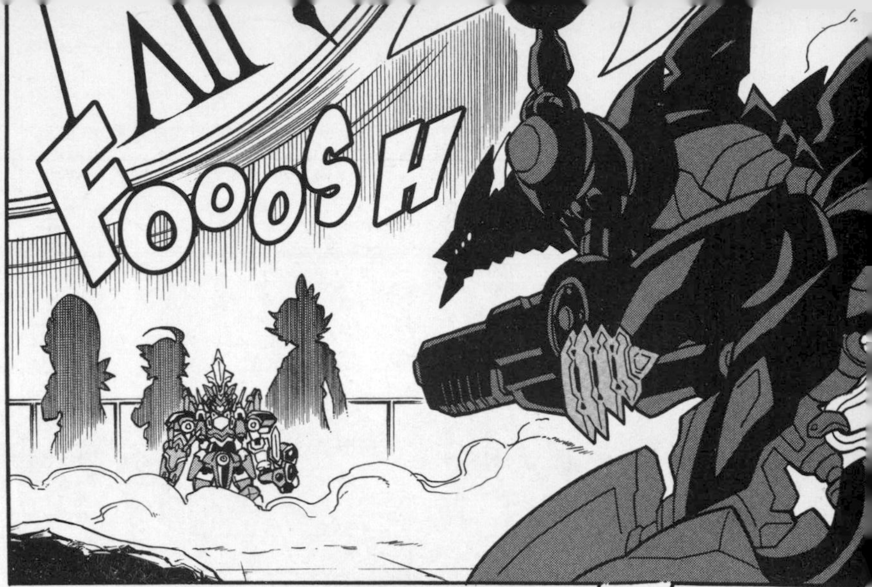
FOOOSH

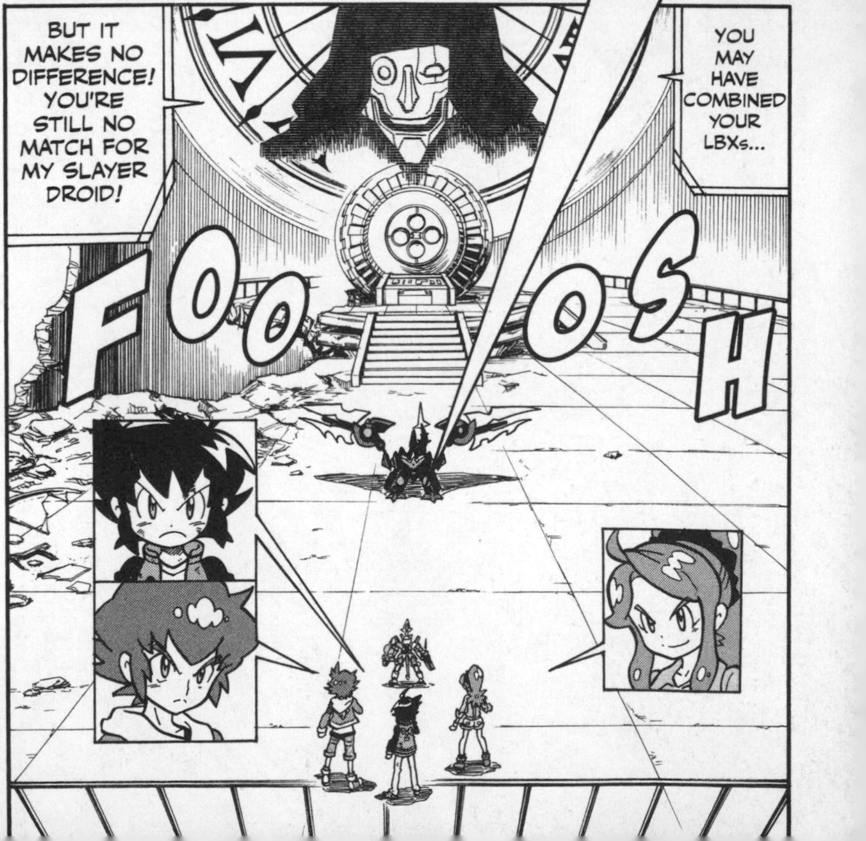
YOU MAY HAVE COMBINED YOUR LBXs...
BUT IT MAKES NO DIFFERENCE! YOU'RE STILL NO MATCH FOR MY SLAYER DROID!
FOOOOSH

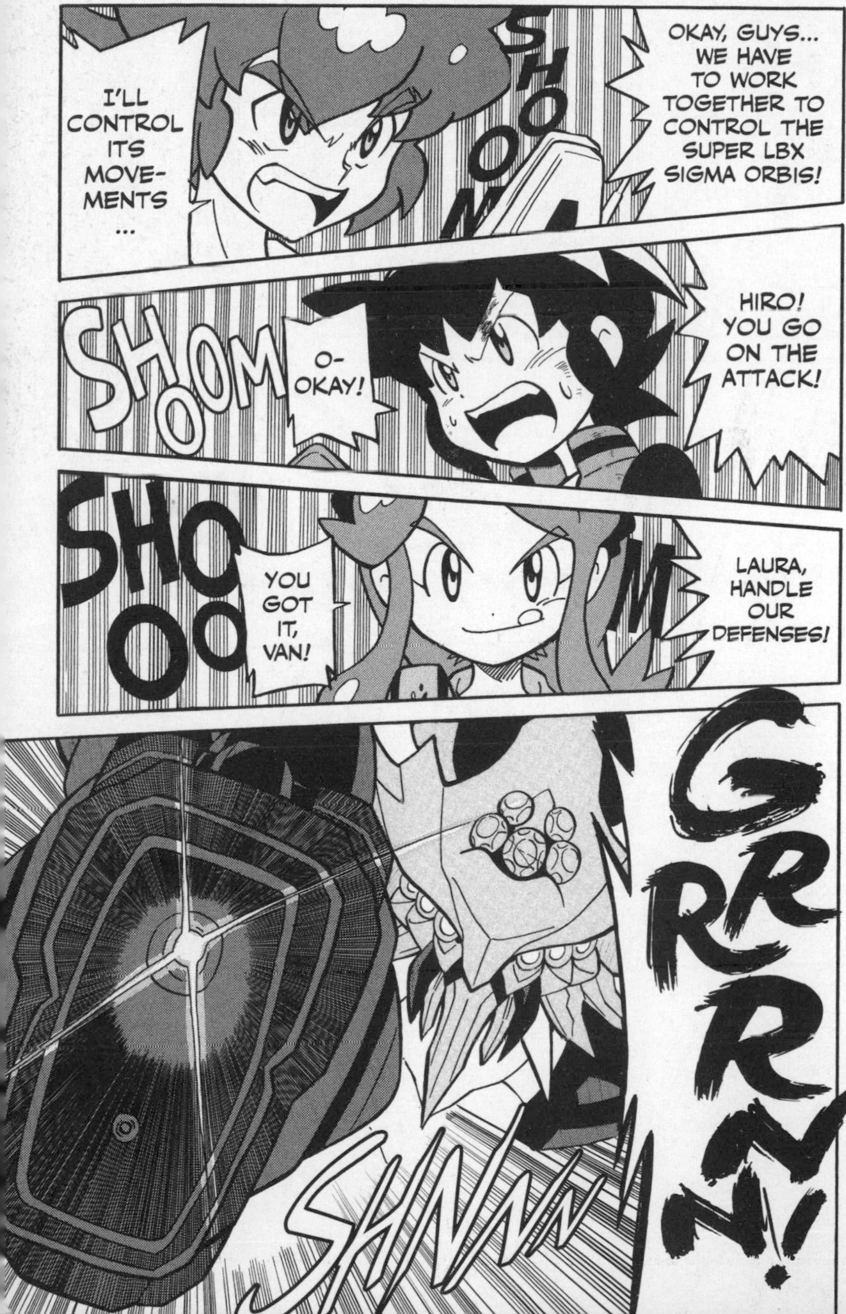
OKAY, GUYS... WE HAVE TO WORK TOGETHER TO CONTROL THE SUPER LBX SIGMA ORBIS!
SHOOOM
I'LL CONTROL ITS MOVEMENTS...
HIRO! YOU GO ON THE ATTACK!
O-OKAY!
SHOOOM
LAURA, HANDLE OUR DEFENSES!
SHOOOM
YOU GOT IT, VAN!
GRRRNN!
SHNNN!

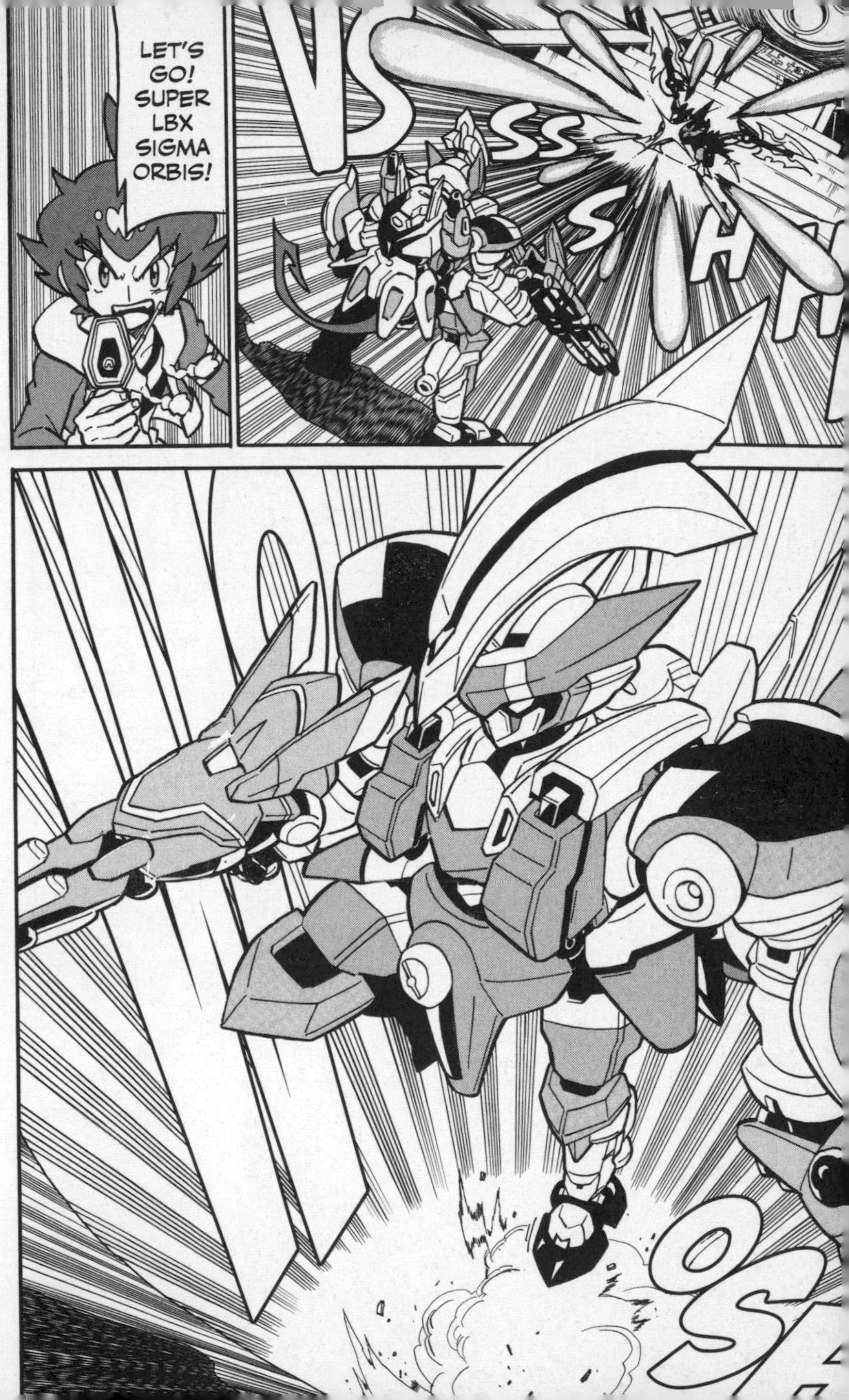
LET'S GO! SUPER LBX SIGMA ORBIS!

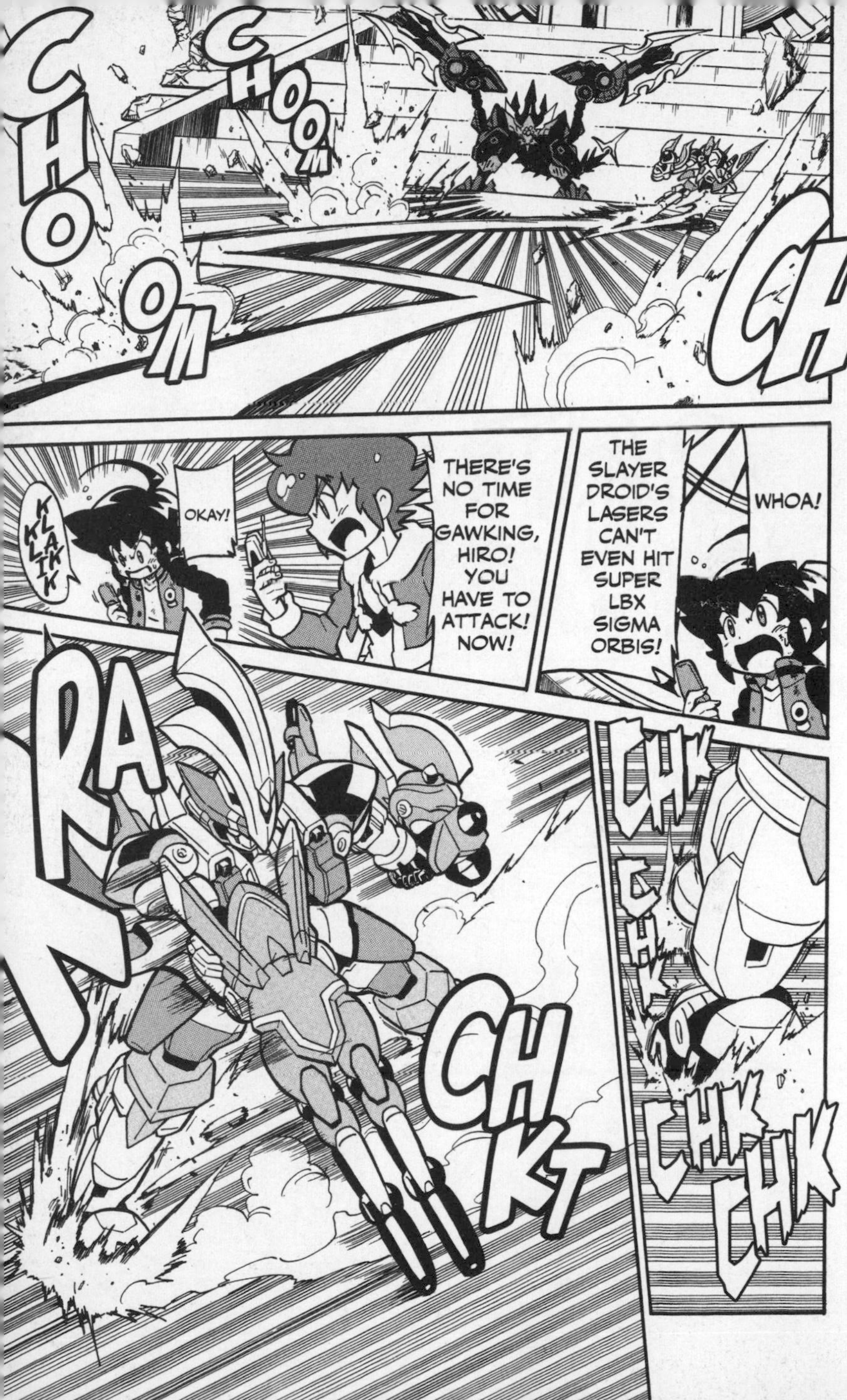
CH
CHOOM
CHOOOM
WHOA!
THE SLAYER DROID'S LASERS CAN'T EVEN HIT SUPER LBX SIGMA ORBIS!
THERE'S NO TIME FOR GAWKING, HIRO! YOU HAVE TO ATTACK! NOW!
OKAY!
KLAK KLIK
CHK
CHK
CHK
CHK
CHKT
PA

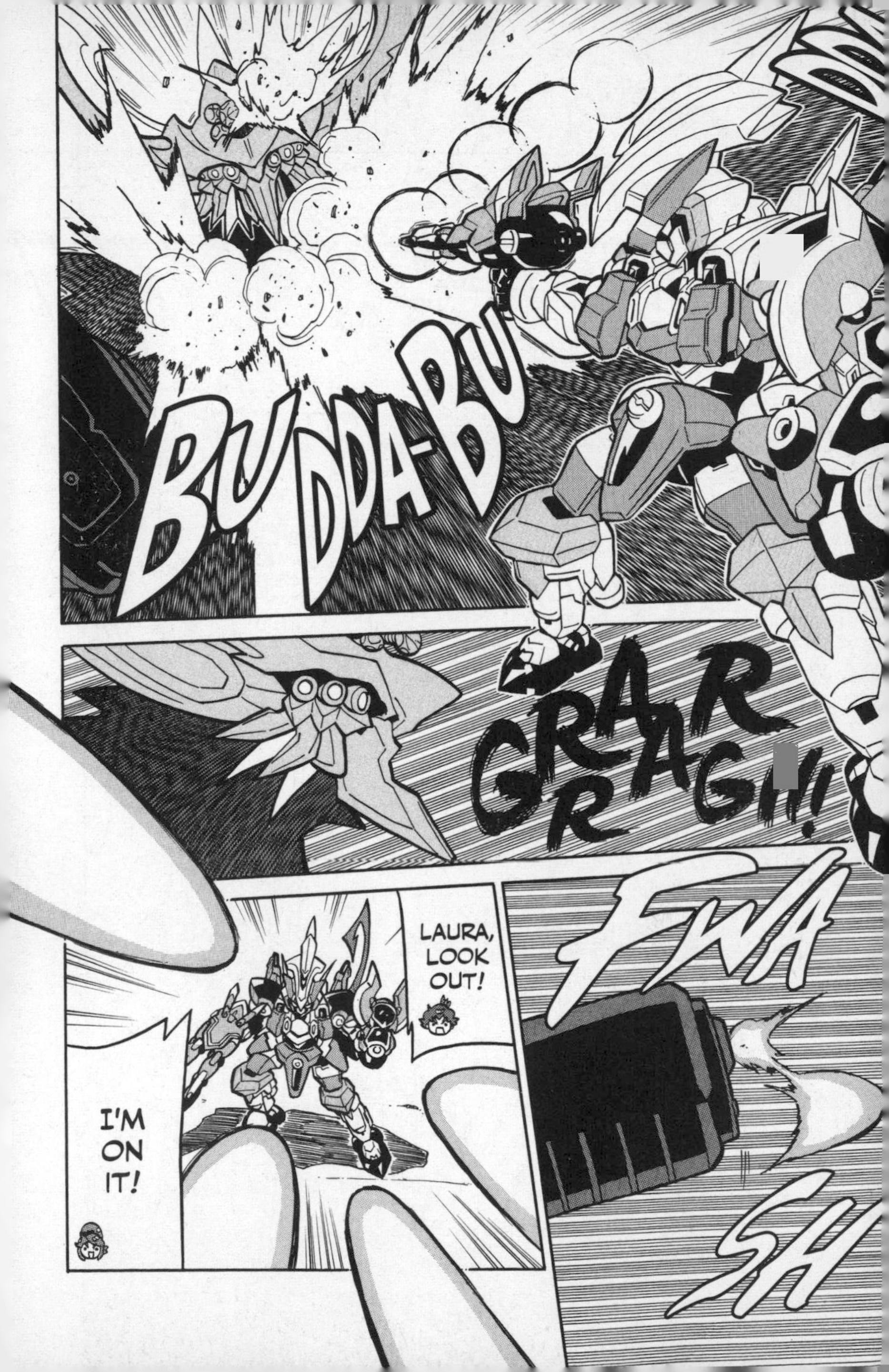
BUDDA-BU
GRAR RAGH!!
FWASH
LAURA, LOOK OUT!
I'M ON IT!

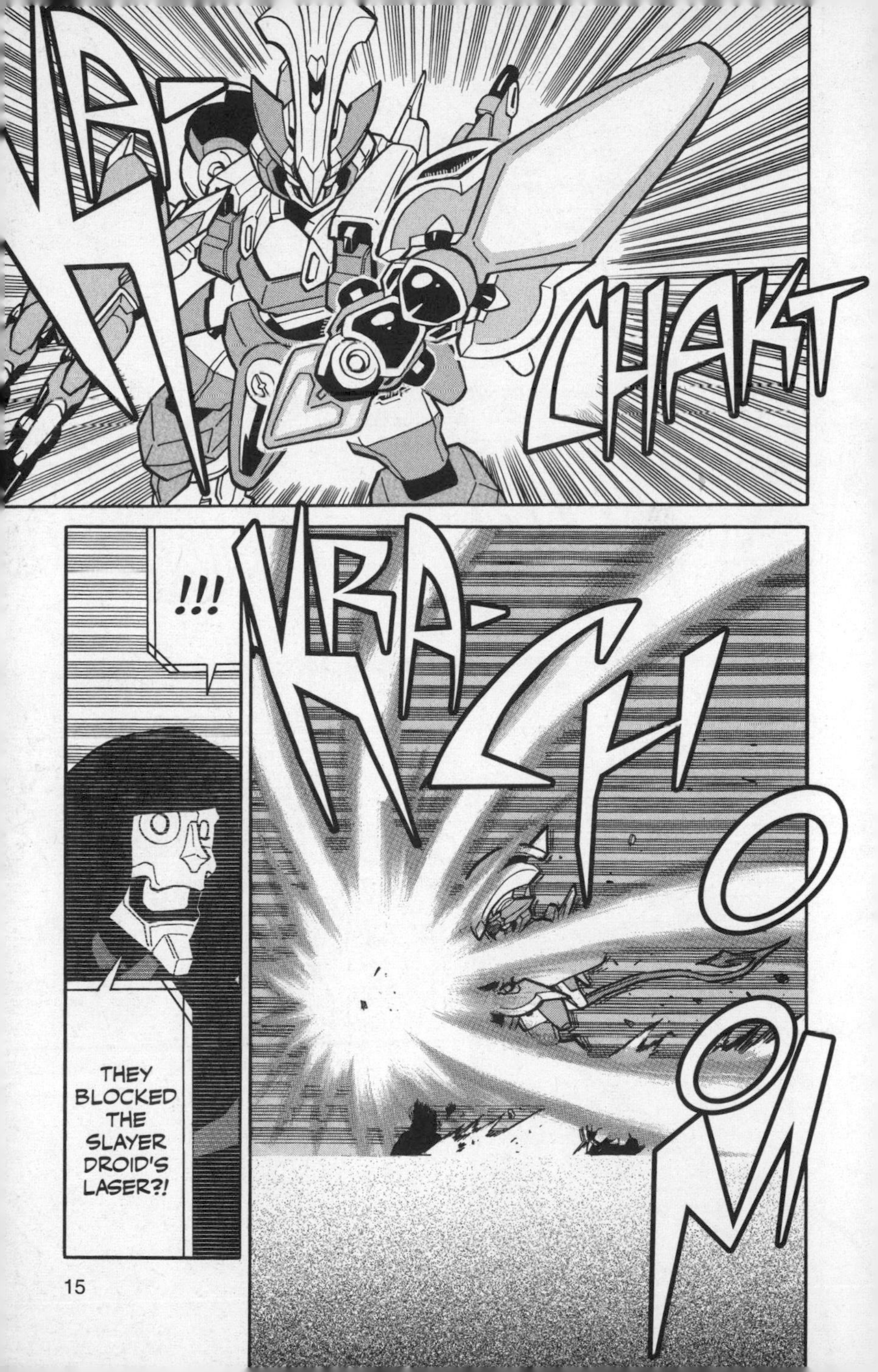

VRA
CHAKT
!!!
VRA-CHOOOM
THEY BLOCKED THE SLAYER DROID'S LASER?!

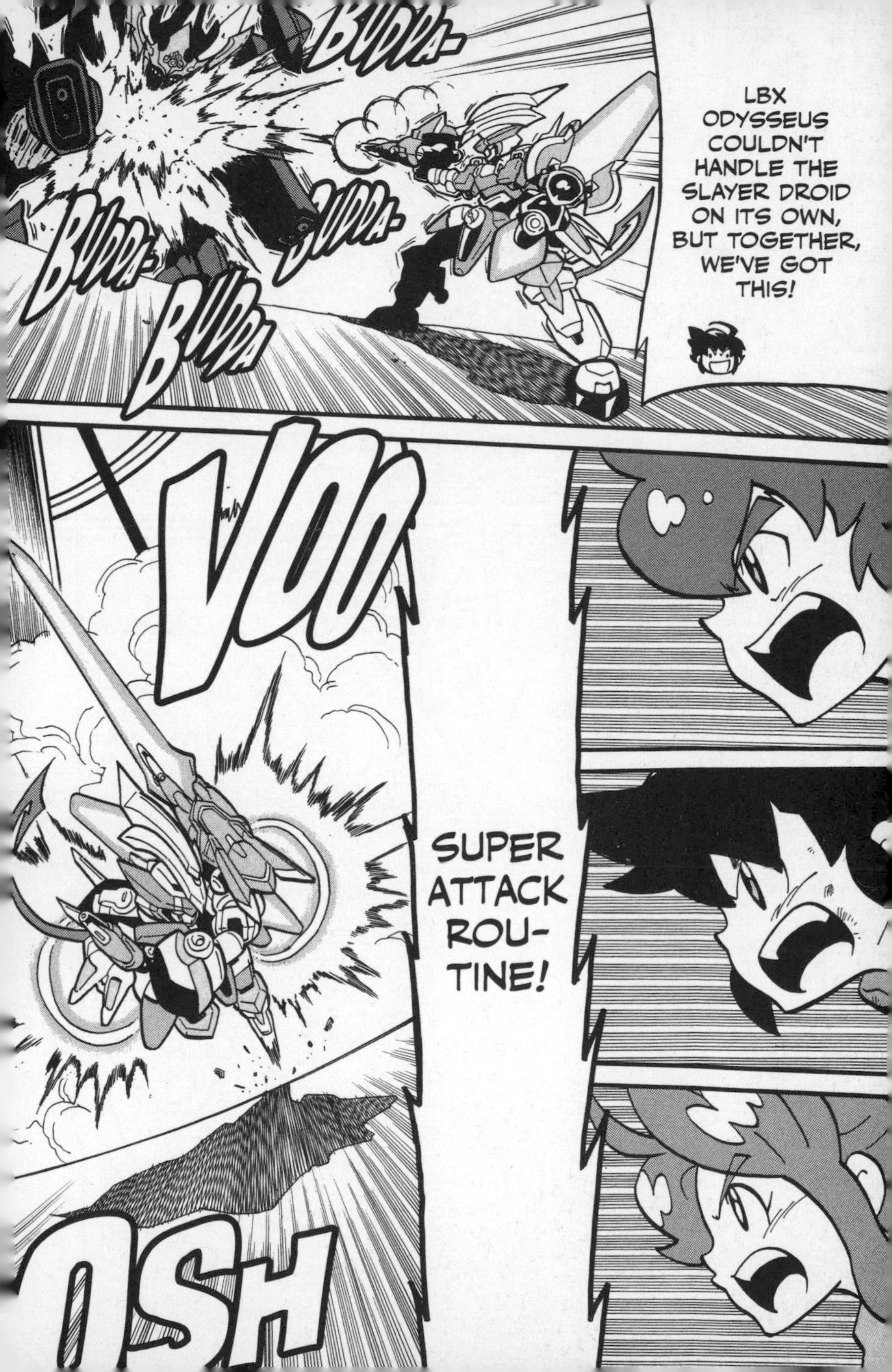
BUDDA-
LBX ODYSSEUS COULDN'T HANDLE THE SLAYER DROID ON ITS OWN, BUT TOGETHER, WE'VE GOT THIS!
BUDDA-
BUDDA-
BUDDA
VOO
SUPER ATTACK ROU-TINE!
OSH

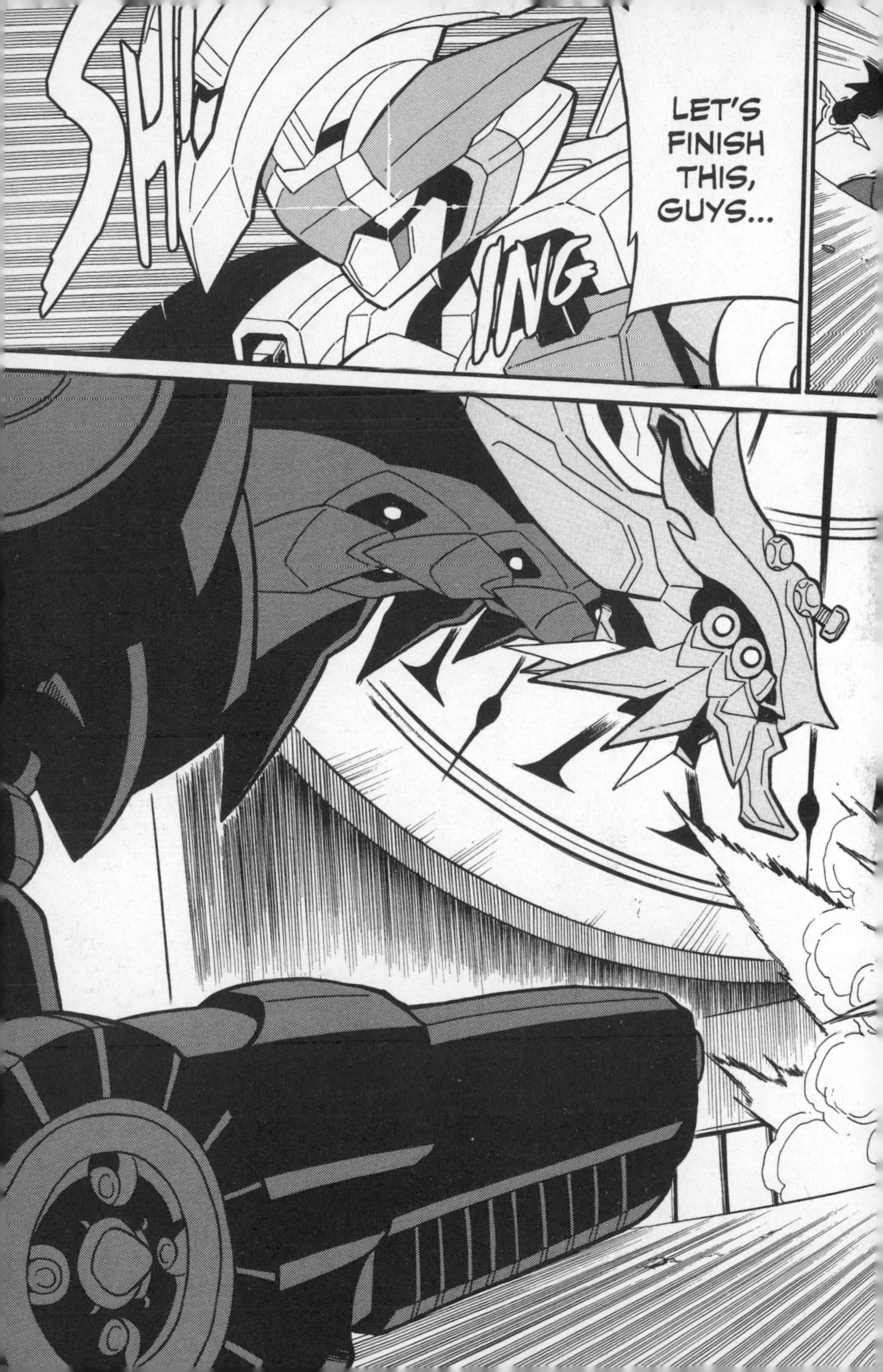
LET'S FINISH THIS, GUYS...
SHING

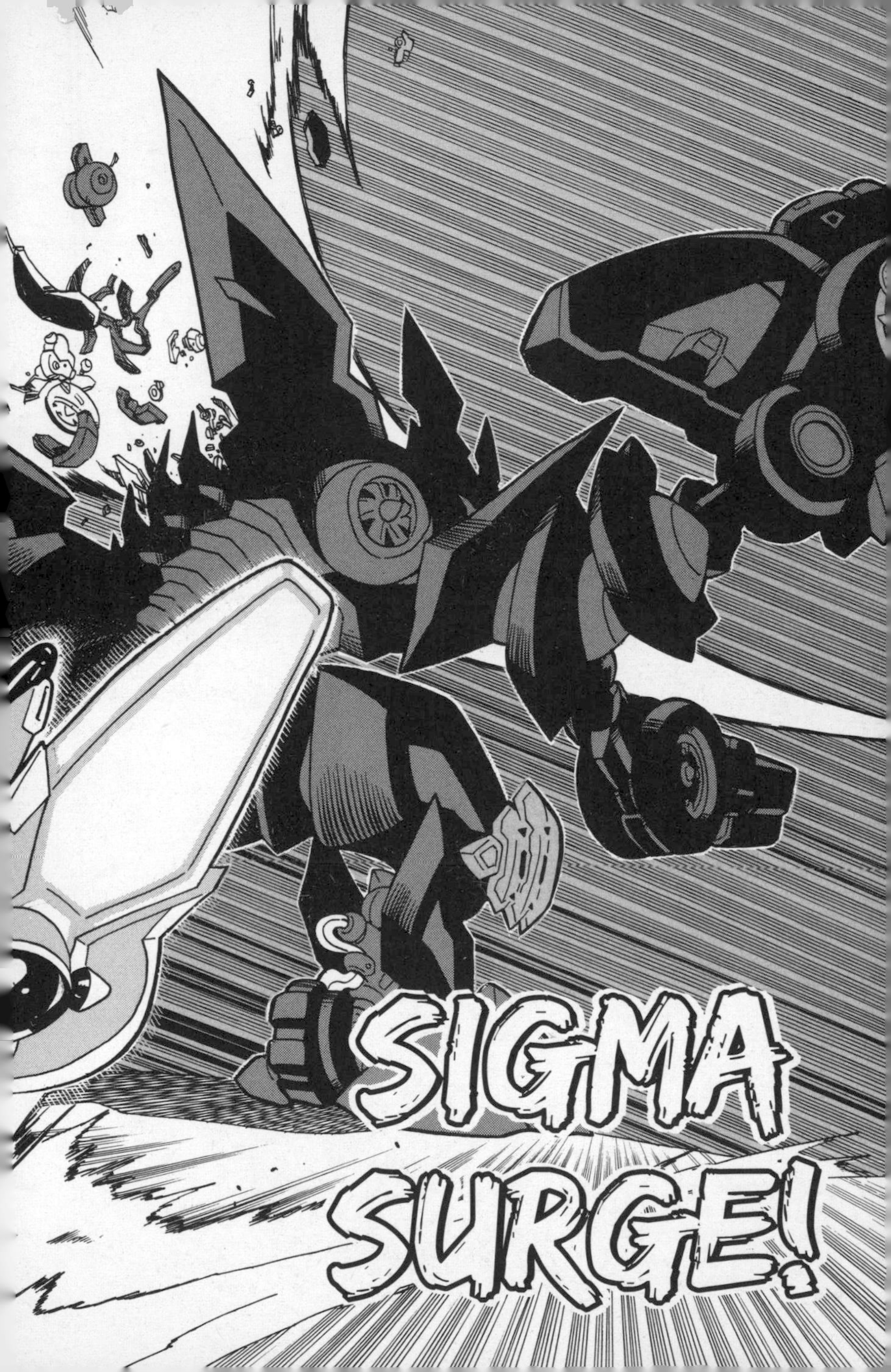
SIGMA SURGE!

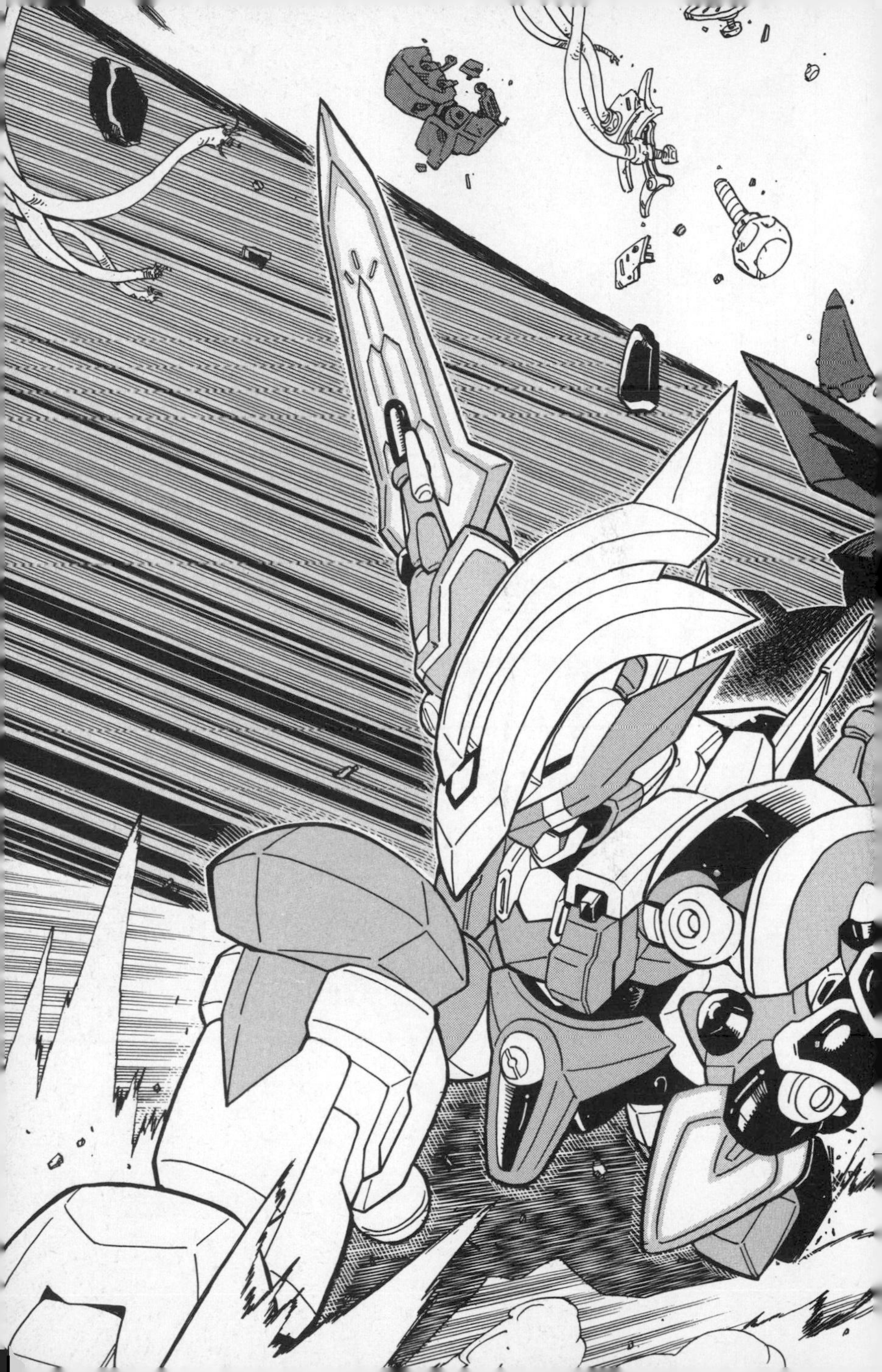

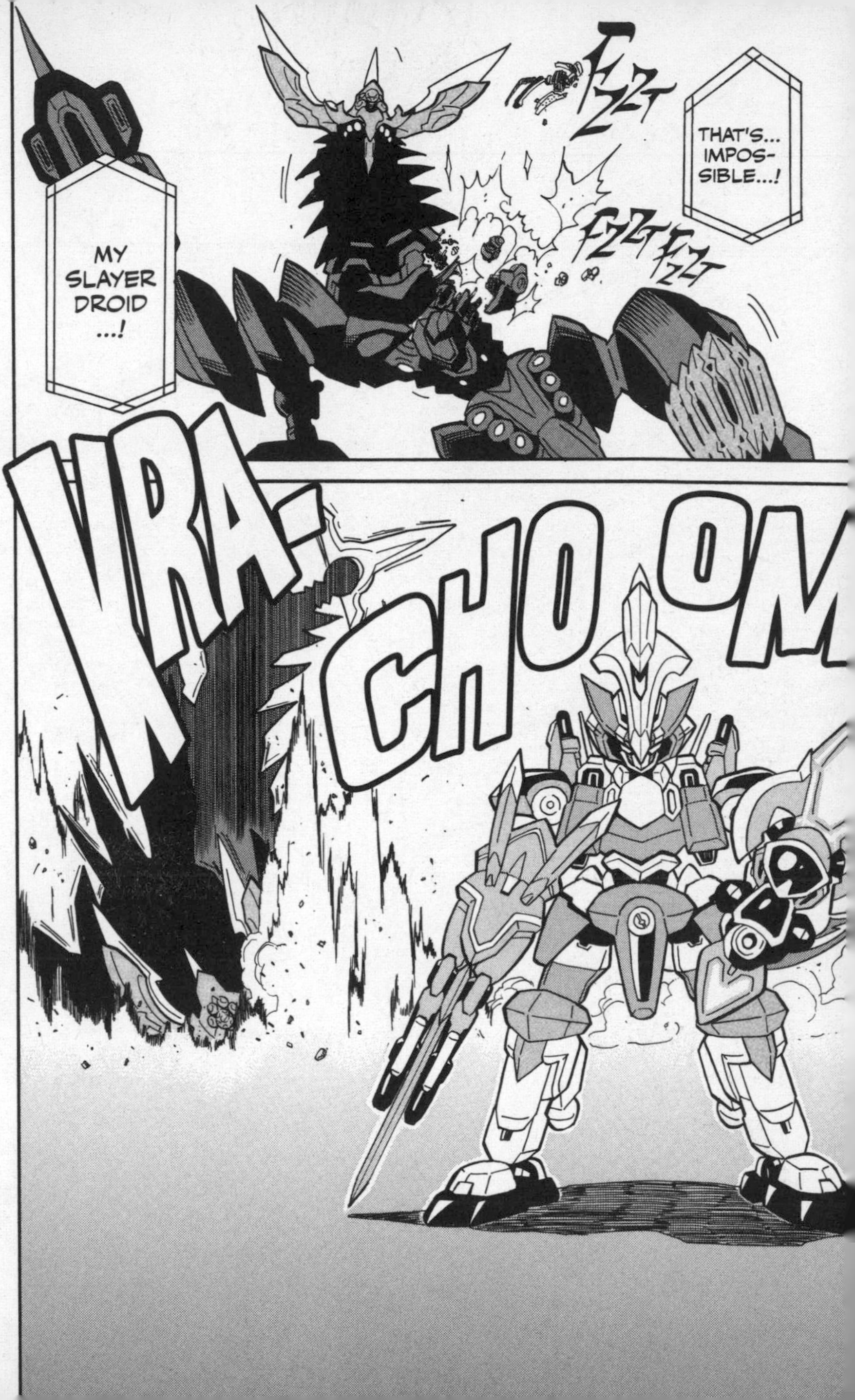
FZZT
THAT'S... IMPOSSIBLE...!
FZZT FZZT
MY SLAYER DROID ...!
VRA-CHOOM

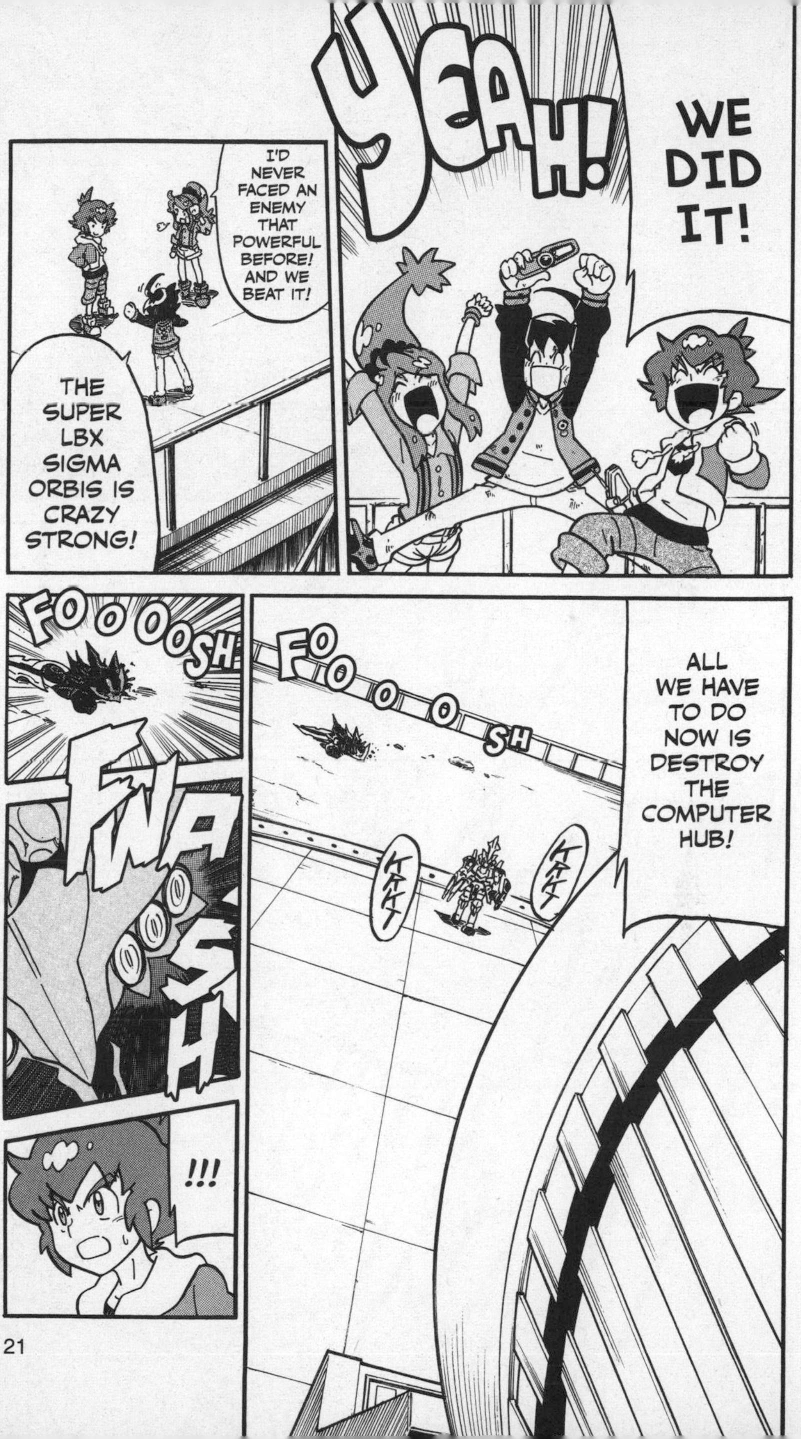
YEAH!
WE DID IT!
I'D NEVER FACED AN ENEMY THAT POWERFUL BEFORE! AND WE BEAT IT!
THE SUPER LBX SIGMA ORBIS IS CRAZY STRONG!
ALL WE HAVE TO DO NOW IS DESTROY THE COMPUTER HUB!
FOOOOOSH
KRKT
KRKT
FOOOOSH
FWASH
!!!

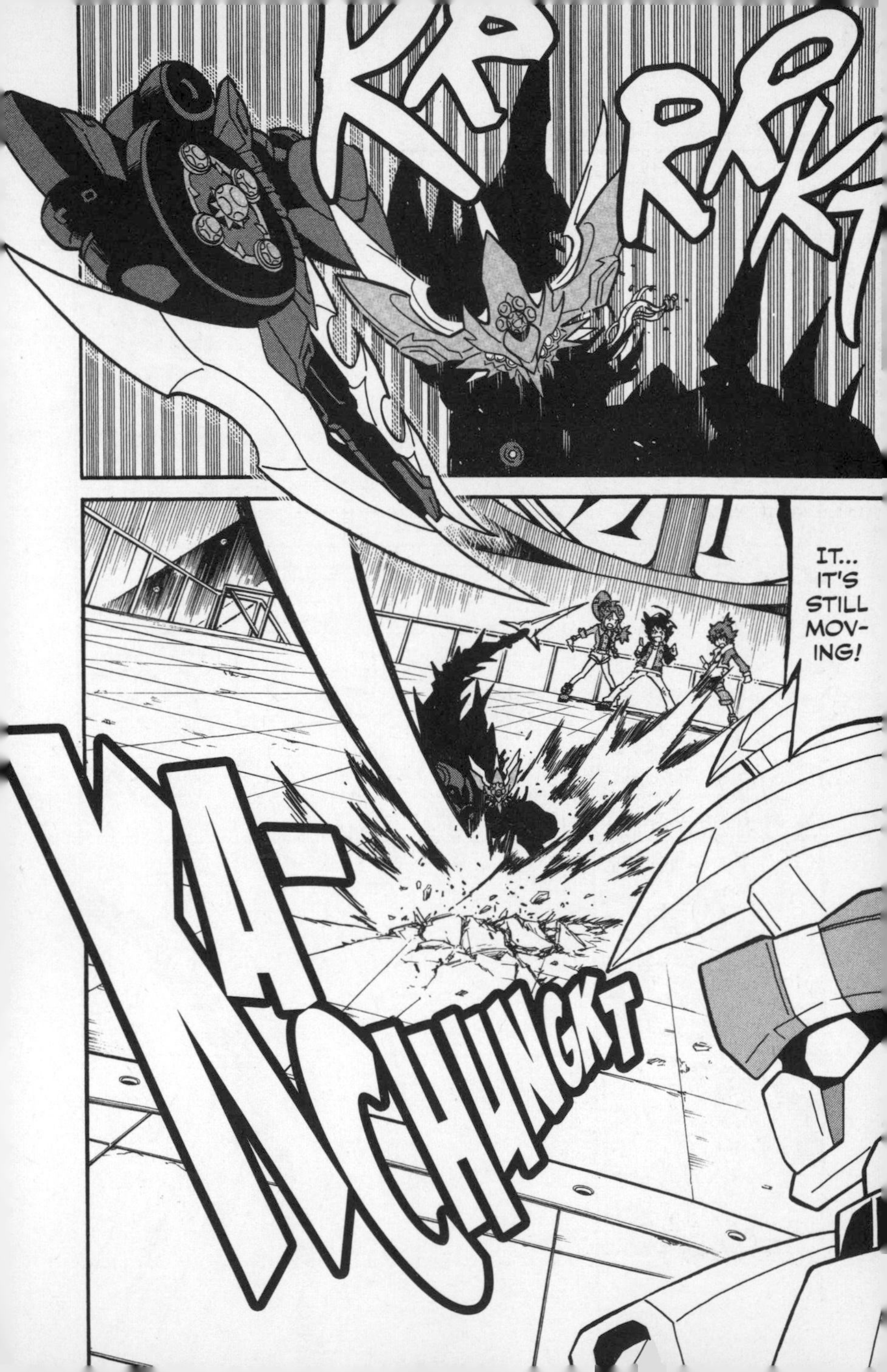
KRRRK
IT... IT'S STILL MOVING!
KA-CHUNGKT

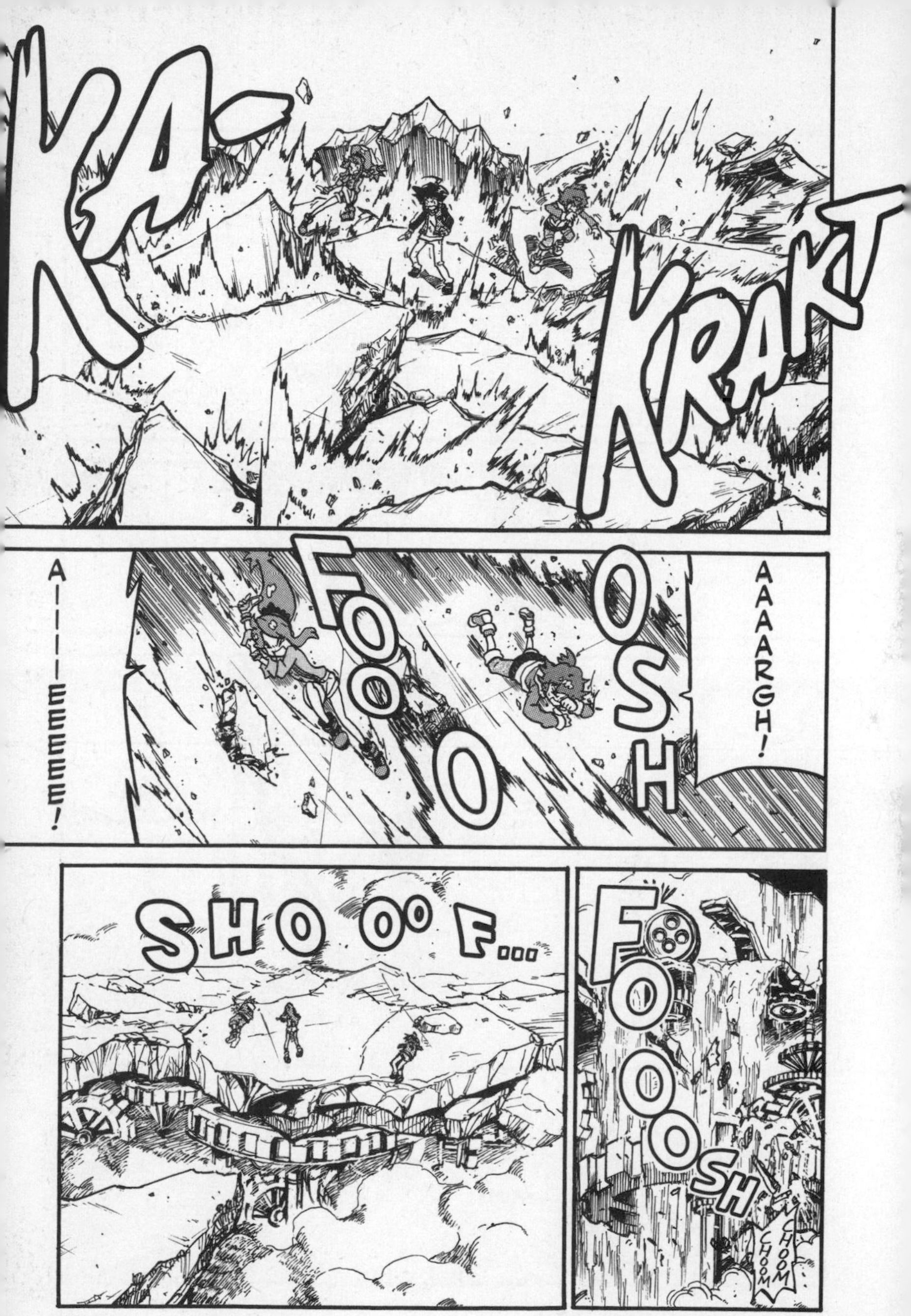
KA-
KRAKT
AAAARGH!
FOOOOSH
A-IIIEEEEE!
FOOOOOSH
CHOOM CHOOM
SHOOOF...

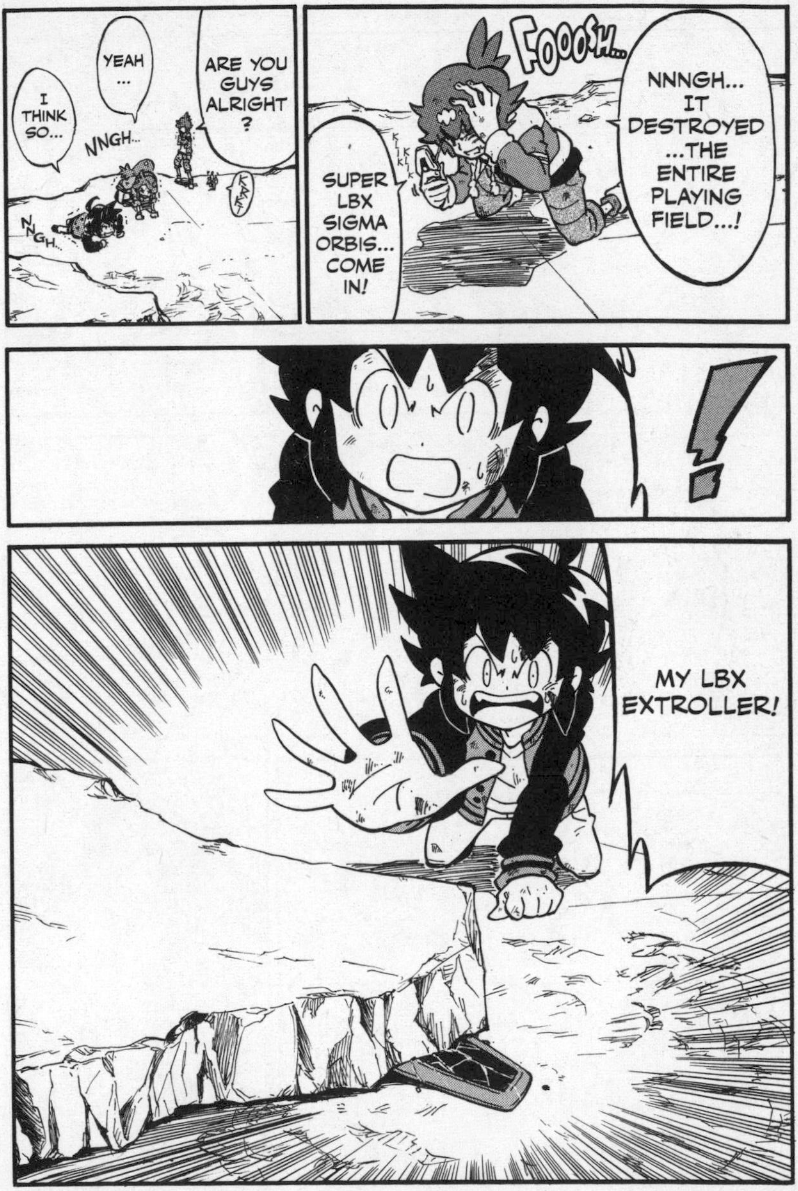
FOOOSH...
NNNGH... IT DESTROYED ...THE ENTIRE PLAYING FIELD...!
KLIK KLIK
SUPER LBX SIGMA ORBIS... COME IN!
ARE YOU GUYS ALRIGHT?
YEAH ...
I THINK SO...
NNGH...
NNGH...
!
MY LBX EXTROLLER!

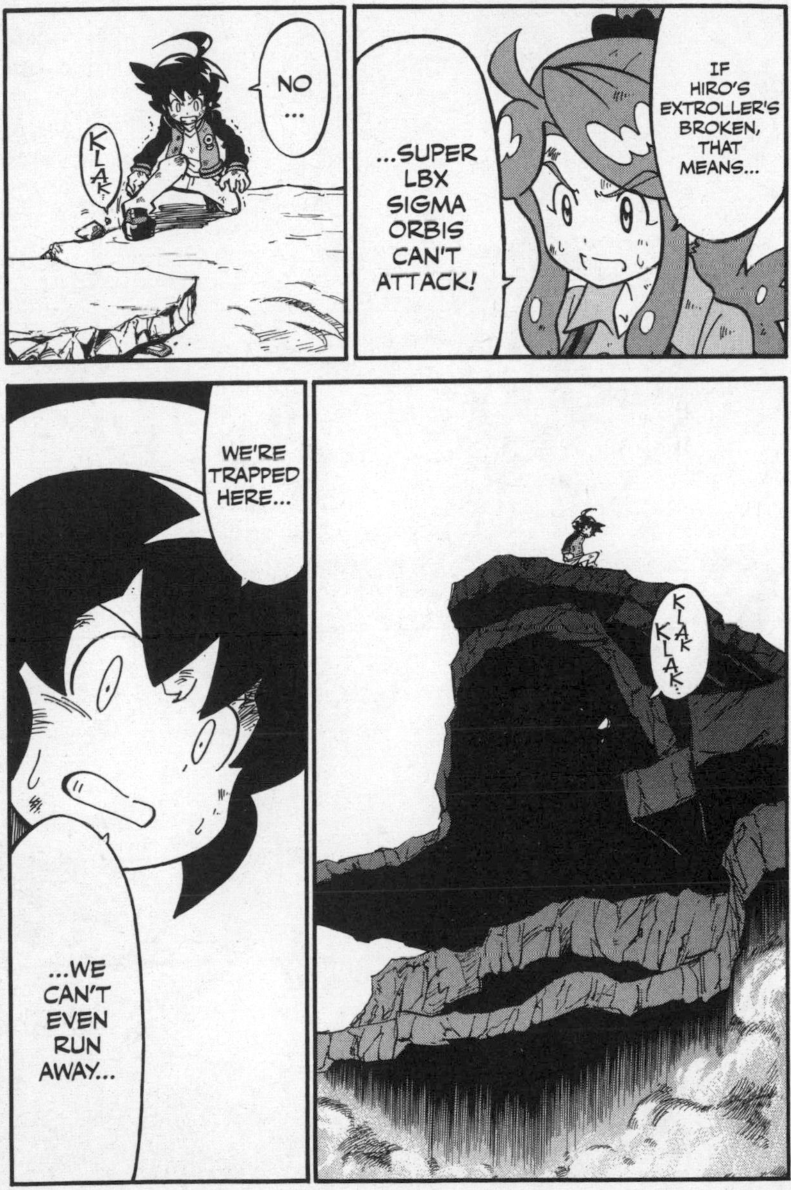
IF HIRO'S EXTROLLER'S BROKEN, THAT MEANS...
...SUPER LBX SIGMA ORBIS CAN'T ATTACK!
NO ...
KLAK
KLAK KLAK...
WE'RE TRAPPED HERE...
...WE CAN'T EVEN RUN AWAY...

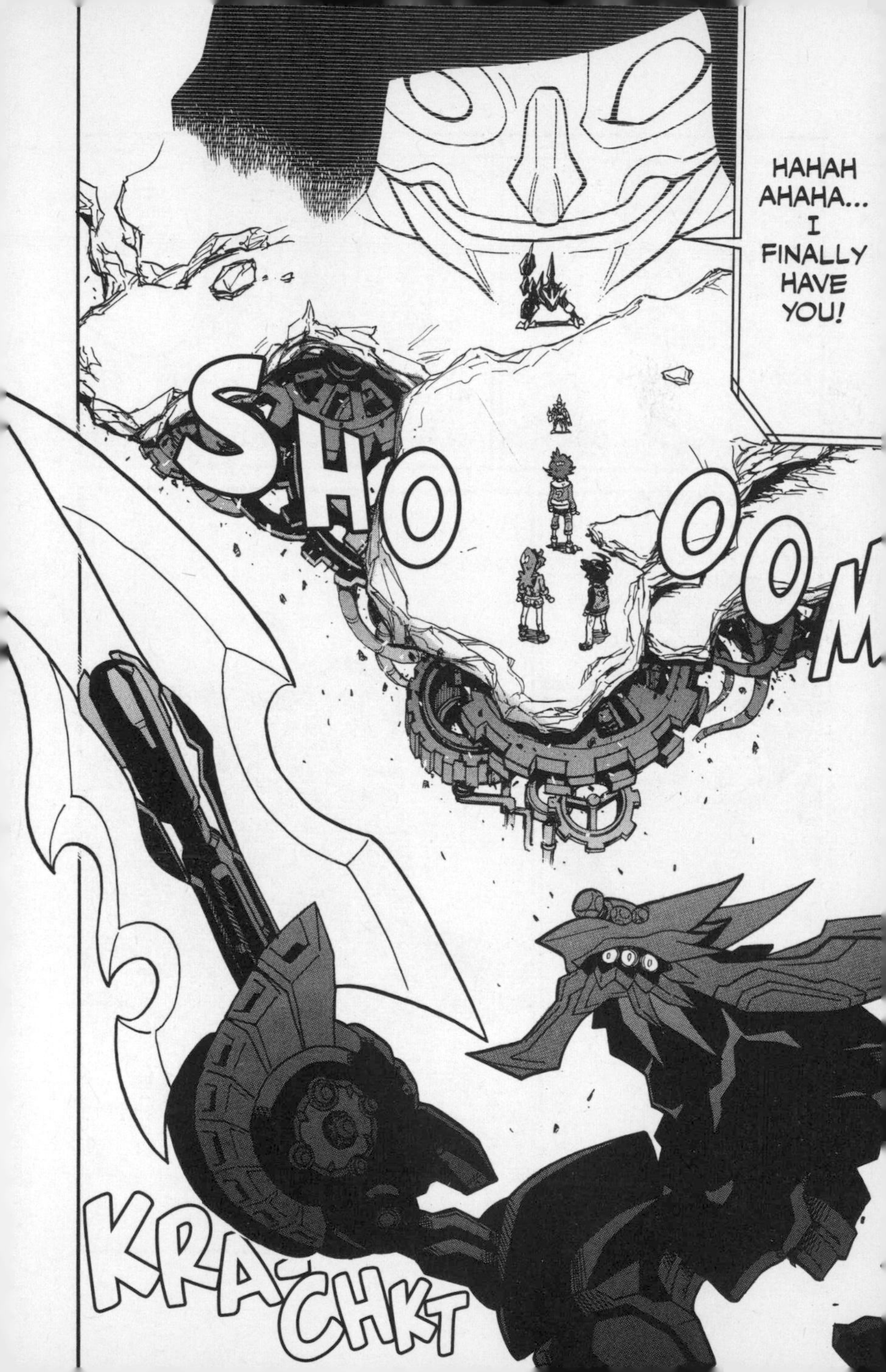
HAHAH AHAHA... I FINALLY HAVE YOU!
SHOOOOM
KRA-CHKT

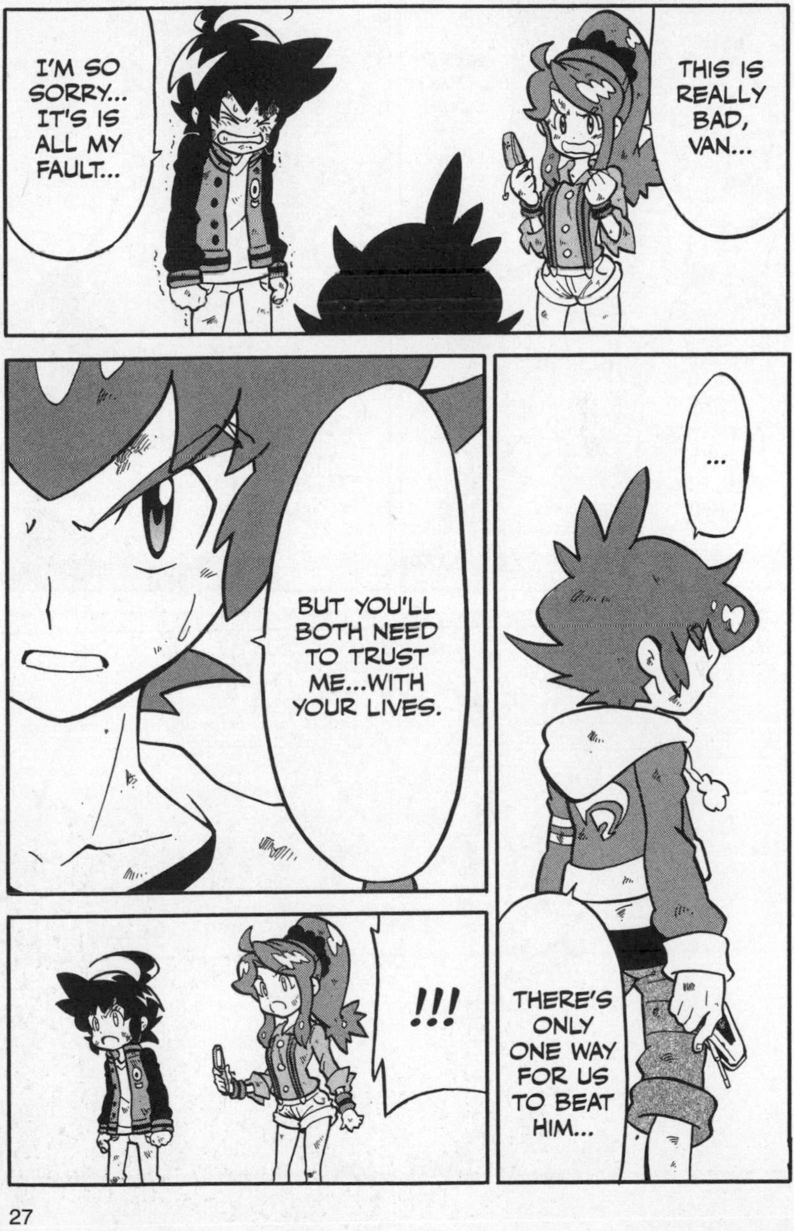
THIS IS REALLY BAD, VAN...
I'M SO SORRY... IT'S IS ALL MY FAULT...
...
THERE'S ONLY ONE WAY FOR US TO BEAT HIM...
BUT YOU'LL BOTH NEED TO TRUST ME...WITH YOUR LIVES.
!!!

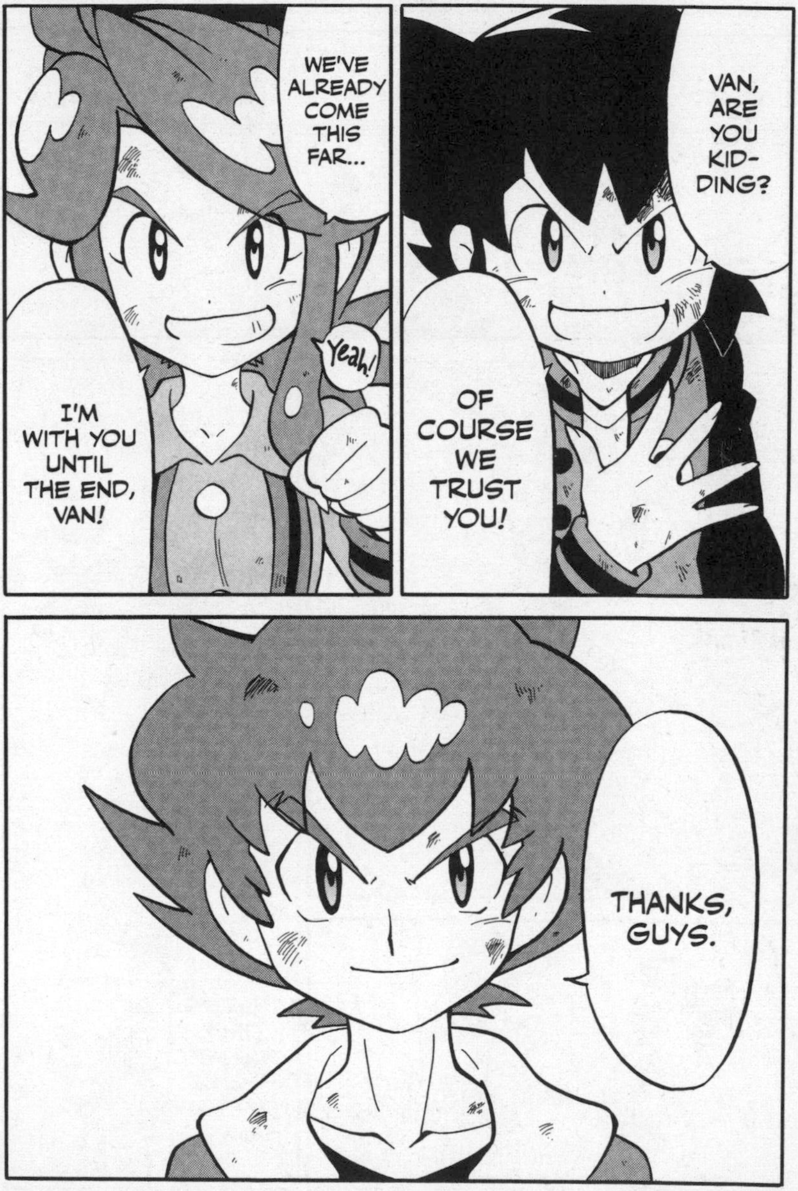
VAN, ARE YOU KID-DING?
OF COURSE WE TRUST YOU!
WE'VE ALREADY COME THIS FAR...
Yeah!
I'M WITH YOU UNTIL THE END, VAN!
THANKS, GUYS.

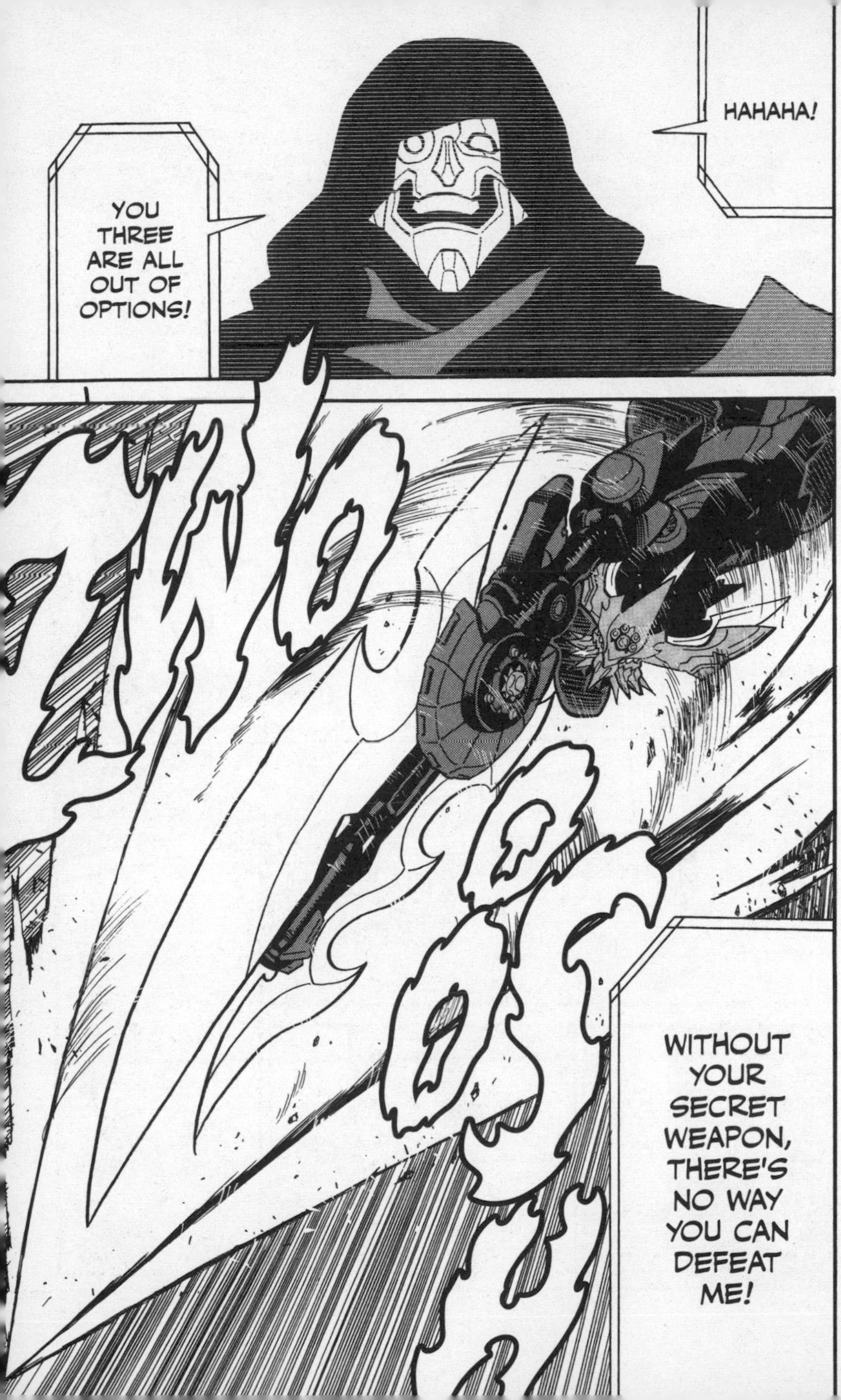
HAHAHA!
YOU THREE ARE ALL OUT OF OPTIONS!
WITHOUT YOUR SECRET WEAPON, THERE'S NO WAY YOU CAN DEFEAT ME!

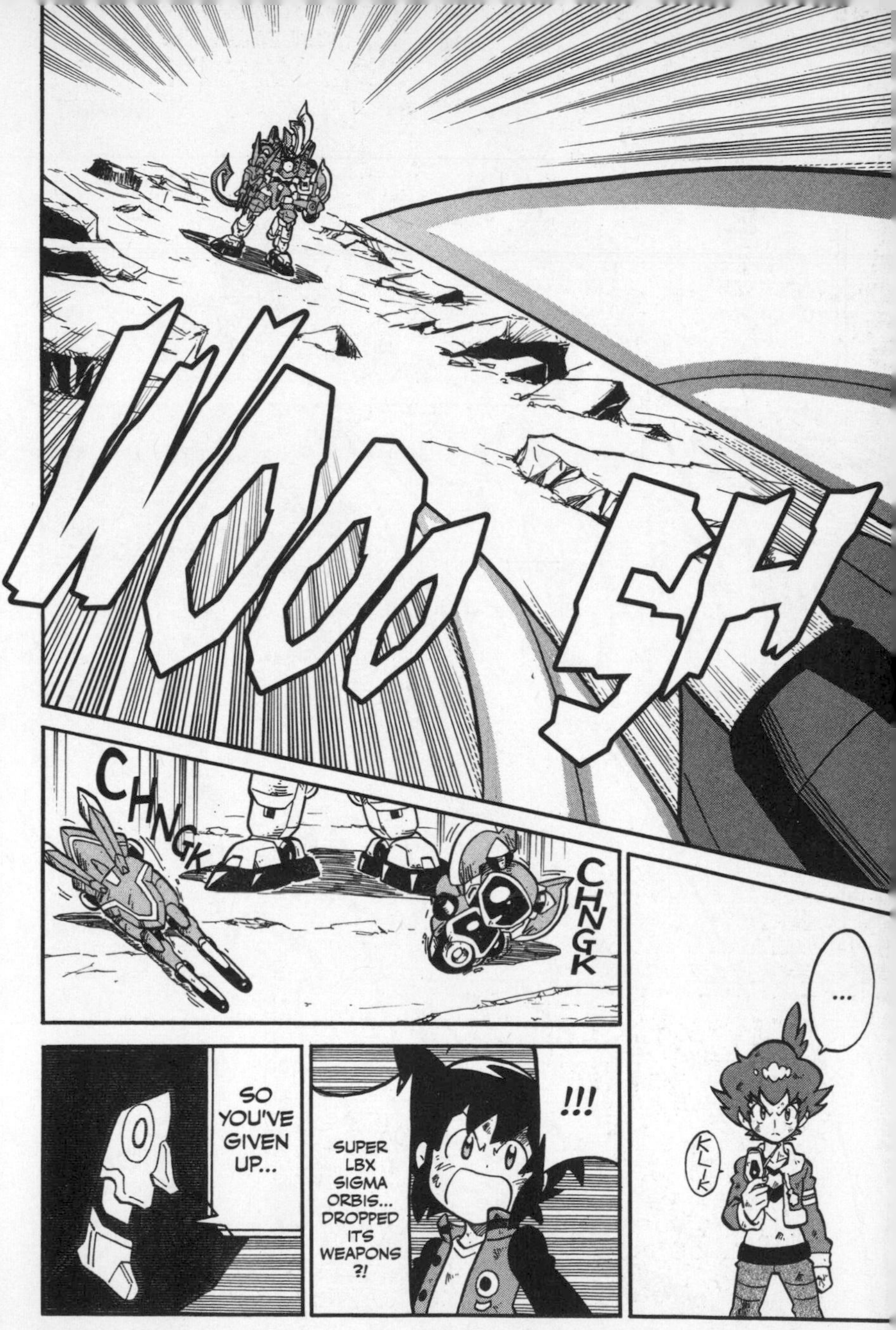
WOOOSH
...
KLIK
CHNGK
CHNGK
!!!
SUPER LBX SIGMA ORBIS... DROPPED ITS WEAPONS?!
SO YOU'VE GIVEN UP...

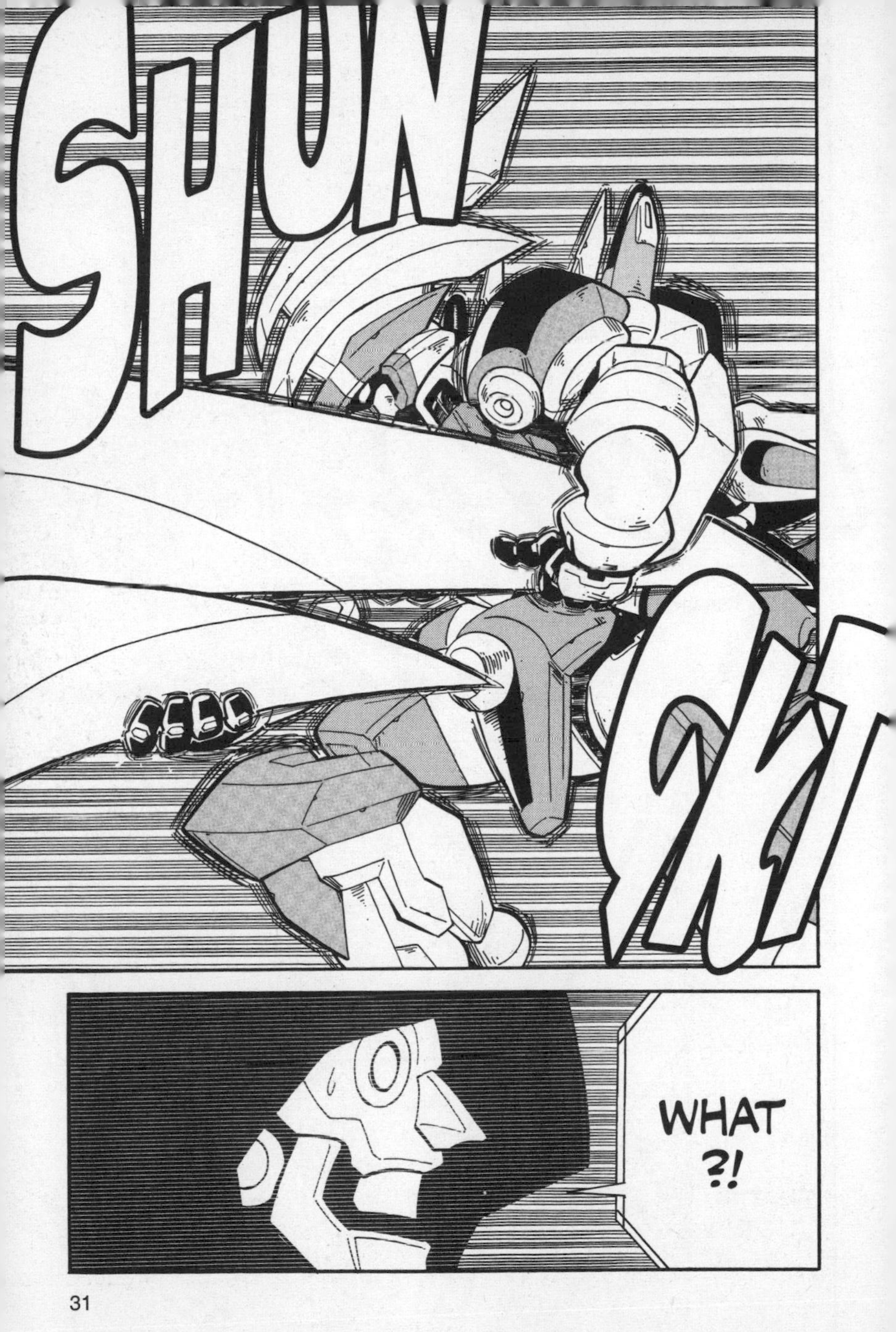
SHUN
GKI
WHAT ?!

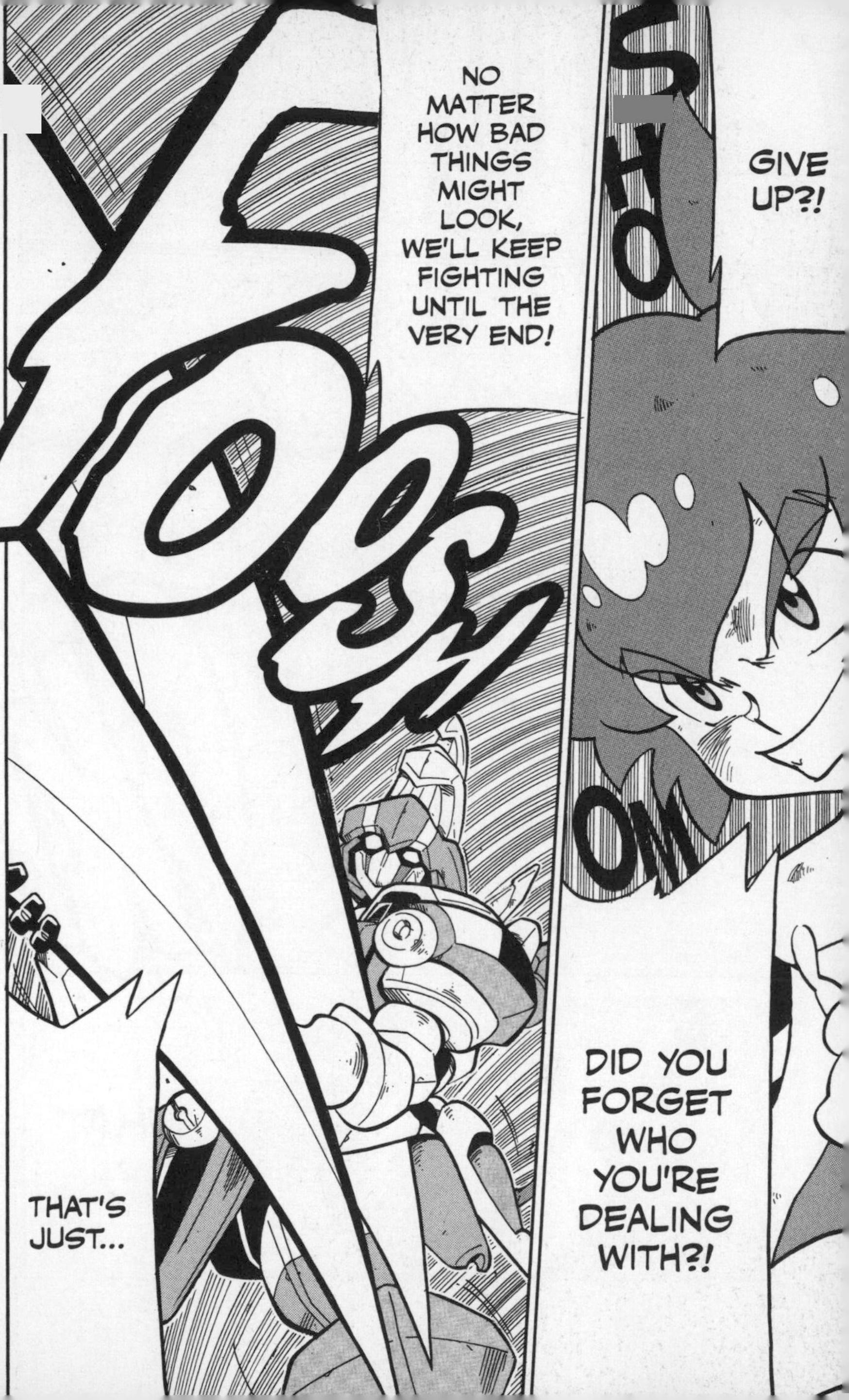
THAT'S JUST...
NO MATTER HOW BAD THINGS MIGHT LOOK, WE'LL KEEP FIGHTING UNTIL THE VERY END!
SHOOM
GIVE UP?!
DID YOU FORGET WHO YOU'RE DEALING WITH?!

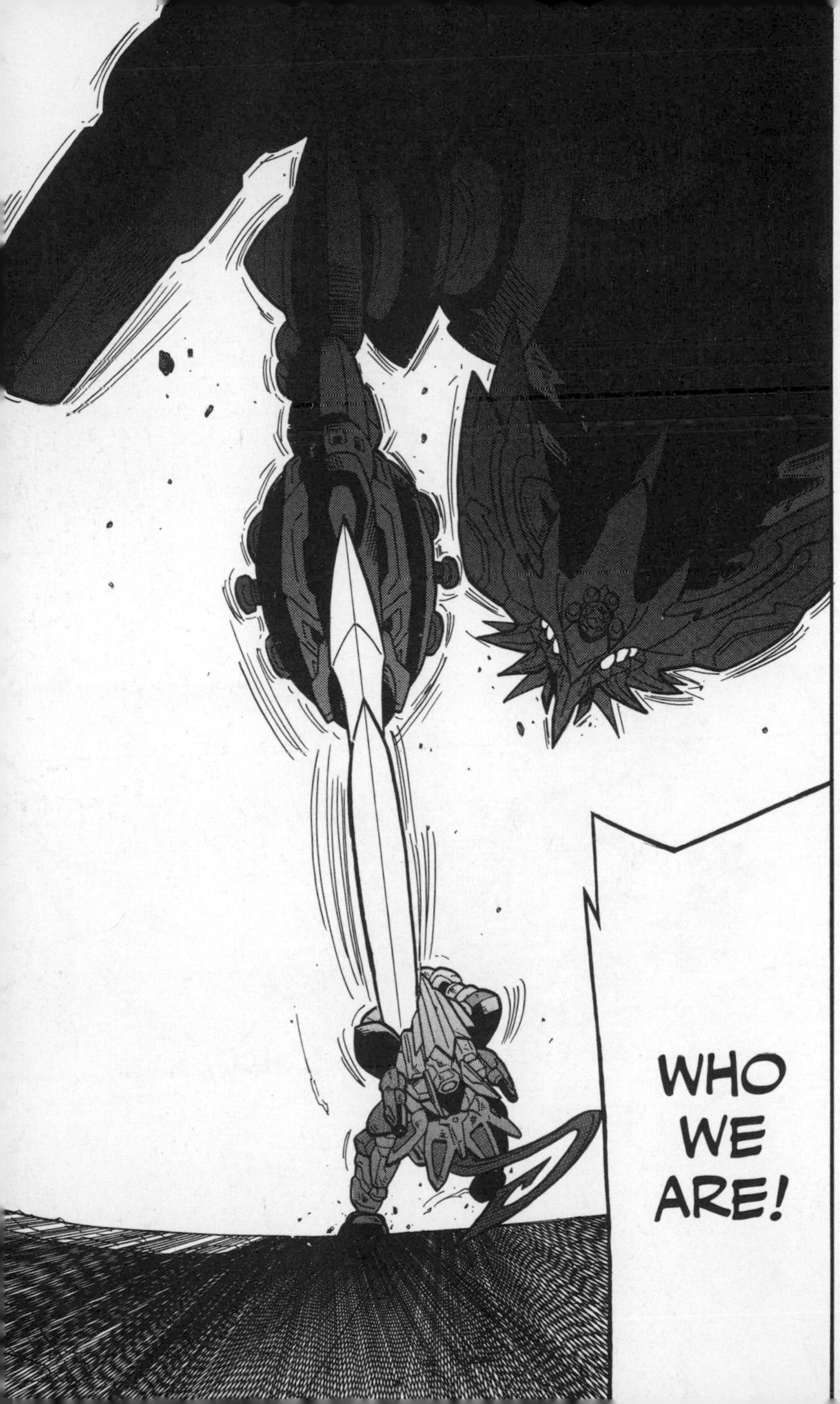
WHO WE ARE!

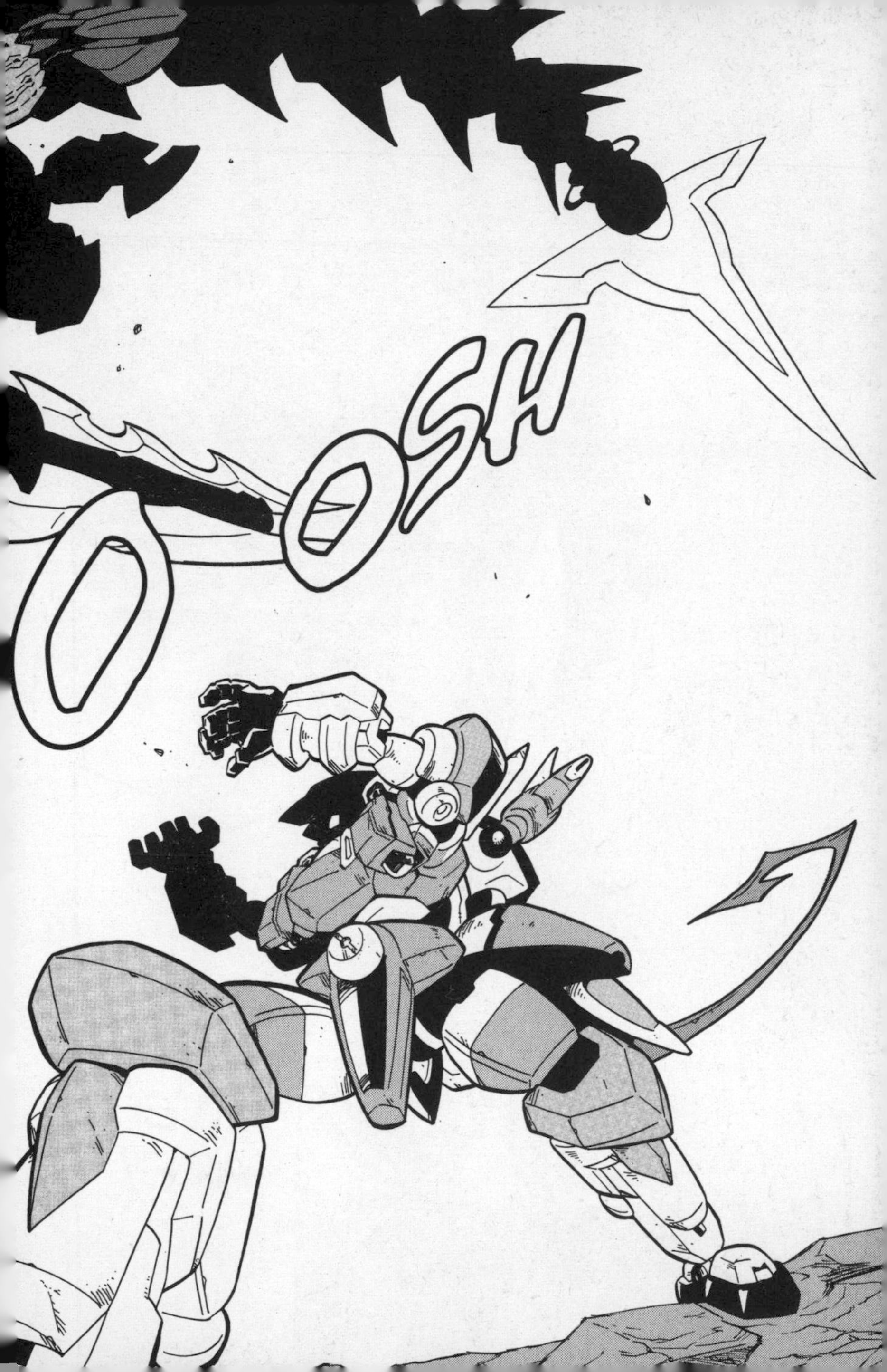
OOSH

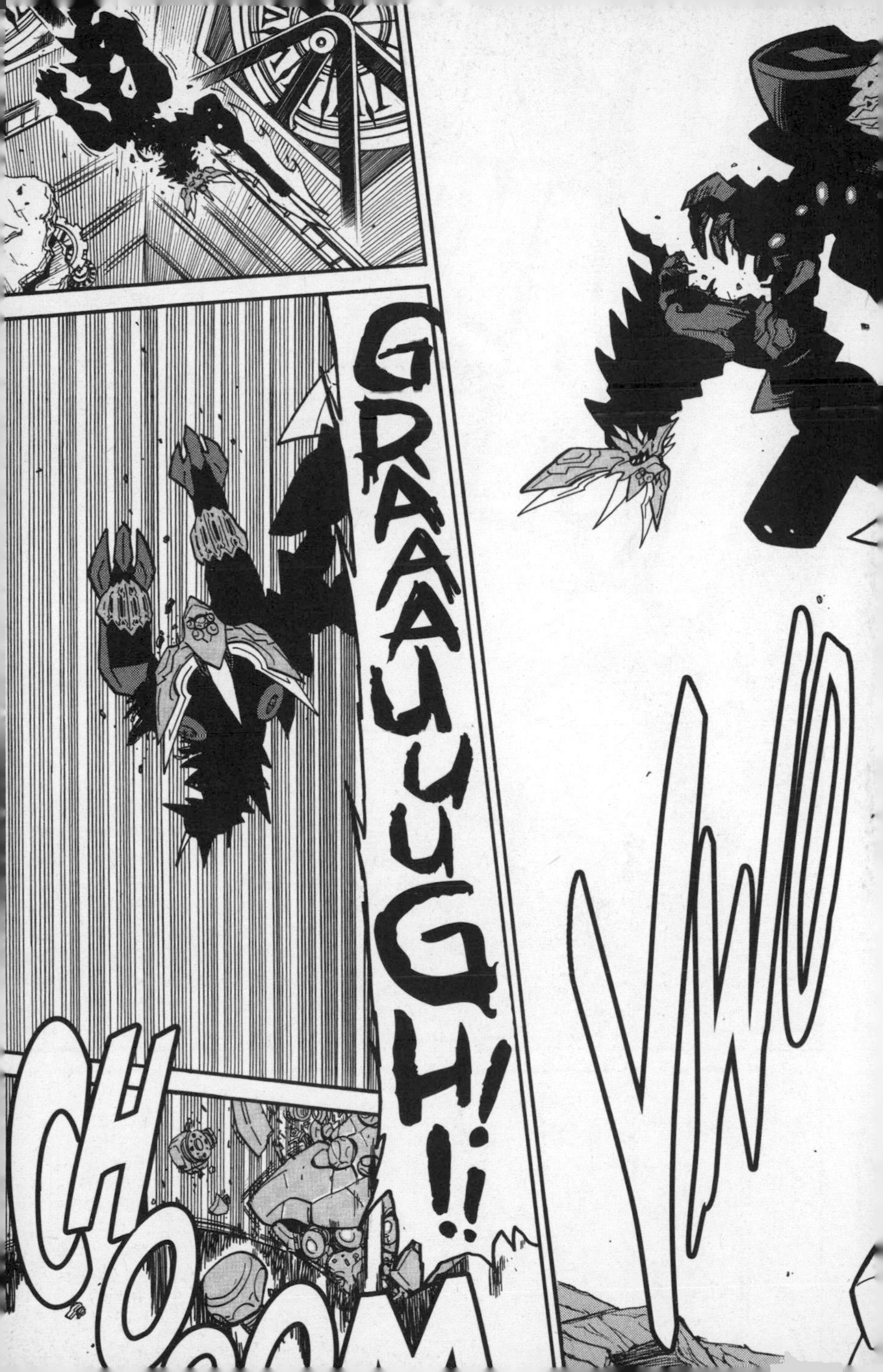
VWOO
GRAAAUUUGH!!
CHOOOM

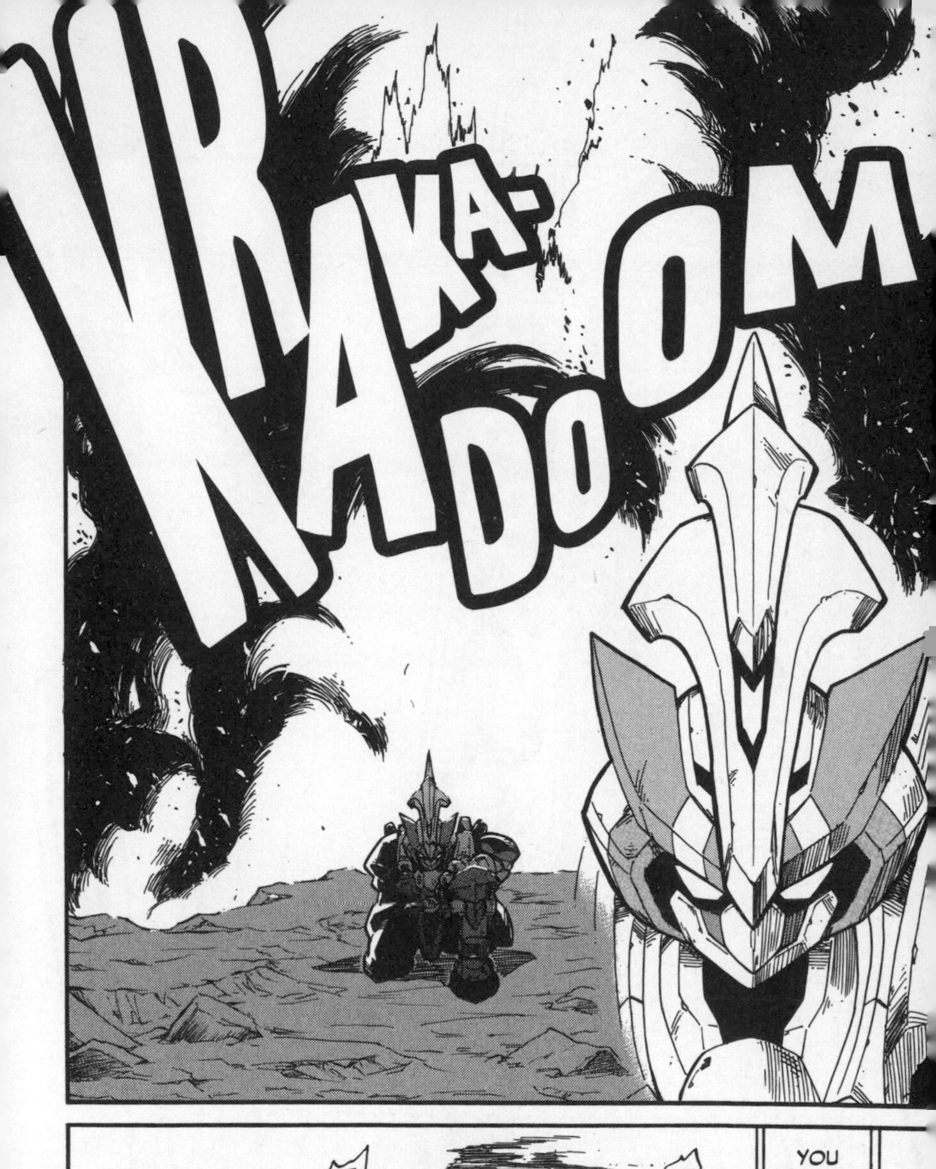
VRAKA-KADOOM

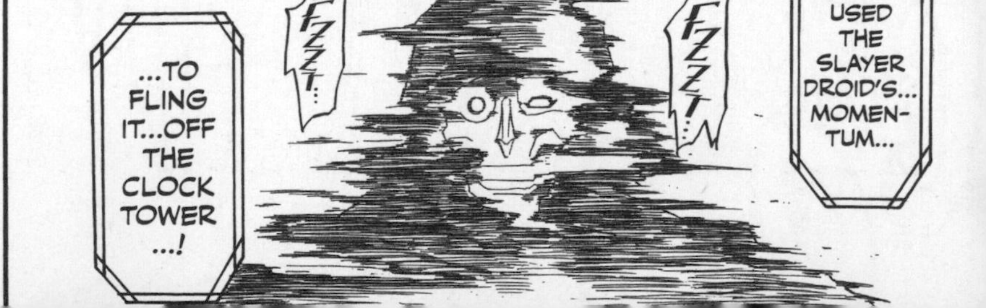
YOU USED THE SLAYER DROID'S... MOMENTUM...
FZZZT...
FZZZT...
...TO FLING IT...OFF THE CLOCK TOWER ...!

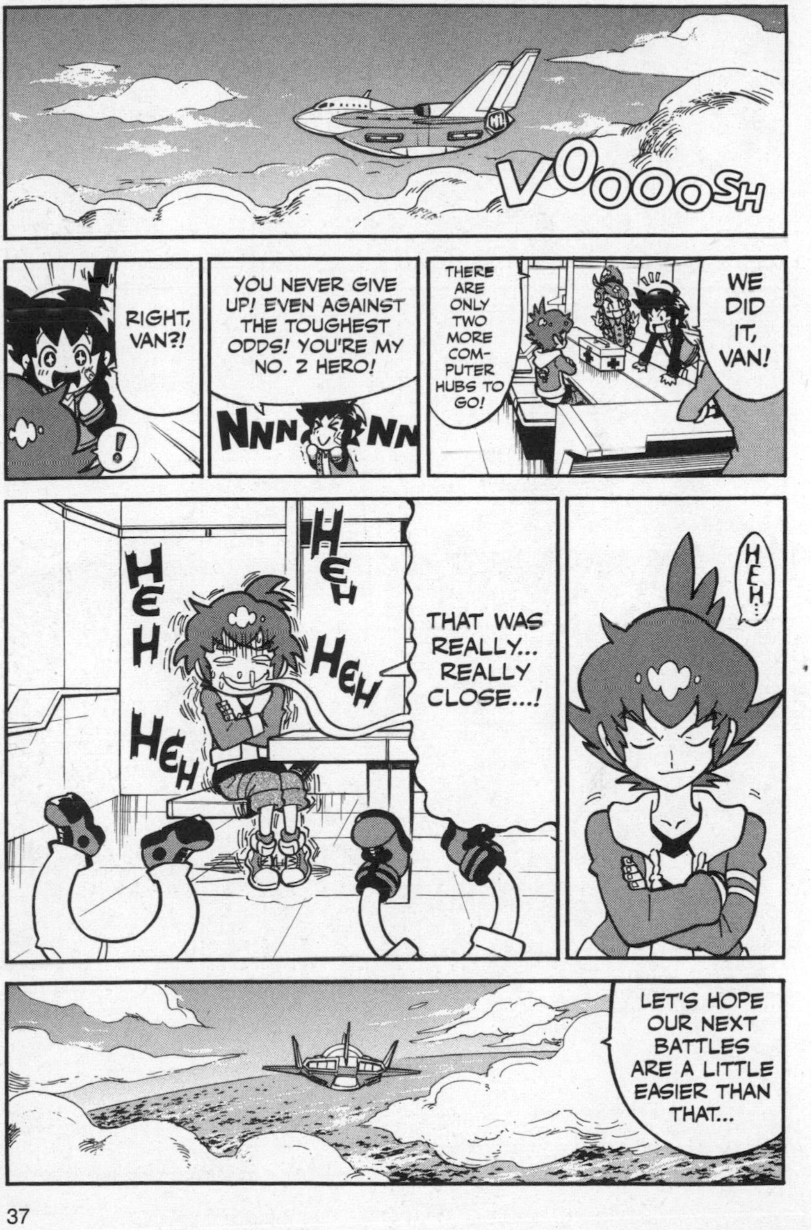
VOOOOSH
WE DID IT, VAN!
THERE ARE ONLY TWO MORE COMPUTER HUBS TO GO!
YOU NEVER GIVE UP! EVEN AGAINST THE TOUGHEST ODDS! YOU'RE MY NO. 2 HERO!
NNN NN
RIGHT, VAN?!
!
HEH...
THAT WAS REALLY... REALLY CLOSE...!
HEH HEH HEH HEH
LET'S HOPE OUR NEXT BATTLES ARE A LITTLE EASIER THAN THAT...

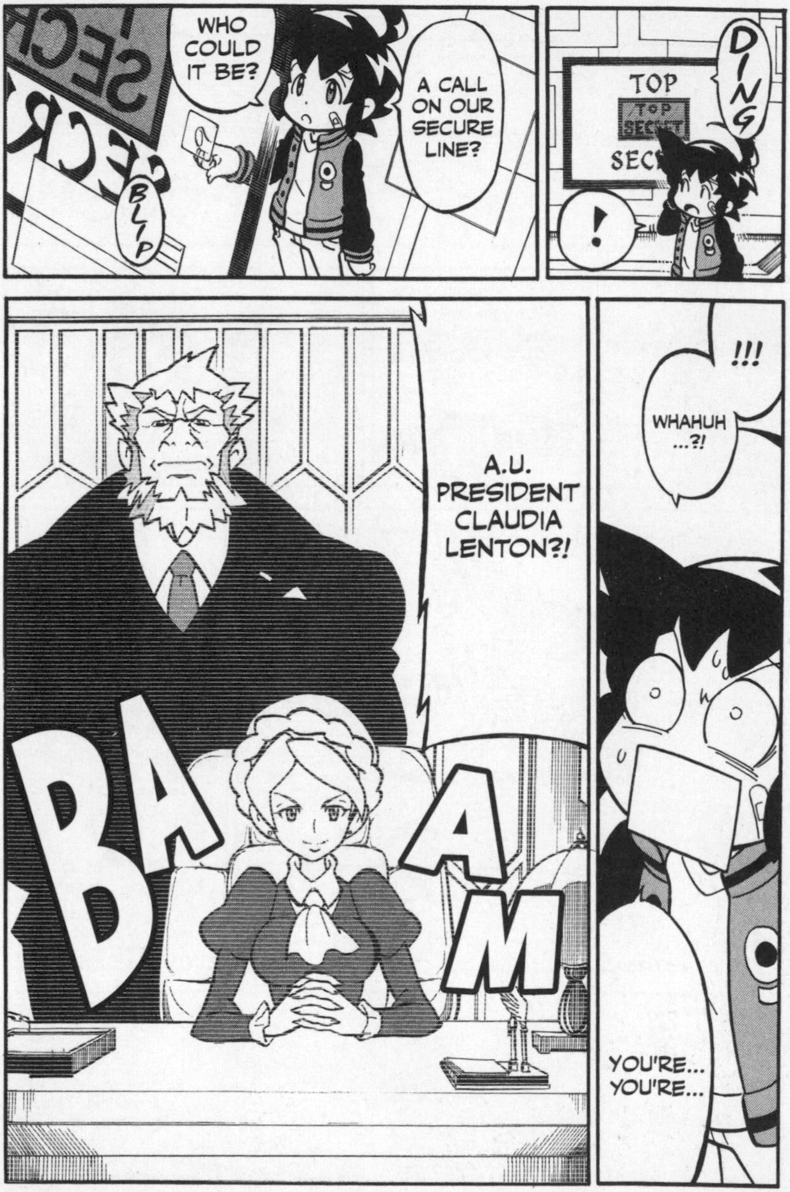
DING
TOP
!
WHO COULD IT BE?
A CALL ON OUR SECURE LINE?
BLIP
!!!
WHAHUH ...?!
YOU'RE... YOU'RE...
A.U. PRESIDENT CLAUDIA LENTON?!
BAAM

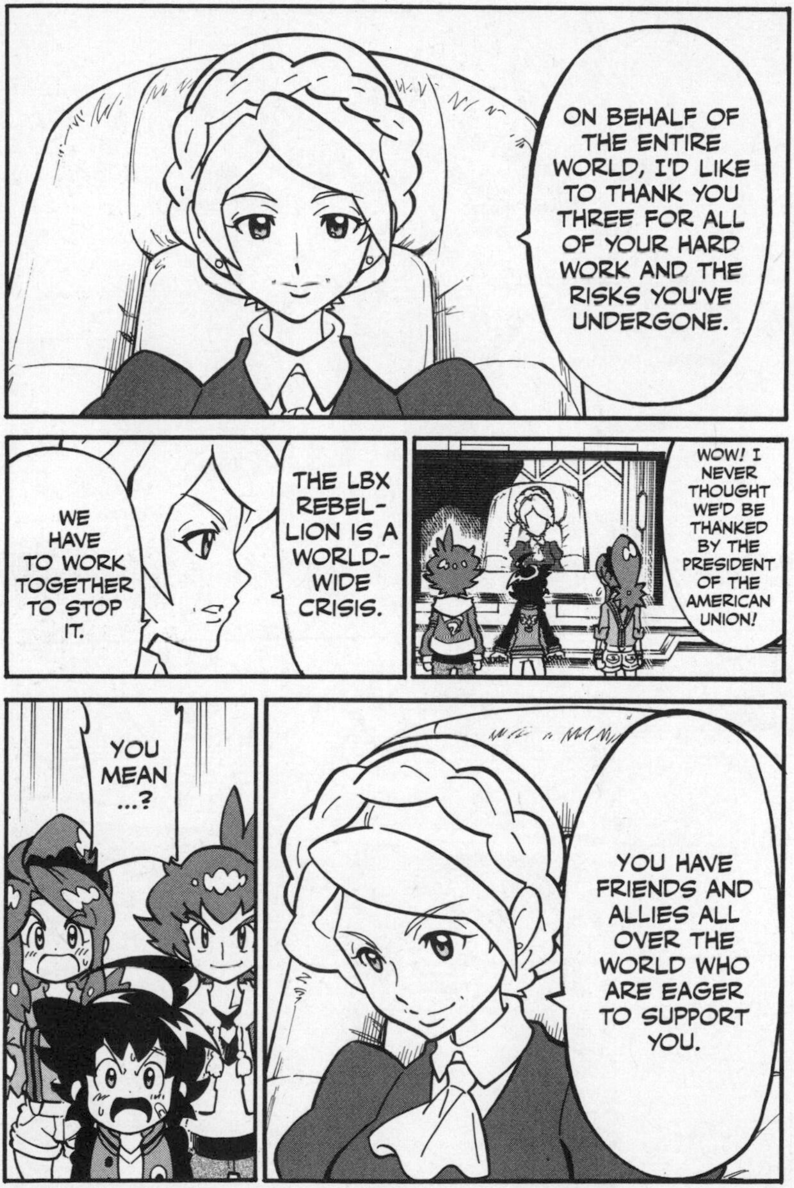
ON BEHALF OF THE ENTIRE WORLD, I'D LIKE TO THANK YOU THREE FOR ALL OF YOUR HARD WORK AND THE RISKS YOU'VE UNDERGONE.
WOW! I NEVER THOUGHT WE'D BE THANKED BY THE PRESIDENT OF THE AMERICAN UNION!
THE LBX REBEL-LION IS A WORLD-WIDE CRISIS.
WE HAVE TO WORK TOGETHER TO STOP IT.
YOU HAVE FRIENDS AND ALLIES ALL OVER THE WORLD WHO ARE EAGER TO SUPPORT YOU.
YOU MEAN ...?

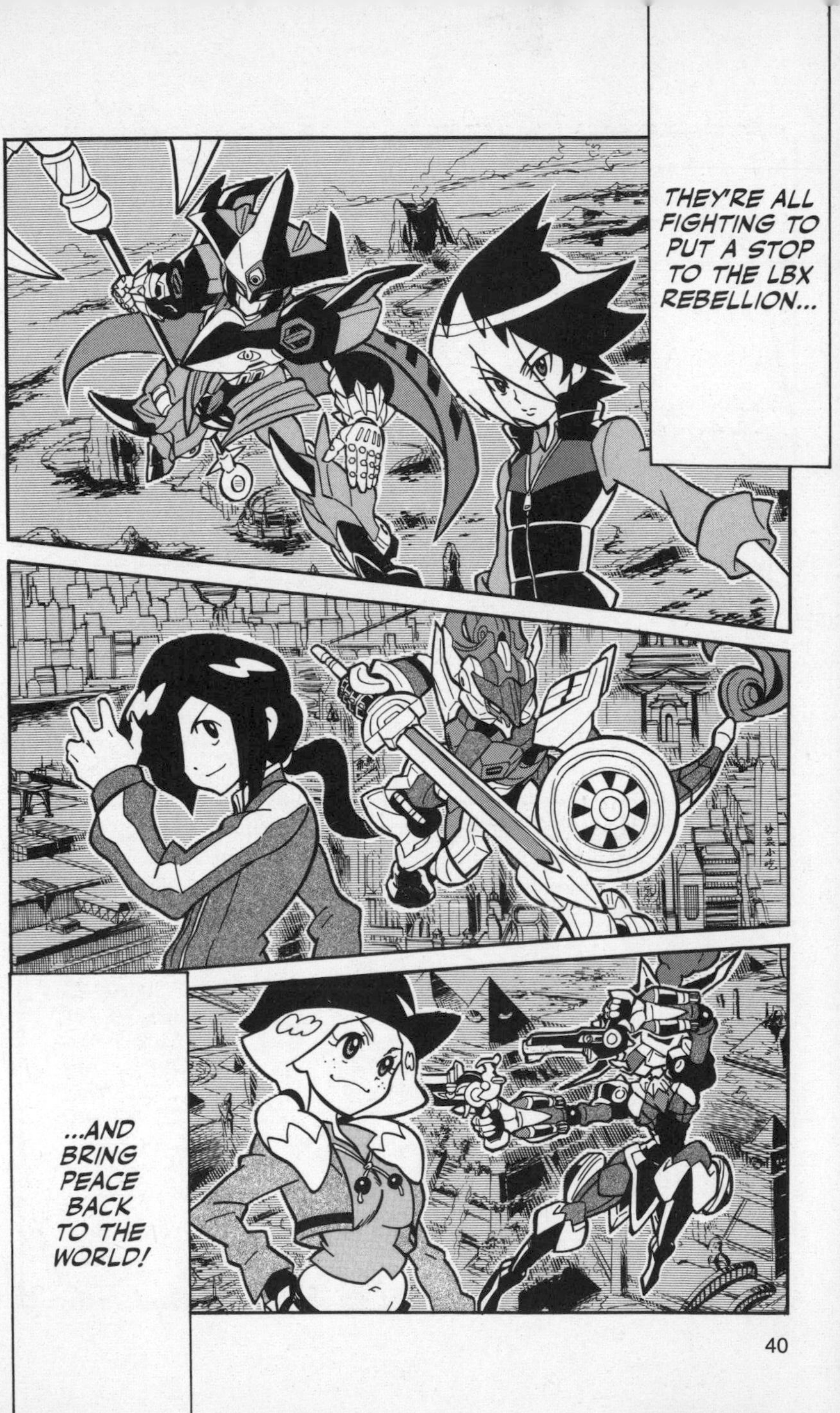
THEY'RE ALL FIGHTING TO PUT A STOP TO THE LBX REBELLION...
...AND BRING PEACE BACK TO THE WORLD!

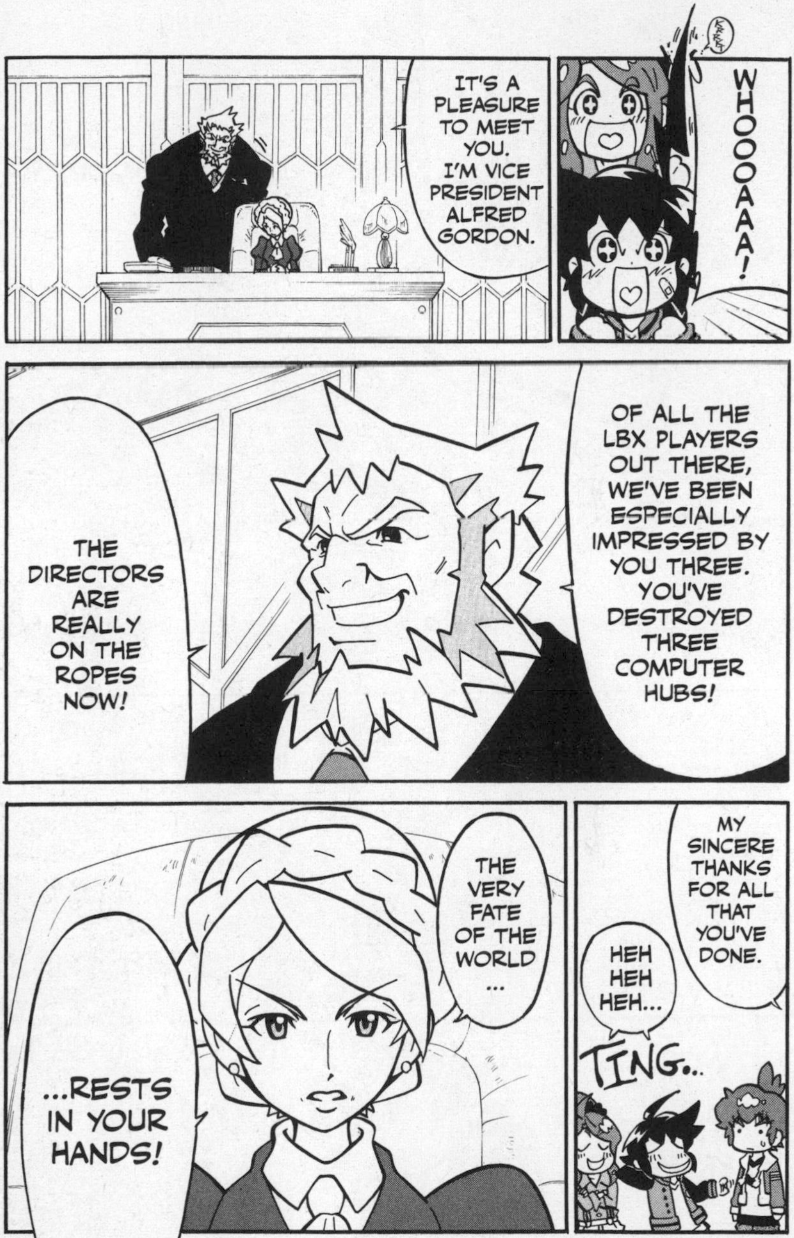
WHOOOAAA!
IT'S A PLEASURE TO MEET YOU. I'M VICE PRESIDENT ALFRED GORDON.
OF ALL THE LBX PLAYERS OUT THERE, WE'VE BEEN ESPECIALLY IMPRESSED BY YOU THREE. YOU'VE DESTROYED THREE COMPUTER HUBS!
THE DIRECTORS ARE REALLY ON THE ROPES NOW!
MY SINCERE THANKS FOR ALL THAT YOU'VE DONE.
HEH HEH HEH...
TING...
THE VERY FATE OF THE WORLD ...
...RESTS IN YOUR HANDS!

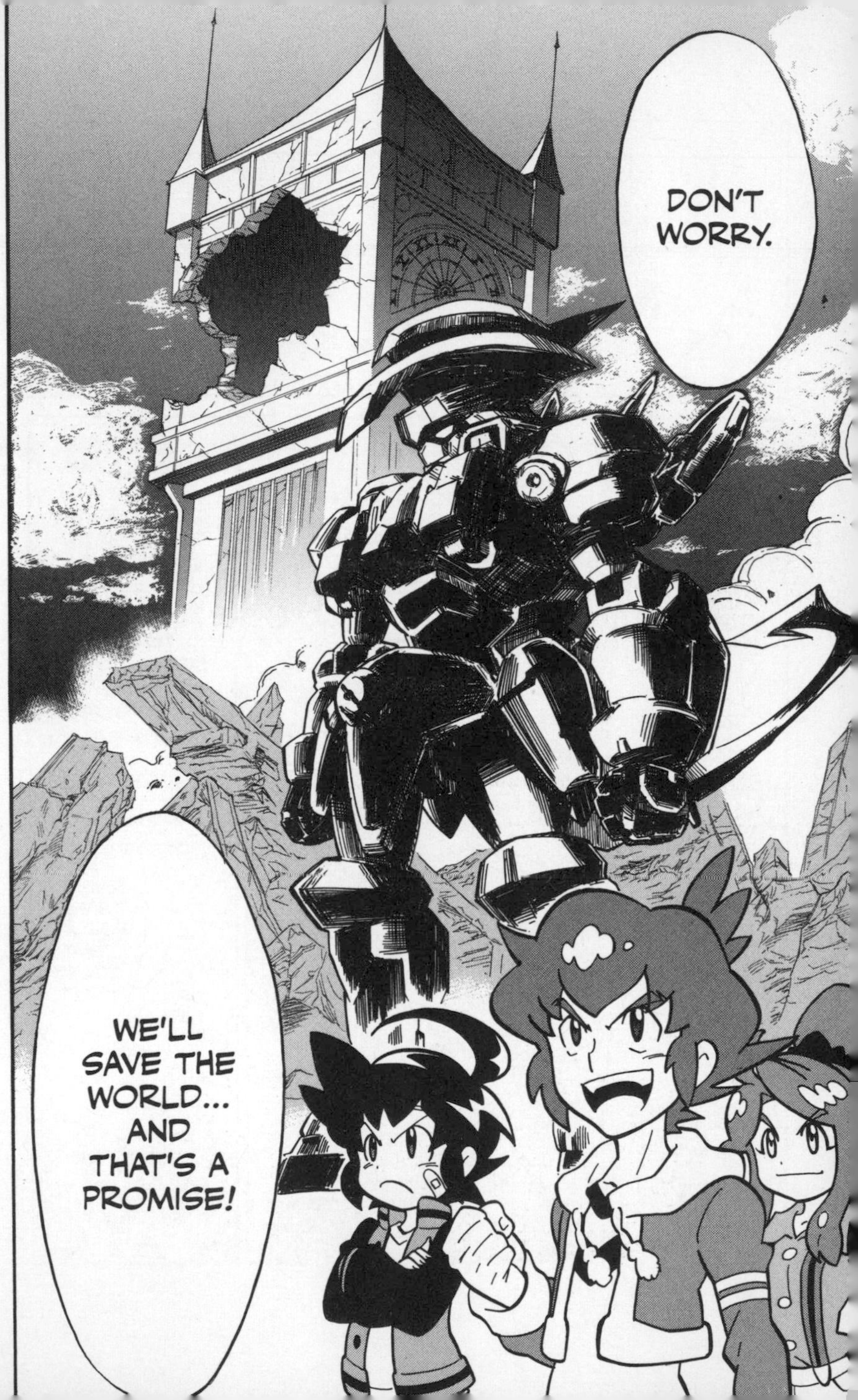
DON'T WORRY.
WE'LL SAVE THE WORLD... AND THAT'S A PROMISE!

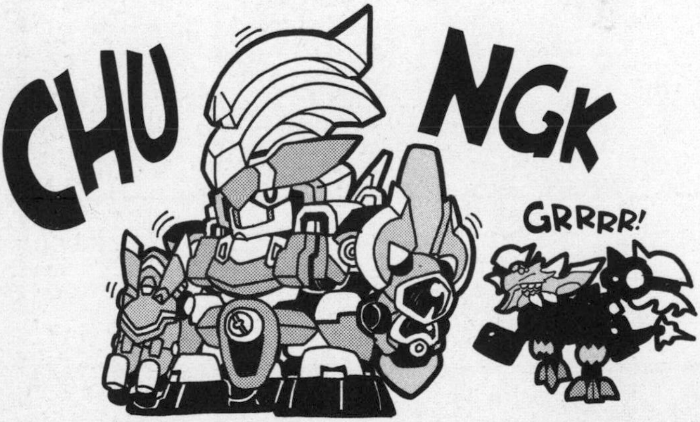
CHU NGK
GRRRR!

BONUS ILLUSTRATION GALLERY

PART 1

ENJOY ONE OF OUR SPECIAL CHAPTER TITLE PAGES FROM VOLUME 4!

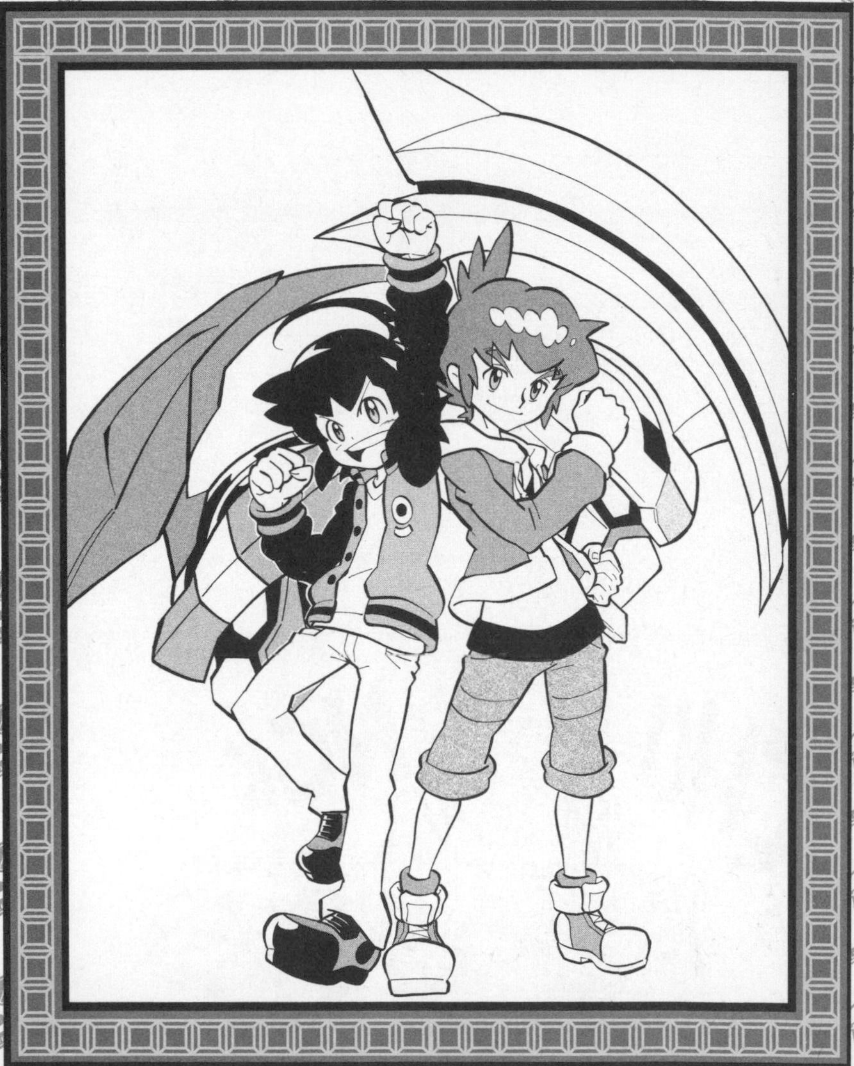

MONTHLY COROCORO COMICS, 2013
MARCH ISSUE

CHAPTER 19: TARGET: THE FINAL COMPUTER HUB

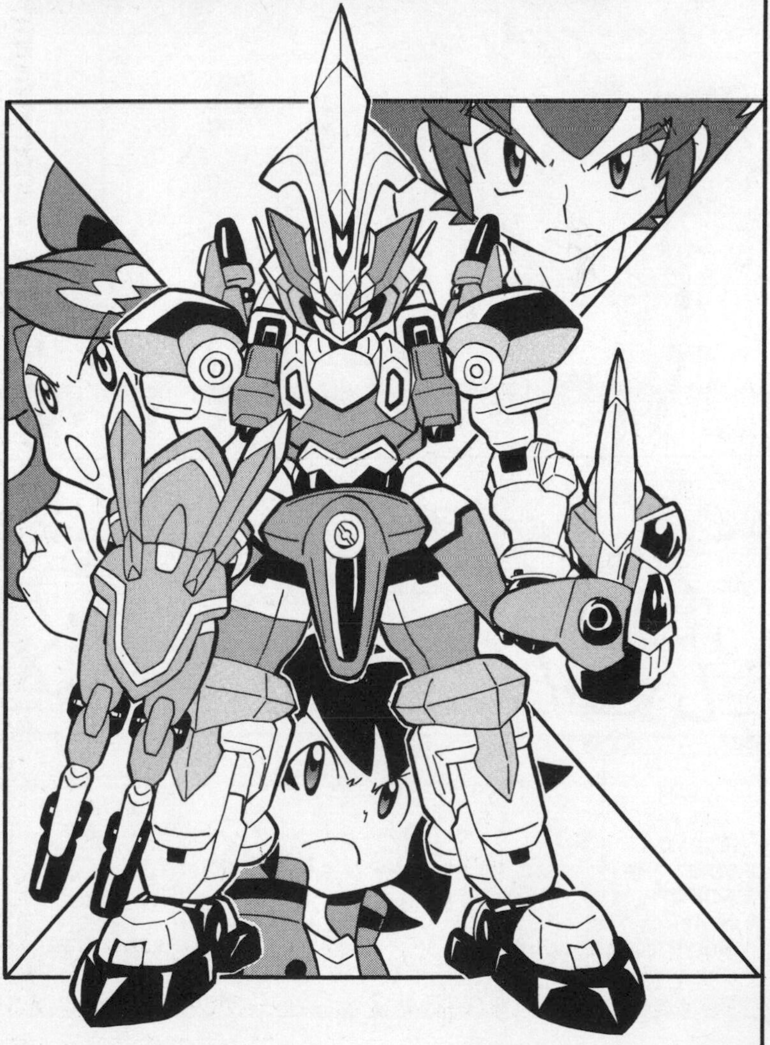

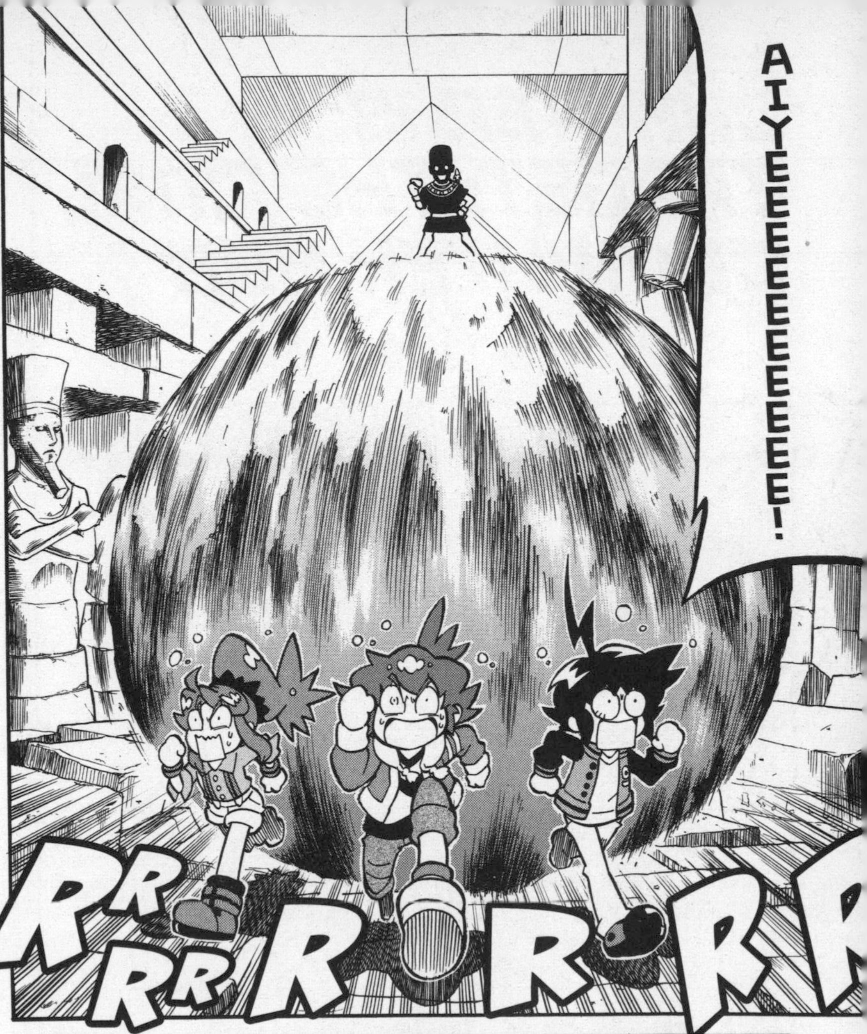
AIYEEEEEEEEEEEE!
RRRRR R R R
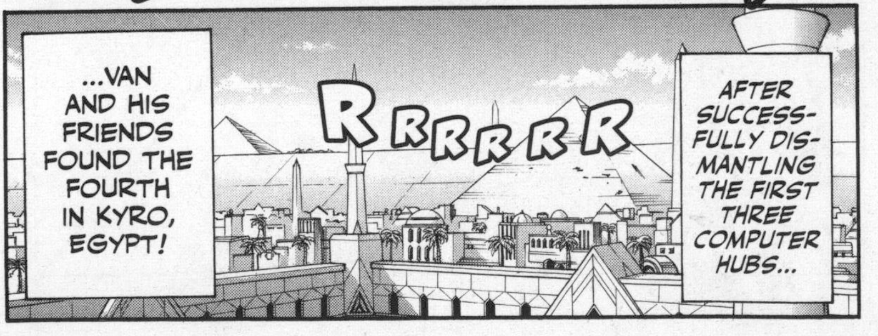
AFTER SUCCESSFULLY DISMANTLING THE FIRST THREE COMPUTER HUBS...
...VAN AND HIS FRIENDS FOUND THE FOURTH IN KYRO, EGYPT!
RRRRRRR

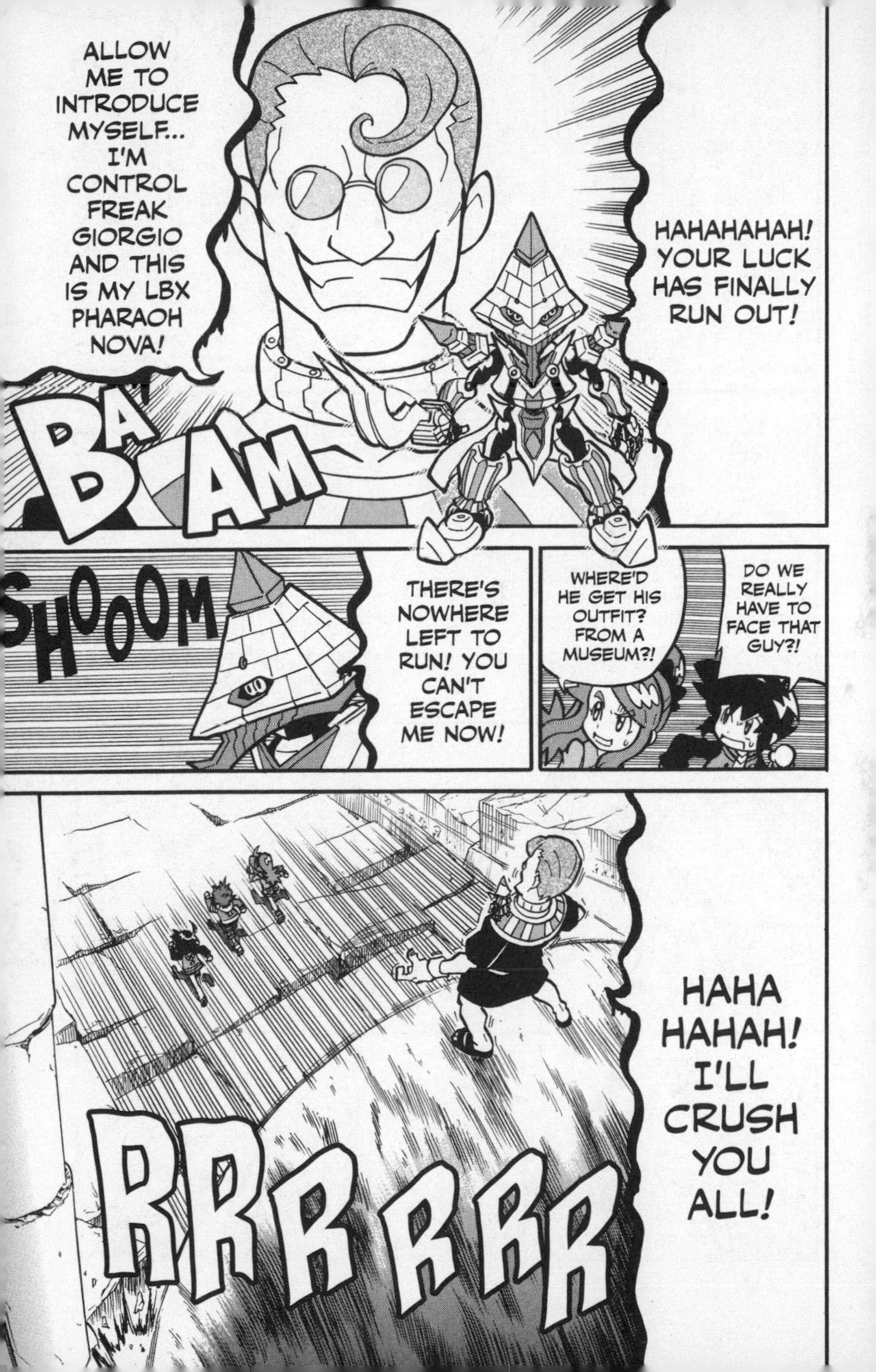
ALLOW ME TO INTRODUCE MYSELF... I'M CONTROL FREAK GIORGIO AND THIS IS MY LBX PHARAOH NOVA!
HAHAHAHAH! YOUR LUCK HAS FINALLY RUN OUT!
BAAM
DO WE REALLY HAVE TO FACE THAT GUY?!
WHERE'D HE GET HIS OUTFIT? FROM A MUSEUM?!
THERE'S NOWHERE LEFT TO RUN! YOU CAN'T ESCAPE ME NOW!
SHOOOM
HAHA HAHAH! I'LL CRUSH YOU ALL!
RRRRRR

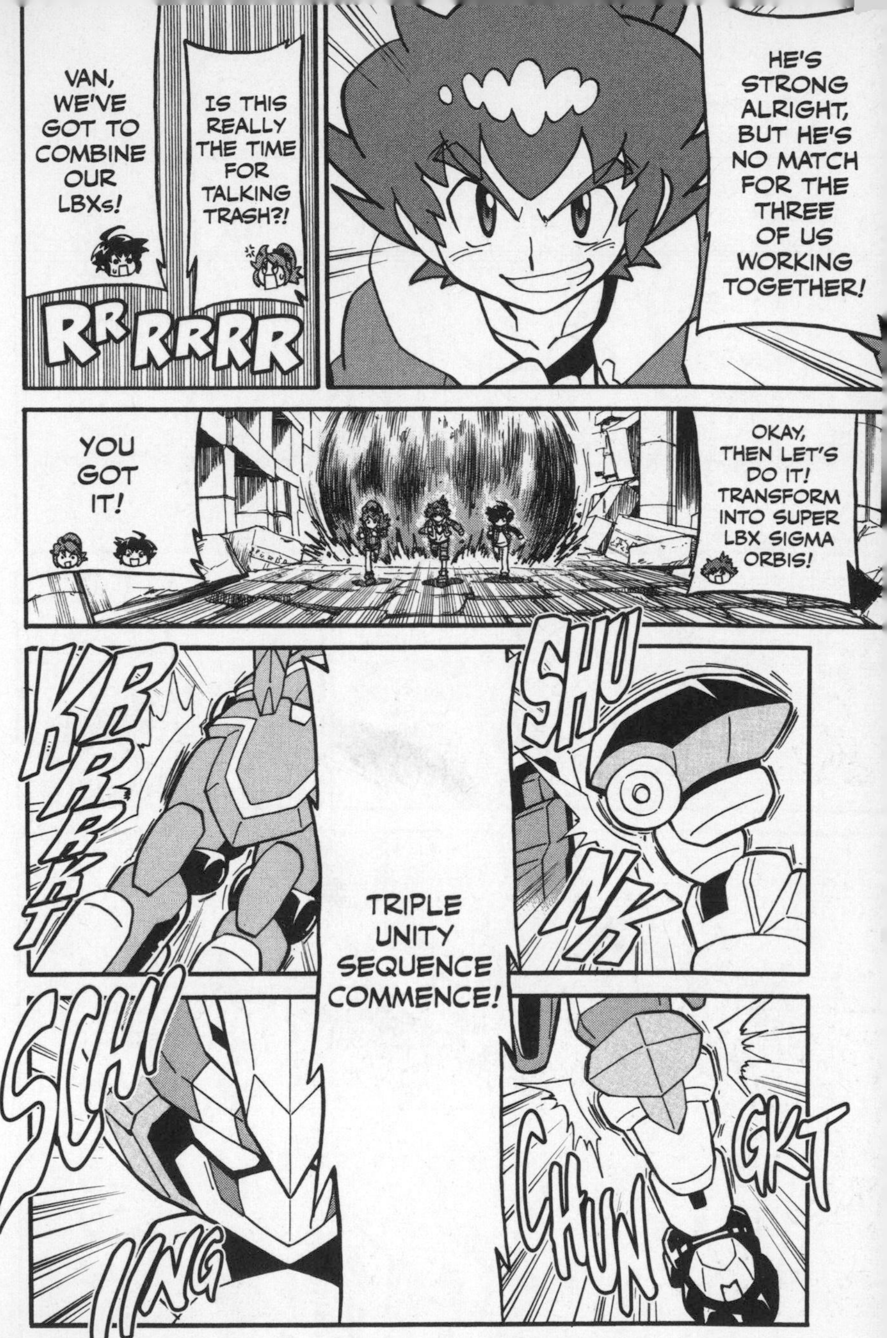
HE'S STRONG ALRIGHT, BUT HE'S NO MATCH FOR THE THREE OF US WORKING TOGETHER!
IS THIS REALLY THE TIME FOR TALKING TRASH?!
VAN, WE'VE GOT TO COMBINE OUR LBXs!
RRRRRR
OKAY, THEN LET'S DO IT! TRANSFORM INTO SUPER LBX SIGMA ORBIS!
YOU GOT IT!
SHUNK
KRRRT
TRIPLE UNITY SEQUENCE COMMENCE!
CHUNGKT
SCHING

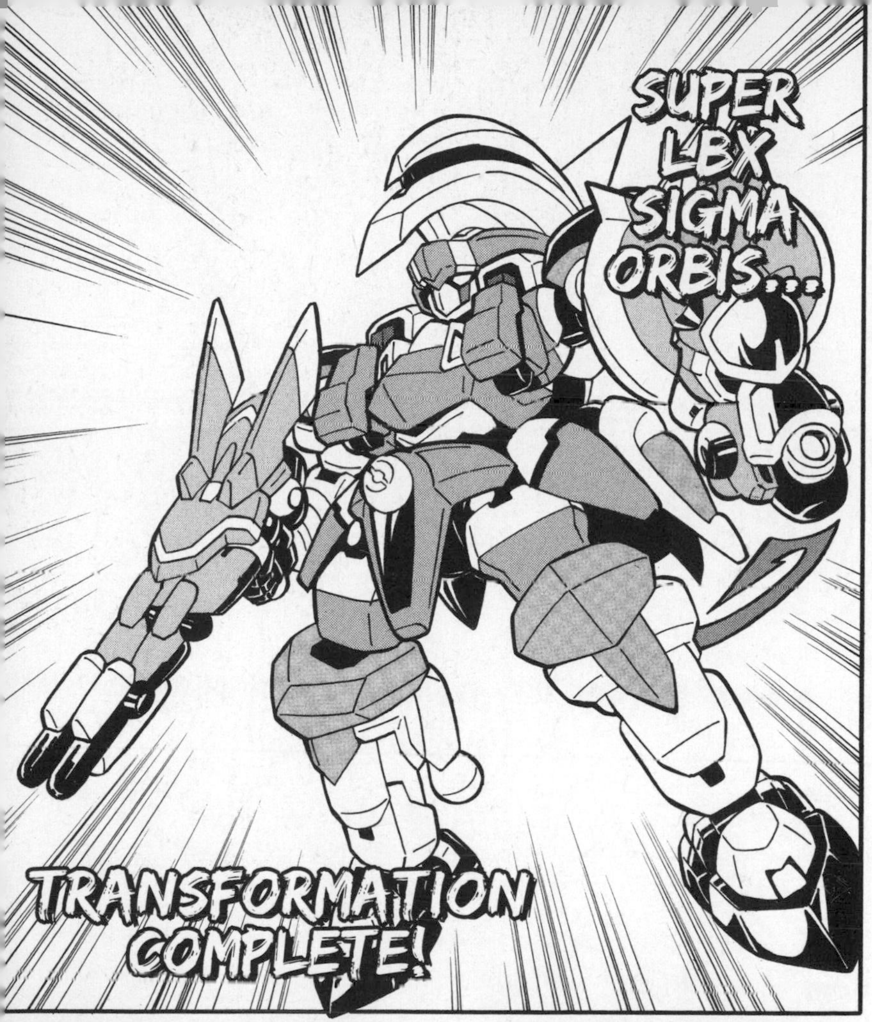
SUPER LBX SIGMA ORBIS...
TRANSFORMATION COMPLETE!
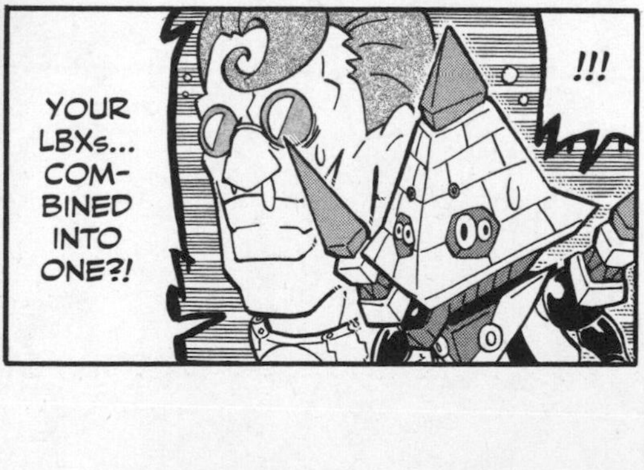
!!!
YOUR LBXs... COM-BINED INTO ONE?!
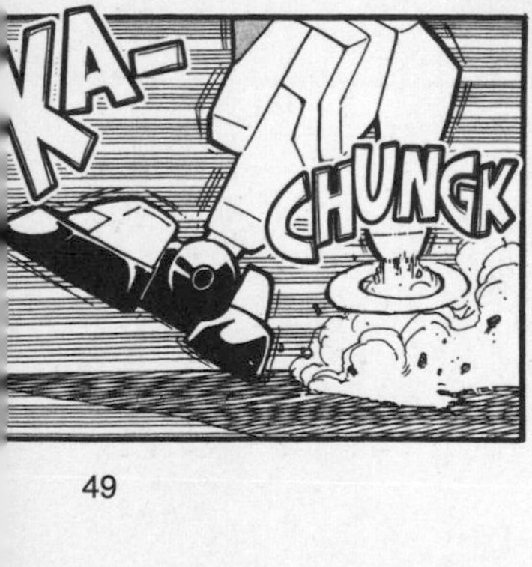
KA-
CHUNCK

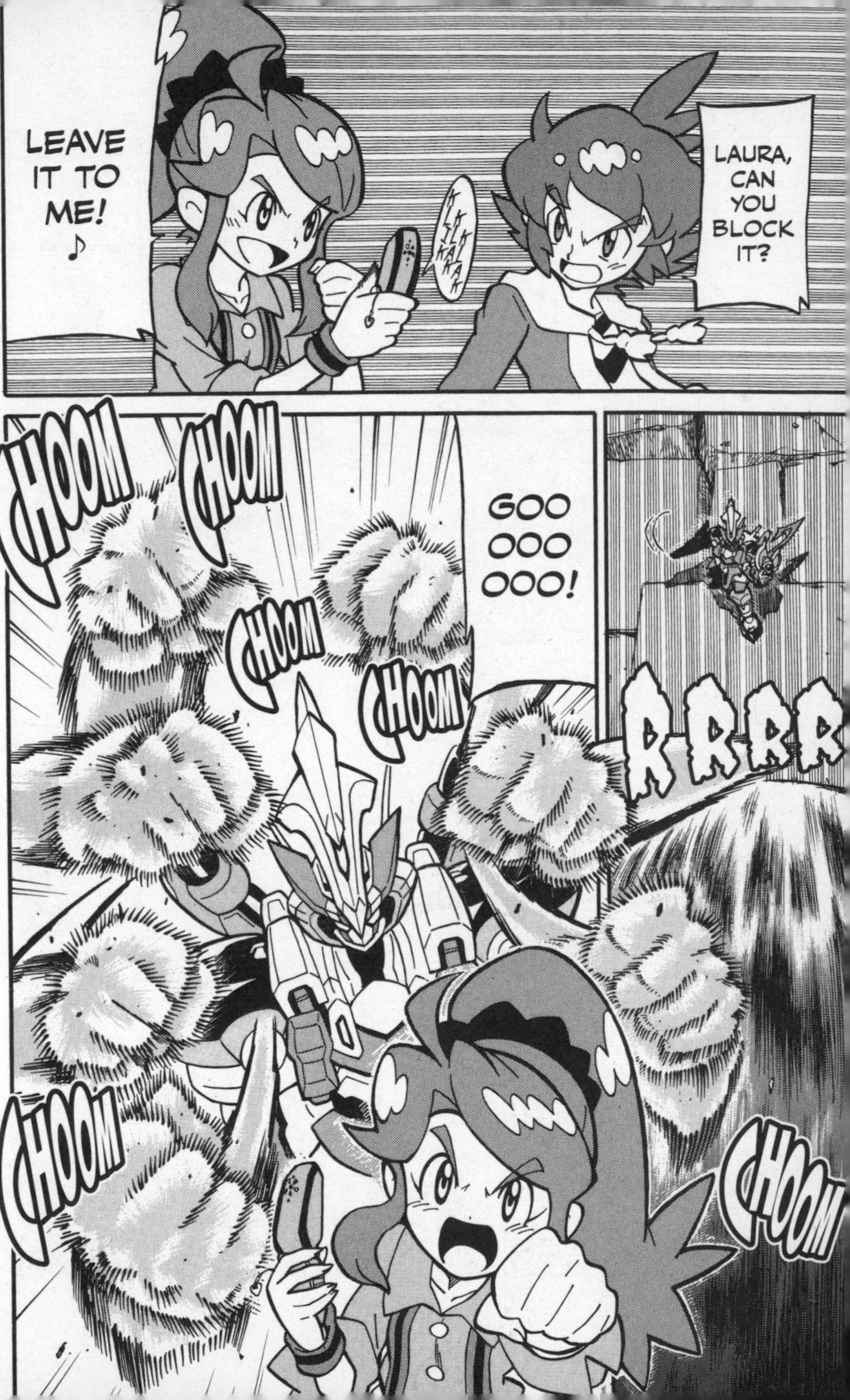
LAURA, CAN YOU BLOCK IT?
LEAVE IT TO ME! ♪
RRRR
CHOOM
CHOOM
GOO OOO OOO!
CHOOM
CHOOM
CHOOM
CHOOM
CHOOM

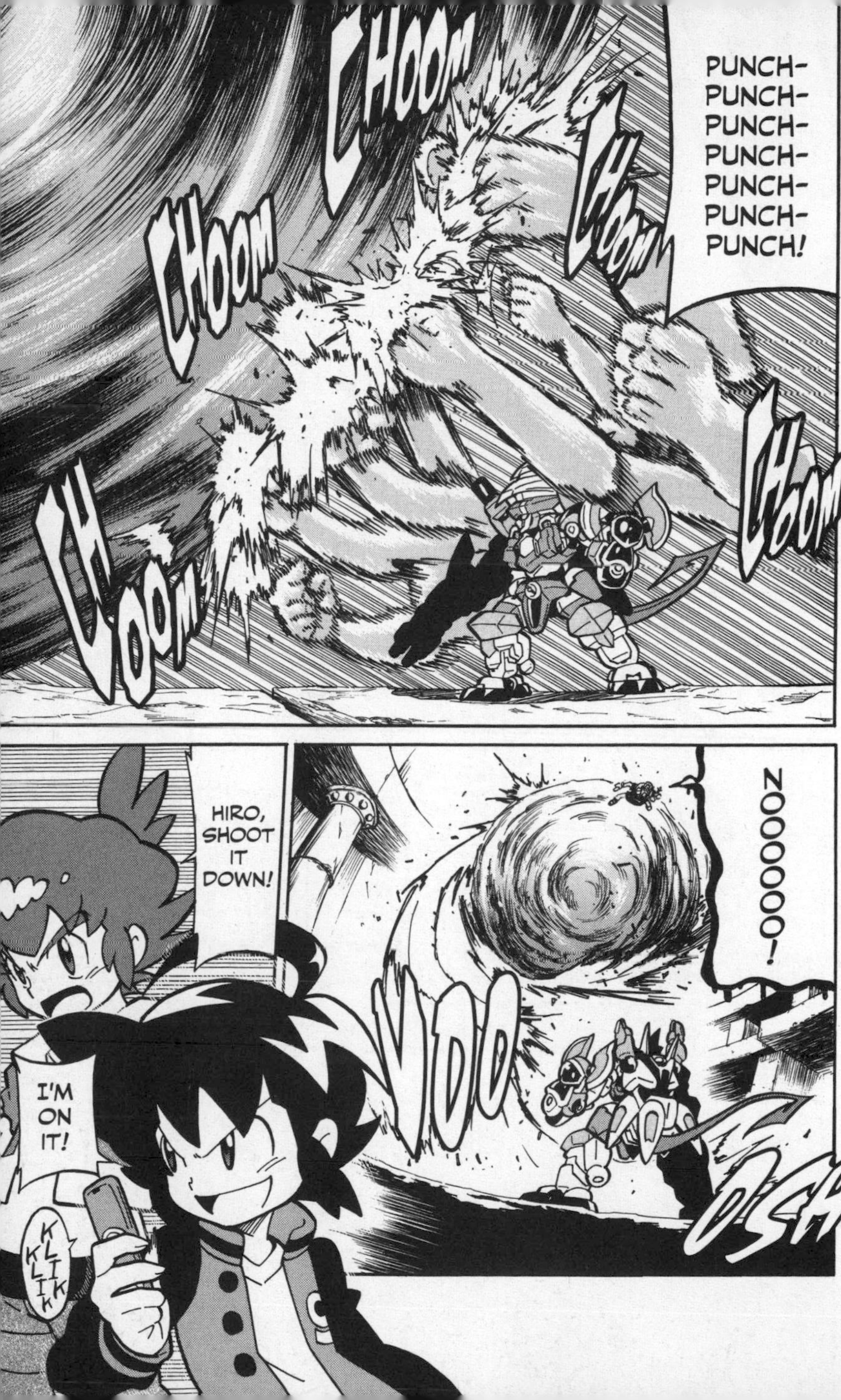
PUNCH-PUNCH-PUNCH-PUNCH-PUNCH-PUNCH-PUNCH!
CHOOM
CHOOM
CHOOM
CHOOM
CHOOM
CHOOM
NOOOOOOO!
HIRO, SHOOT IT DOWN!
VDOO
OSH
I'M ON IT!
KLIK KLIK

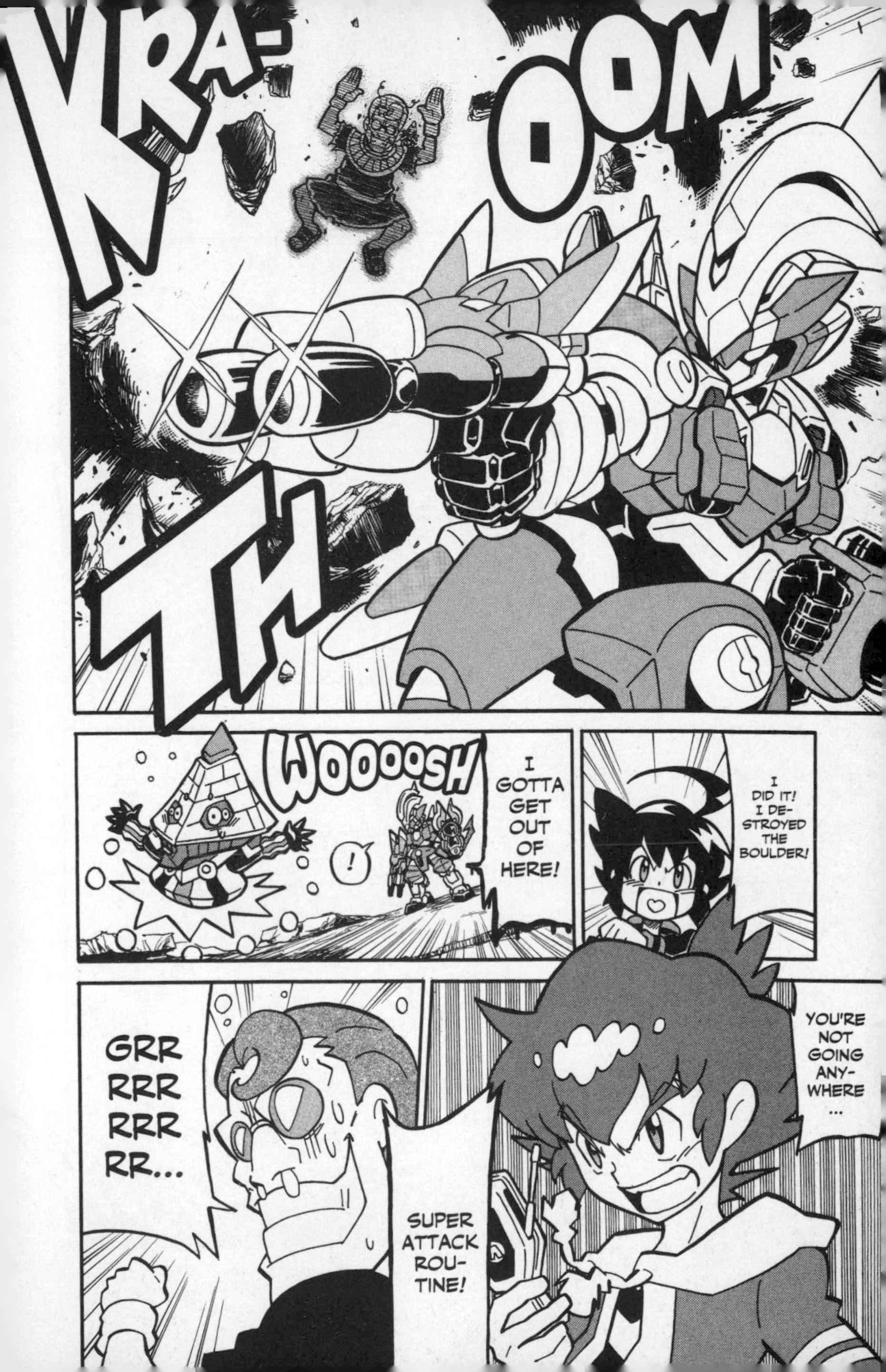
KRA-
OOM
TH
I DID IT! I DESTROYED THE BOULDER!
I GOTTA GET OUT OF HERE!
WOOOOSH
!
YOU'RE NOT GOING ANYWHERE...
SUPER ATTACK ROUTINE!
GRR RRR RRR RR...

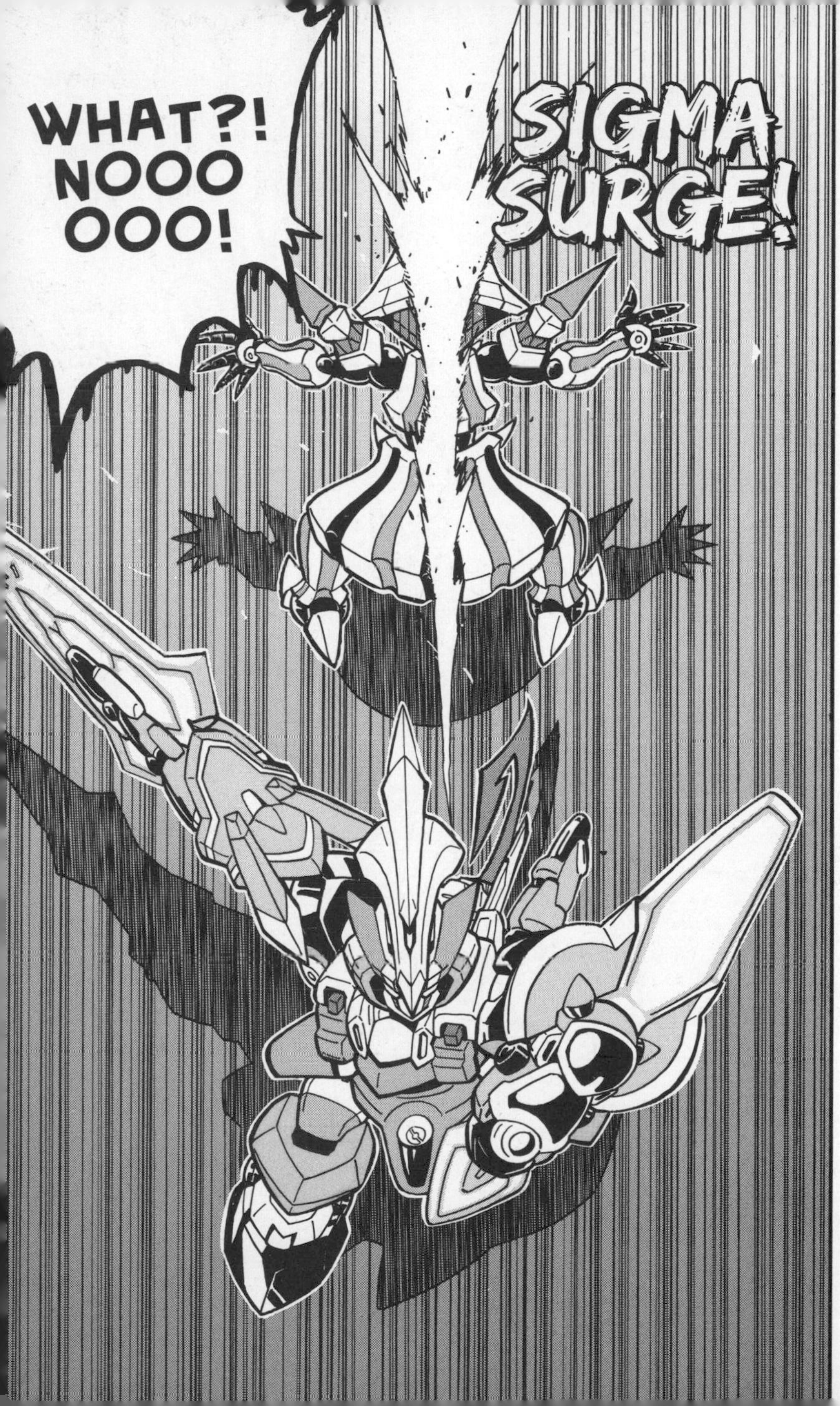
SIGMA SURGE!
WHAT?! NOOOOOO!

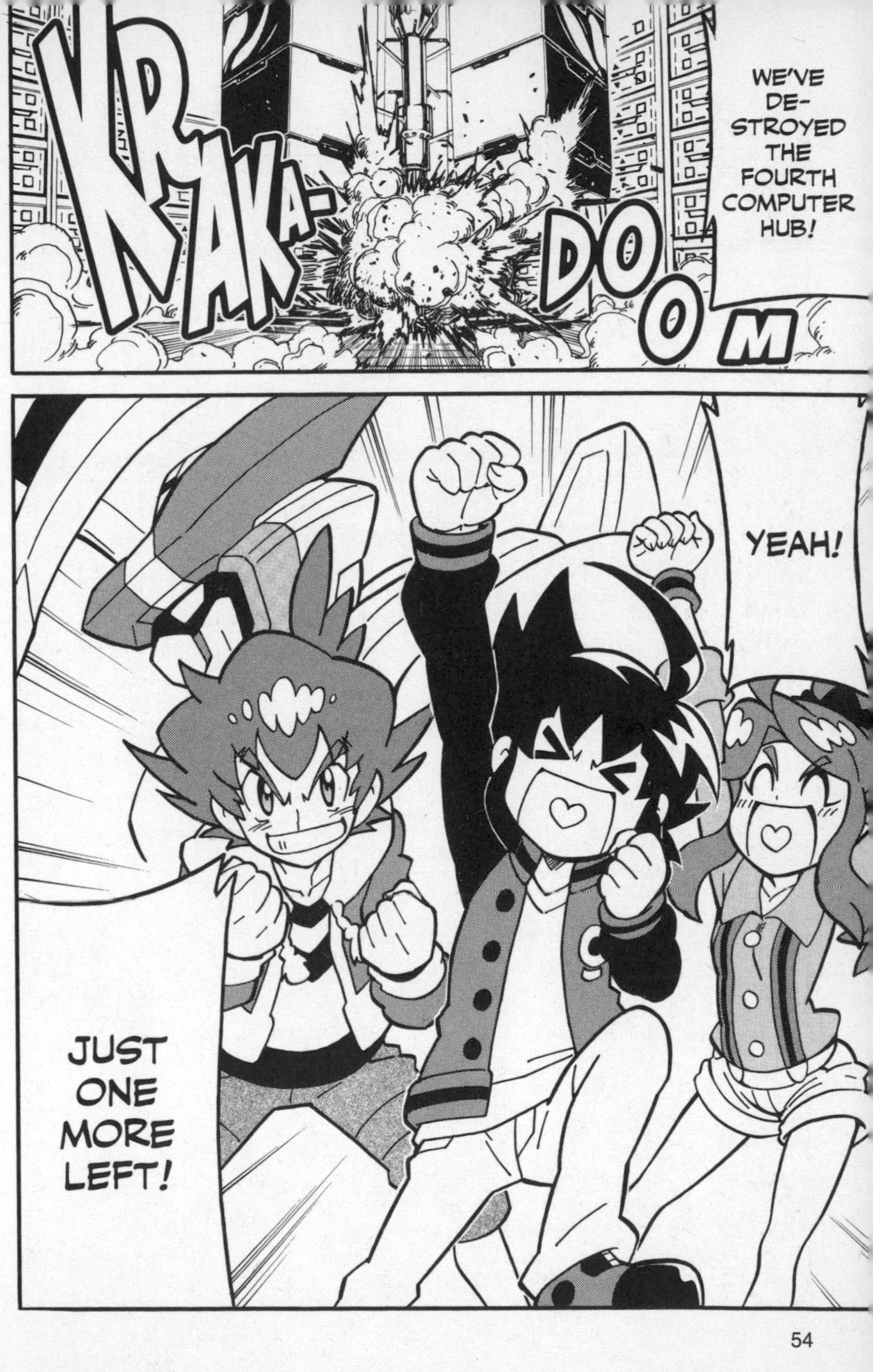
WE'VE DE-STROYED THE FOURTH COMPUTER HUB!
KRAKA-DOOOM
YEAH!
JUST ONE MORE LEFT!

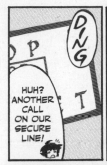

FOOOSH...
DING
HUH? ANOTHER CALL ON OUR SECURE LINE!
EXCELLENT WORK, YOU THREE!
VICE PRESIDENT GORDON!
MADAM PRESIDENT IS HARD AT WORK ON OFFICIAL BUSINESS, BUT SHE WANTED ME TO CALL AND THANK YOU.
ARE YOU SURPRISED THAT YOU DIDN'T GET BOTH OF US THIS TIME? I HOPE I'M NOT A DISAPPOINTMENT...
HA HA HA
WHAAAAA
NO NO NO NO! NOT AT ALL!

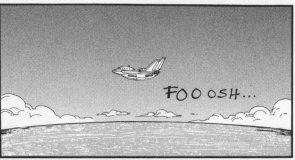

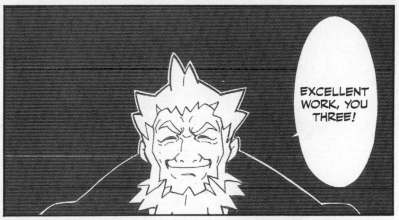

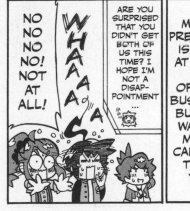

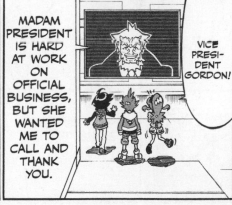

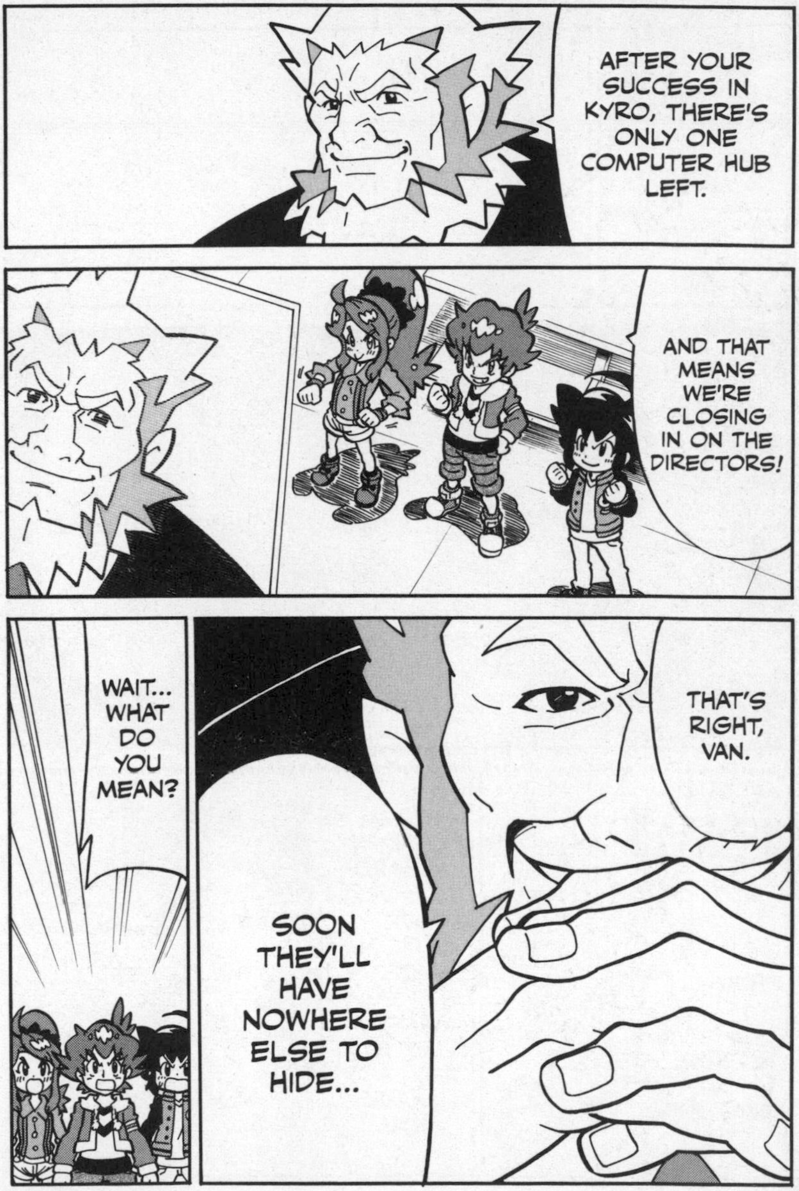
AFTER YOUR SUCCESS IN KYRO, THERE'S ONLY ONE COMPUTER HUB LEFT.
AND THAT MEANS WE'RE CLOSING IN ON THE DIRECTORS!
THAT'S RIGHT, VAN.
SOON THEY'LL HAVE NOWHERE ELSE TO HIDE...
WAIT... WHAT DO YOU MEAN?

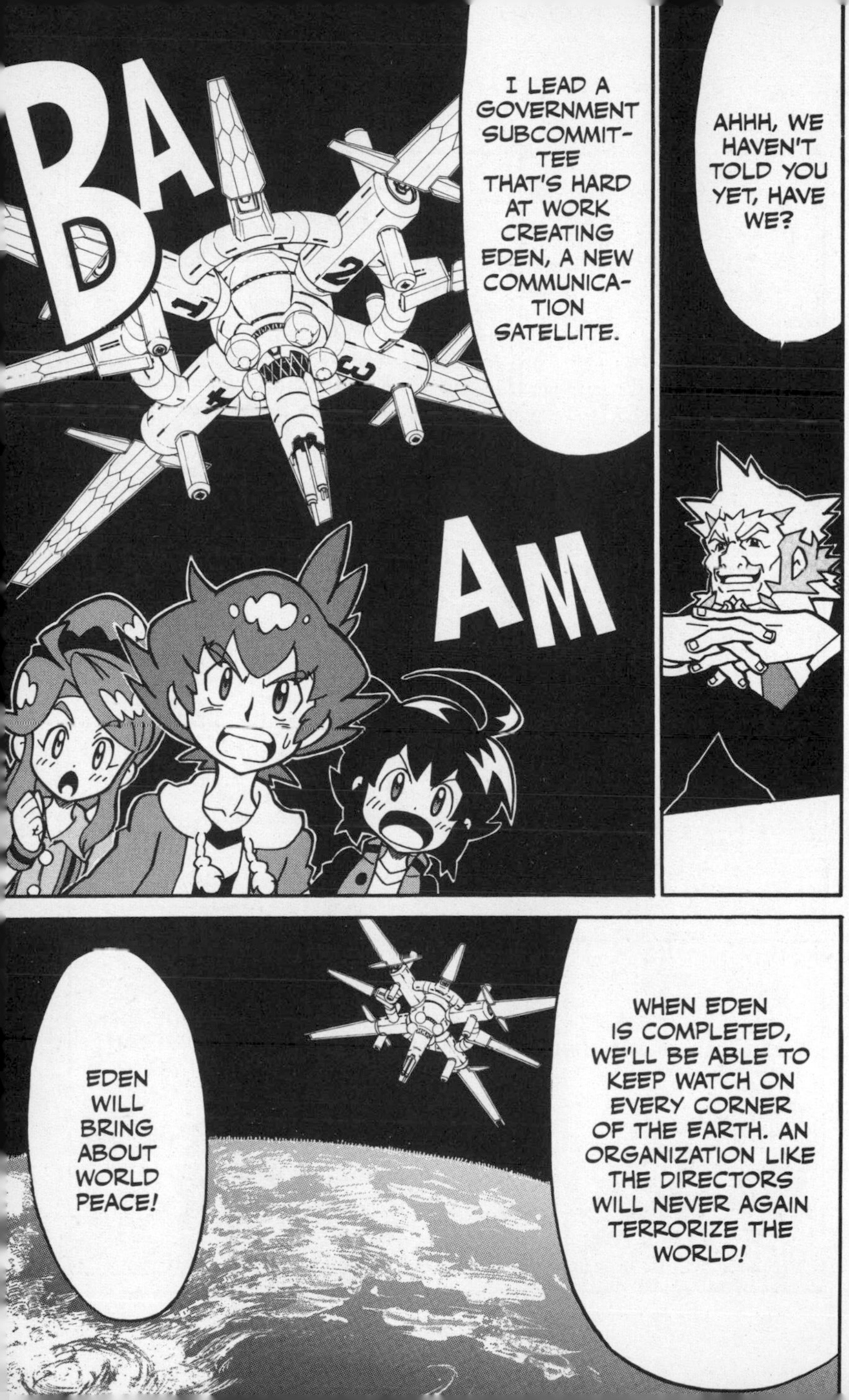

AHHH, WE HAVEN'T TOLD YOU YET, HAVE WE?
I LEAD A GOVERNMENT SUBCOMMIT-TEE THAT'S HARD AT WORK CREATING EDEN, A NEW COMMUNICA-TION SATELLITE.
BADAM
WHEN EDEN IS COMPLETED, WE'LL BE ABLE TO KEEP WATCH ON EVERY CORNER OF THE EARTH. AN ORGANIZATION LIKE THE DIRECTORS WILL NEVER AGAIN TERRORIZE THE WORLD!
EDEN WILL BRING ABOUT WORLD PEACE!

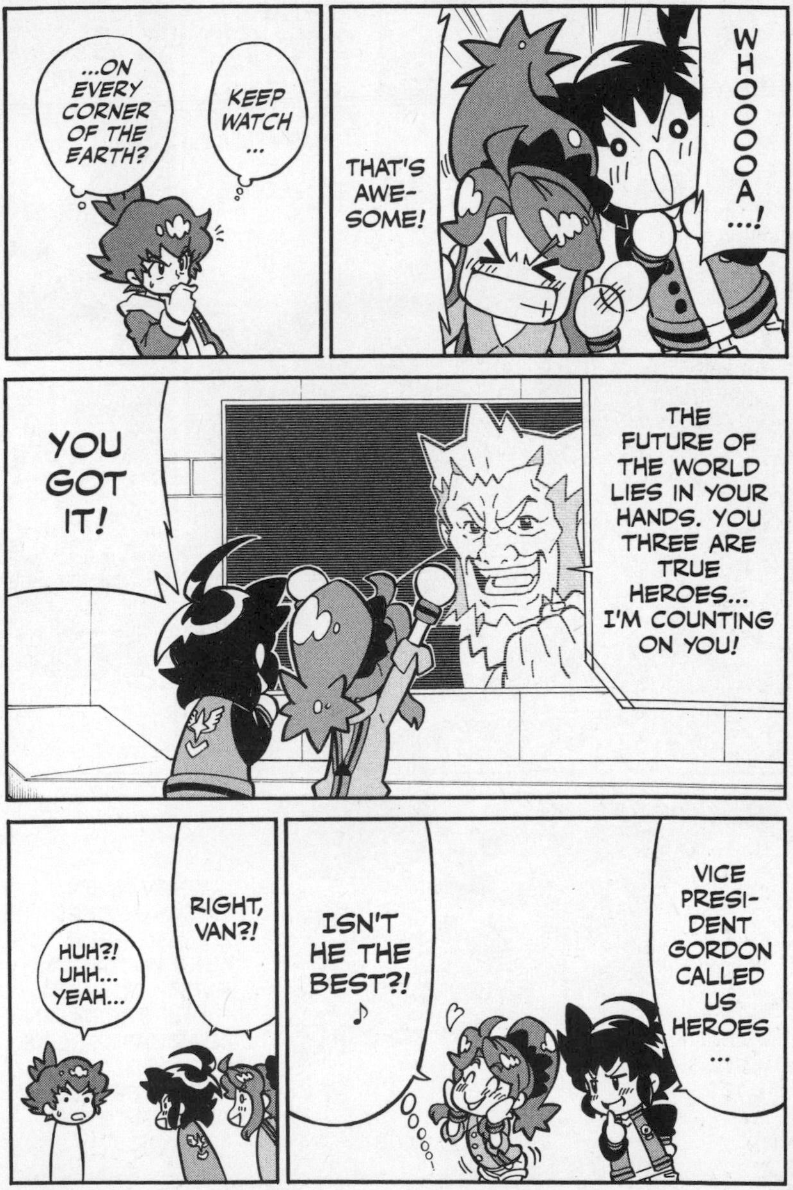
WHOOOOA...!
THAT'S AWE-SOME!
KEEP WATCH...
...ON EVERY CORNER OF THE EARTH?
THE FUTURE OF THE WORLD LIES IN YOUR HANDS. YOU THREE ARE TRUE HEROES... I'M COUNTING ON YOU!
YOU GOT IT!
VICE PRESI-DENT GORDON CALLED US HEROES...
ISN'T HE THE BEST?! ♪
RIGHT, VAN?!
HUH?! UHH... YEAH...

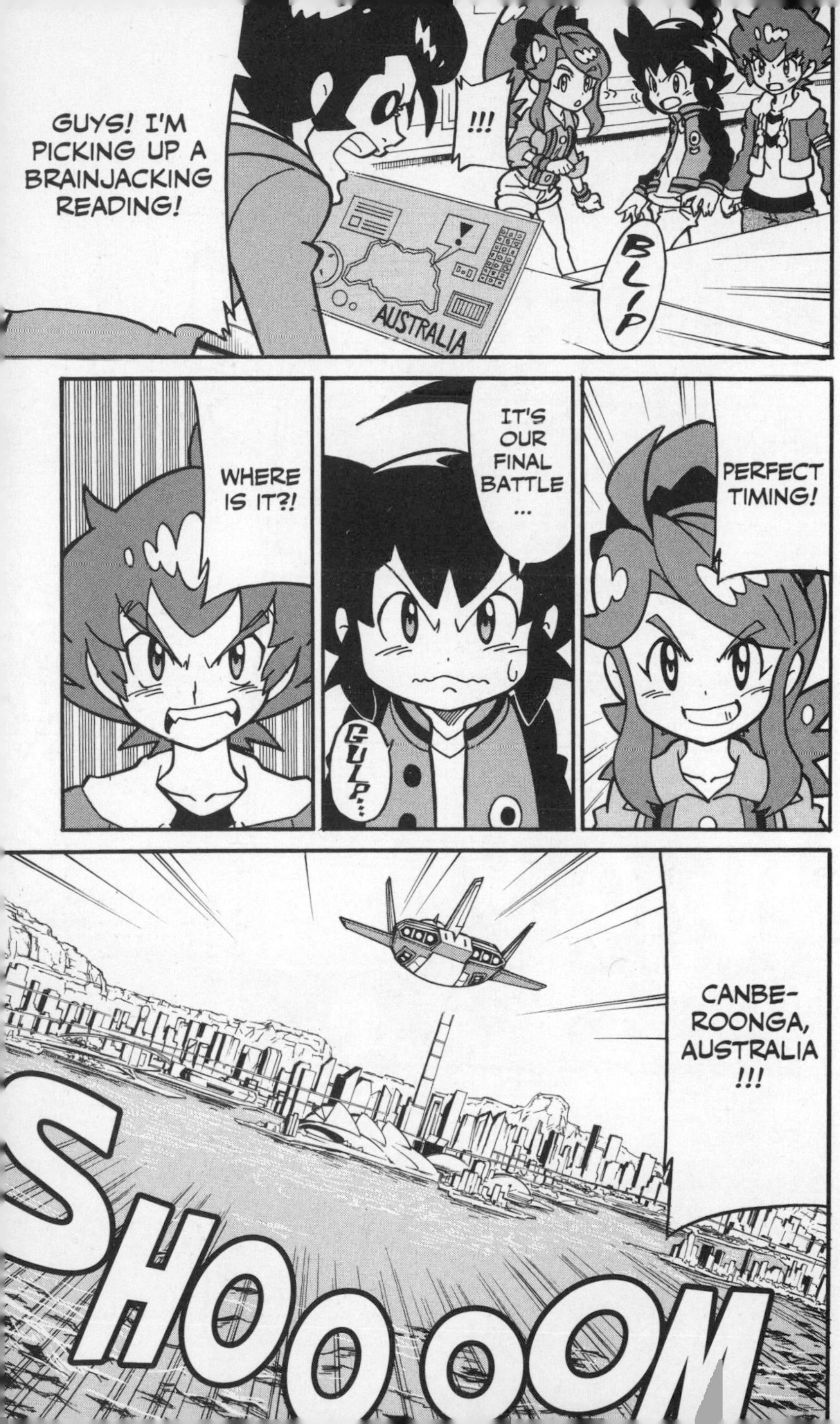
GUYS! I'M PICKING UP A BRAINJACKING READING!
!!!
AUSTRALIA
BLIP
PERFECT TIMING!
IT'S OUR FINAL BATTLE ...
GULP...
WHERE IS IT?!
CANBE-ROONGA, AUSTRALIA !!!
SHOOOOM

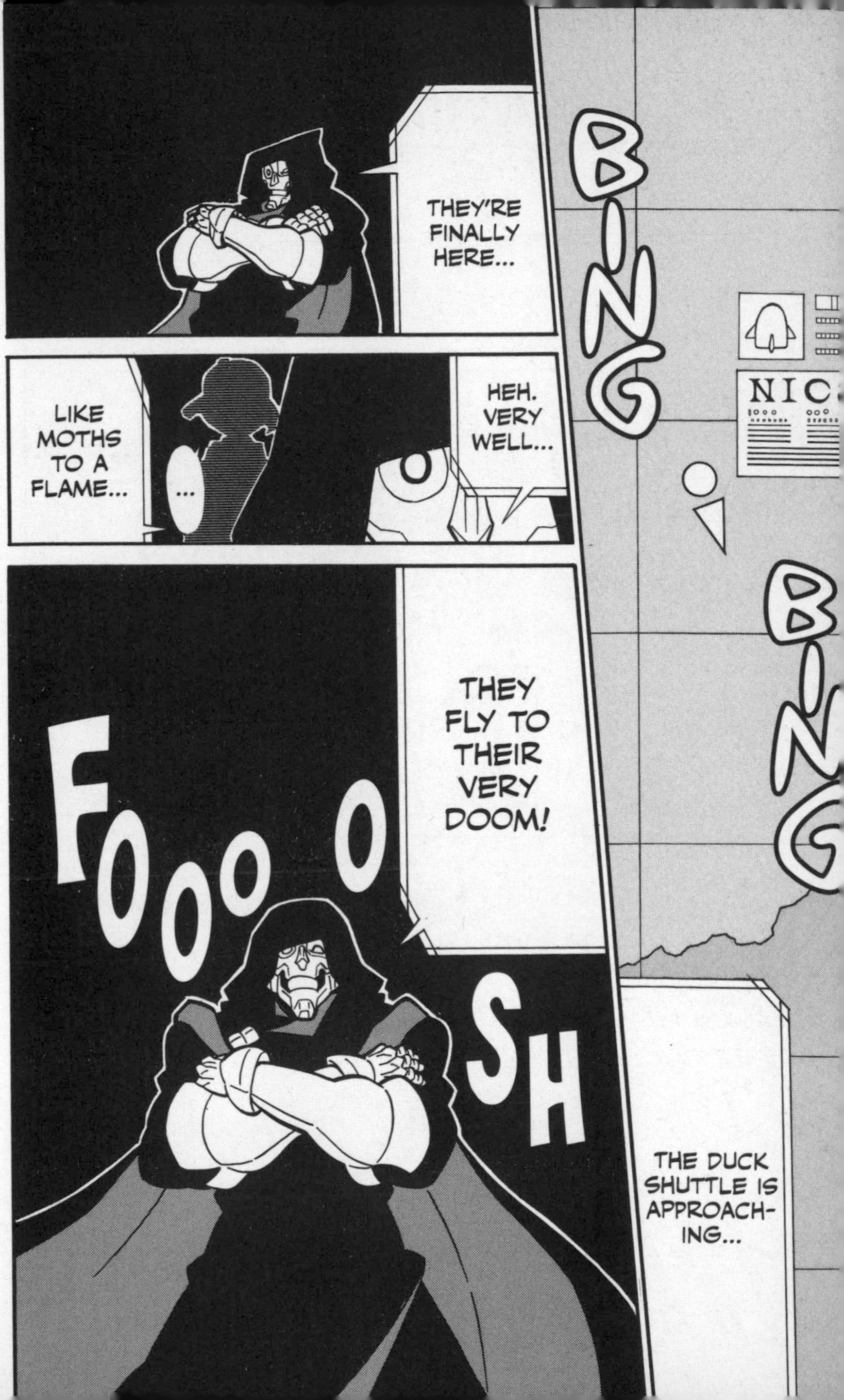
BING
BING
THE DUCK SHUTTLE IS APPROACHING...
THEY'RE FINALLY HERE...
HEH. VERY WELL...
...
LIKE MOTHS TO A FLAME...
THEY FLY TO THEIR VERY DOOM!
FOOOOOSH

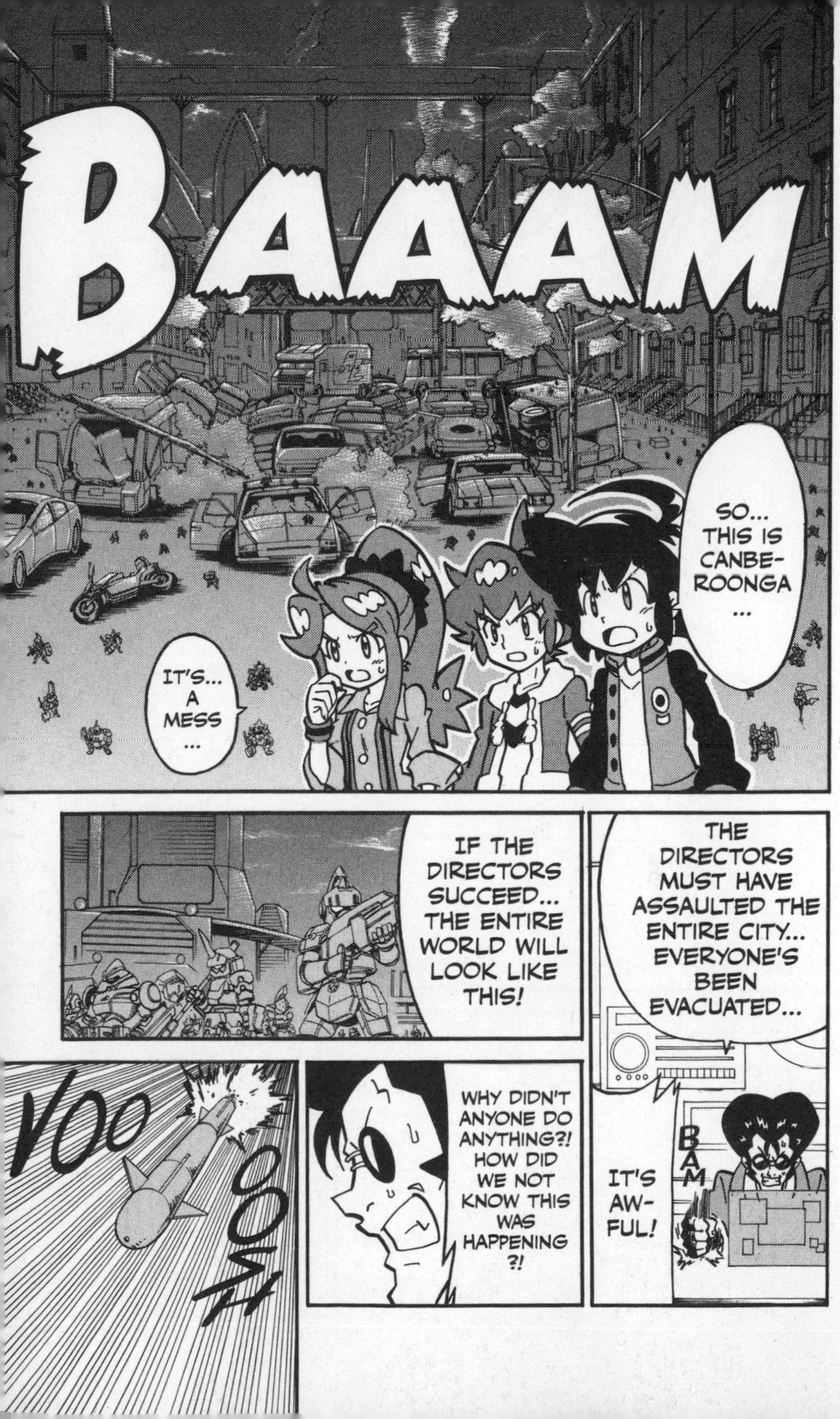
BAAAM
SO... THIS IS CANBE-ROONGA ...
IT'S... A MESS ...
THE DIRECTORS MUST HAVE ASSAULTED THE ENTIRE CITY... EVERYONE'S BEEN EVACUATED...
IF THE DIRECTORS SUCCEED... THE ENTIRE WORLD WILL LOOK LIKE THIS!
BAM
IT'S AW-FUL!
WHY DIDN'T ANYONE DO ANYTHING?! HOW DID WE NOT KNOW THIS WAS HAPPENING ?!
VOOOOM

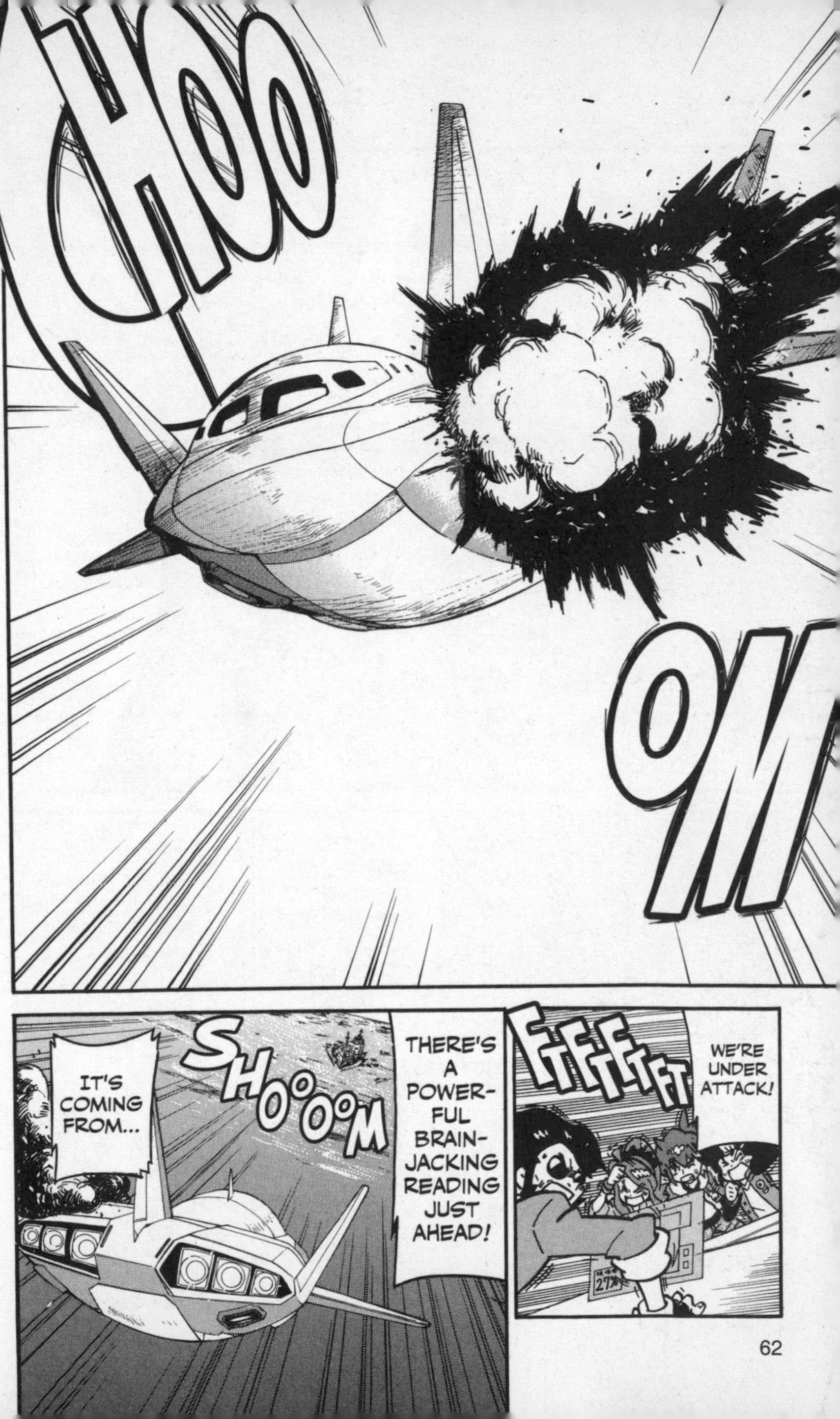
CHOO
WE'RE UNDER ATTACK!
FTFTFTFTFT
THERE'S A POWER-FUL BRAIN-JACKING READING JUST AHEAD!
SHOOOOM
IT'S COMING FROM...

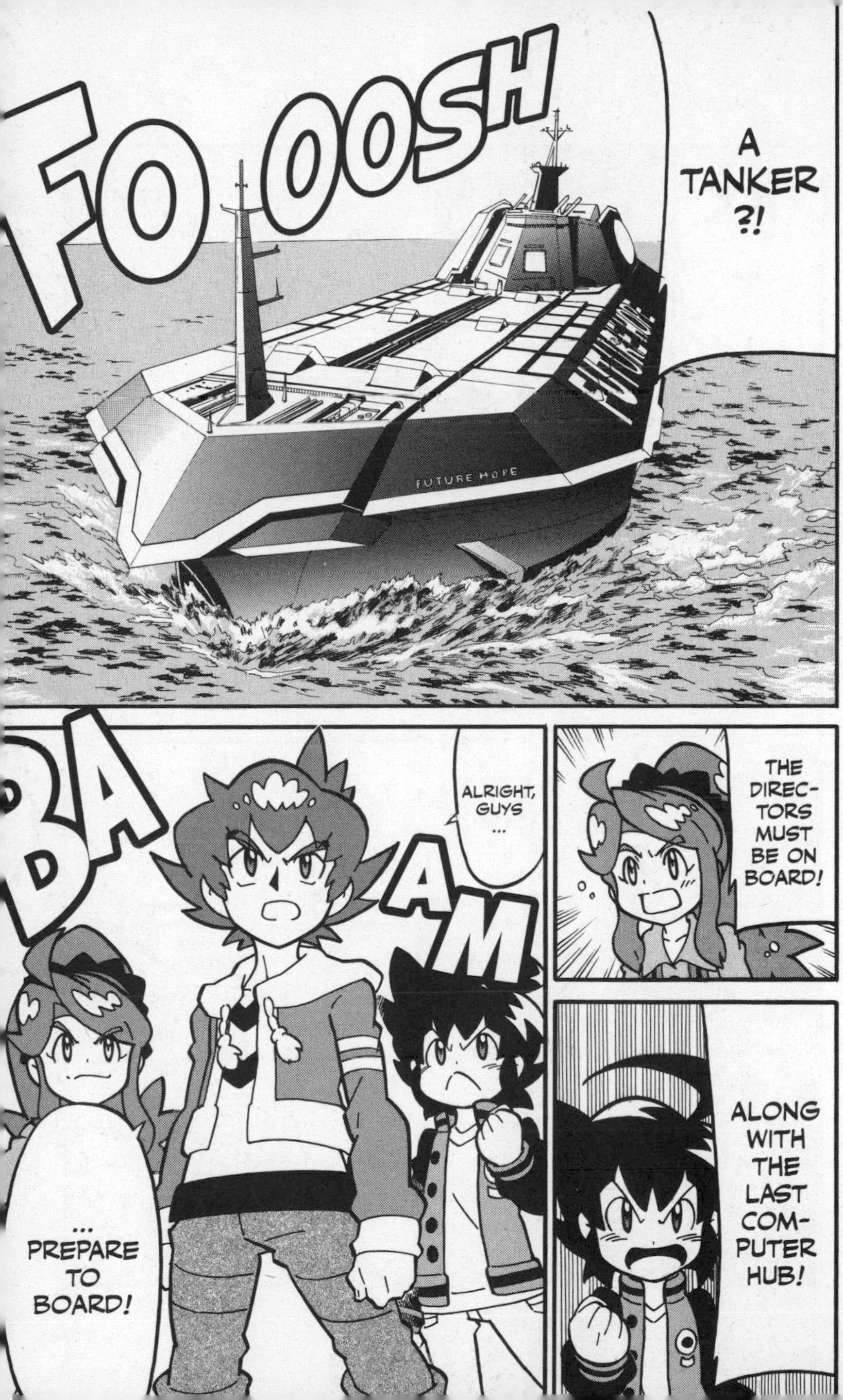
FOOOSH
FUTURE HOPE
A TANKER ?!
THE DIREC-TORS MUST BE ON BOARD!
ALONG WITH THE LAST COM-PUTER HUB!
ALRIGHT, GUYS ...
BAAM
... PREPARE TO BOARD!

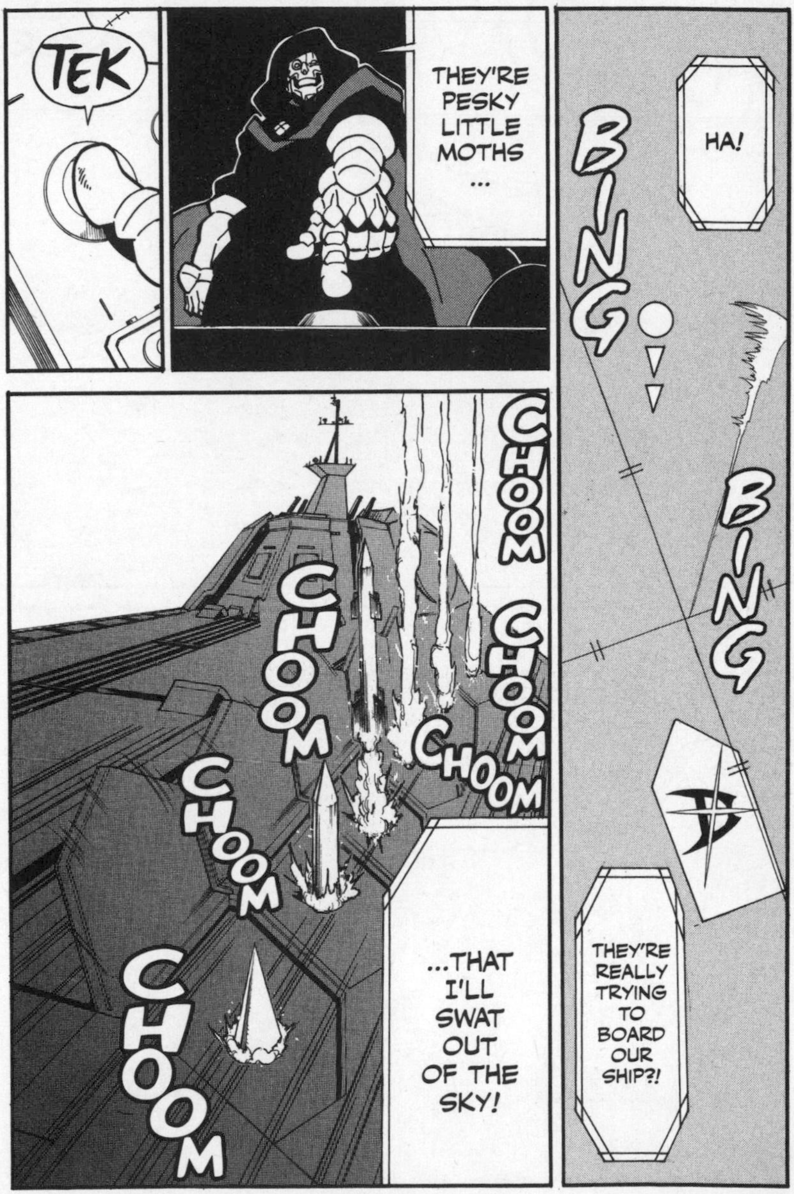
HA!
BING
BING
THEY'RE REALLY TRYING TO BOARD OUR SHIP?!
THEY'RE PESKY LITTLE MOTHS ...
TEK
CHOOM
CHOOM
CHOOM
CHOOM
CHOOM
CHOOM
...THAT I'LL SWAT OUT OF THE SKY!

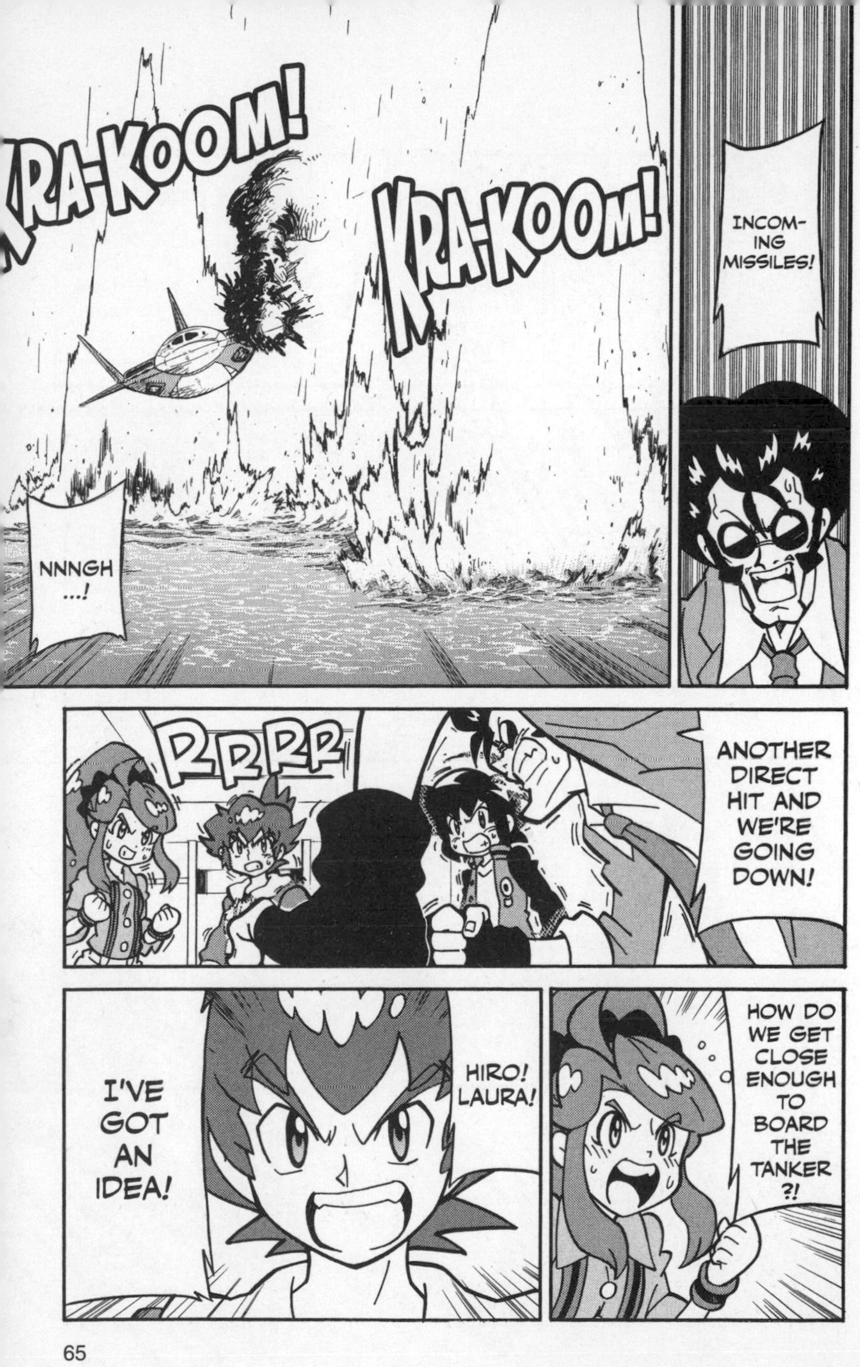
INCOMING MISSILES!
KRA-KOOM!
KRA-KOOM!
NNNGH ...!
ANOTHER DIRECT HIT AND WE'RE GOING DOWN!
RRRR
HOW DO WE GET CLOSE ENOUGH TO BOARD THE TANKER?!
HIRO! LAURA!
I'VE GOT AN IDEA!

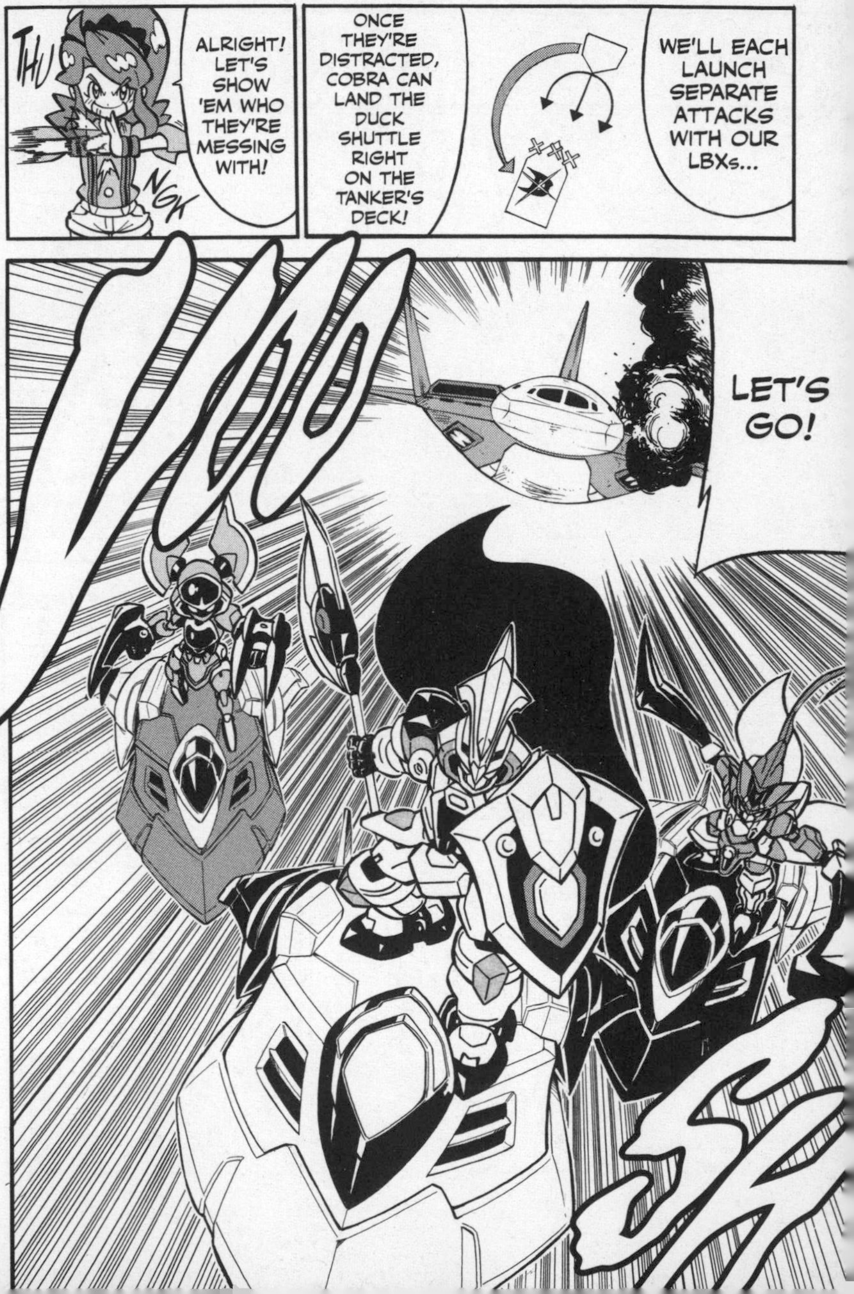
WE'LL EACH LAUNCH SEPARATE ATTACKS WITH OUR LBXs...
ONCE THEY'RE DISTRACTED, COBRA CAN LAND THE DUCK SHUTTLE RIGHT ON THE TANKER'S DECK!
ALRIGHT! LET'S SHOW 'EM WHO THEY'RE MESSING WITH!
THU
NGK
LET'S GO!

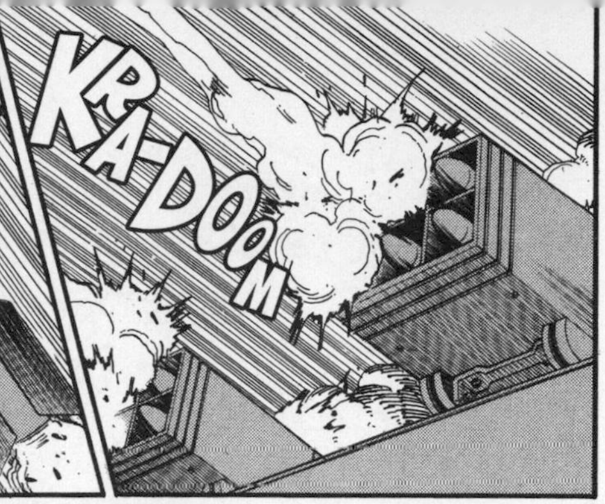
KRA-DOOOM

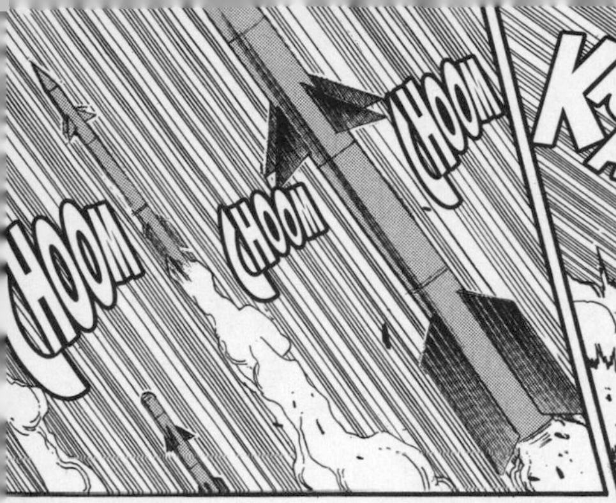
CHOOM
CHOOM
CHOOM

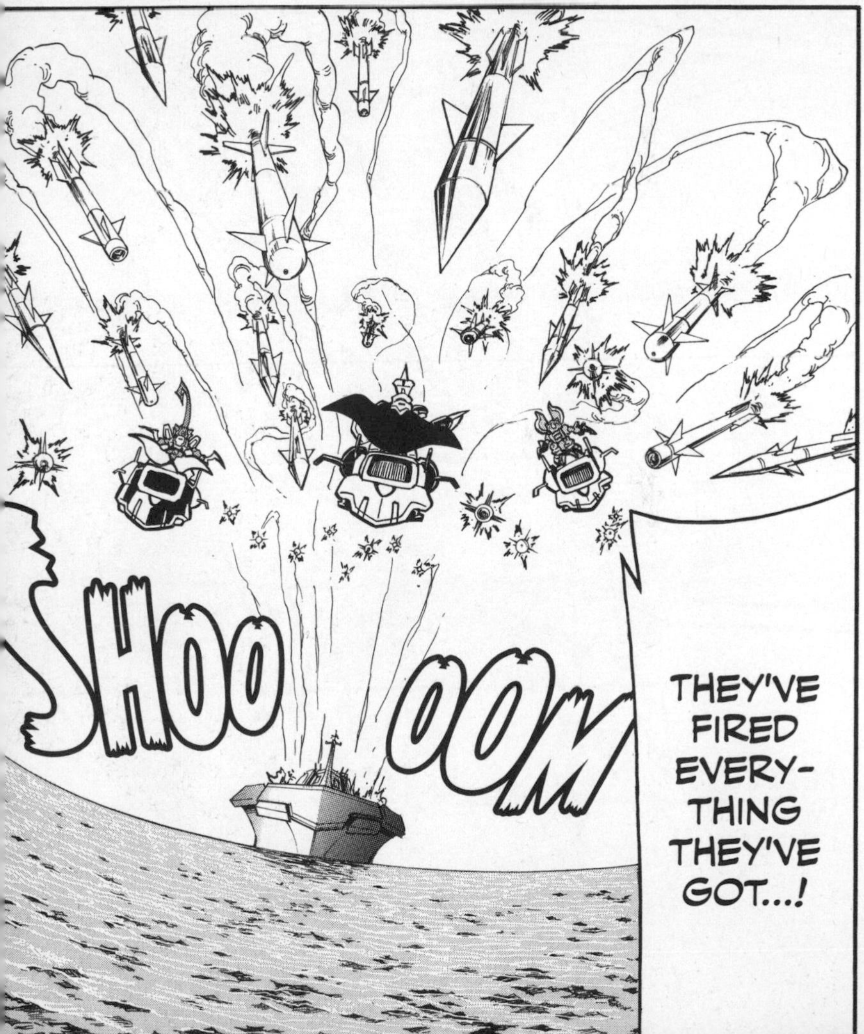
SHOOOOM
THEY'VE FIRED EVERY-THING THEY'VE GOT...!

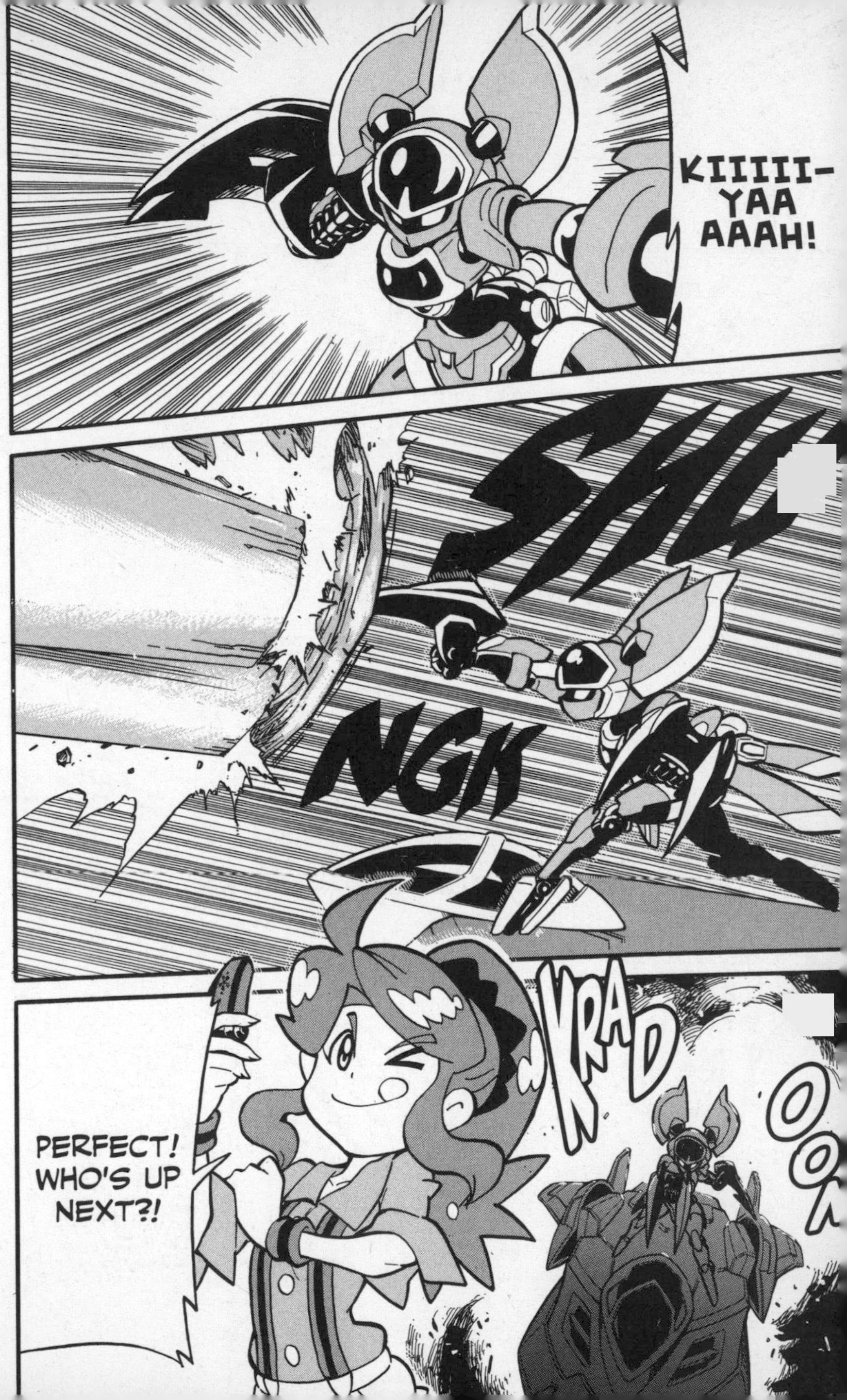
KIIIII-YAA AAAH!
NGK
KRAD
PERFECT! WHO'S UP NEXT?!

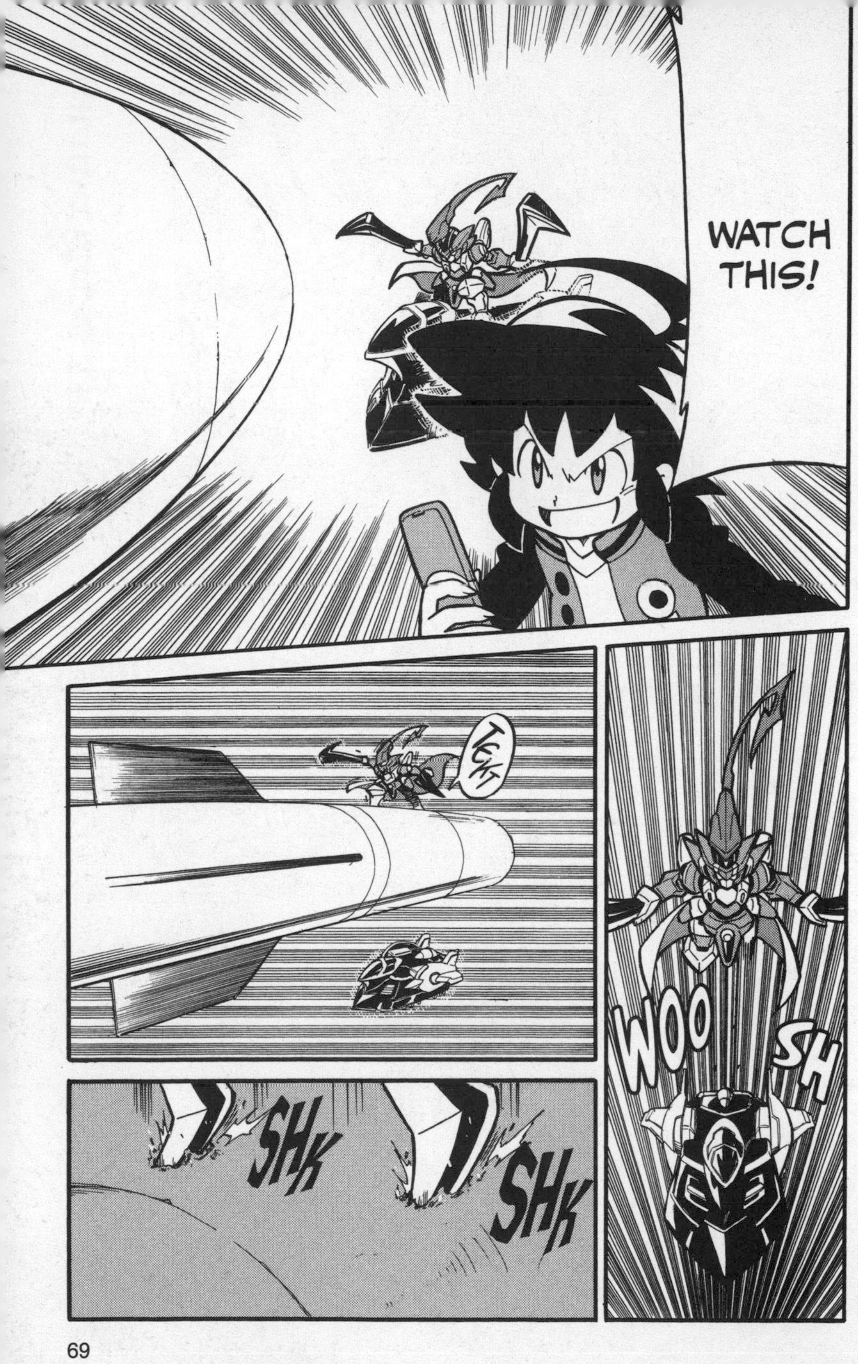
WATCH THIS!
WOOSH
TCKT
SHK
SHK

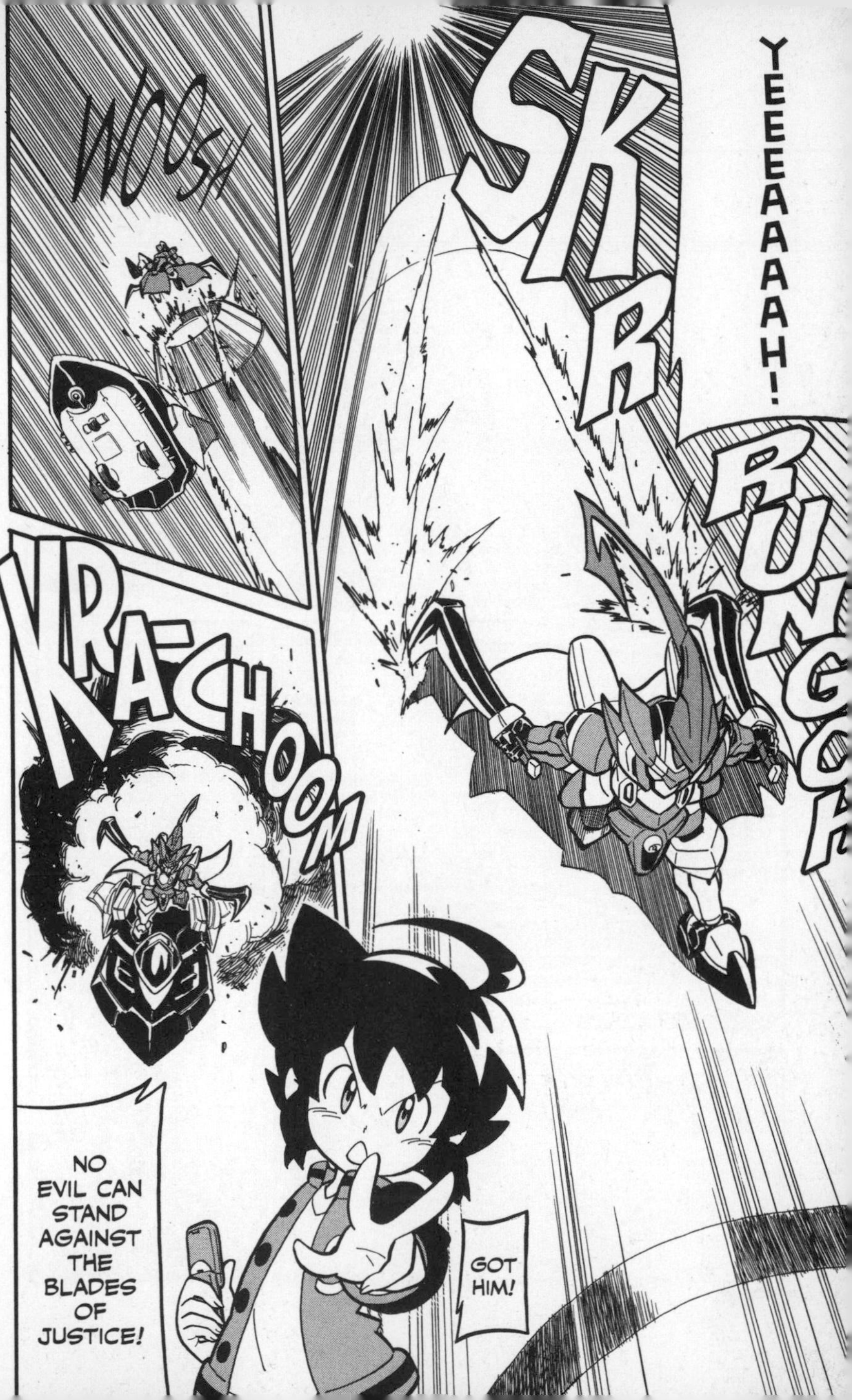
YEEEAAAAAH!
SKRR
RUNCCH
WOOSH
KRA-CHOOM
GOT HIM!
NO EVIL CAN STAND AGAINST THE BLADES OF JUSTICE!

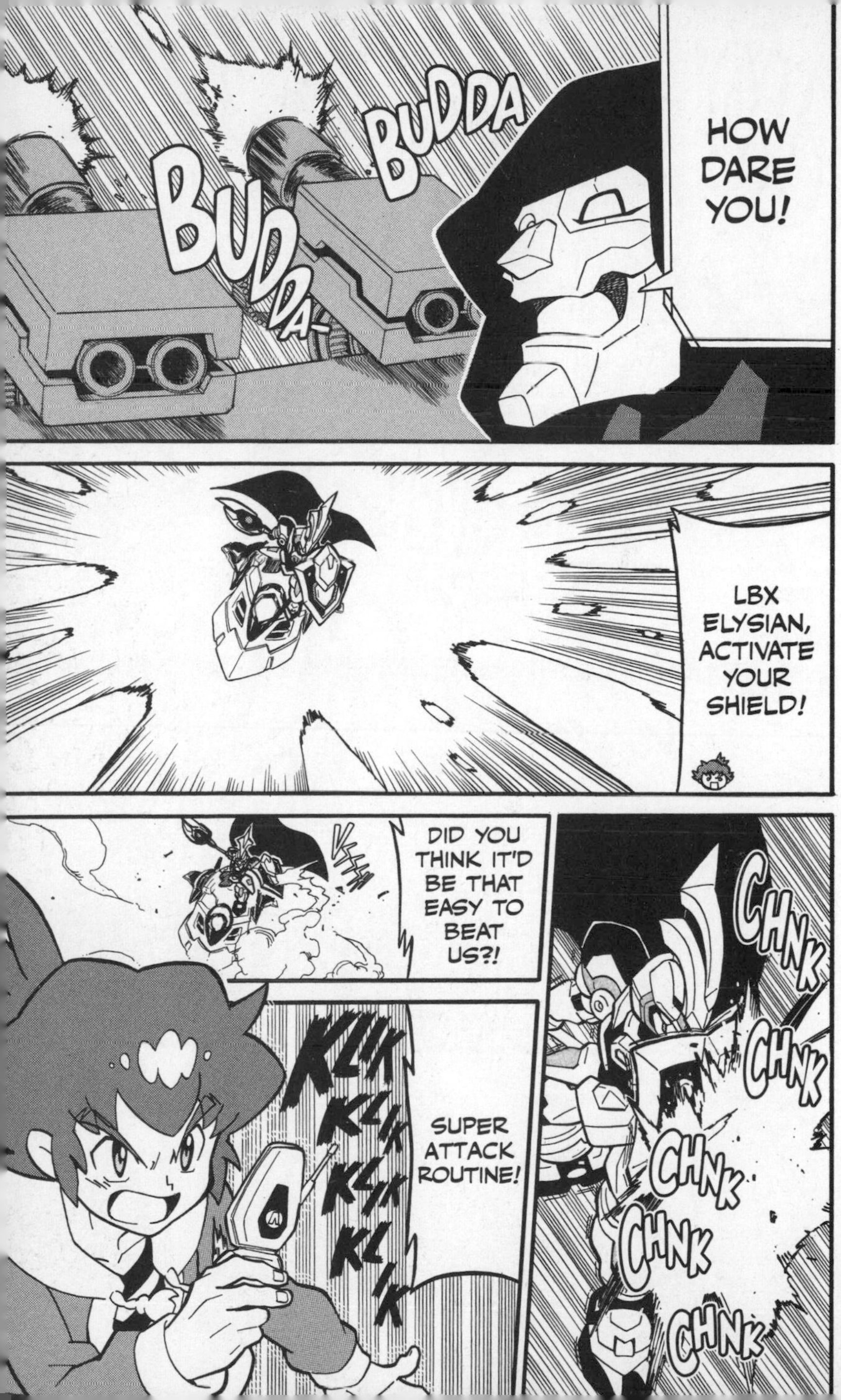
HOW DARE YOU!
BUDDA
BUDDA-
LBX ELYSIAN, ACTIVATE YOUR SHIELD!
CHNK
CHNK
CHNK
CHNK
CHNK
DID YOU THINK IT'D BE THAT EASY TO BEAT US?!
SUPER ATTACK ROUTINE!
KLIK KLIK KLIK KLIK KLIK

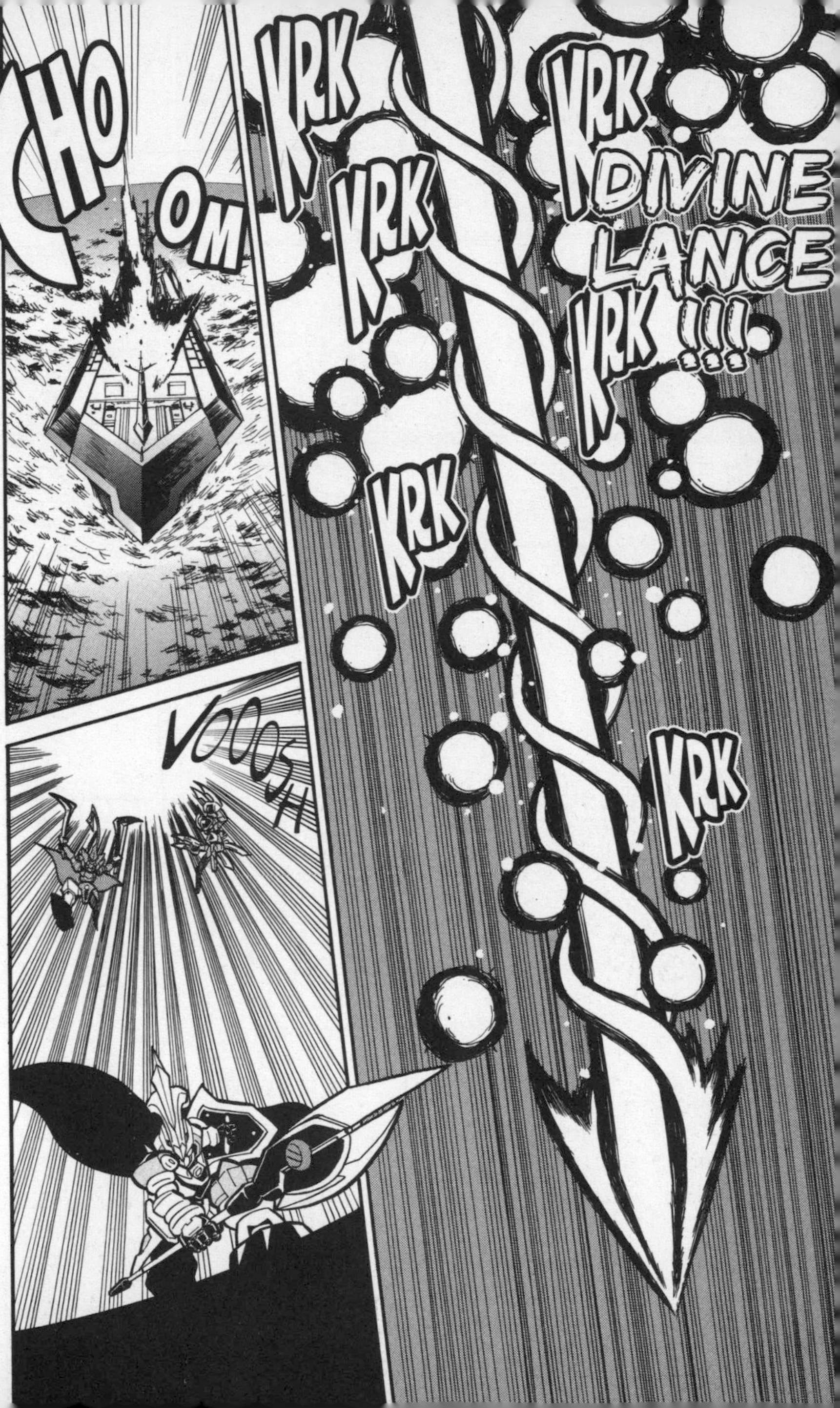
KRK
DIVINE LANCE!!!
KRK
KRK
KRK
KRK
KRK
KRK
CHOOM
VOOOSH

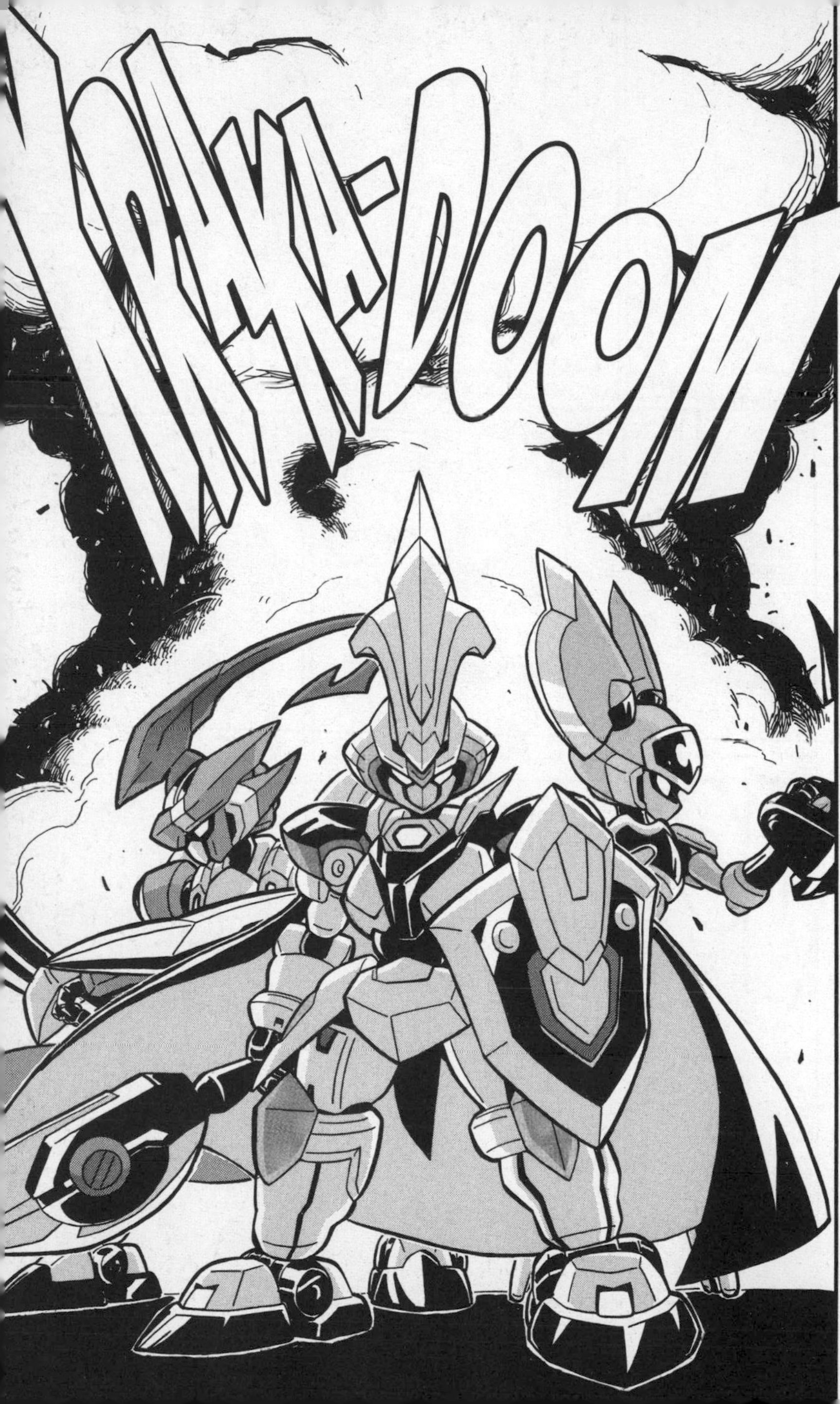
KA-DOOM

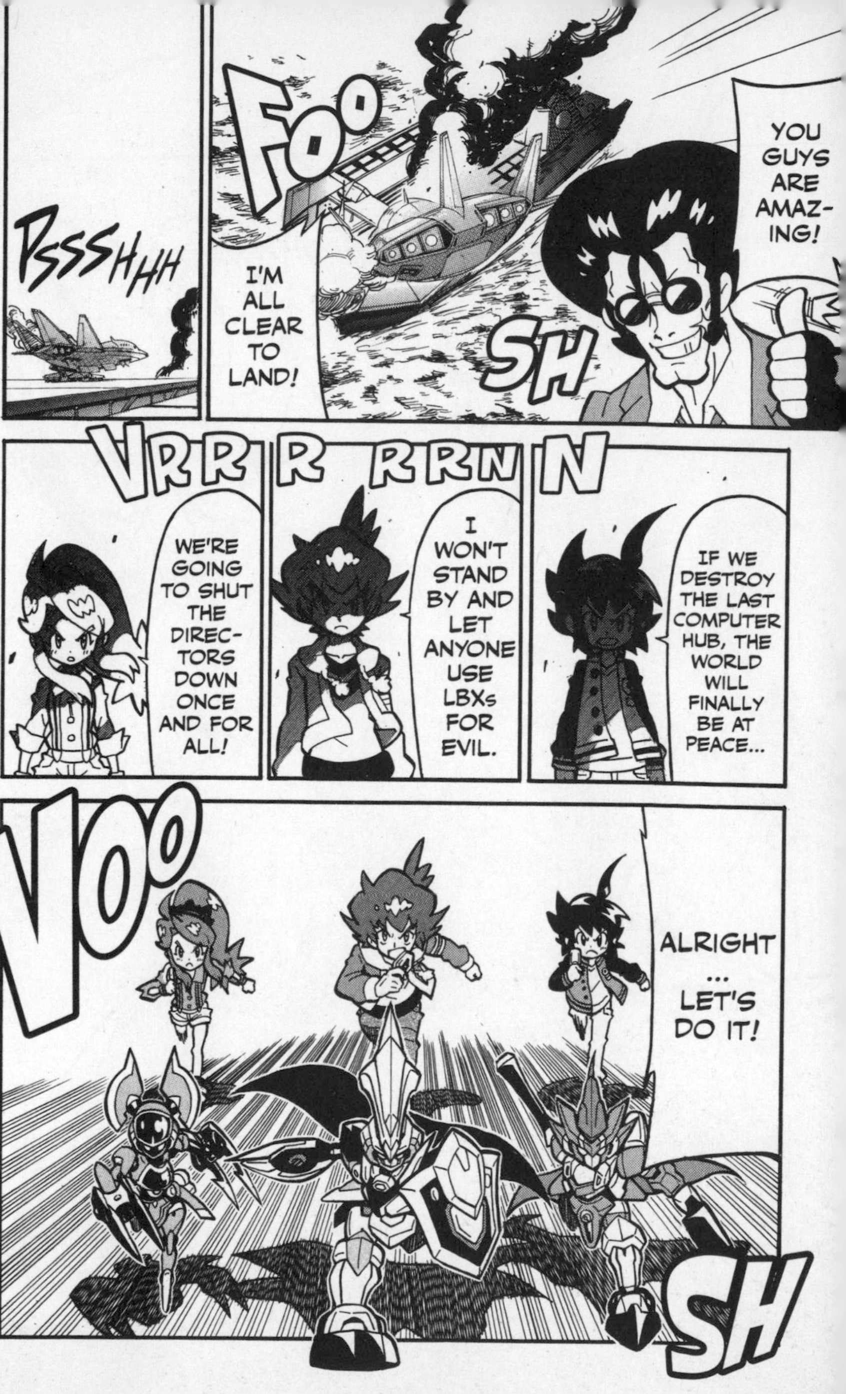
PSSSHHH
FOO
I'M ALL CLEAR TO LAND!
SH
YOU GUYS ARE AMAZ-ING!
VRRRRRRN
WE'RE GOING TO SHUT THE DIREC-TORS DOWN ONCE AND FOR ALL!
I WON'T STAND BY AND LET ANYONE USE LBXs FOR EVIL.
IF WE DESTROY THE LAST COMPUTER HUB, THE WORLD WILL FINALLY BE AT PEACE...
VOO
ALRIGHT ... LET'S DO IT!
SH

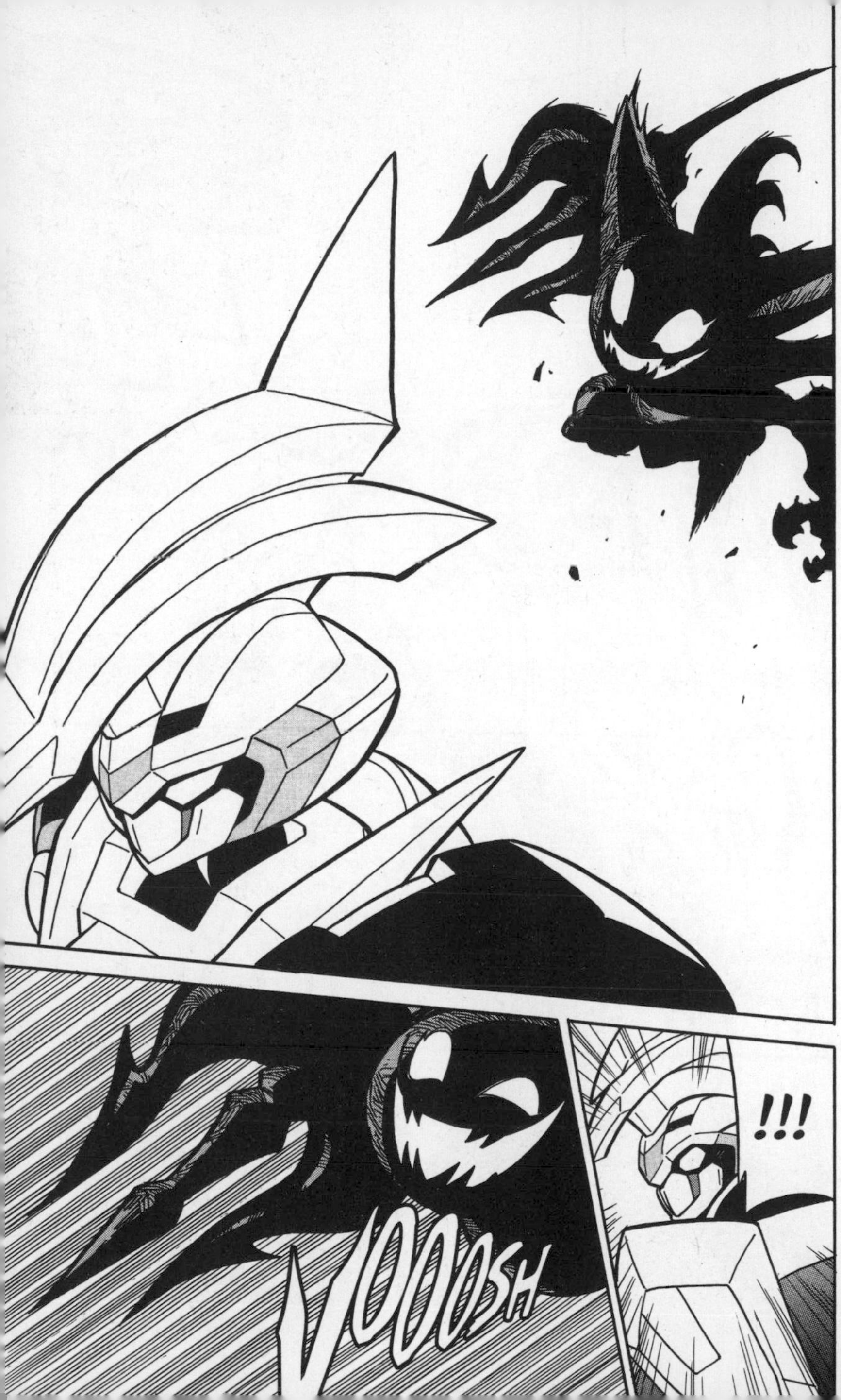
!!!
VOOOSH

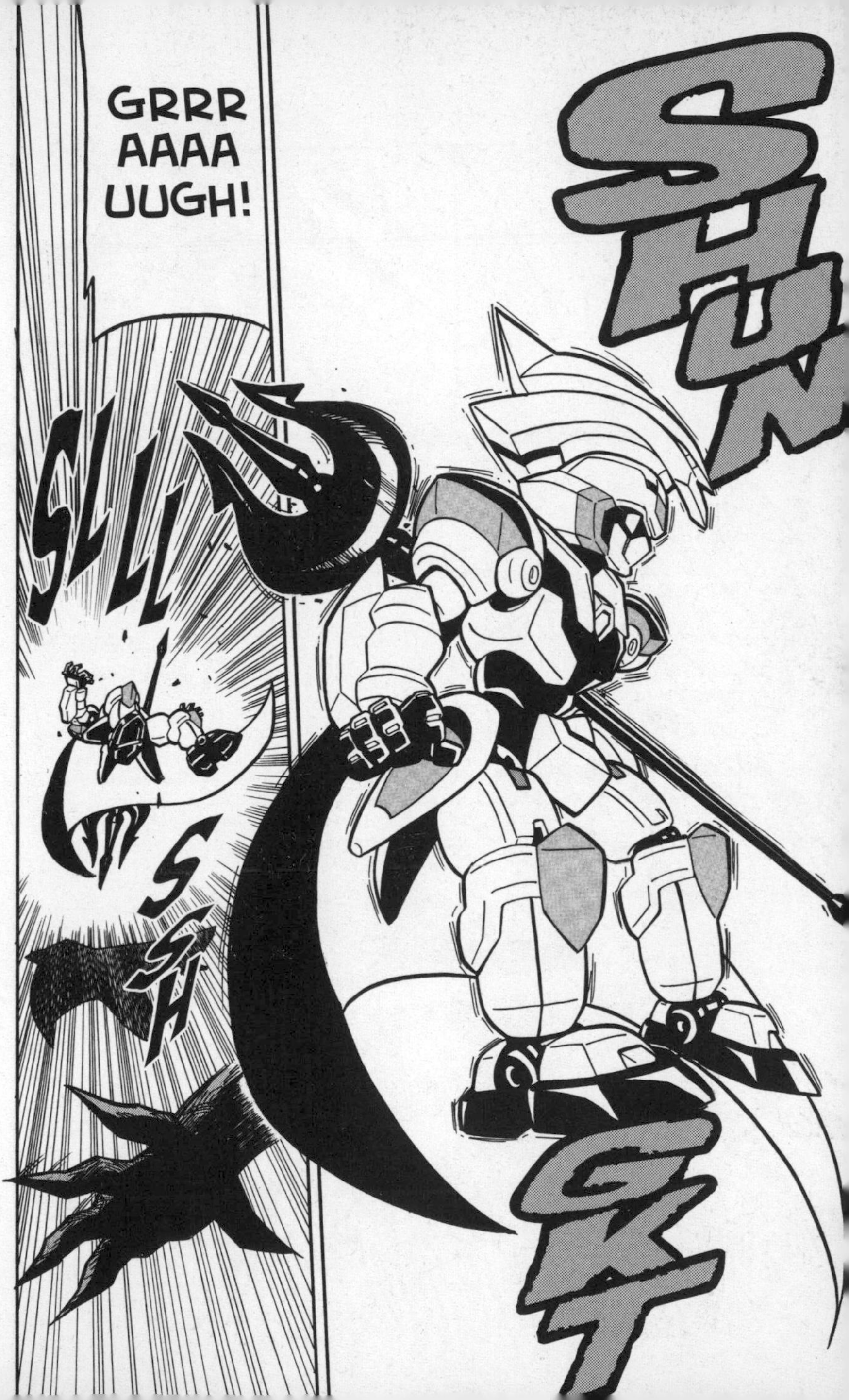
SHUN
GRRR
AAAA
UUGH!
SLLL
SSH
GKT

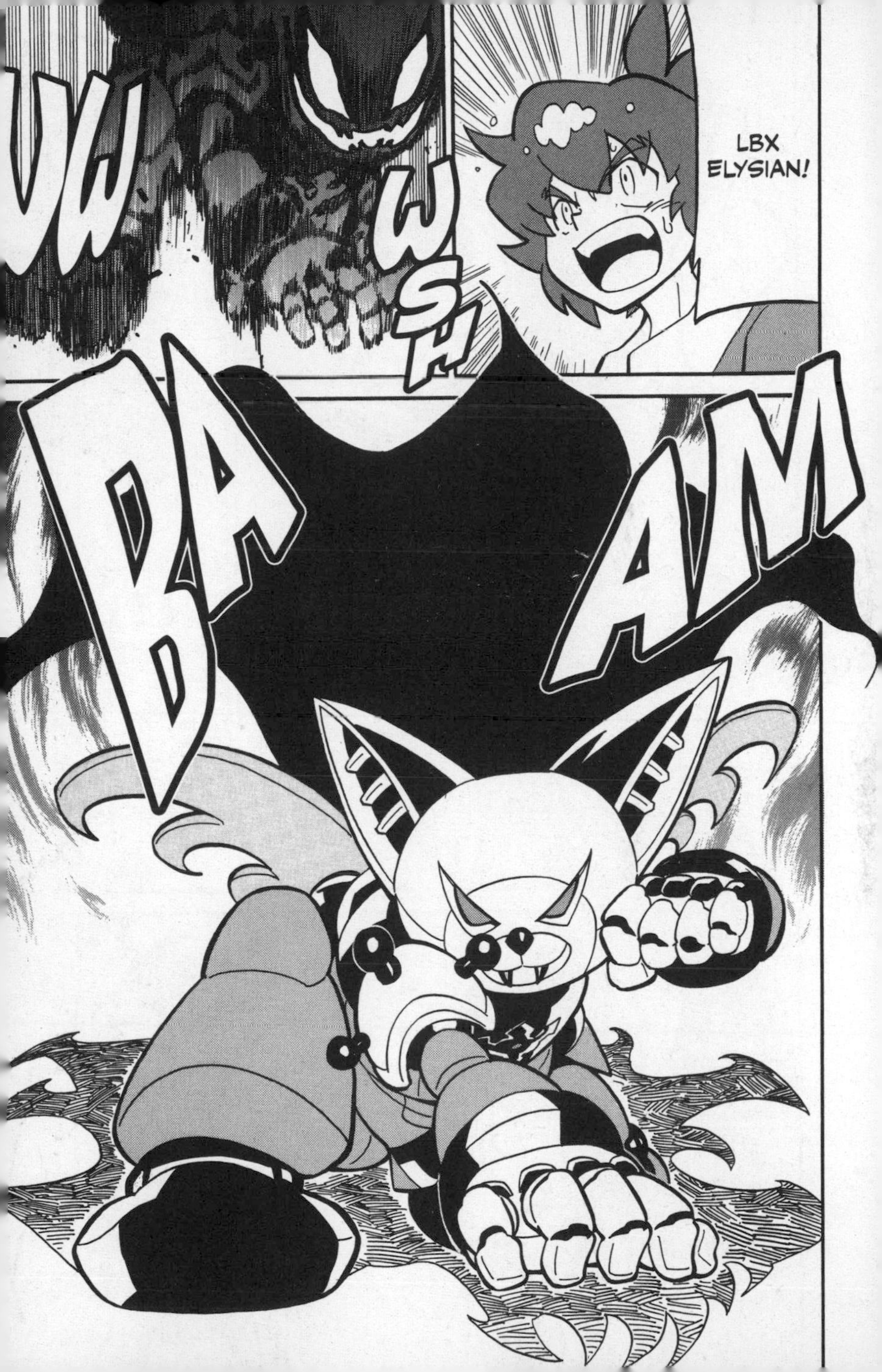
LBX ELYSIAN!
BAAM

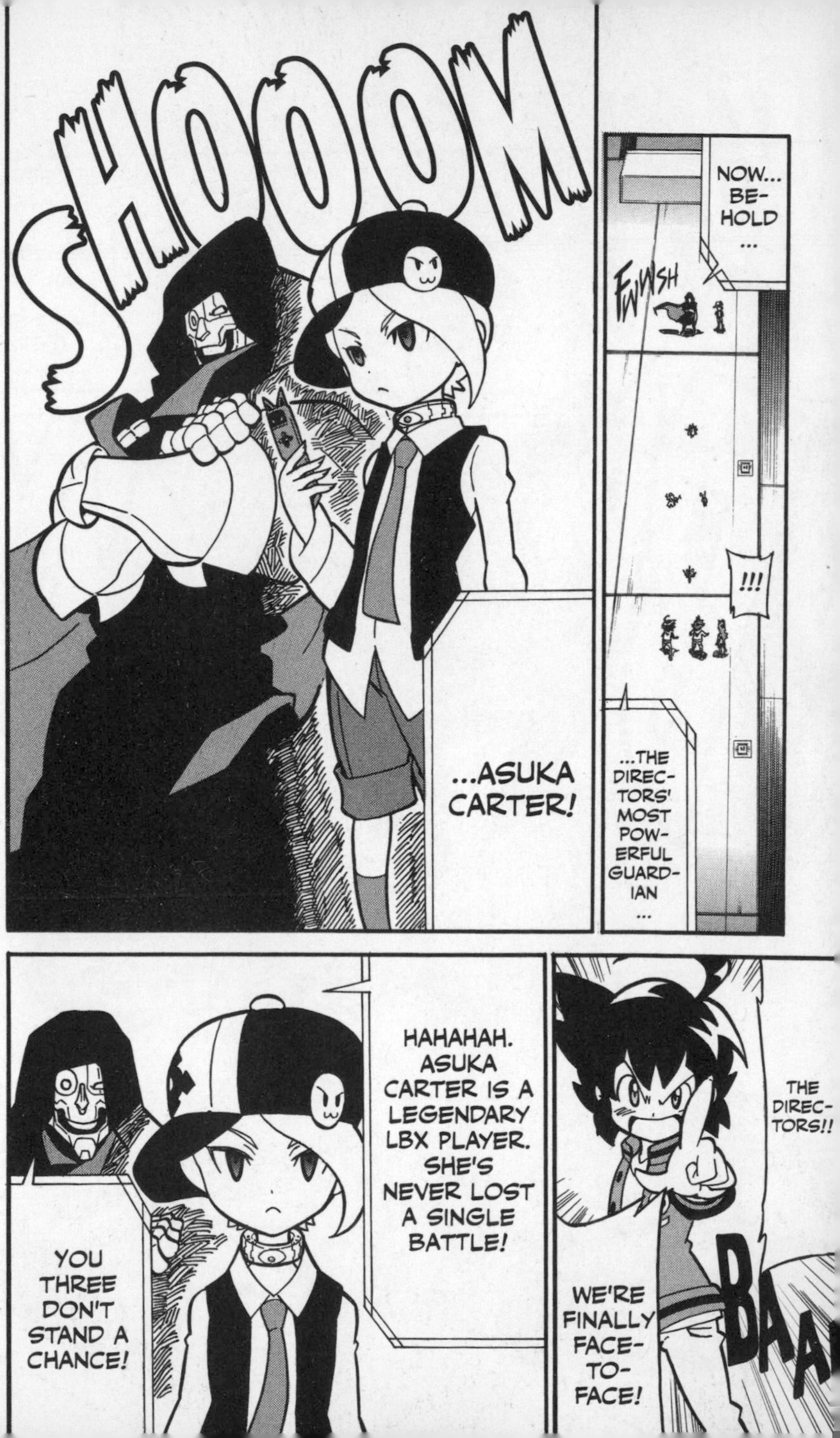
NOW... BE-HOLD ...
FWWSH
!!!
...THE DIREC-TORS' MOST POW-ERFUL GUARD-IAN ...
SHOOOM
...ASUKA CARTER!
THE DIREC-TORS!!
WE'RE FINALLY FACE-TO-FACE!
HAHAHAH. ASUKA CARTER IS A LEGENDARY LBX PLAYER. SHE'S NEVER LOST A SINGLE BATTLE!
YOU THREE DON'T STAND A CHANCE!

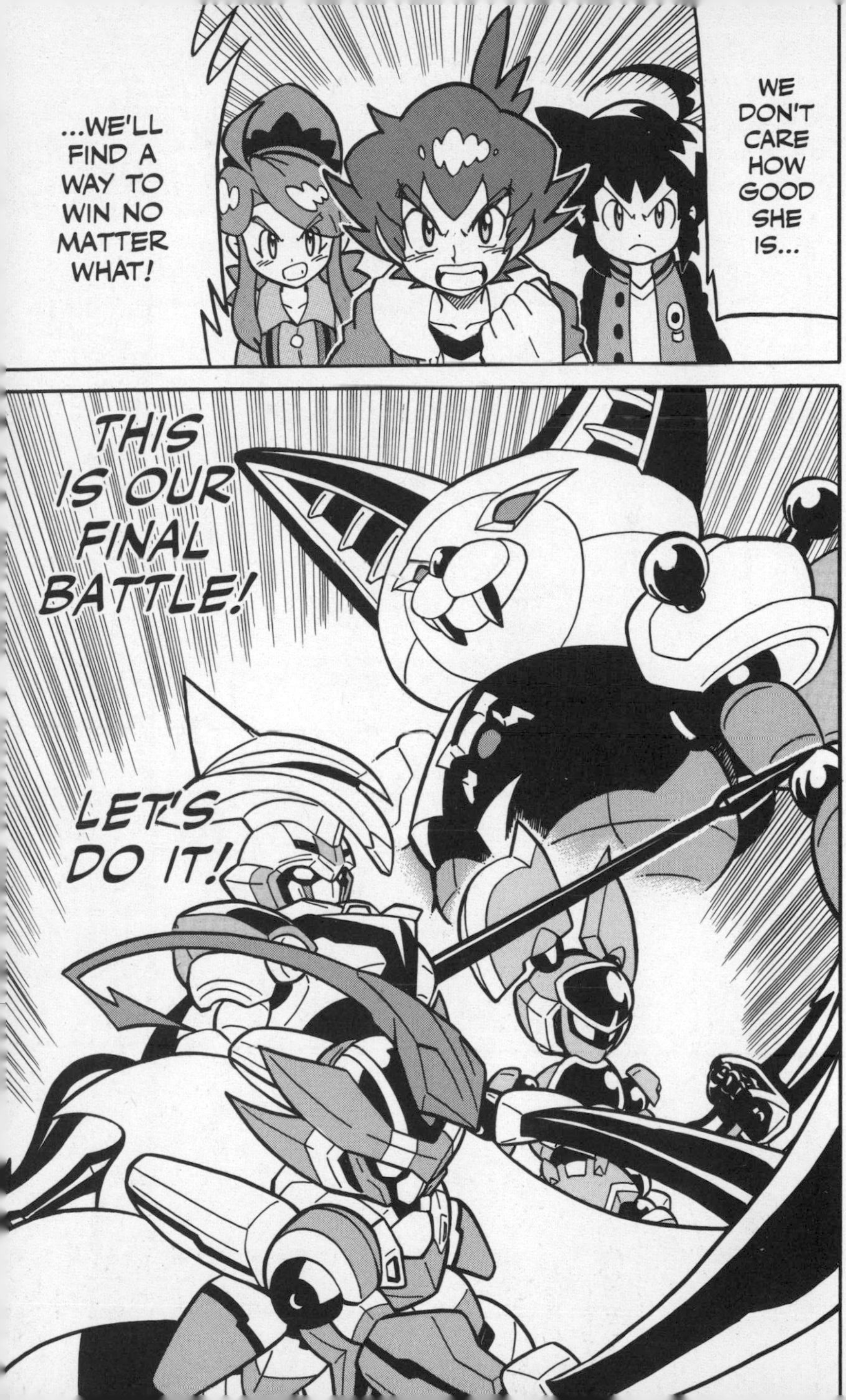
WE DON'T CARE HOW GOOD SHE IS...
...WE'LL FIND A WAY TO WIN NO MATTER WHAT!
THIS IS OUR FINAL BATTLE!
LET'S DO IT!

BONUS ILLUSTRATION GALLERY

PART 2

ENJOY ANOTHER ONE OF OUR SPECIAL
CHAPTER TITLE PAGES FROM VOLUME 4!

MONTHLY COROCORO COMICS, 2012
MAY ISSUE

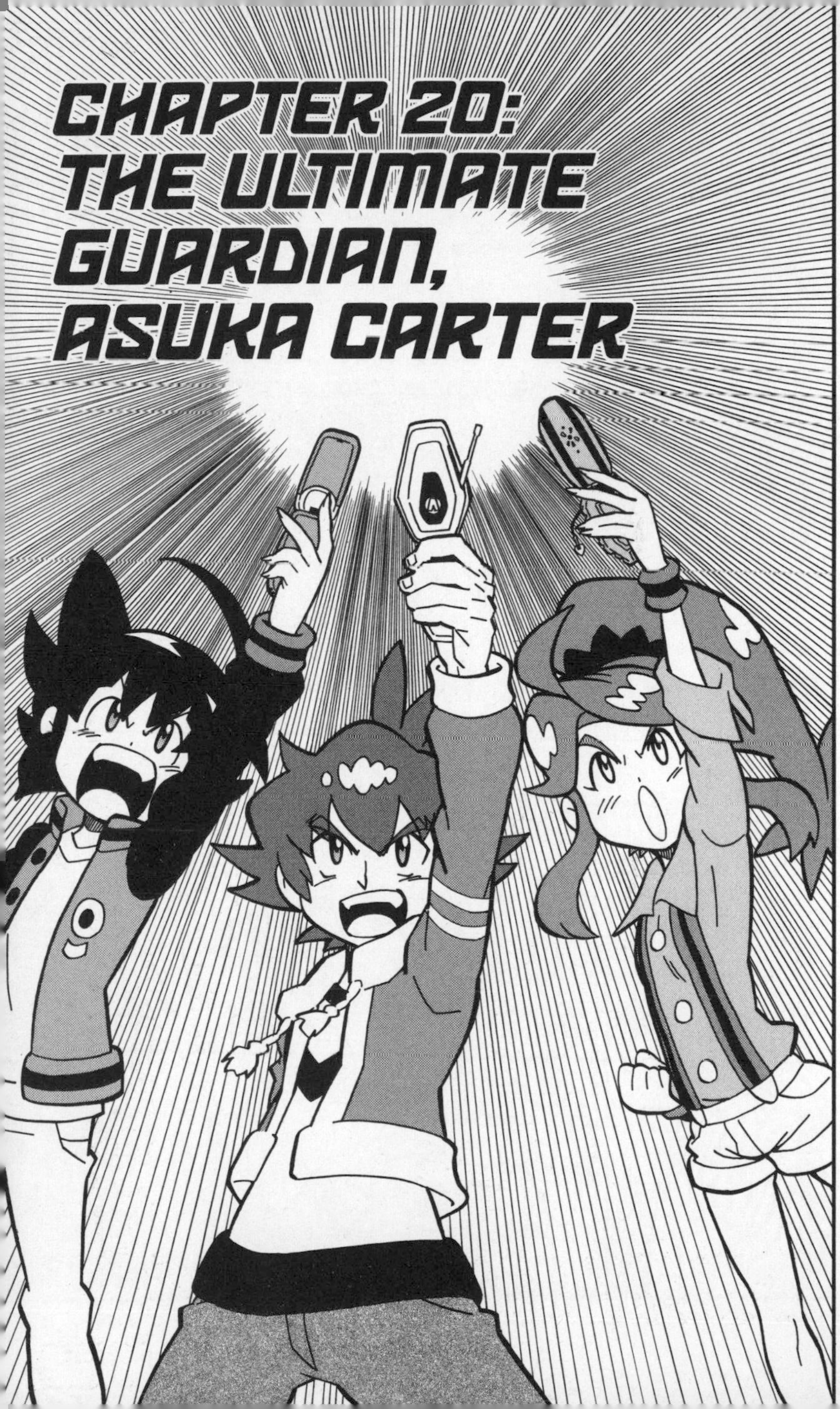
CHAPTER 20:
THE ULTIMATE GUARDIAN, ASUKA CARTER

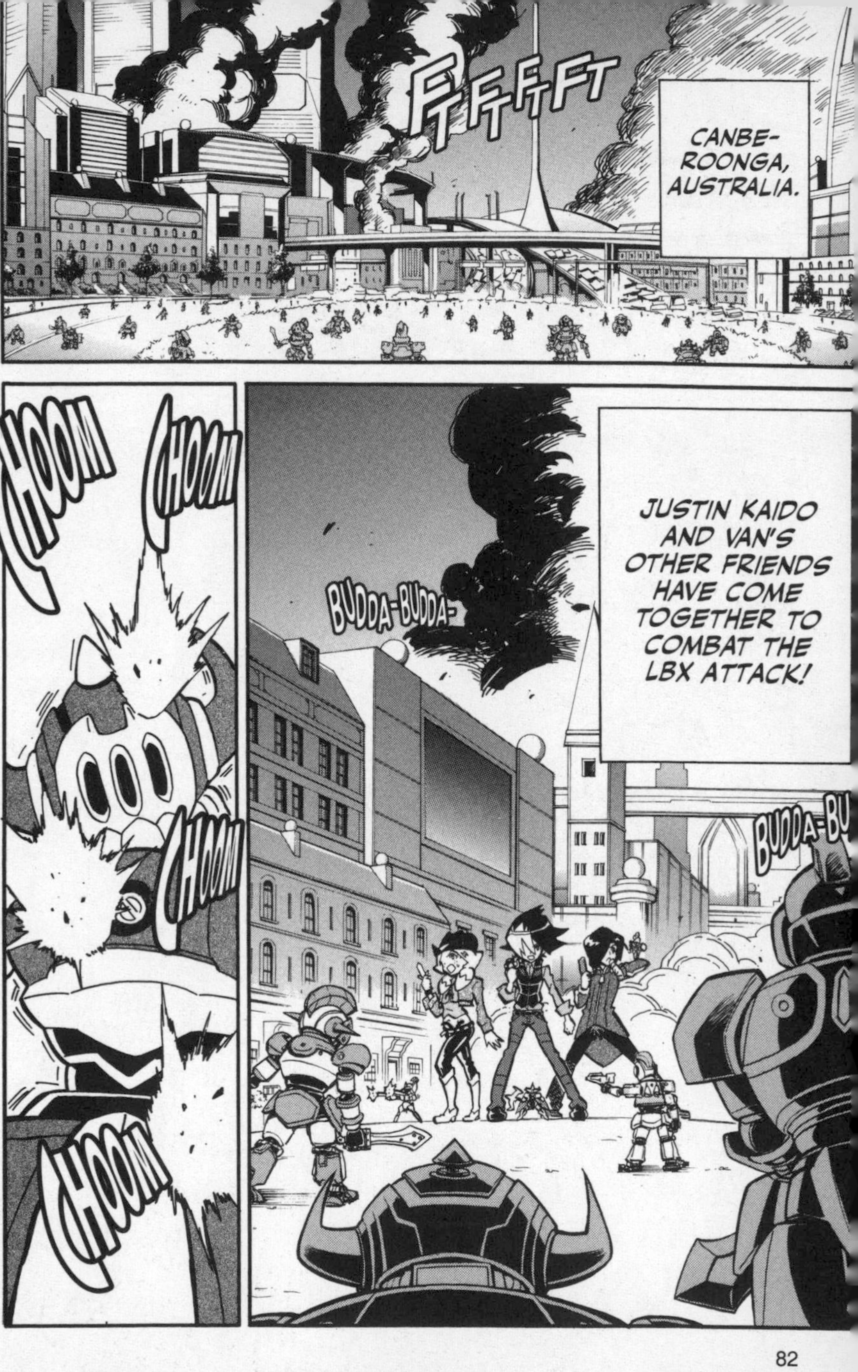
FTFTFTFT
CANBE-ROONGA, AUSTRALIA.
JUSTIN KAIDO AND VAN'S OTHER FRIENDS HAVE COME TOGETHER TO COMBAT THE LBX ATTACK!
BUDDA-BUDDA-
BUDDA-BU
CHOOM
CHOOM
CHOOM
CHOOM

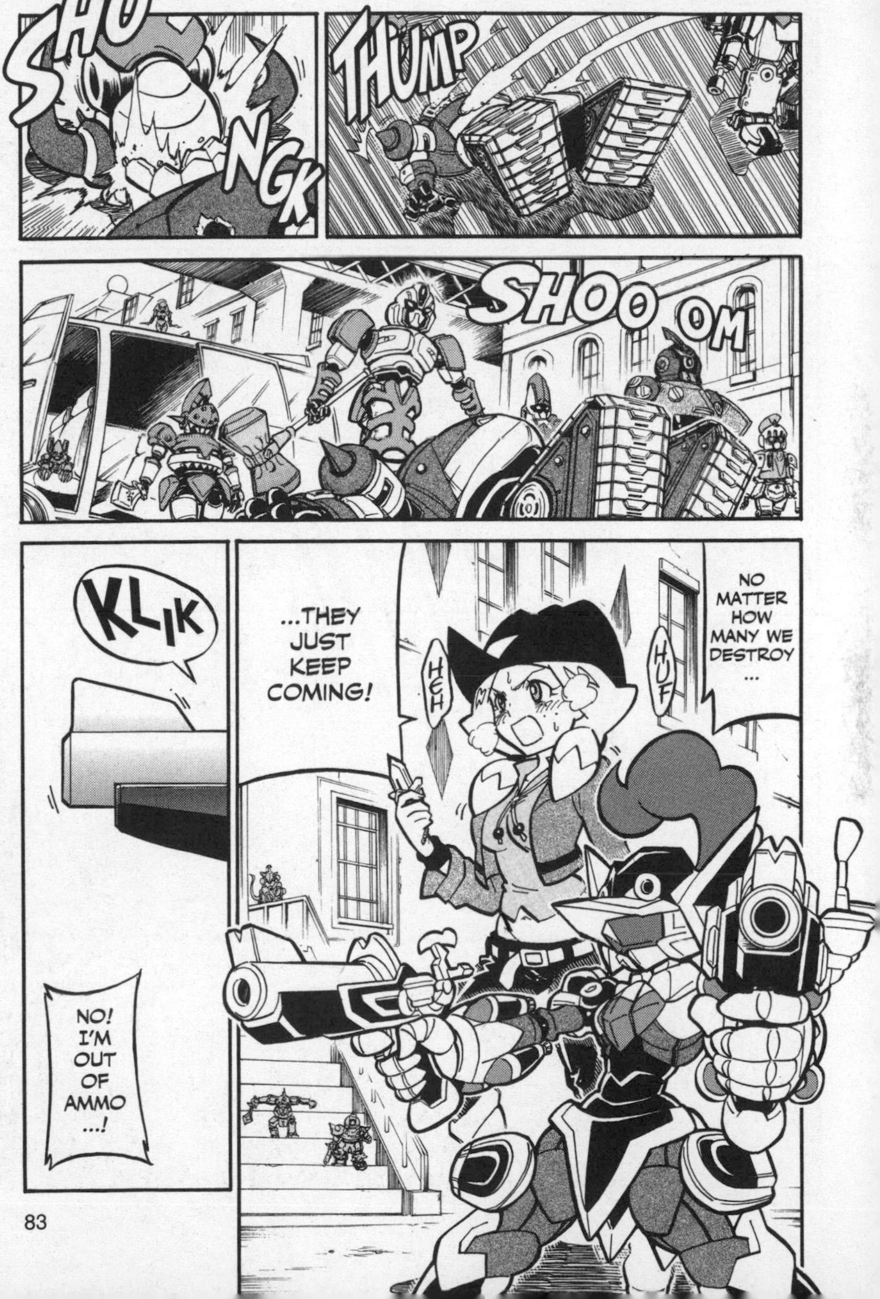
THUMP
SHUNGK
SHOO OM
NO MATTER HOW MANY WE DESTROY ...
HUF
HEH
...THEY JUST KEEP COMING!
KLIK
NO! I'M OUT OF AMMO ...!

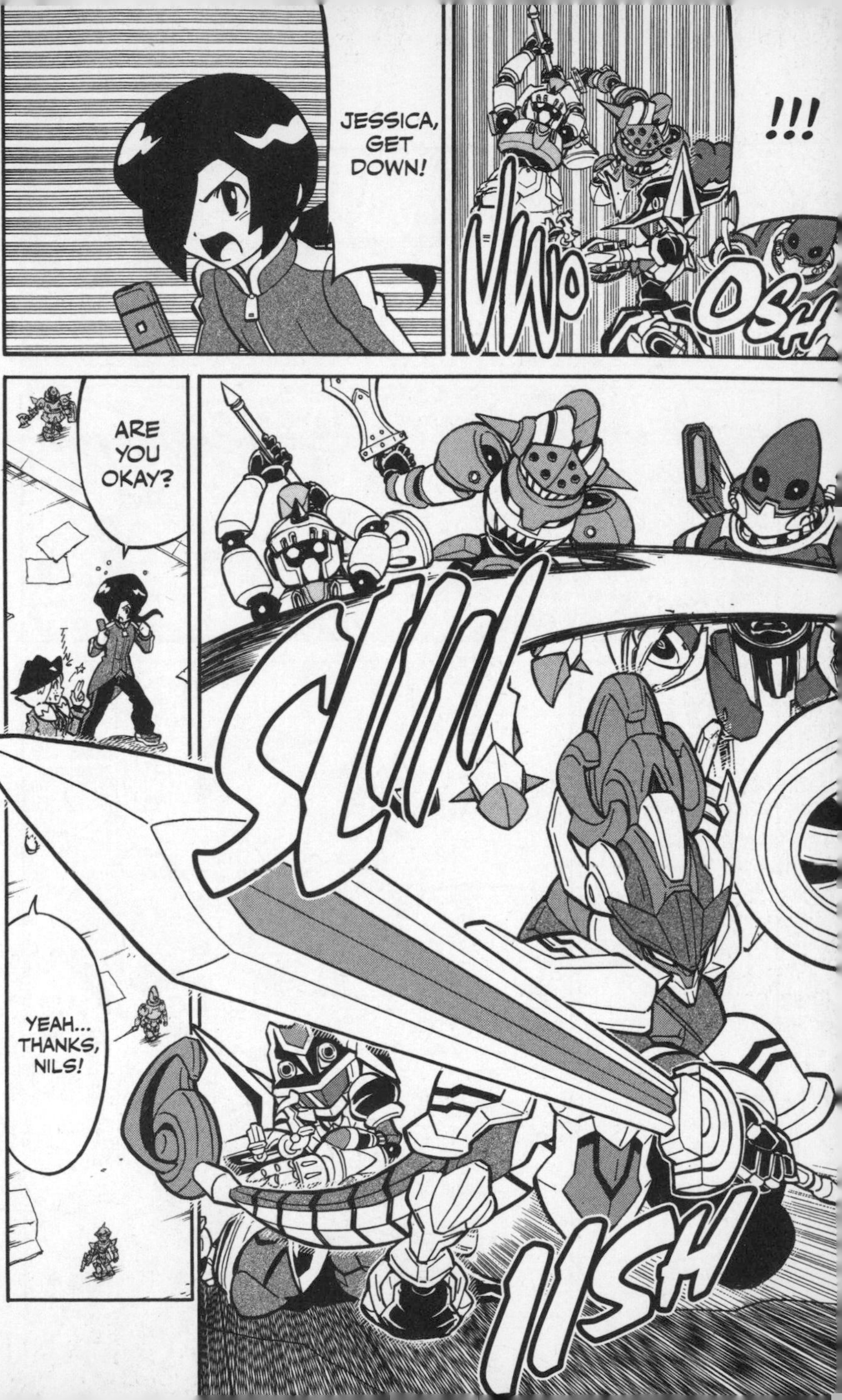
!!!
WHOOSH
JESSICA, GET DOWN!
SHIIIISH
ARE YOU OKAY?
YEAH... THANKS, NILS!

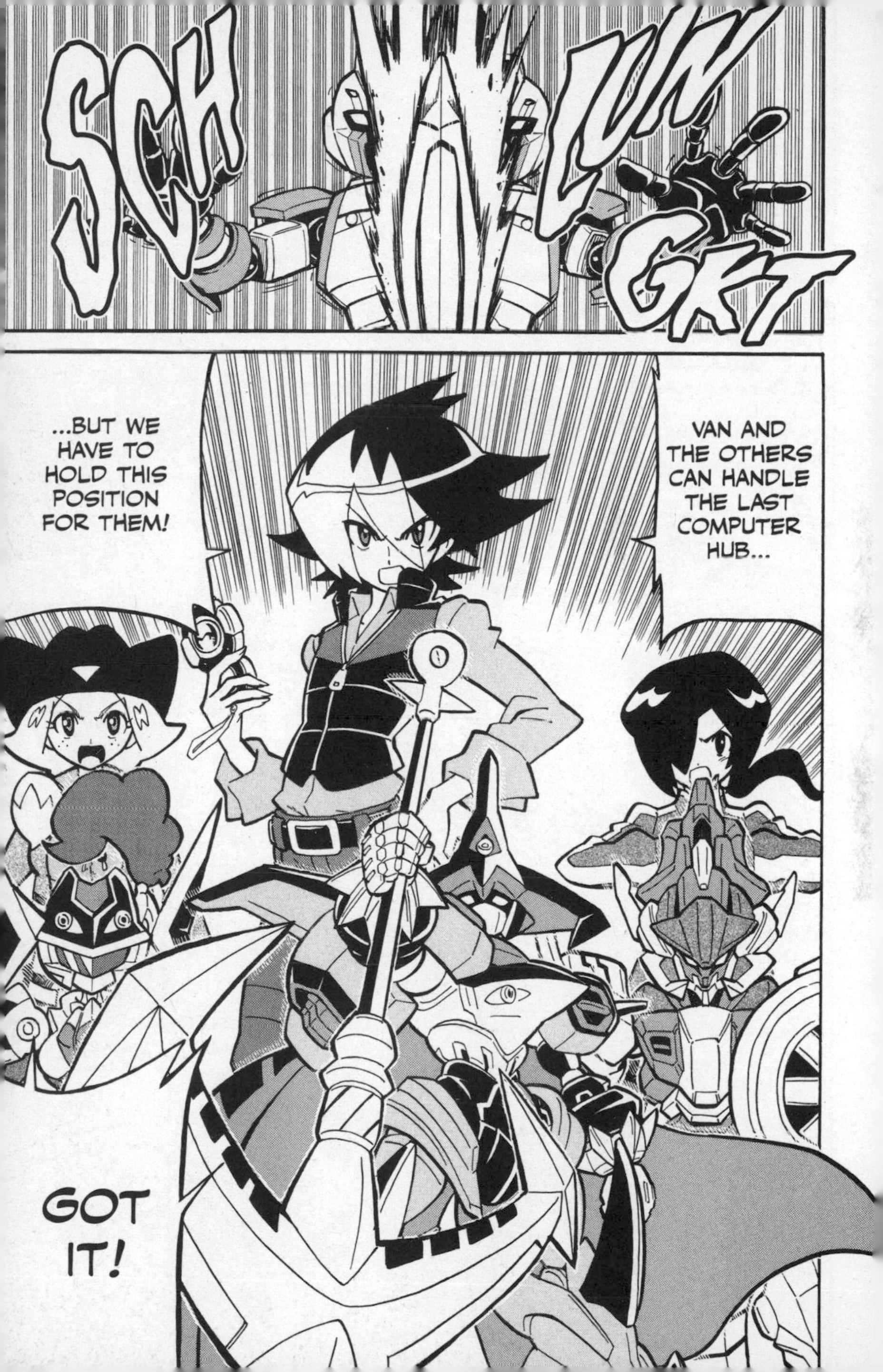
SCH
UN
GKT
VAN AND THE OTHERS CAN HANDLE THE LAST COMPUTER HUB...
...BUT WE HAVE TO HOLD THIS POSITION FOR THEM!
GOT IT!

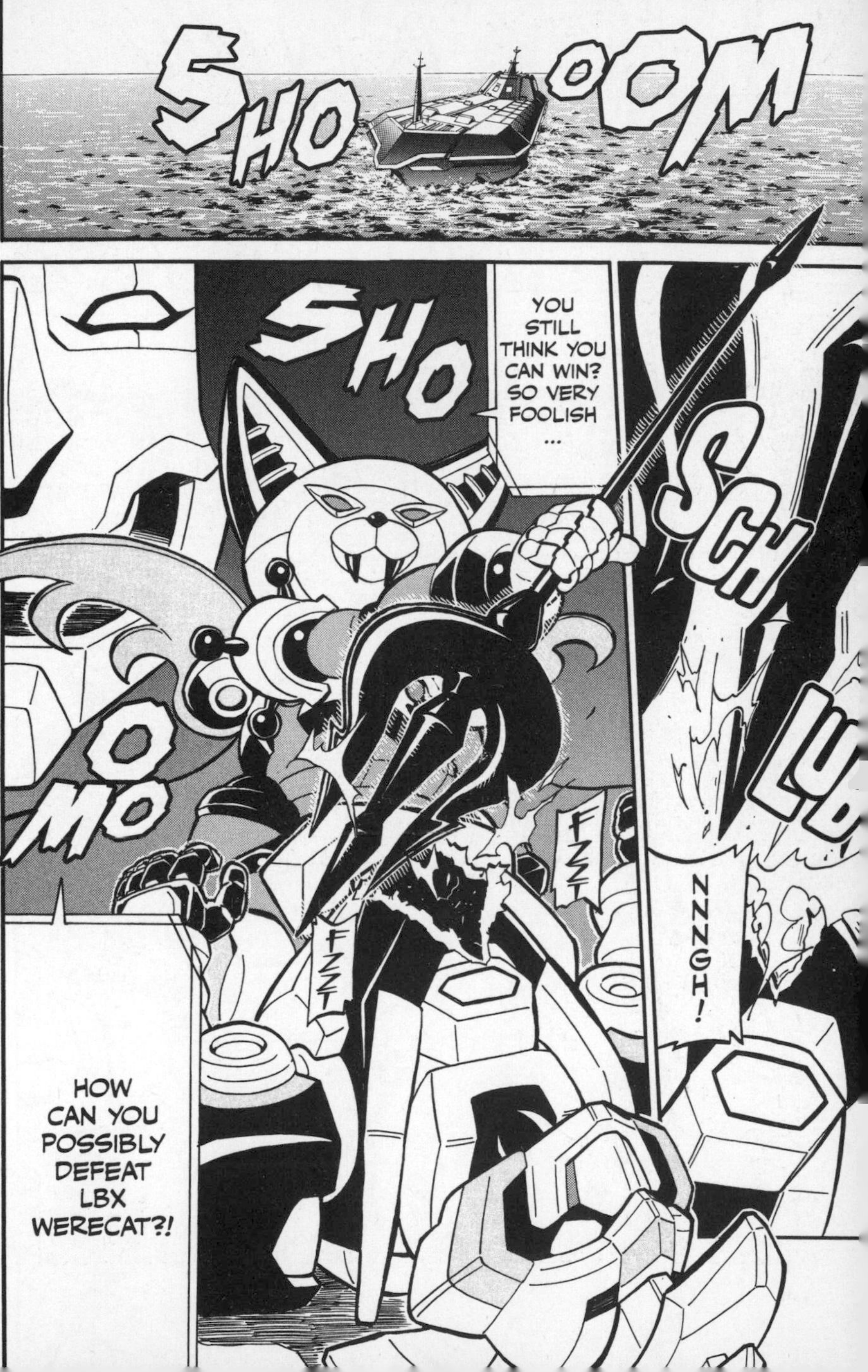
SHOOOOM
SCHLUD
YOU STILL THINK YOU CAN WIN? SO VERY FOOLISH ...
SHOOOMO
NNNGH!
FZZT
FZZT
HOW CAN YOU POSSIBLY DEFEAT LBX WERECAT?!

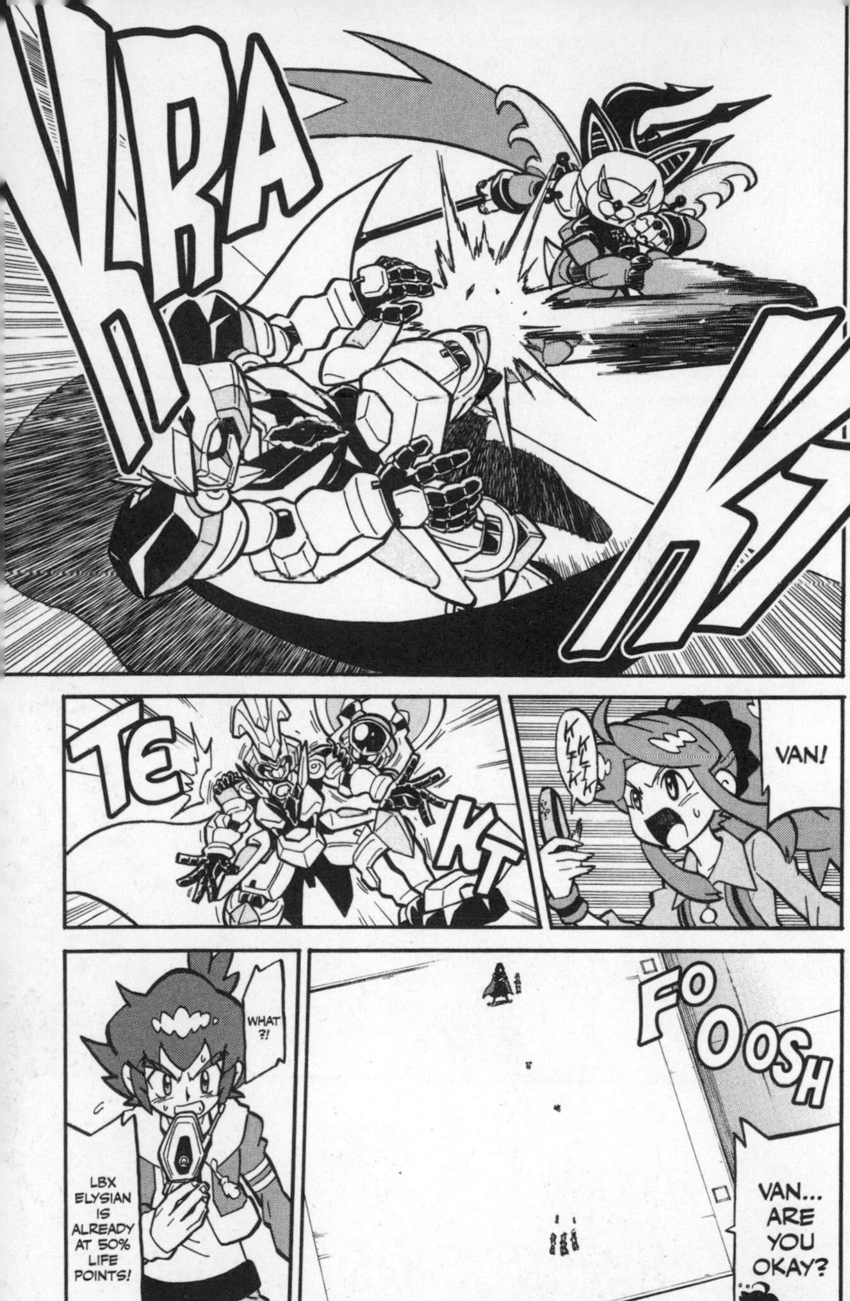
VRA
KT
VAN!
KLIK KLIK
TE
KT
FOOSH
VAN... ARE YOU OKAY?
WHAT?!
LBX ELYSIAN IS ALREADY AT 50% LIFE POINTS!

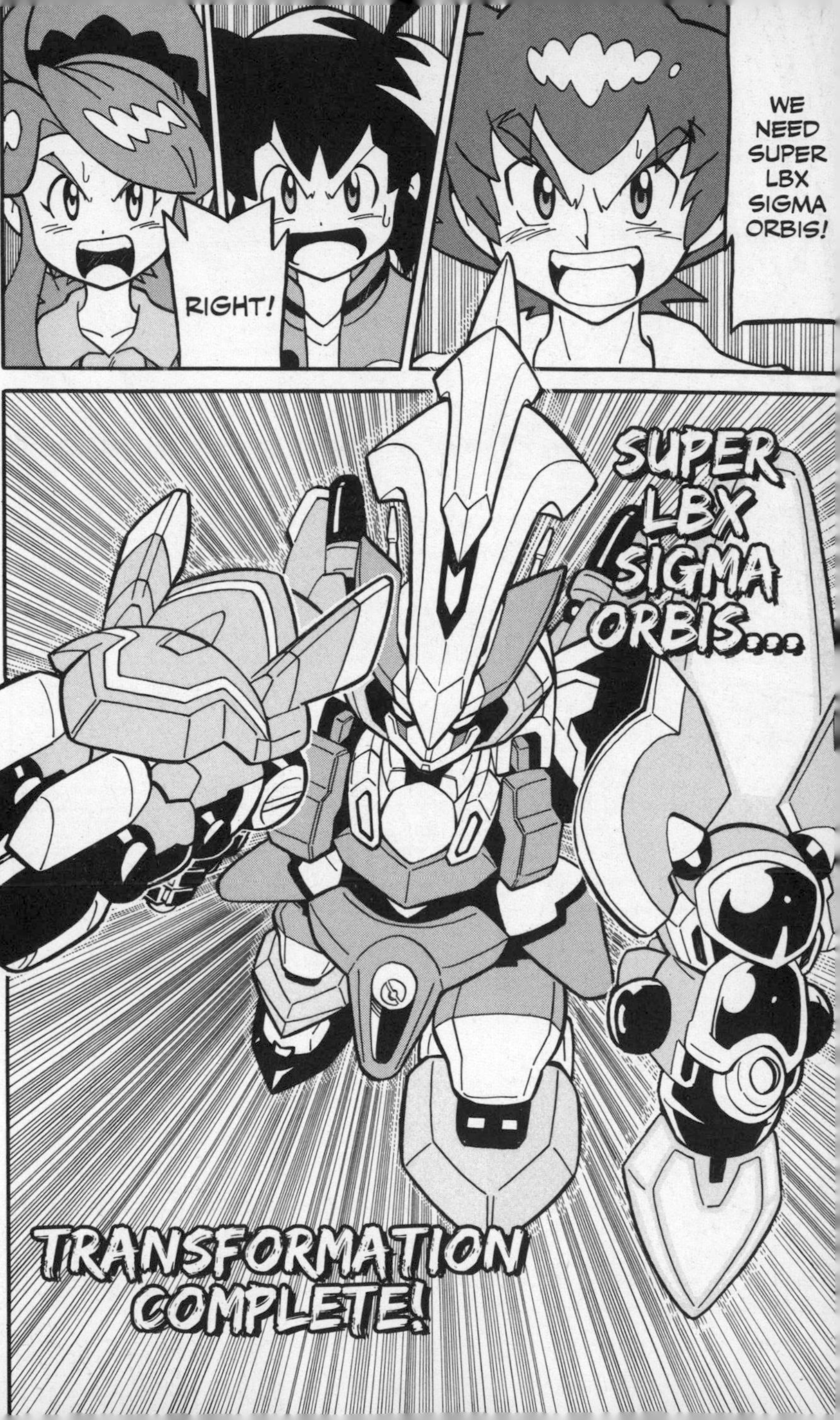
WE NEED SUPER LBX SIGMA ORBIS!
RIGHT!
SUPER LBX SIGMA ORBIS...
TRANSFORMATION COMPLETE!

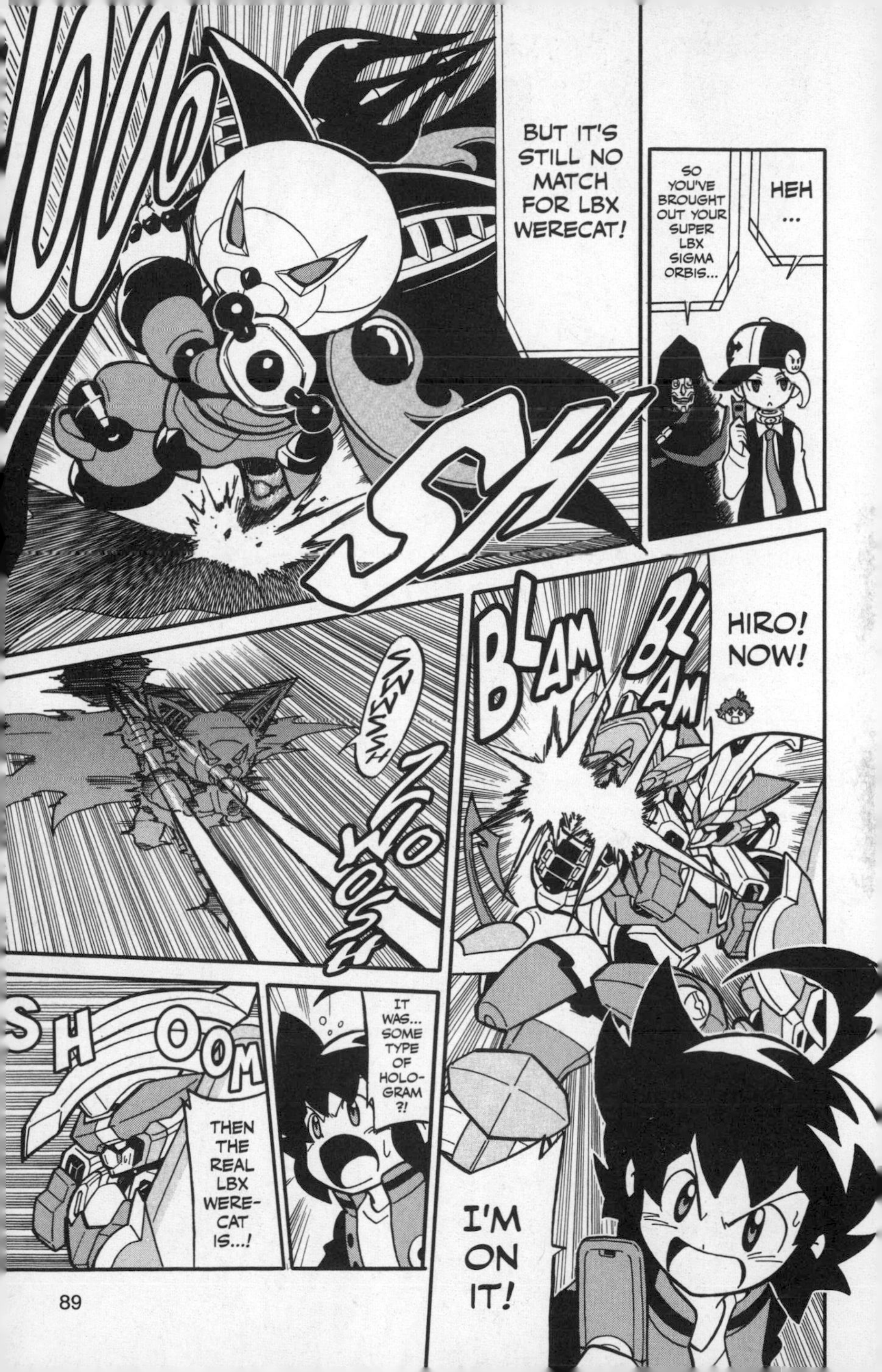
HEH ...
SO YOU'VE BROUGHT OUT YOUR SUPER LBX SIGMA ORBIS...
BUT IT'S STILL NO MATCH FOR LBX WERECAT!
SH
HIRO! NOW!
BLAM BLAM
SWISH
WOOSH
I'M ON IT!
IT WAS... SOME TYPE OF HOLO-GRAM?!
THEN THE REAL LBX WERE-CAT IS...!
SHOOM

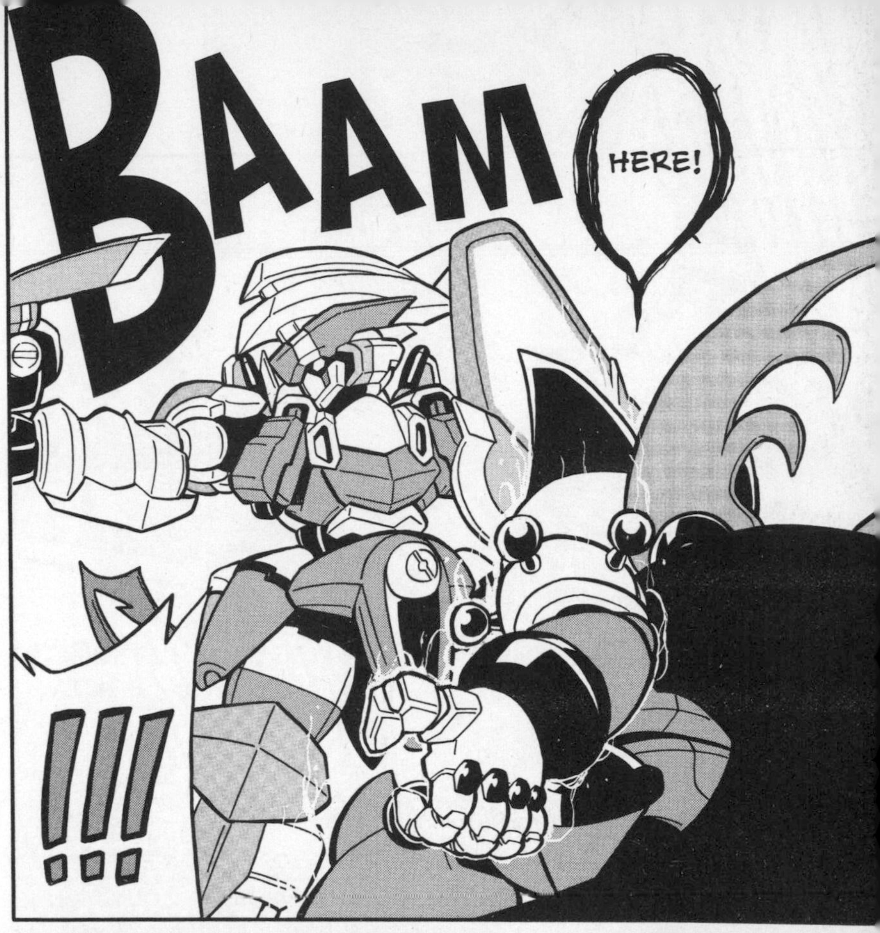
HERE!
BAAM
!!!
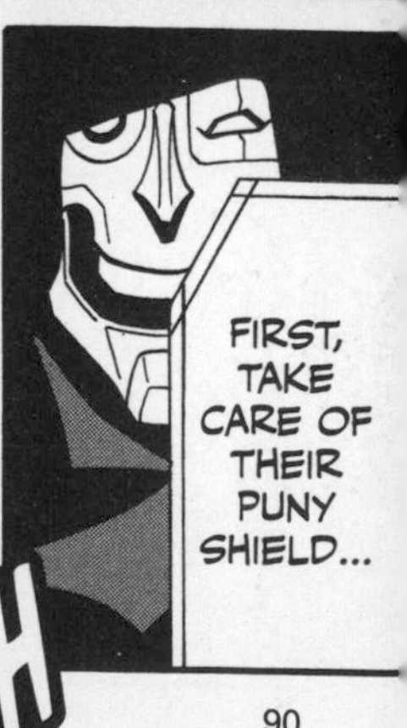
FIRST, TAKE CARE OF THEIR PUNY SHIELD...
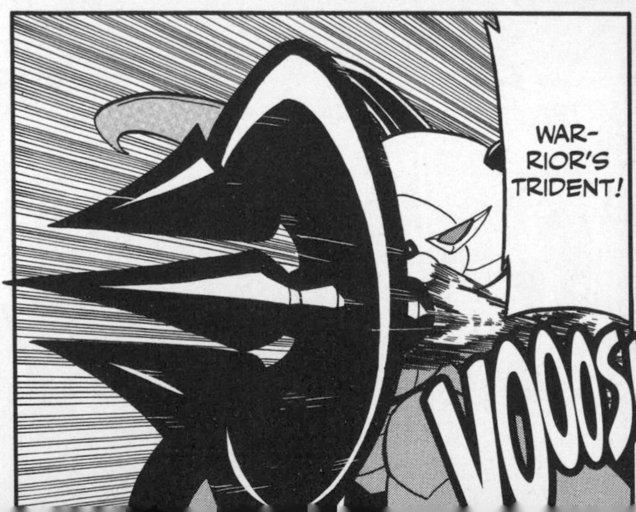
WAR-RIOR'S TRIDENT!
VOOOSH

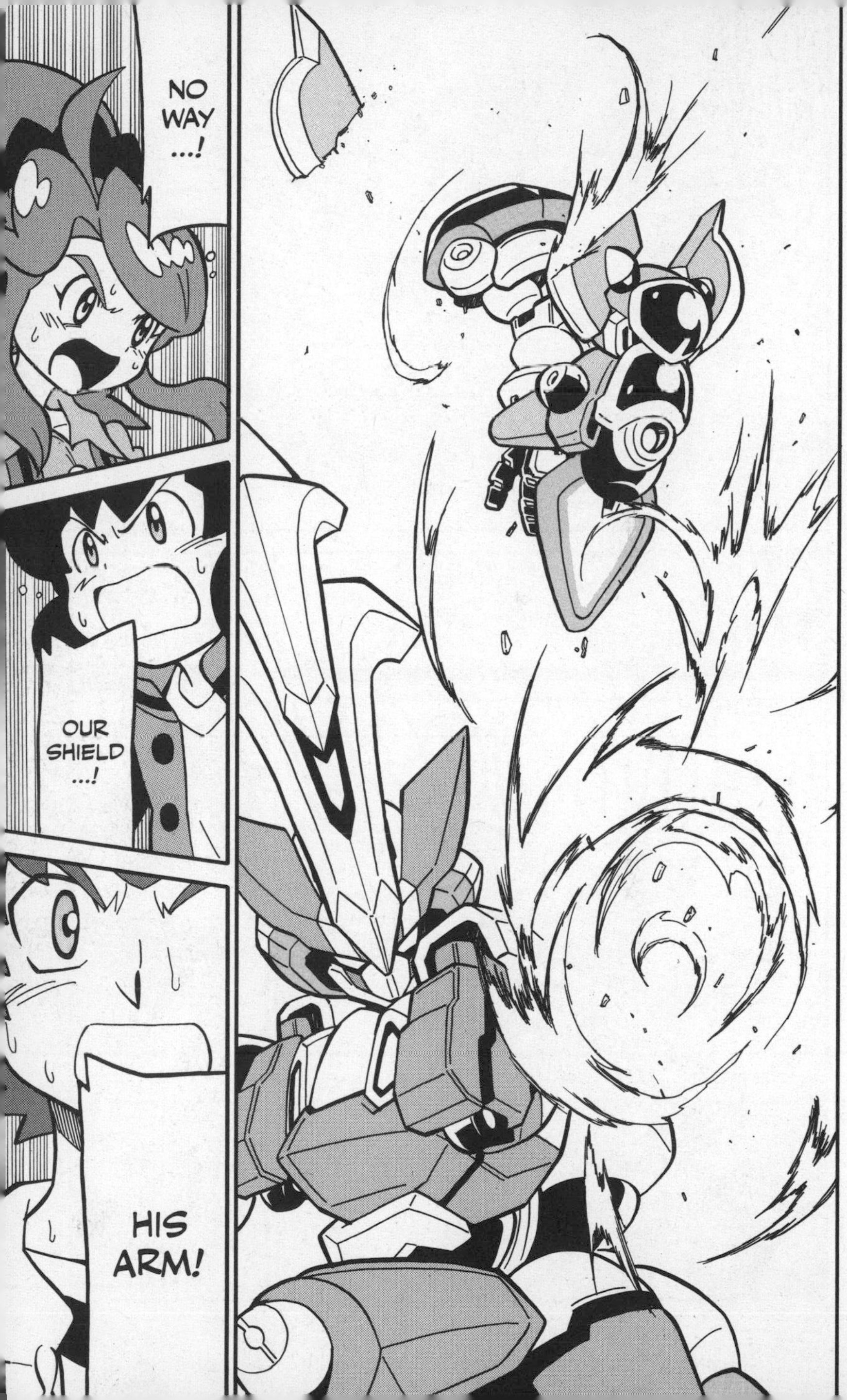
NO WAY ...!
OUR SHIELD ...!
HIS ARM!

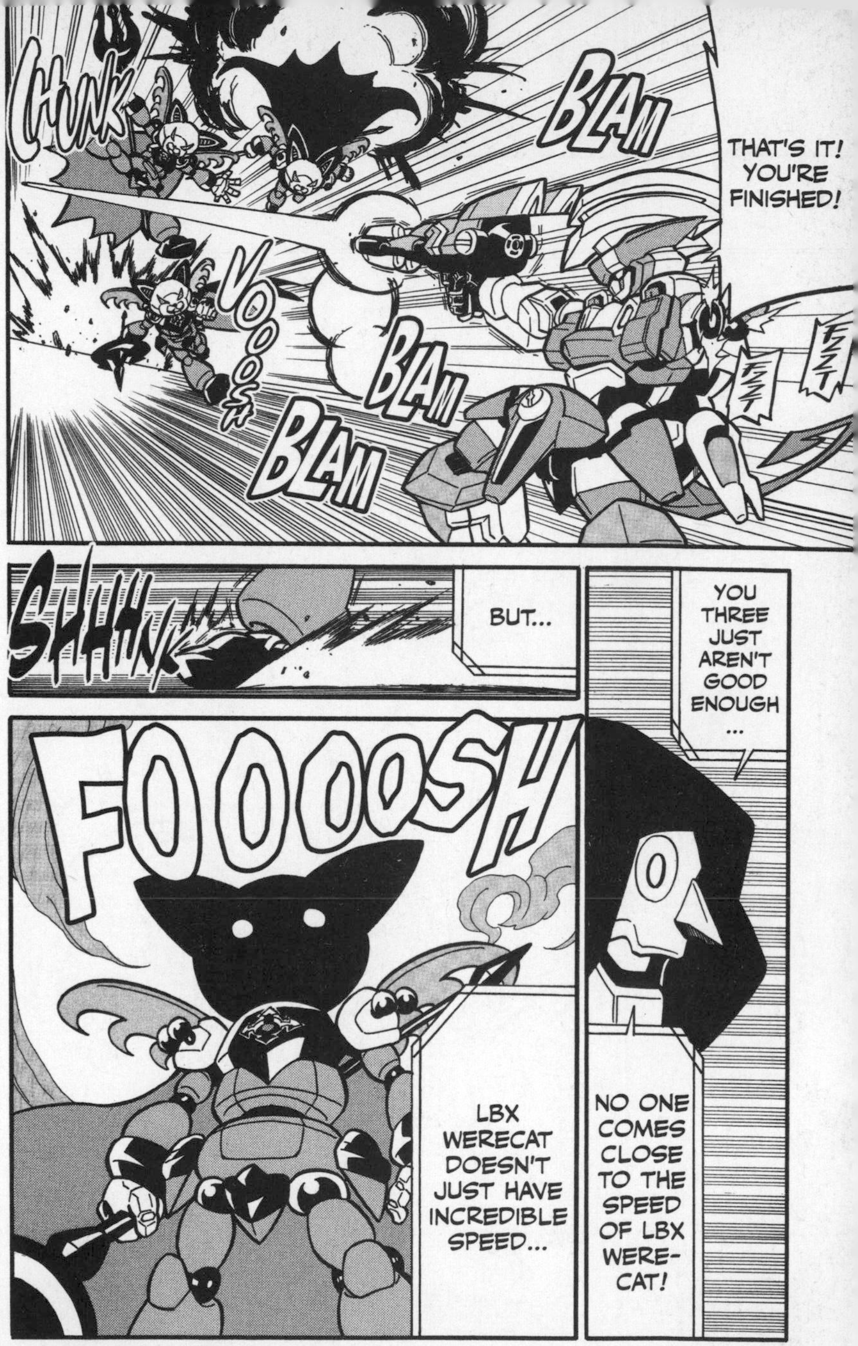
THAT'S IT! YOU'RE FINISHED!
BLAM
CHUNK
FZZZT
FZZT
VOOOOSH
BLAM
BLAM
YOU THREE JUST AREN'T GOOD ENOUGH ...
NO ONE COMES CLOSE TO THE SPEED OF LBX WERE-CAT!
BUT...
SHHHN
LBX WERECAT DOESN'T JUST HAVE INCREDIBLE SPEED...
FOOOOSH

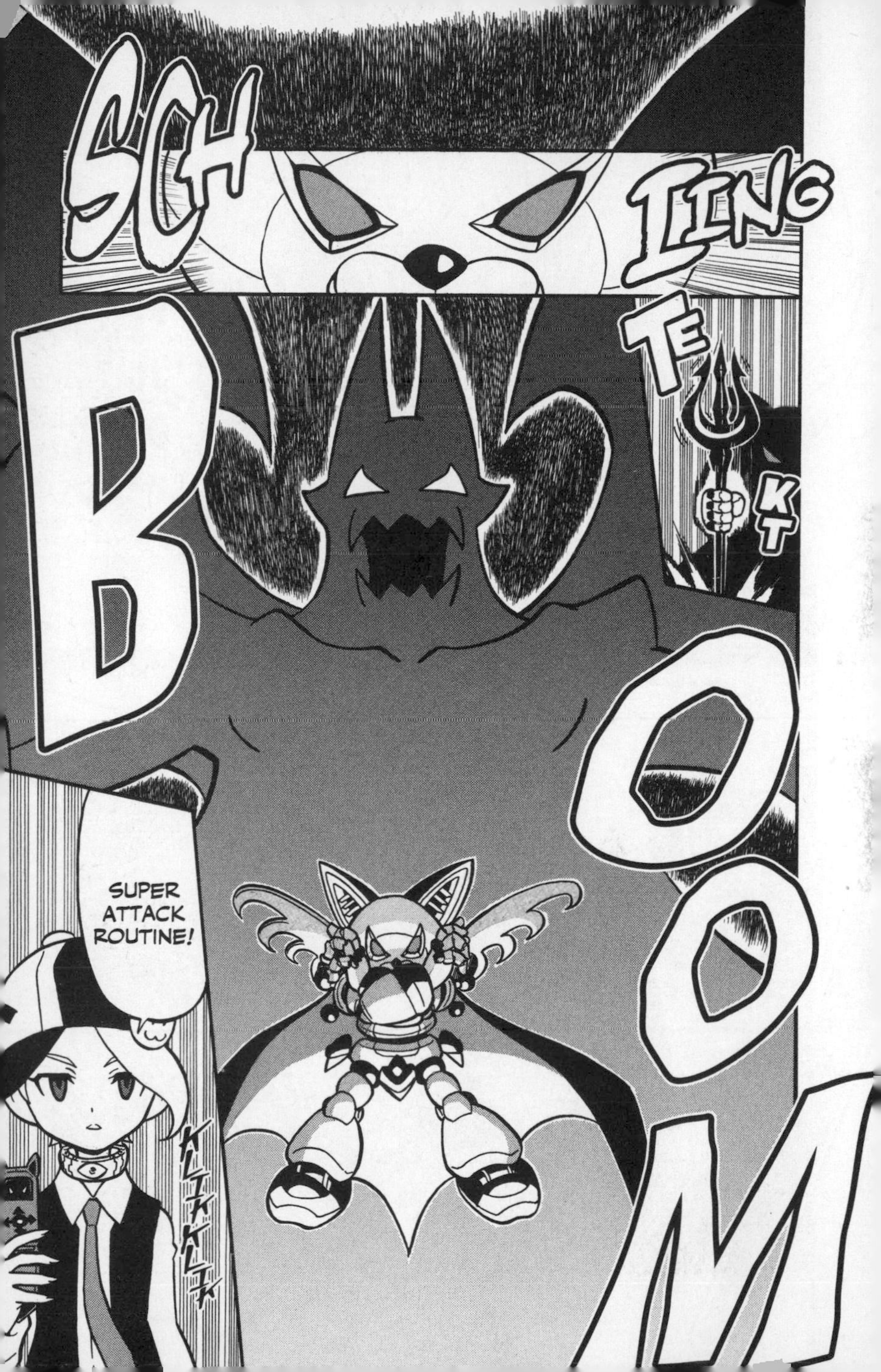
SCH
IING
TE
KT
BOOOM
SUPER ATTACK ROUTINE!
KLIK KLIK

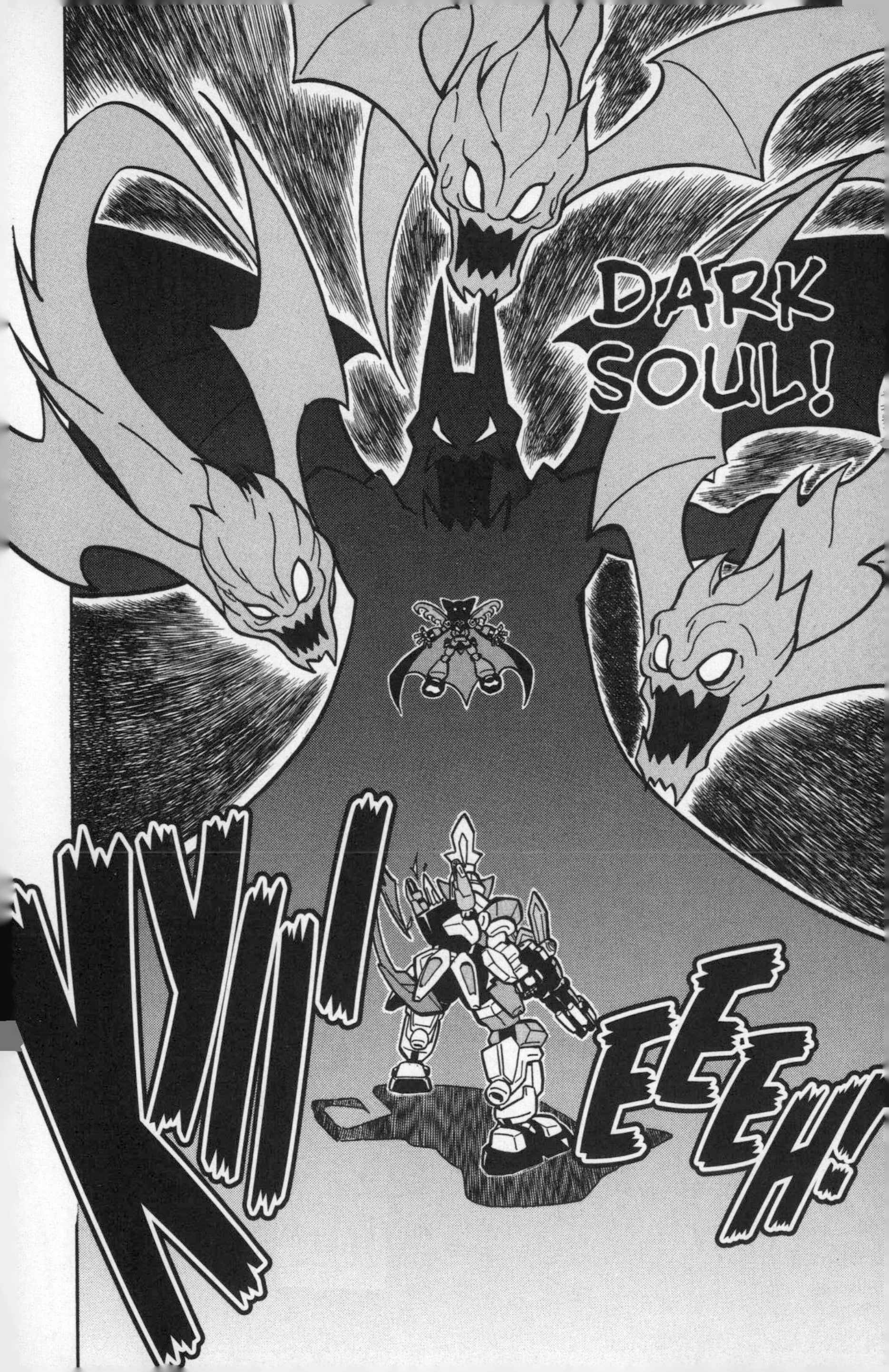
DARK SOUL!
KYIIIEEEH!

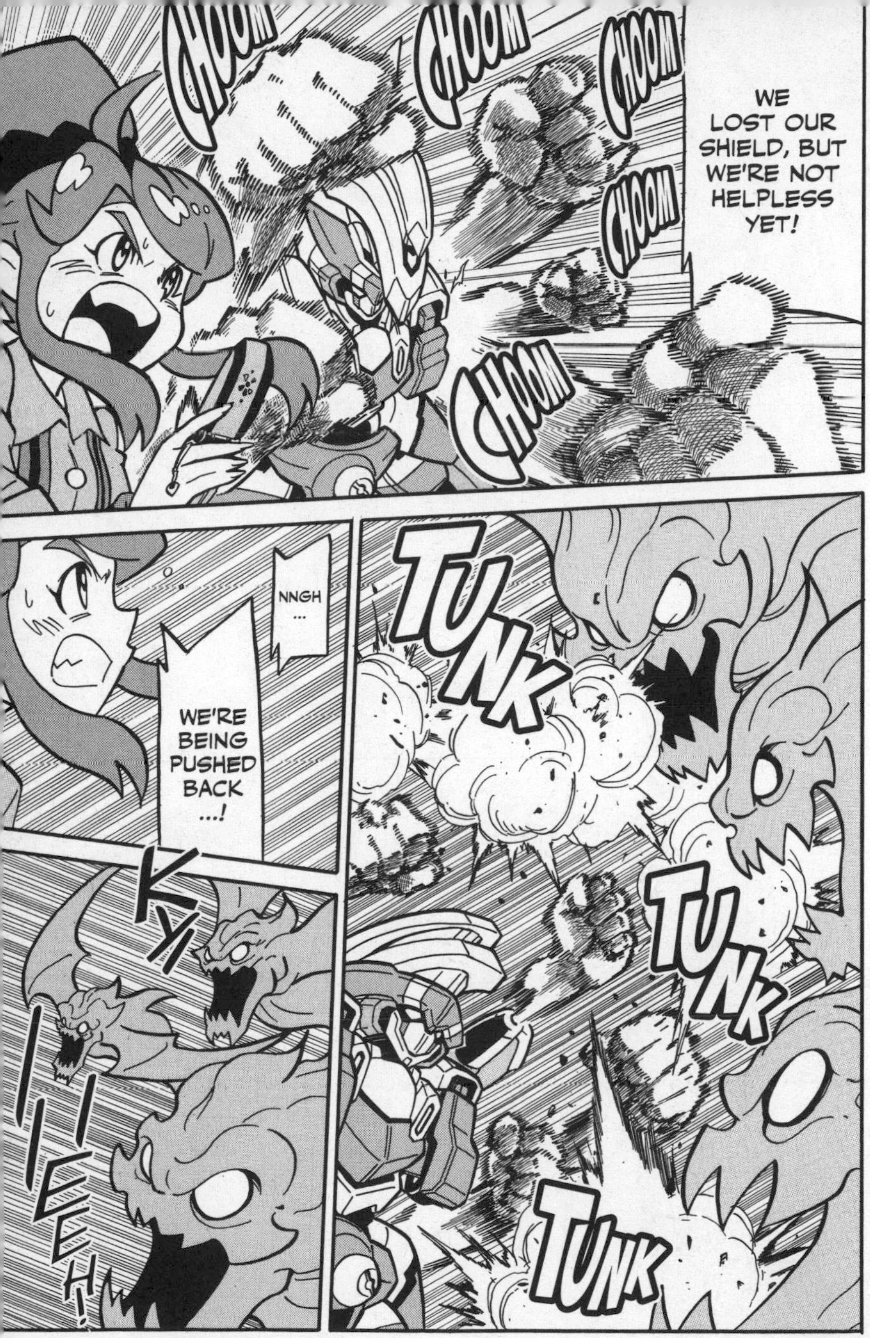
CHOOM
CHOOM
CHOOM
CHOOM
CHOOM
WE LOST OUR SHIELD, BUT WE'RE NOT HELPLESS YET!
TUNK
TUNK
TUNK
NNGH ...
WE'RE BEING PUSHED BACK ...!
KYIIIEEEH!

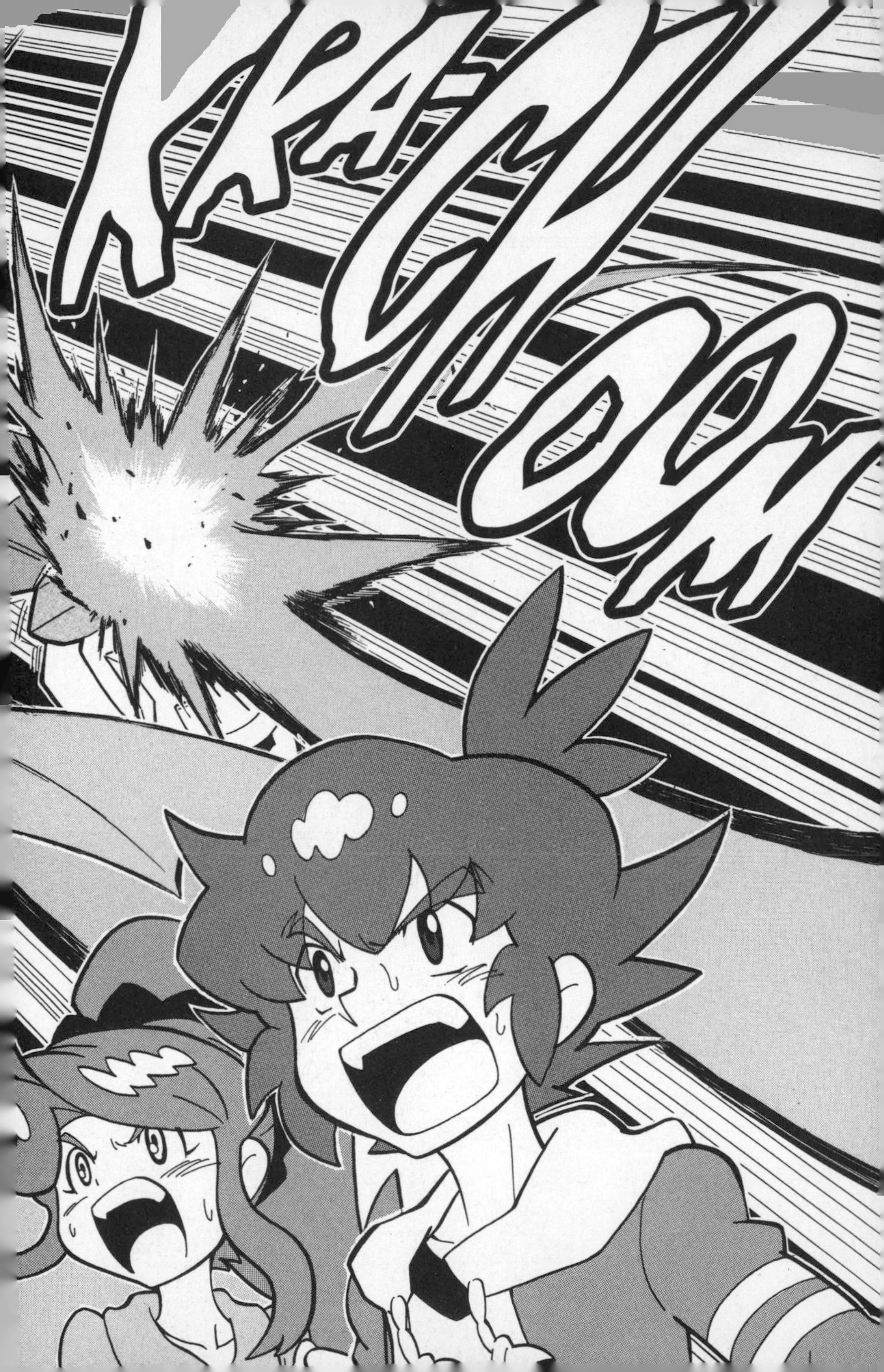

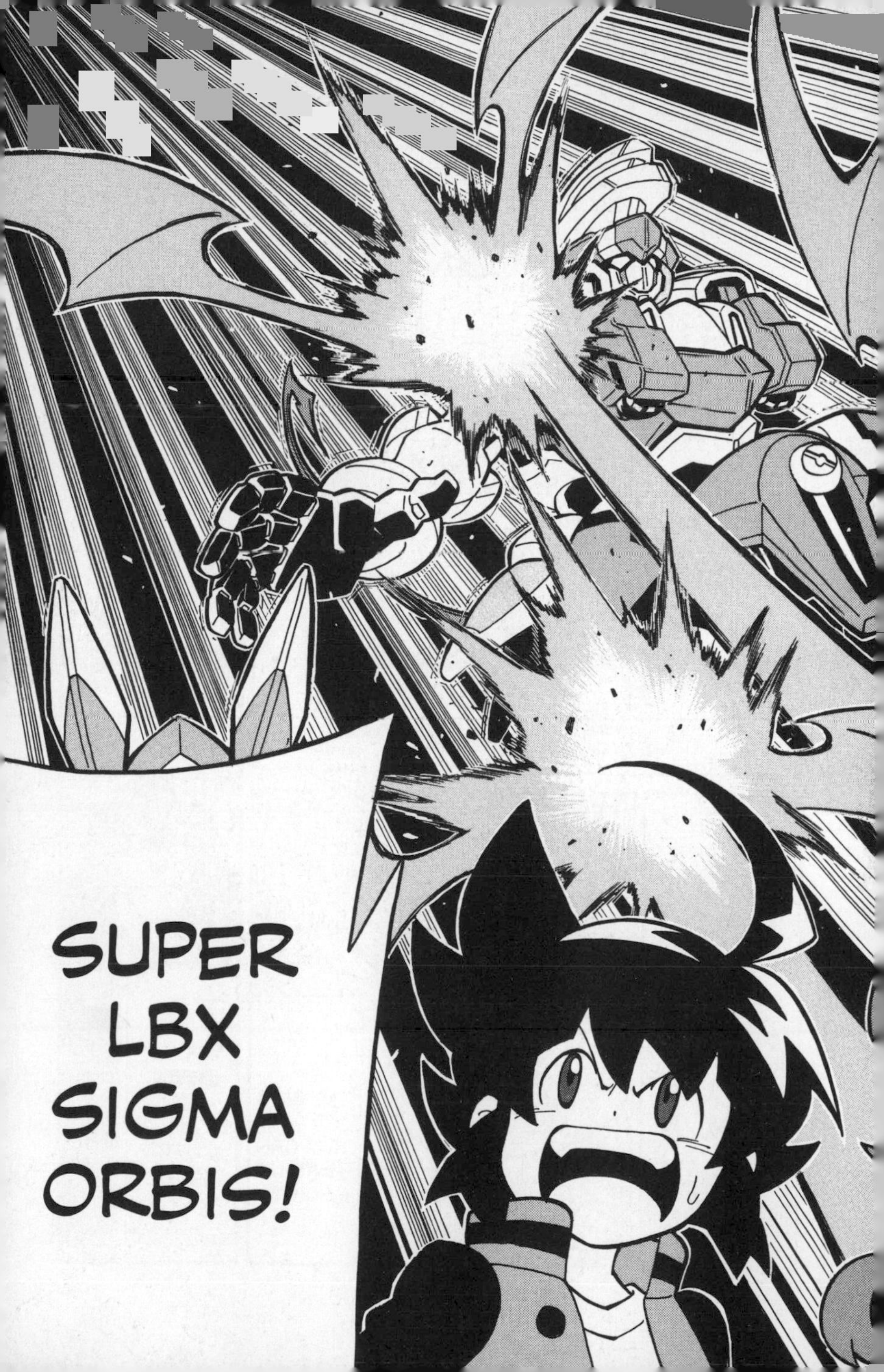
SUPER LBX SIGMA ORBIS!

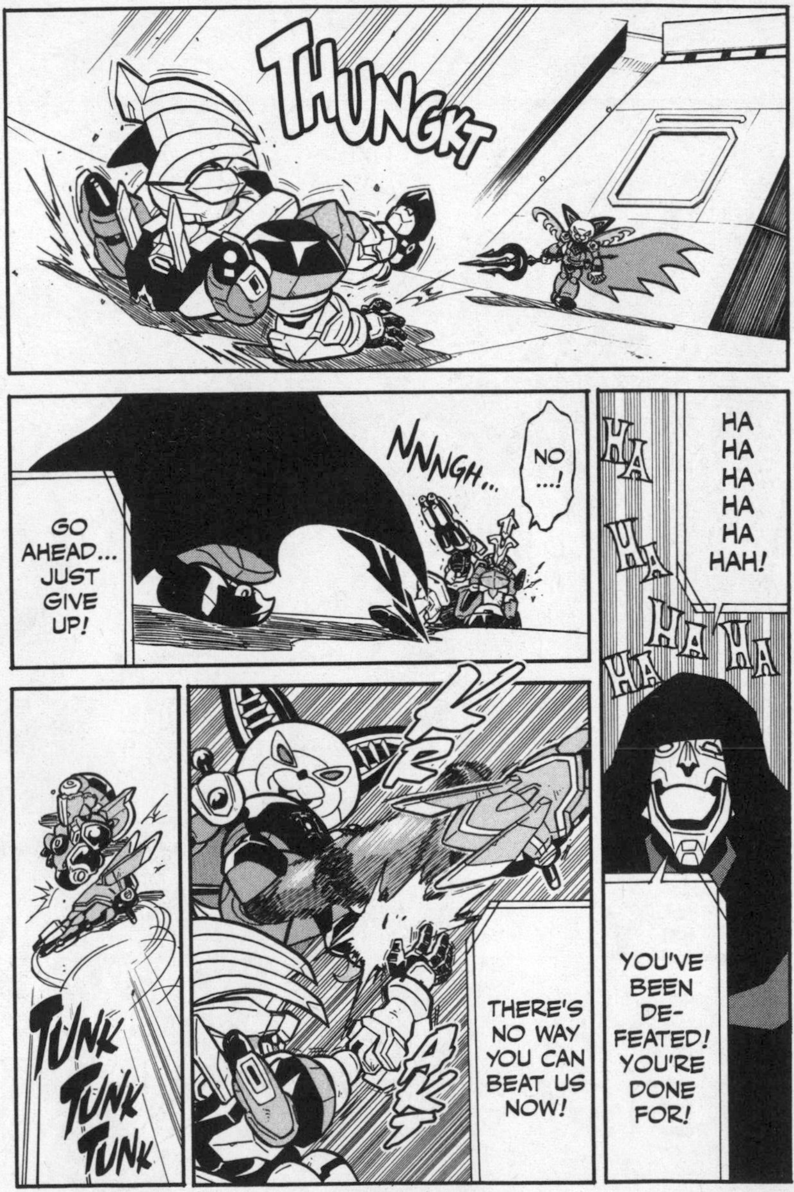
THUNGKT
HA HA HA HA HA HA HAH!
HA HA HA HA HA HA
YOU'VE BEEN DE-FEATED! YOU'RE DONE FOR!
NO ...!
NNNGH...
GO AHEAD... JUST GIVE UP!
THERE'S NO WAY YOU CAN BEAT US NOW!
TUNK TUNK TUNK

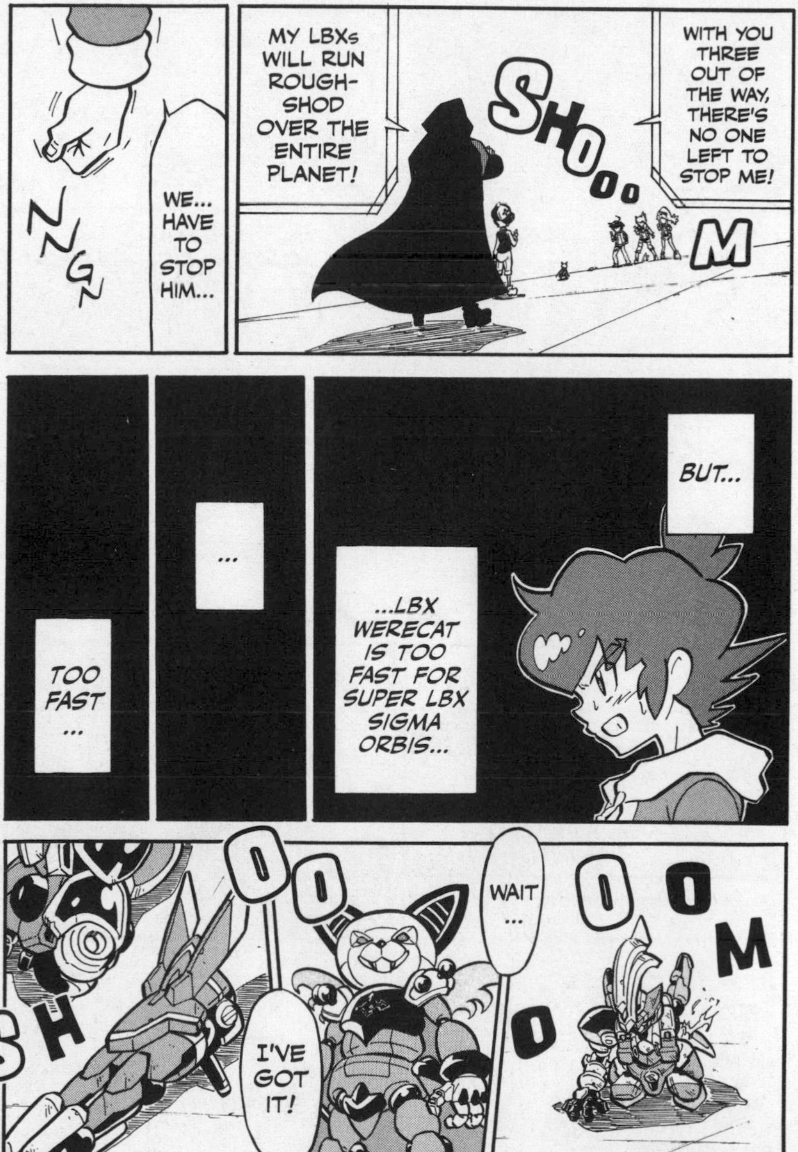
WITH YOU THREE OUT OF THE WAY, THERE'S NO ONE LEFT TO STOP ME!
SHOOOOM
MY LBXs WILL RUN ROUGH-SHOD OVER THE ENTIRE PLANET!
WE... HAVE TO STOP HIM...
NNGN
BUT...
...LBX WERECAT IS TOO FAST FOR SUPER LBX SIGMA ORBIS...
...
TOO FAST...
OOOOM
WAIT...
OO
I'VE GOT IT!
SH

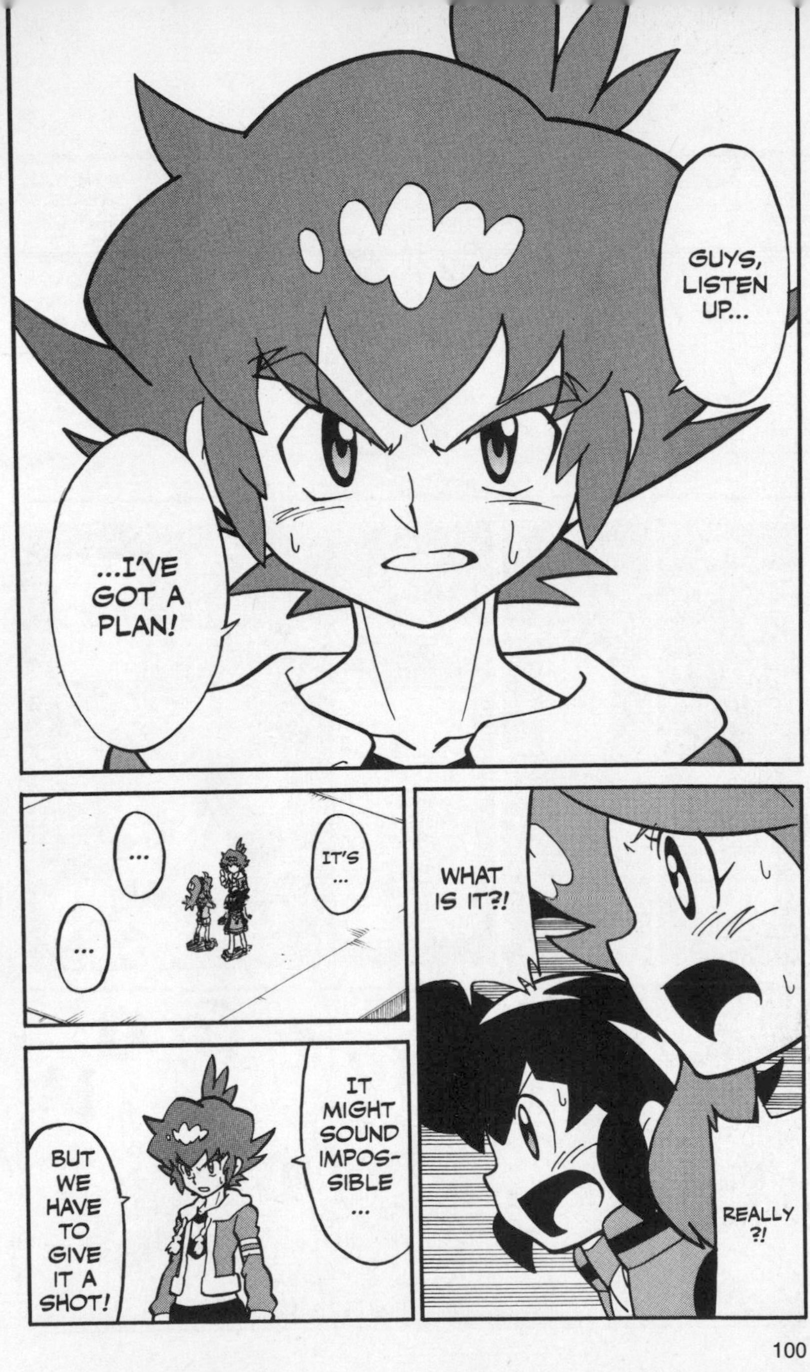
GUYS, LISTEN UP...
...I'VE GOT A PLAN!
WHAT IS IT?!
REALLY ?!
IT'S ...
...
...
IT MIGHT SOUND IMPOSSIBLE ...
BUT WE HAVE TO GIVE IT A SHOT!

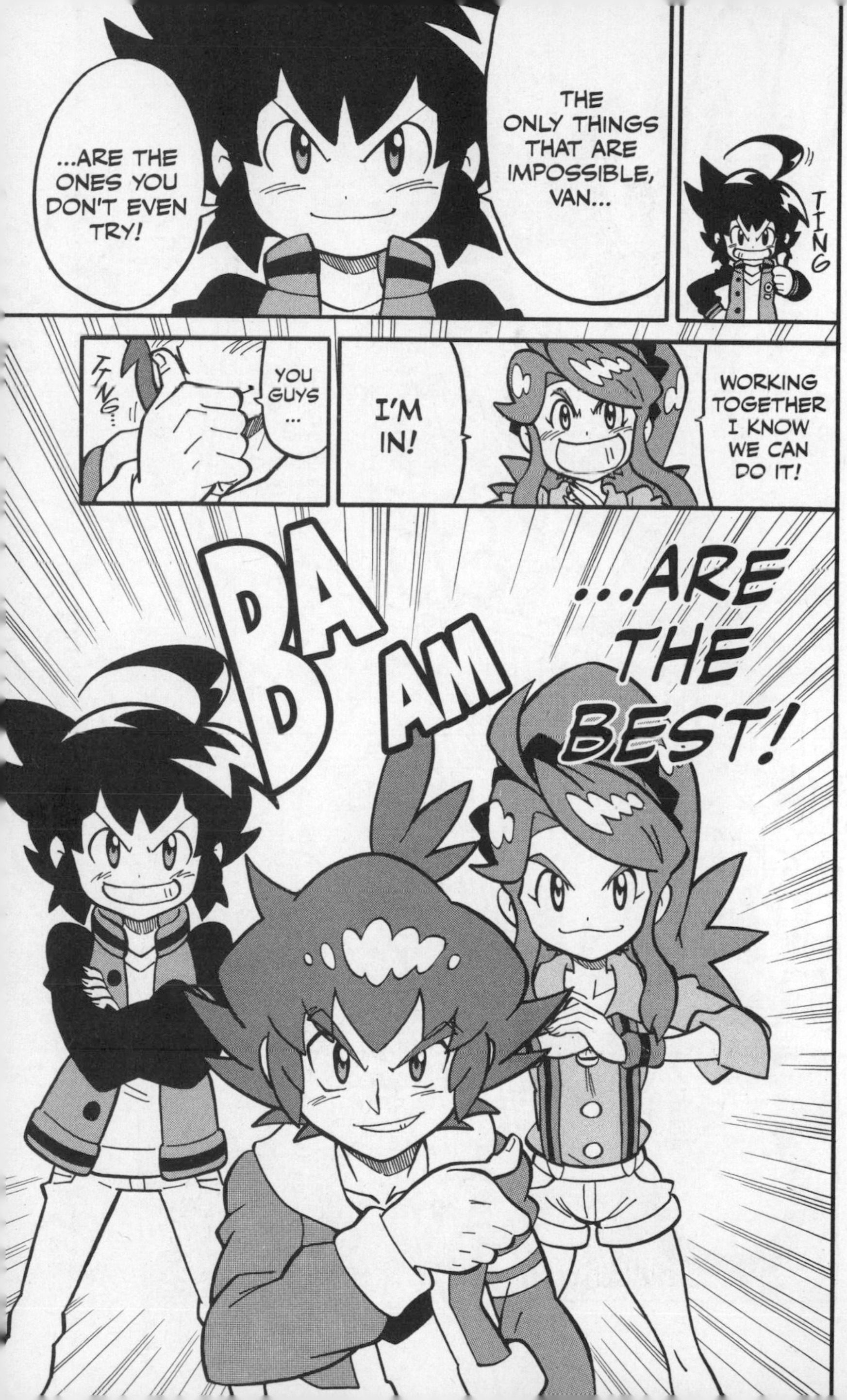
TING
THE ONLY THINGS THAT ARE IMPOSSIBLE, VAN...
...ARE THE ONES YOU DON'T EVEN TRY!
WORKING TOGETHER I KNOW WE CAN DO IT!
I'M IN!
YOU GUYS ...
TING...
...ARE THE BEST!
BADAM

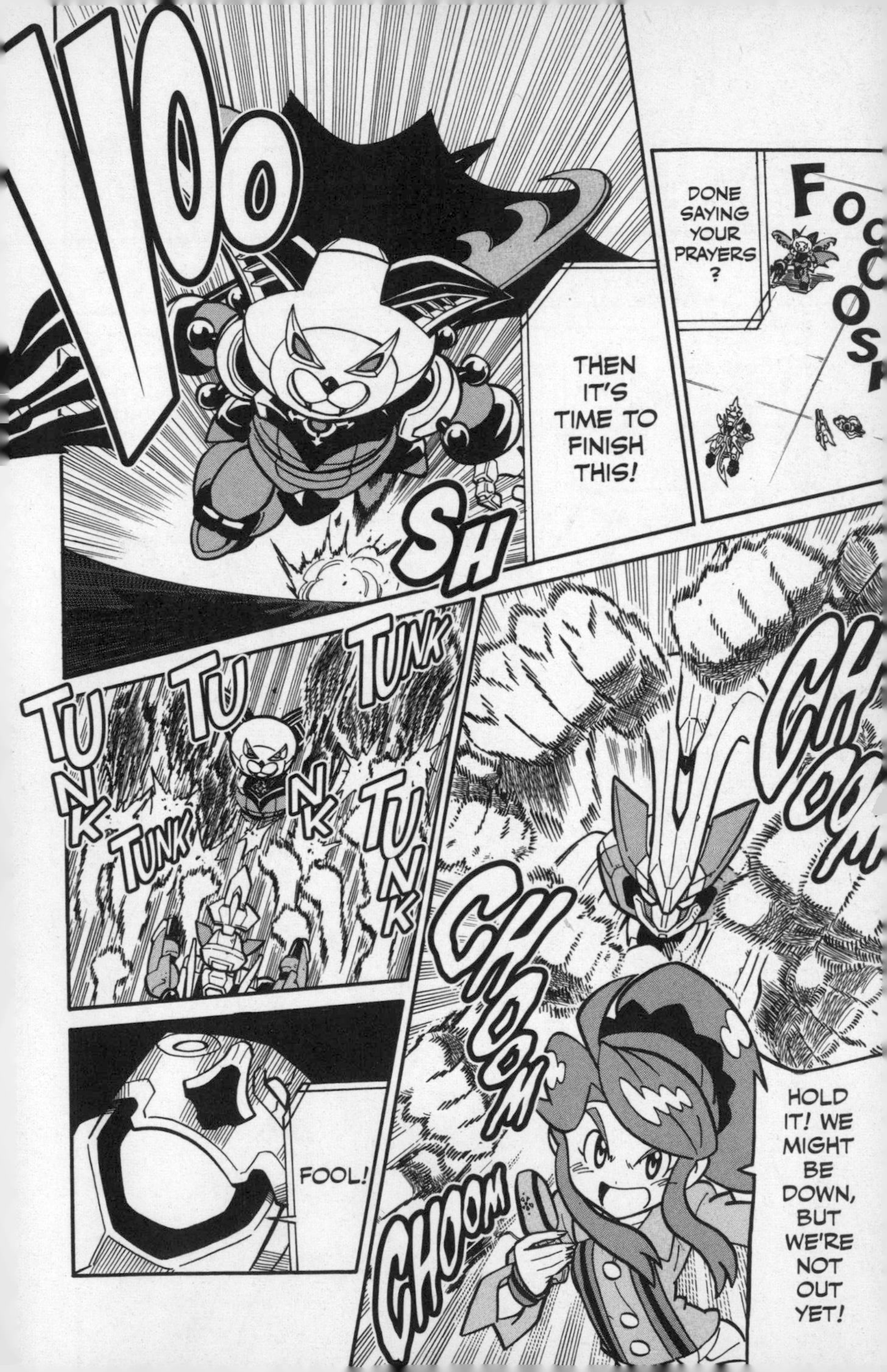
FOOOOSH
DONE SAYING YOUR PRAYERS?
THEN IT'S TIME TO FINISH THIS!
VOOO
SH
TUNK
TU
TUNK
TUNK
TUNK
TUNK
TUNK
FOOL!
HOLD IT! WE MIGHT BE DOWN, BUT WE'RE NOT OUT YET!
CHOOOM
CHOOOM
CHOOM

WITH NO LEFT ARM, THEIR ENTIRE FLANK IS VULNERABLE...

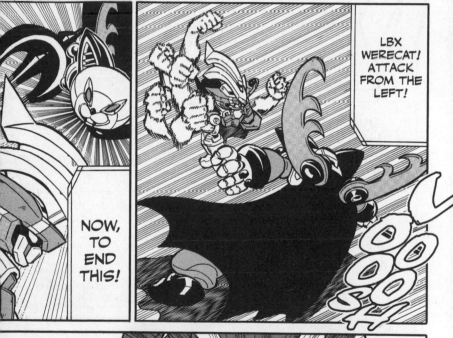

LBX WERECAT! ATTACK FROM THE LEFT!

NOW, TO END THIS!

OOOOSH

OKAY, GUYS...!

UNLOCK TRANSFORMATION!

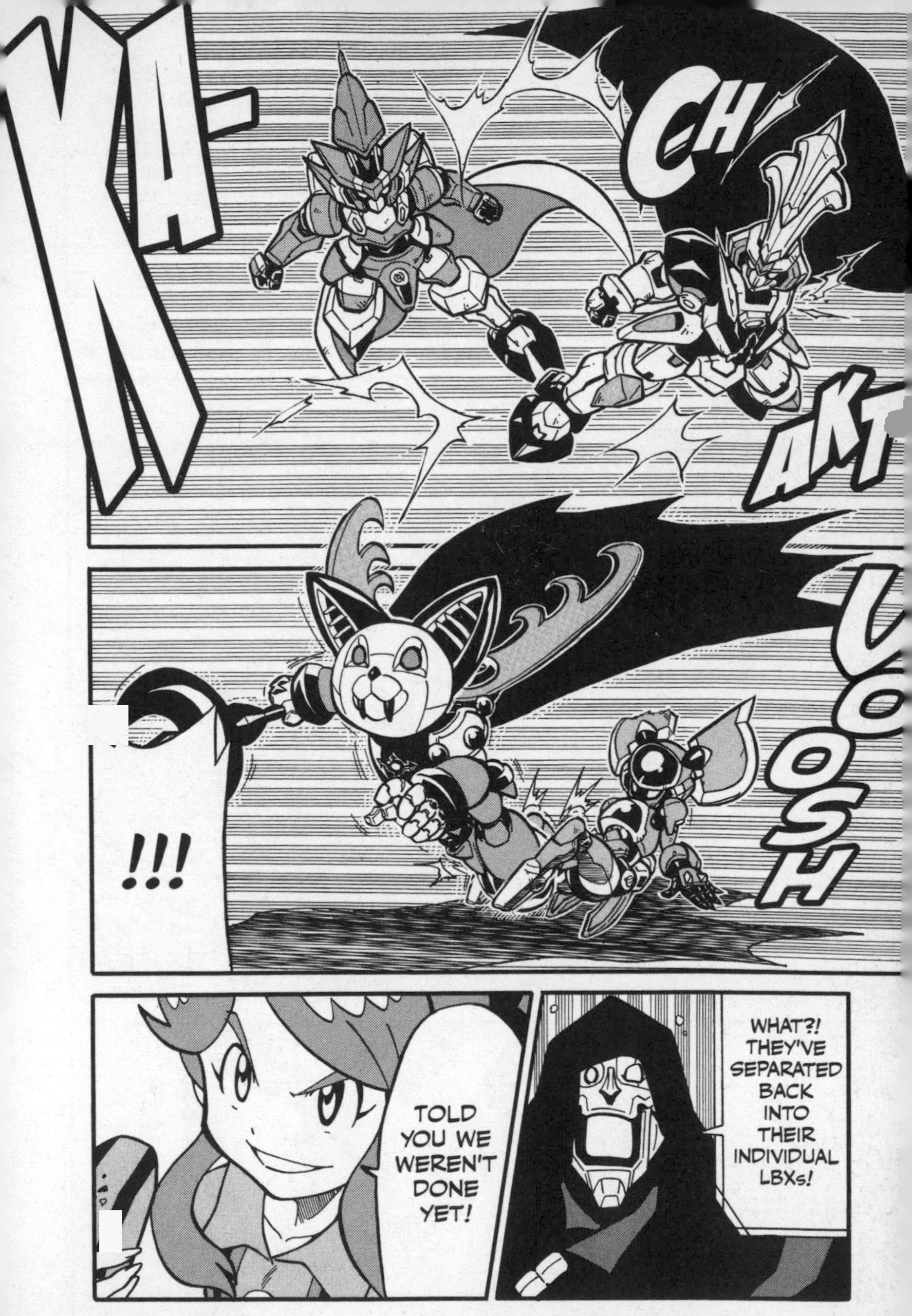
KA-CHAKT
VOOSH
!!!
WHAT?! THEY'VE SEPARATED BACK INTO THEIR INDIVIDUAL LBXs!
TOLD YOU WE WEREN'T DONE YET!

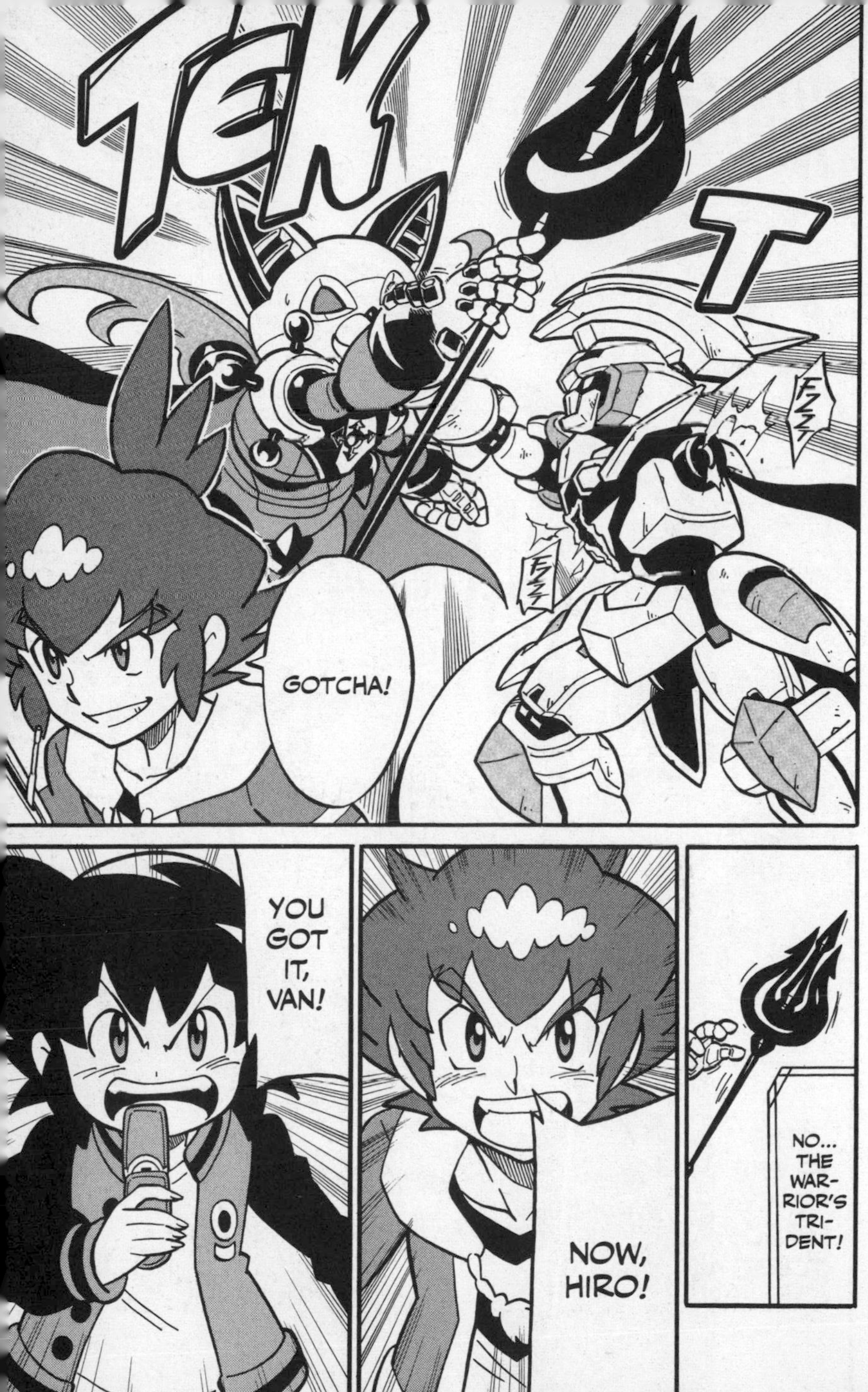
FZZZ
FZZZ
GOTCHA!
NO... THE WARRIOR'S TRIDENT!
NOW, HIRO!
YOU GOT IT, VAN!

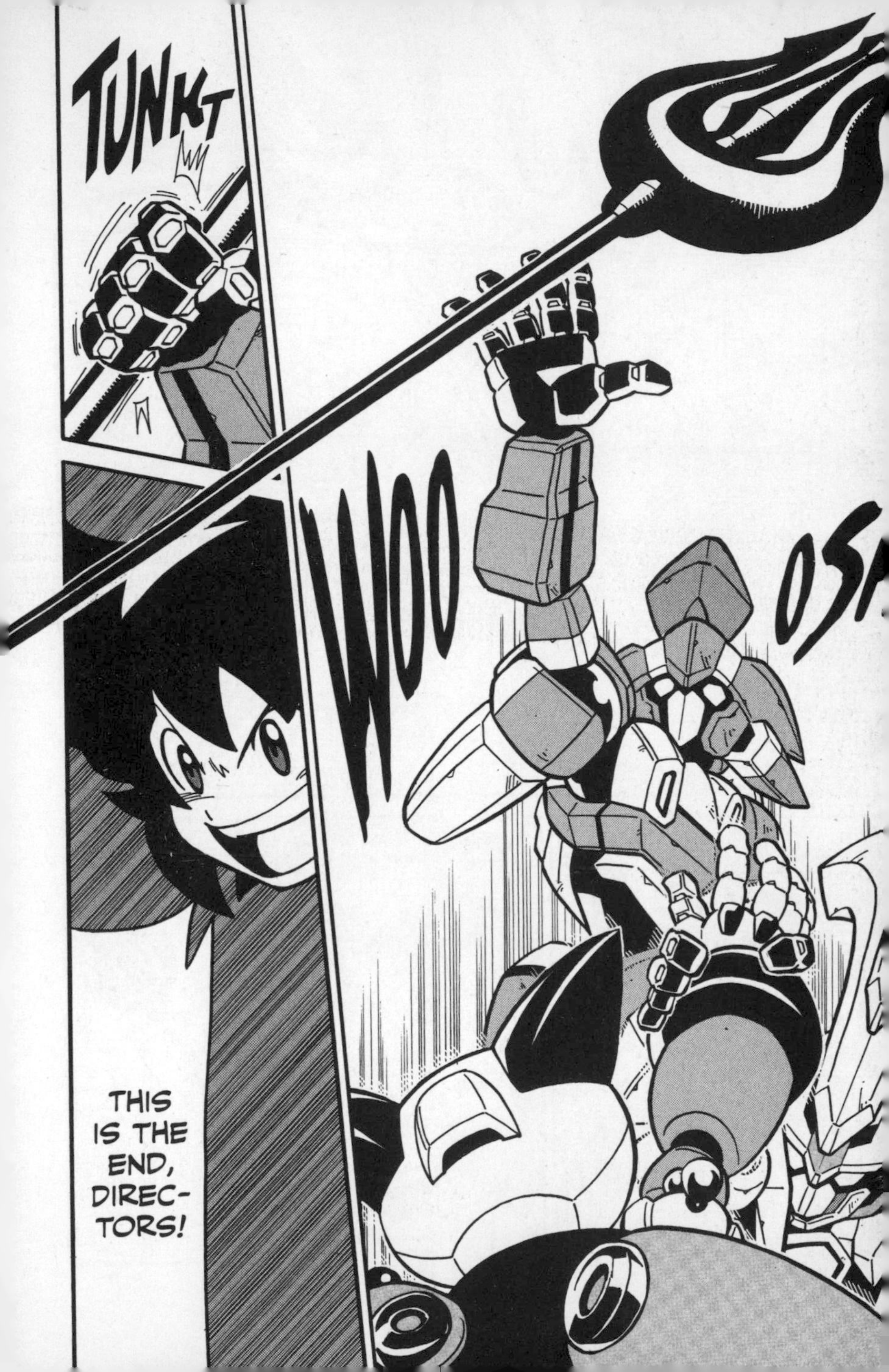
TUNKT
WOOOSH
THIS IS THE END, DIRECTORS!

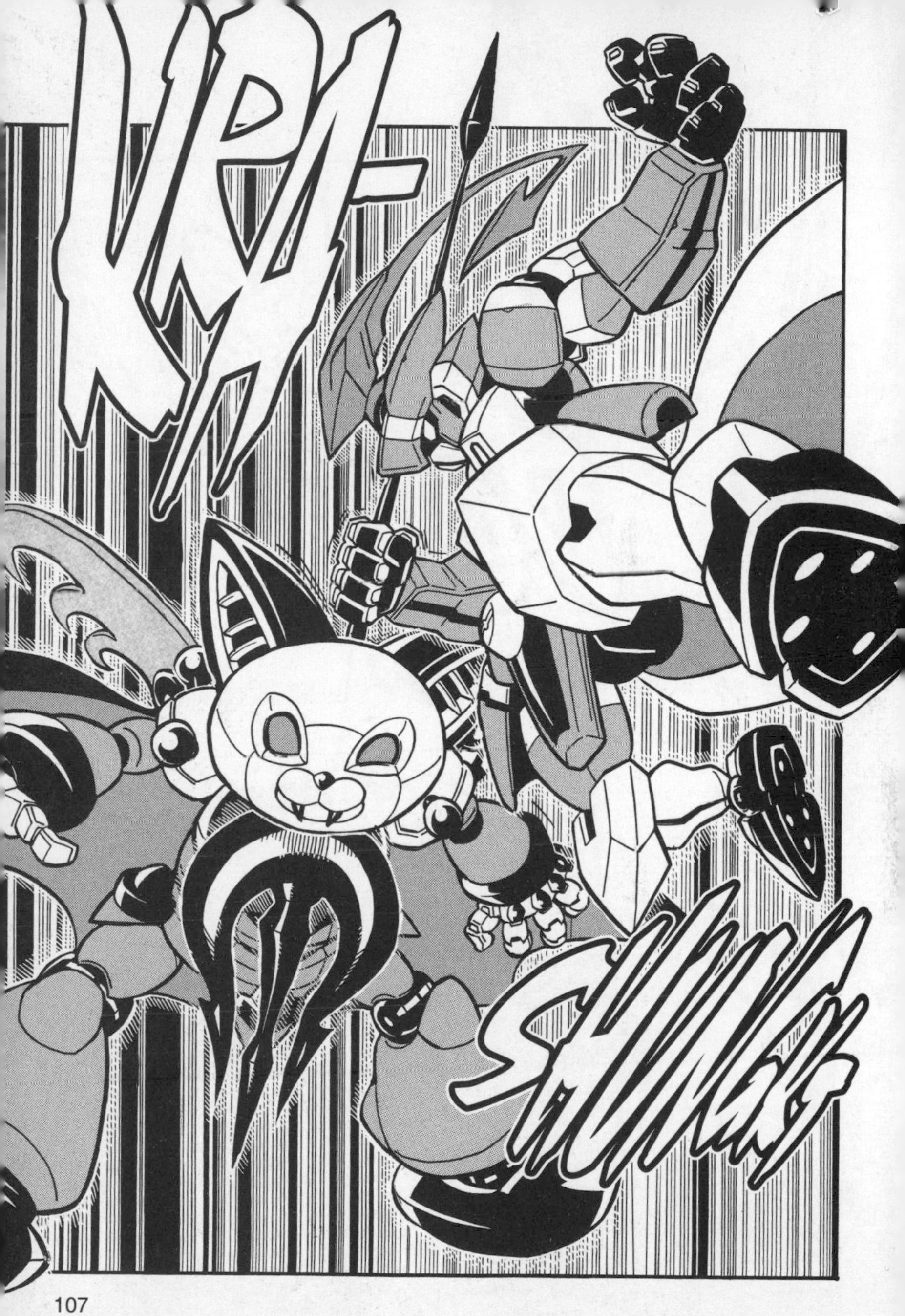

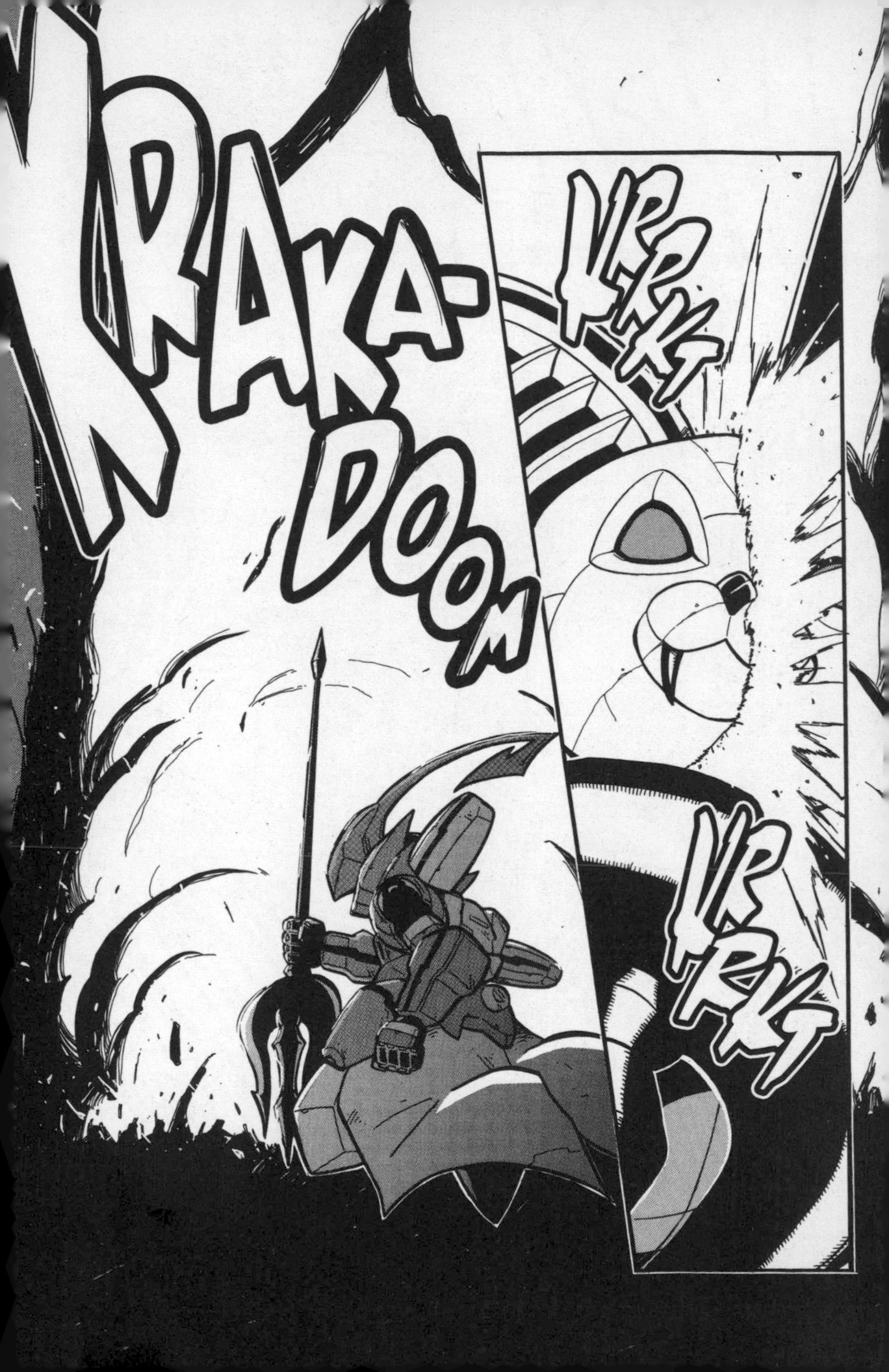
VRRKT
RAKA-DOOM
VRRKT

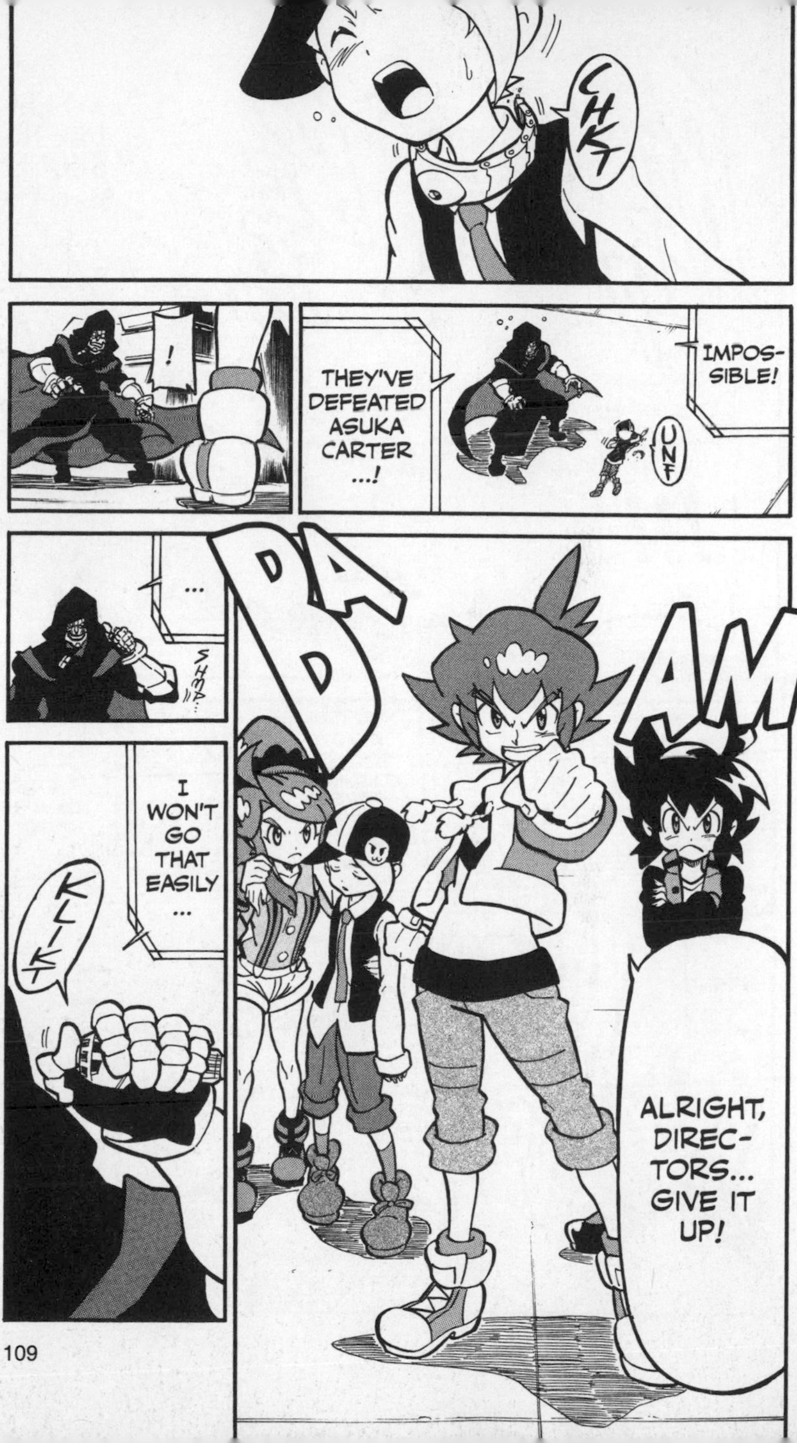
CHKT
IMPOS-SIBLE!
UNF
THEY'VE DEFEATED ASUKA CARTER ...!
!
DA
D
AM
ALRIGHT, DIRECTORS... GIVE IT UP!
...
SHMP...
I WON'T GO THAT EASILY ...
KLIKT

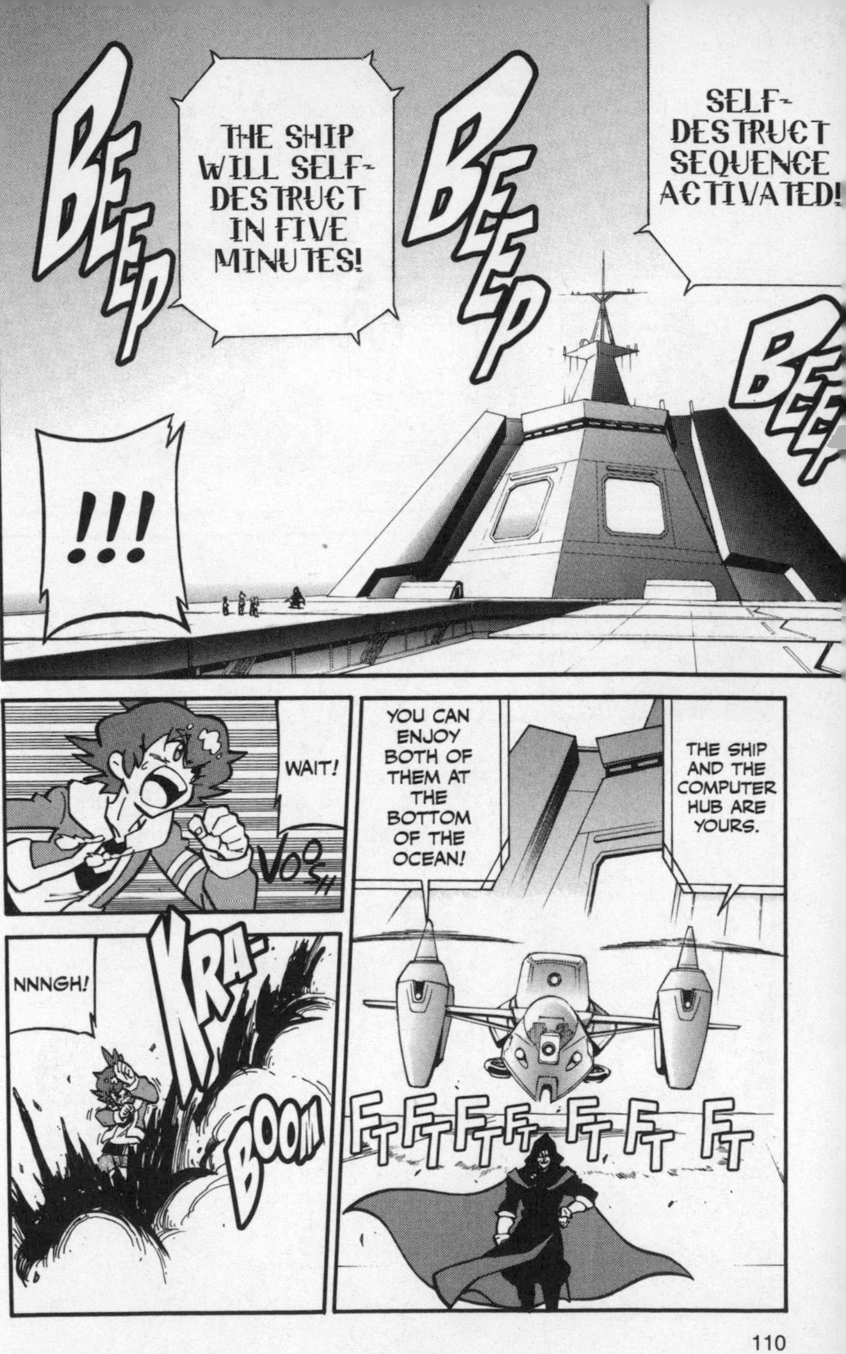
BEEP
SELF-DESTRUCT SEQUENCE ACTIVATED!
BEEP
THE SHIP WILL SELF-DESTRUCT IN FIVE MINUTES!
BEEP
!!!
THE SHIP AND THE COMPUTER HUB ARE YOURS.
YOU CAN ENJOY BOTH OF THEM AT THE BOTTOM OF THE OCEAN!
FT FT FT FT FT FT FT
WAIT!
VOOSH
NNNGH!
KRA-BOOM

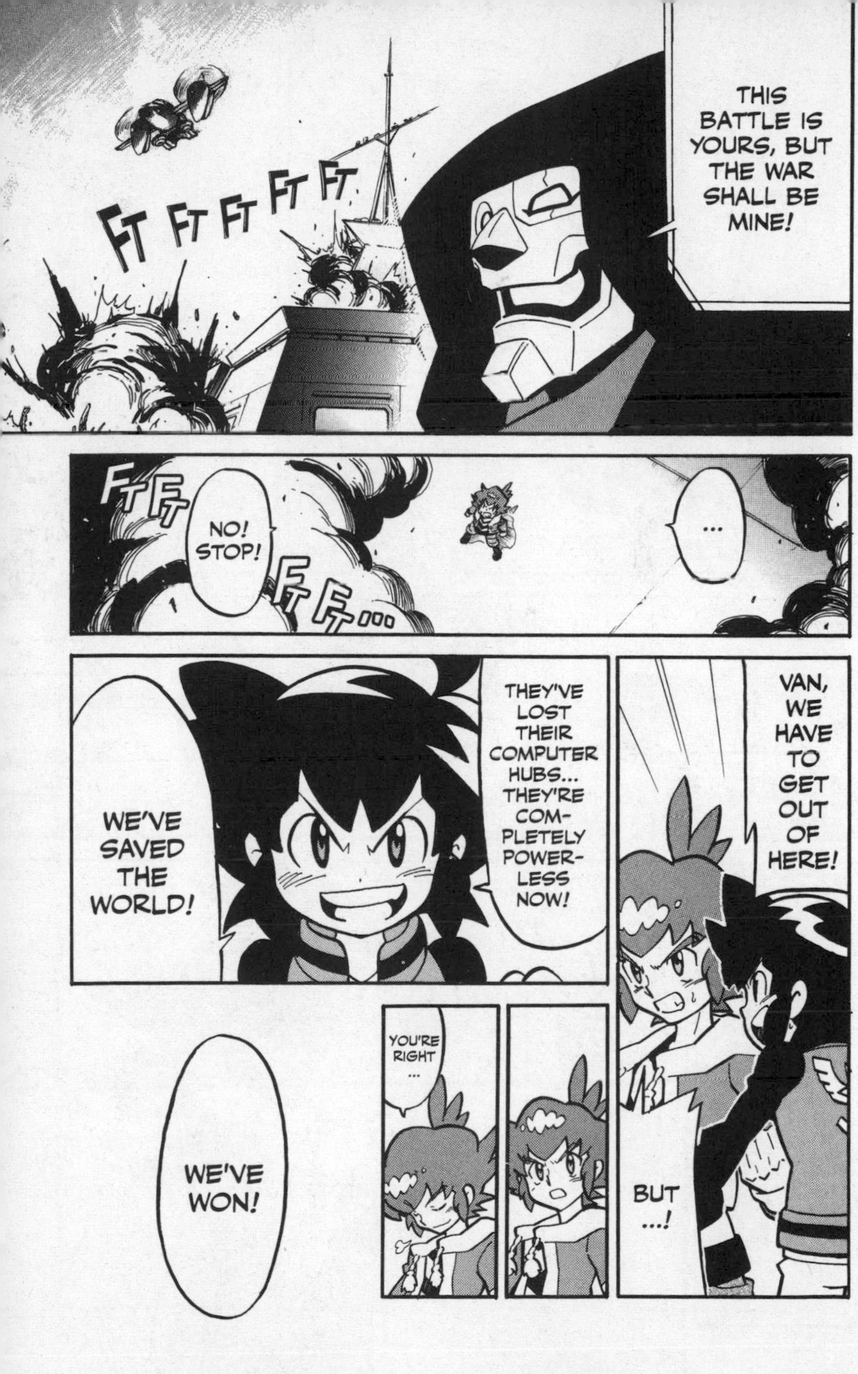
THIS BATTLE IS YOURS, BUT THE WAR SHALL BE MINE!
FT FT FT FT FT
...
NO! STOP!
FT FT
FT FT ooo
VAN, WE HAVE TO GET OUT OF HERE!
BUT ...!
THEY'VE LOST THEIR COMPUTER HUBS... THEY'RE COM-PLETELY POWER-LESS NOW!
WE'VE SAVED THE WORLD!
YOU'RE RIGHT ...
WE'VE WON!

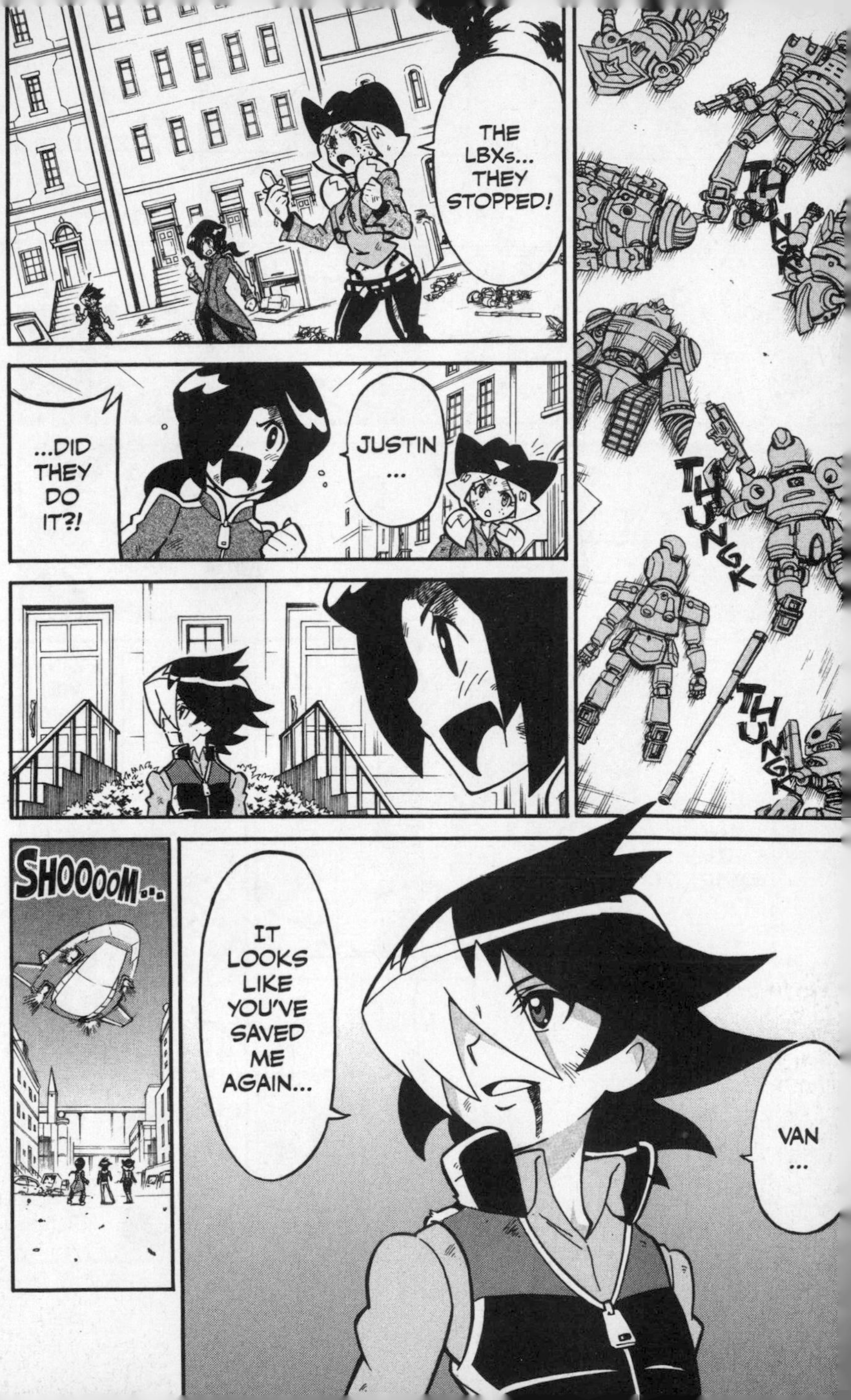
THUNGK
THUNGK
THUNGK
THE LBXs... THEY STOPPED!
JUSTIN ...
...DID THEY DO IT?!
VAN ...
IT LOOKS LIKE YOU'VE SAVED ME AGAIN...
SHOOOOM...

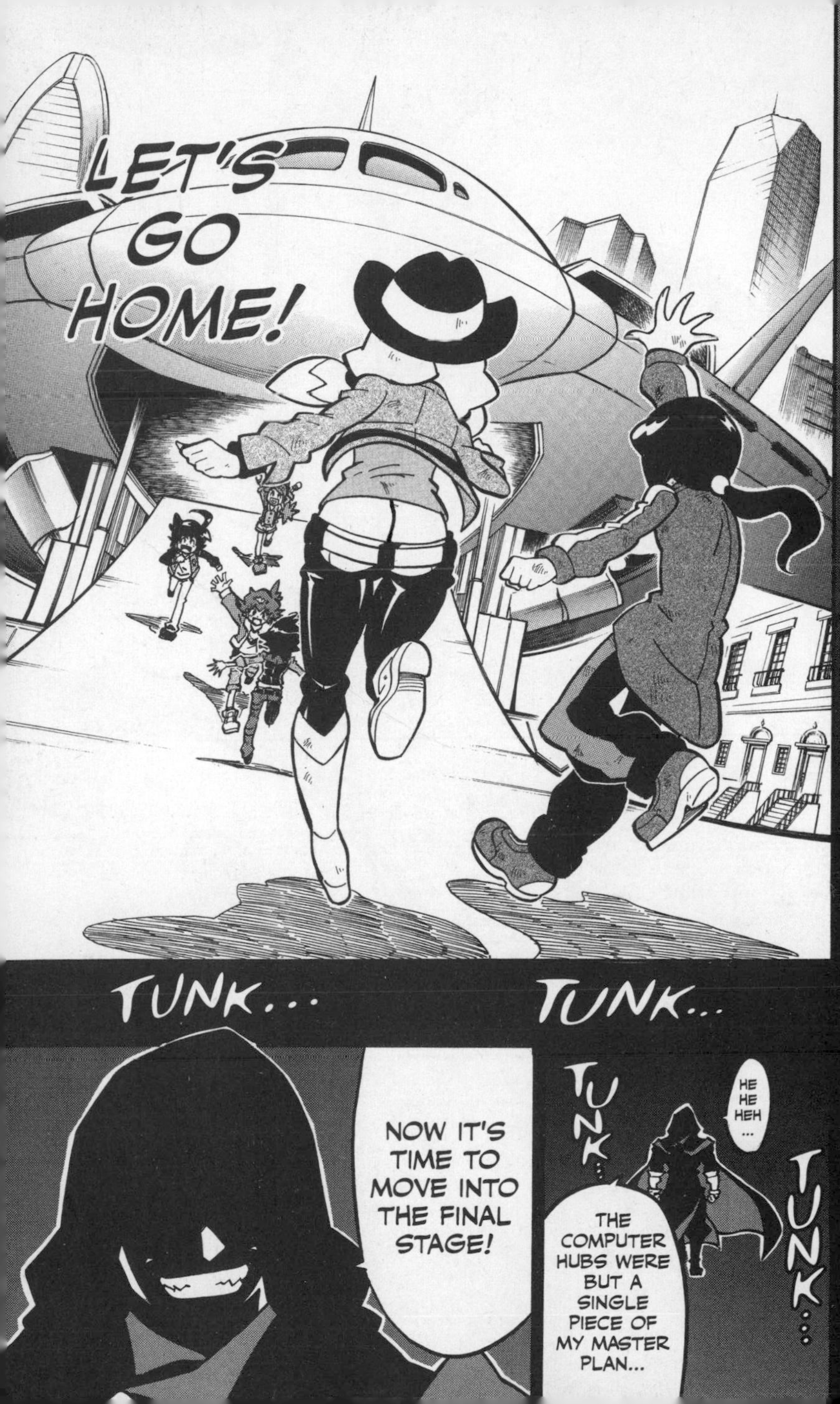
LET'S GO HOME!
TUNK...
TUNK...
TUNK...
HE HE HEH...
TUNK...
THE COMPUTER HUBS WERE BUT A SINGLE PIECE OF MY MASTER PLAN...
NOW IT'S TIME TO MOVE INTO THE FINAL STAGE!

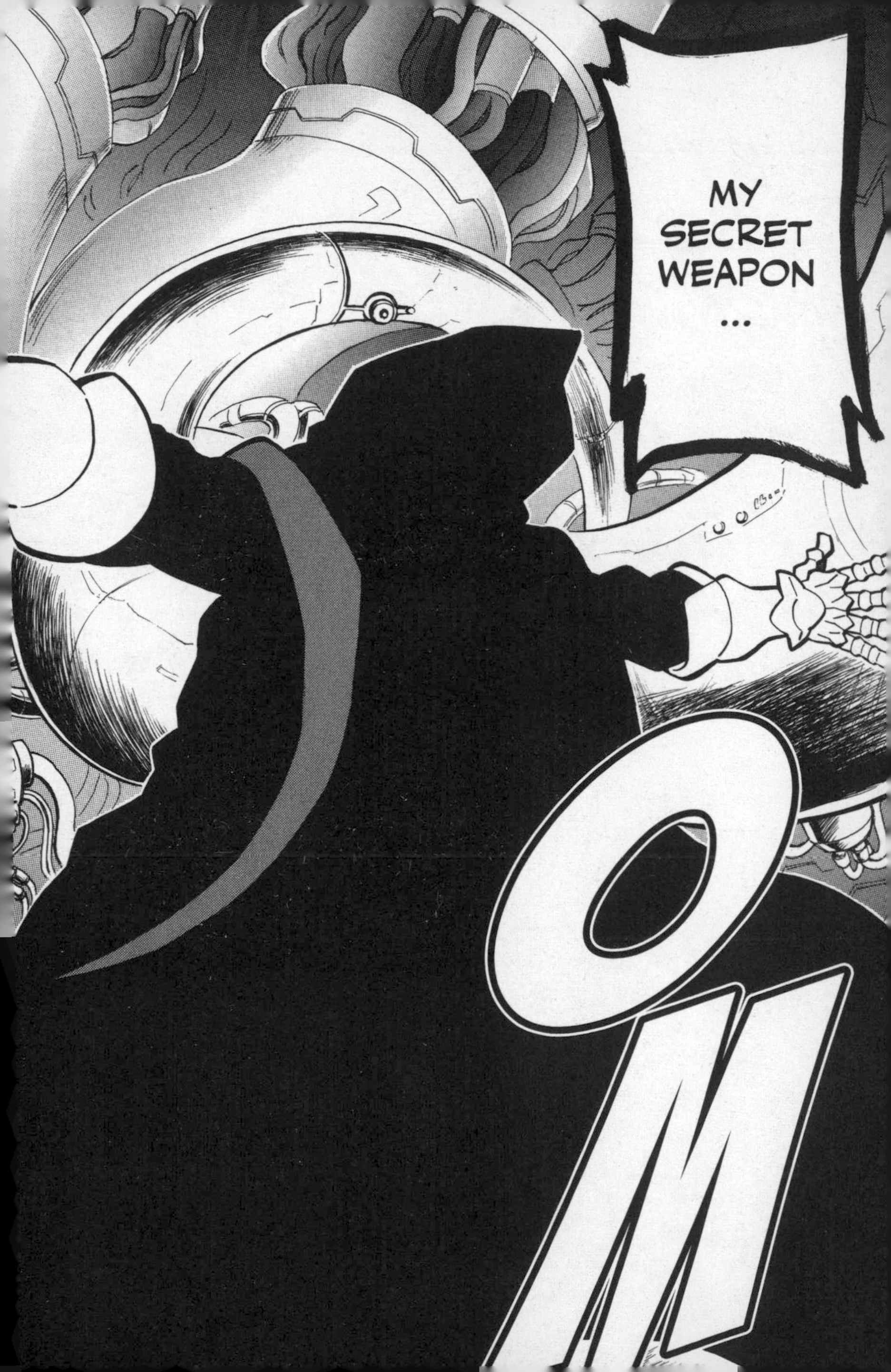
MY SECRET WEAPON ...

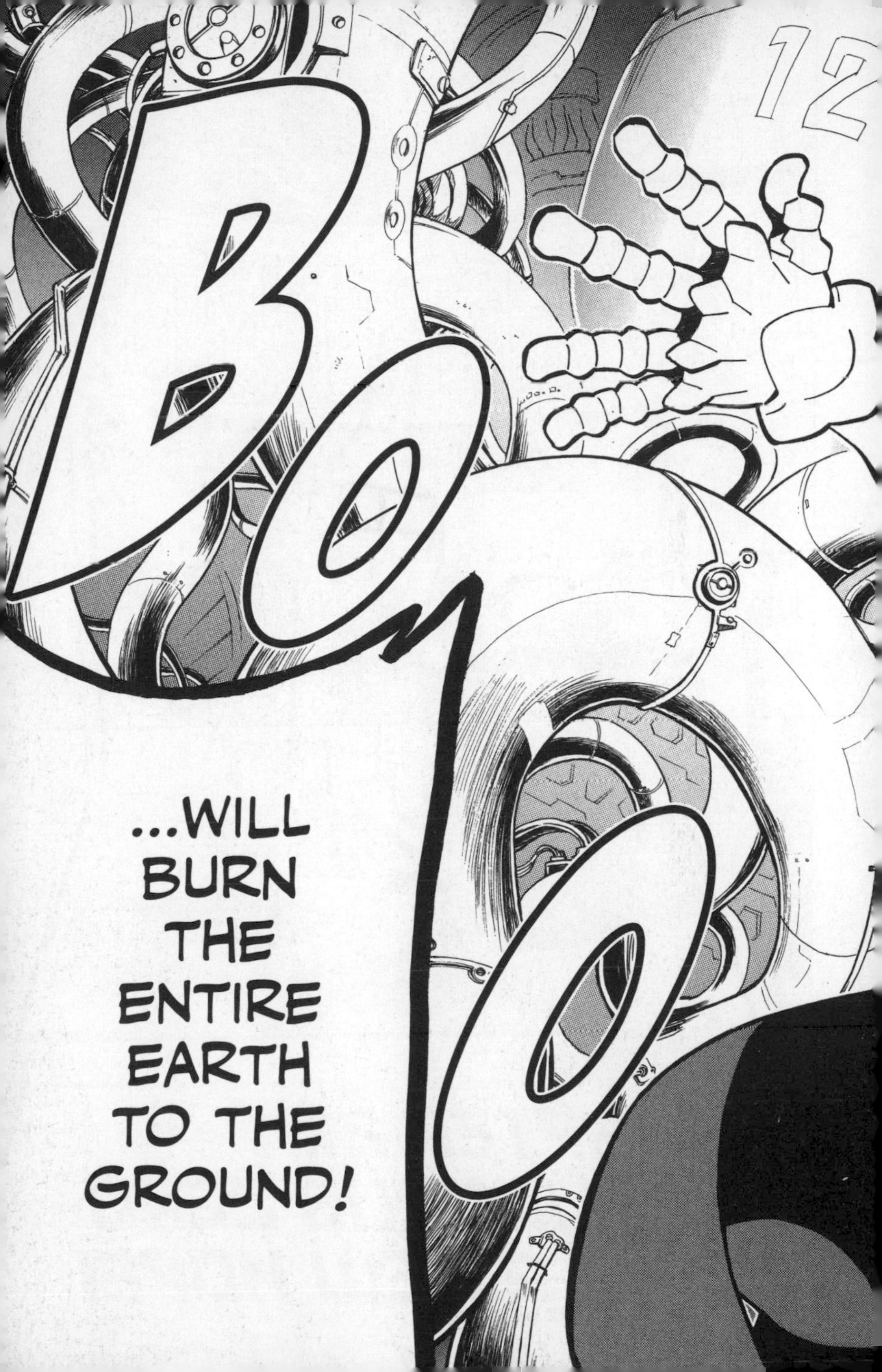
BOOO
...WILL BURN THE ENTIRE EARTH TO THE GROUND!
12

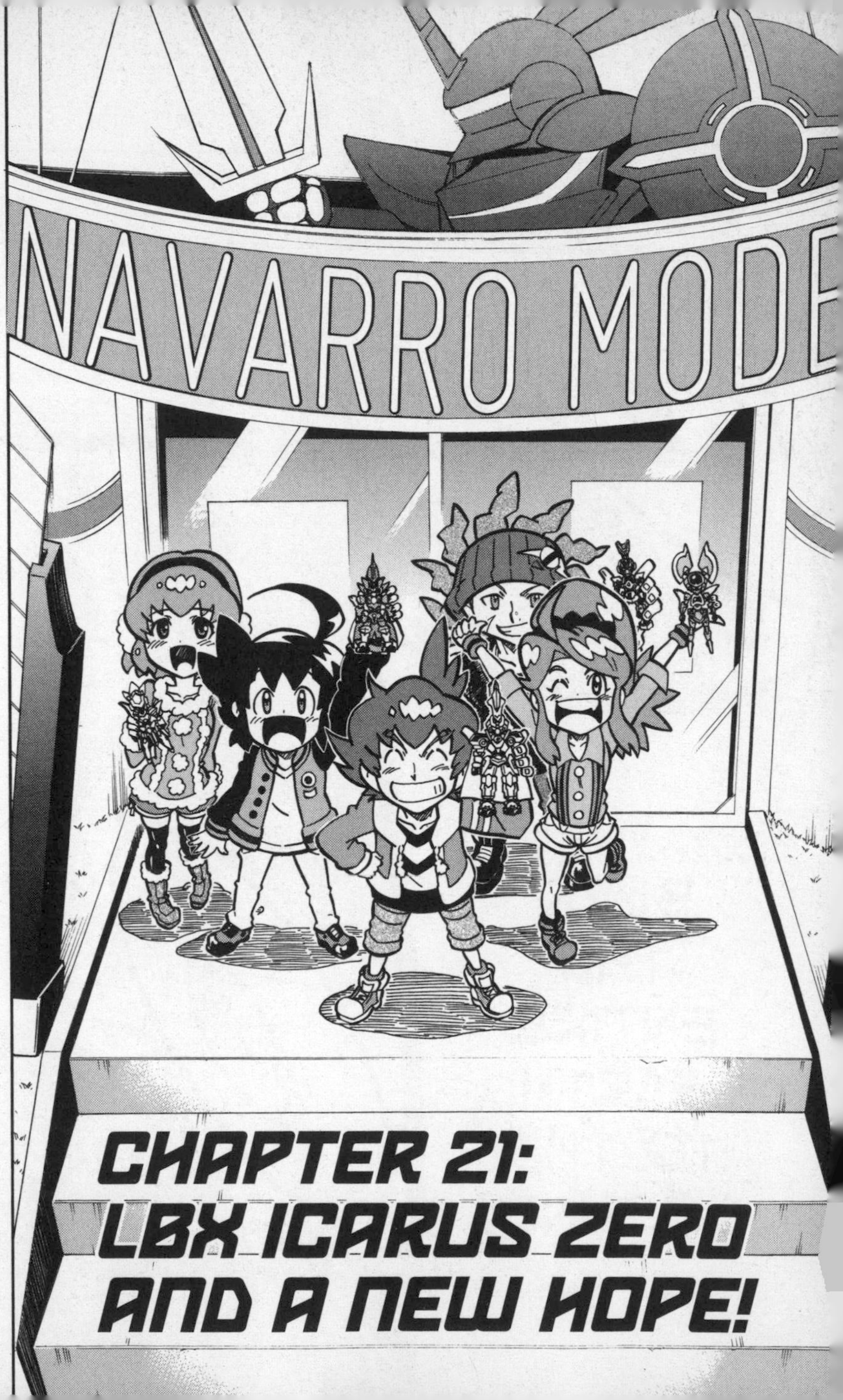
NAVARRO MODE
CHAPTER 21:
LBX ICARUS ZERO
AND A NEW HOPE!

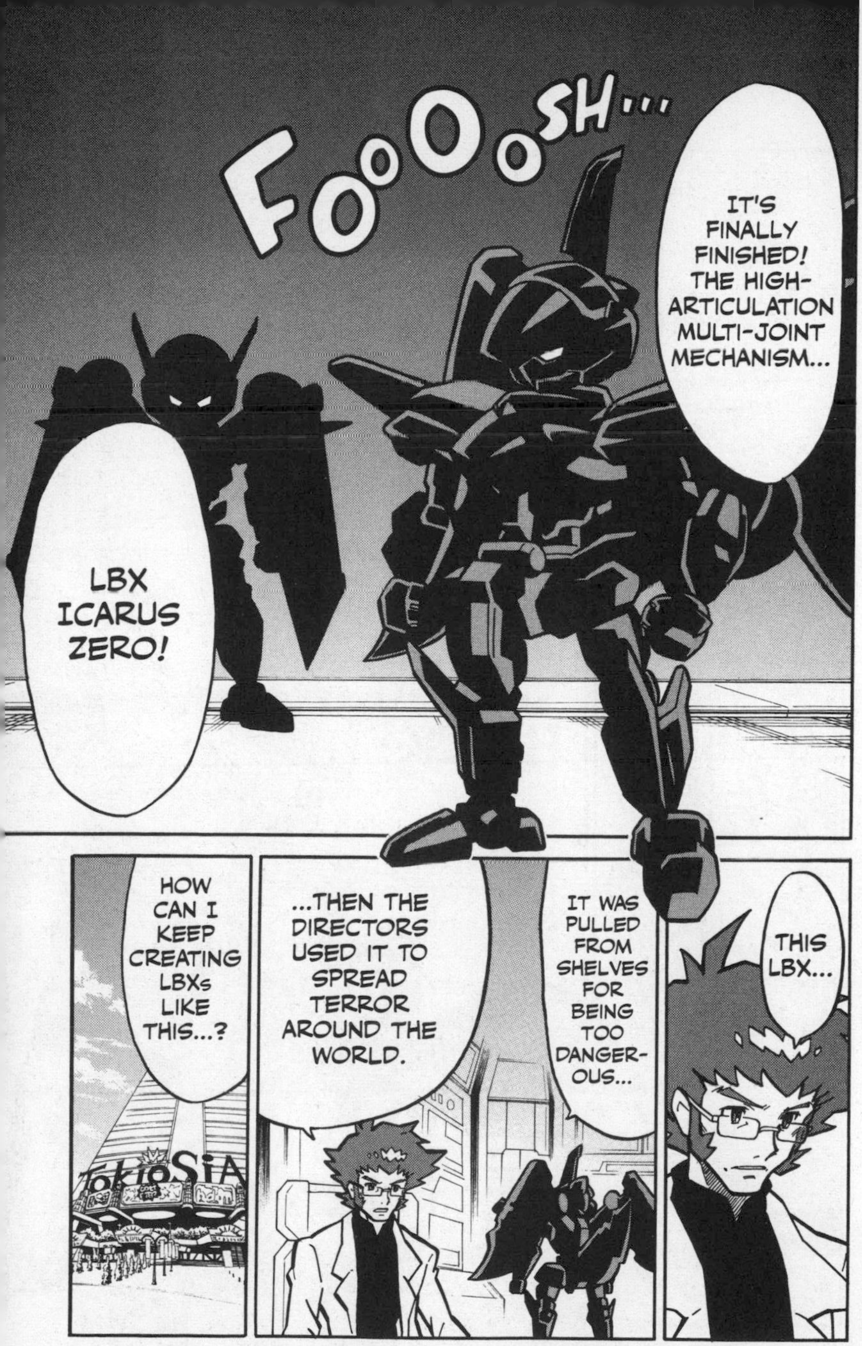
FOOOOSH...
IT'S FINALLY FINISHED! THE HIGH-ARTICULATION MULTI-JOINT MECHANISM...
LBX ICARUS ZERO!
THIS LBX...
IT WAS PULLED FROM SHELVES FOR BEING TOO DANGER-OUS...
...THEN THE DIRECTORS USED IT TO SPREAD TERROR AROUND THE WORLD.
HOW CAN I KEEP CREATING LBXs LIKE THIS...?
TokioSIA

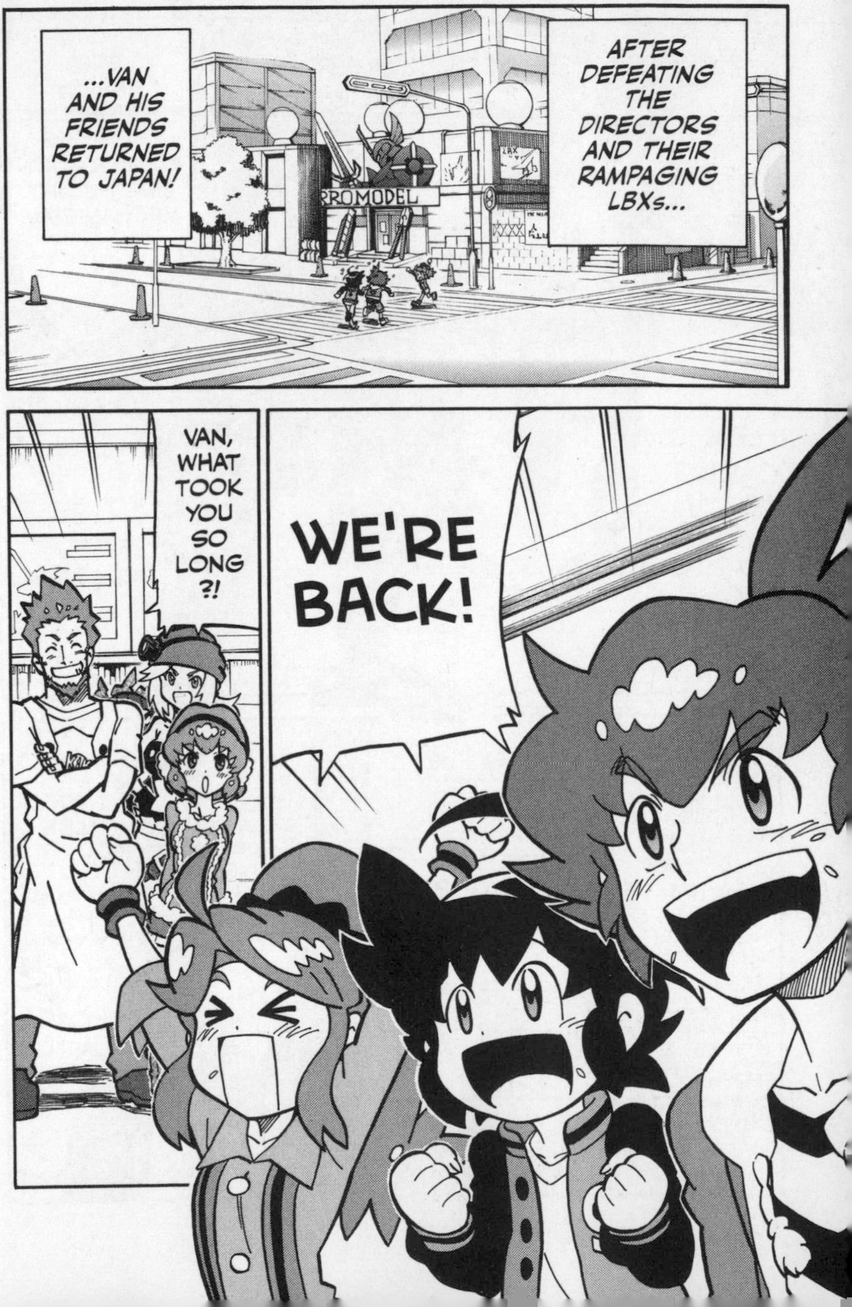
AFTER DEFEATING THE DIRECTORS AND THEIR RAMPAGING LBXs...
...VAN AND HIS FRIENDS RETURNED TO JAPAN!
RROMODEL
WE'RE BACK!
VAN, WHAT TOOK YOU SO LONG?!

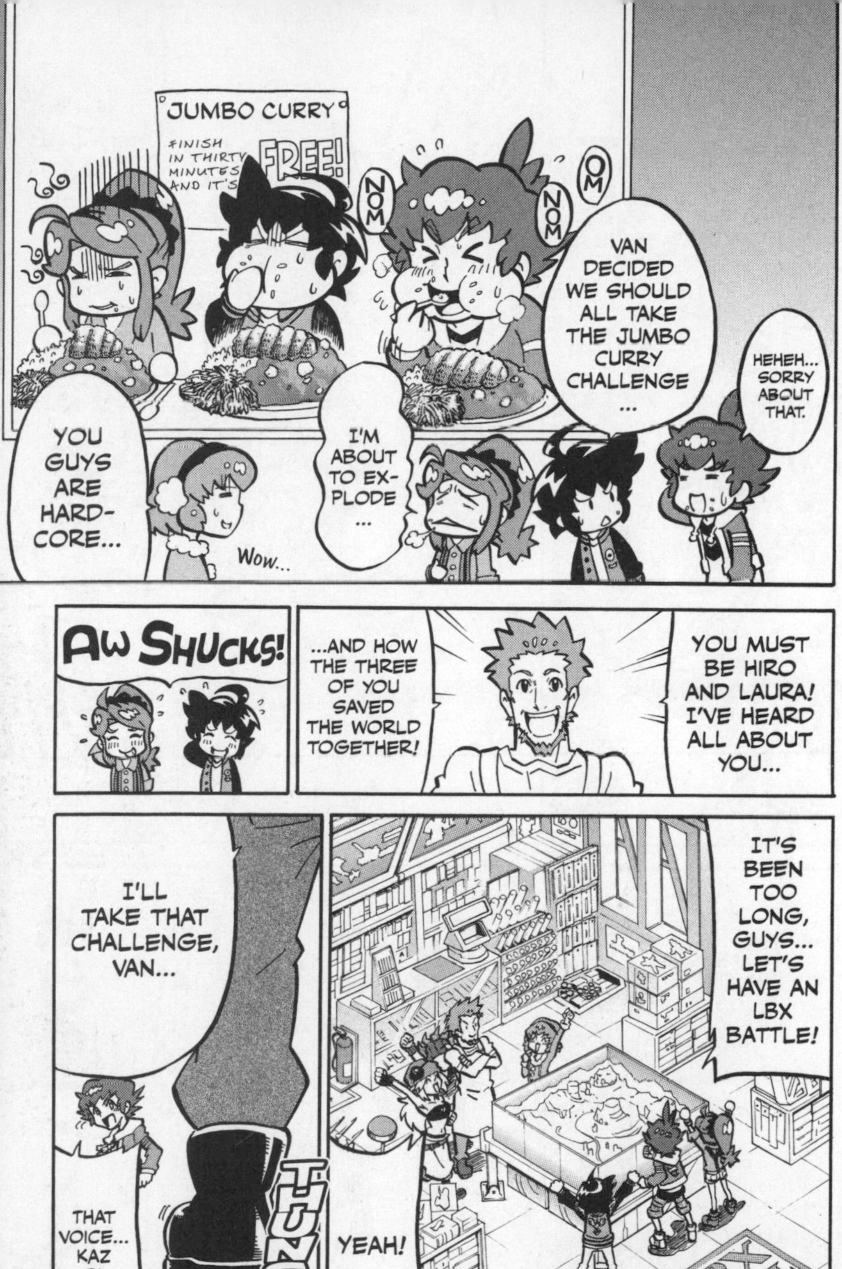
JUMBO CURRY
FINISH IN THIRTY MINUTES AND IT'S FREE!
NOM
NOM
OM
VAN DECIDED WE SHOULD ALL TAKE THE JUMBO CURRY CHALLENGE ...
HEHEH... SORRY ABOUT THAT.
I'M ABOUT TO EX-PLODE ...
YOU GUYS ARE HARD-CORE...
WOW...
YOU MUST BE HIRO AND LAURA! I'VE HEARD ALL ABOUT YOU...
...AND HOW THE THREE OF YOU SAVED THE WORLD TOGETHER!
AW SHUCKS!
IT'S BEEN TOO LONG, GUYS... LET'S HAVE AN LBX BATTLE!
YEAH!
LBX MODEL
I'LL TAKE THAT CHALLENGE, VAN...
THUNK
THAT VOICE... KAZ ?!

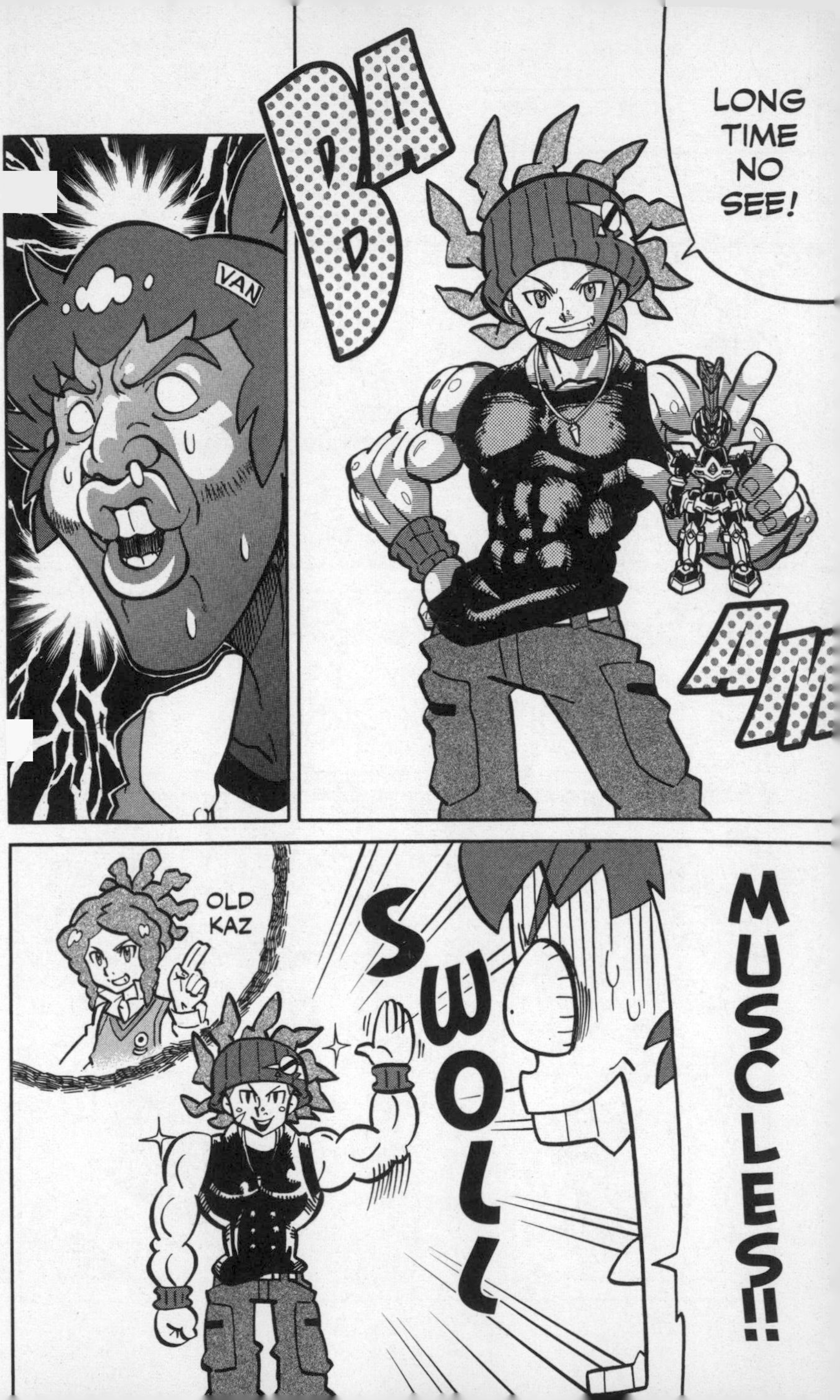
LONG TIME NO SEE!
BADAM
VAN
MUSCLES?!!
SWOLL
OLD KAZ

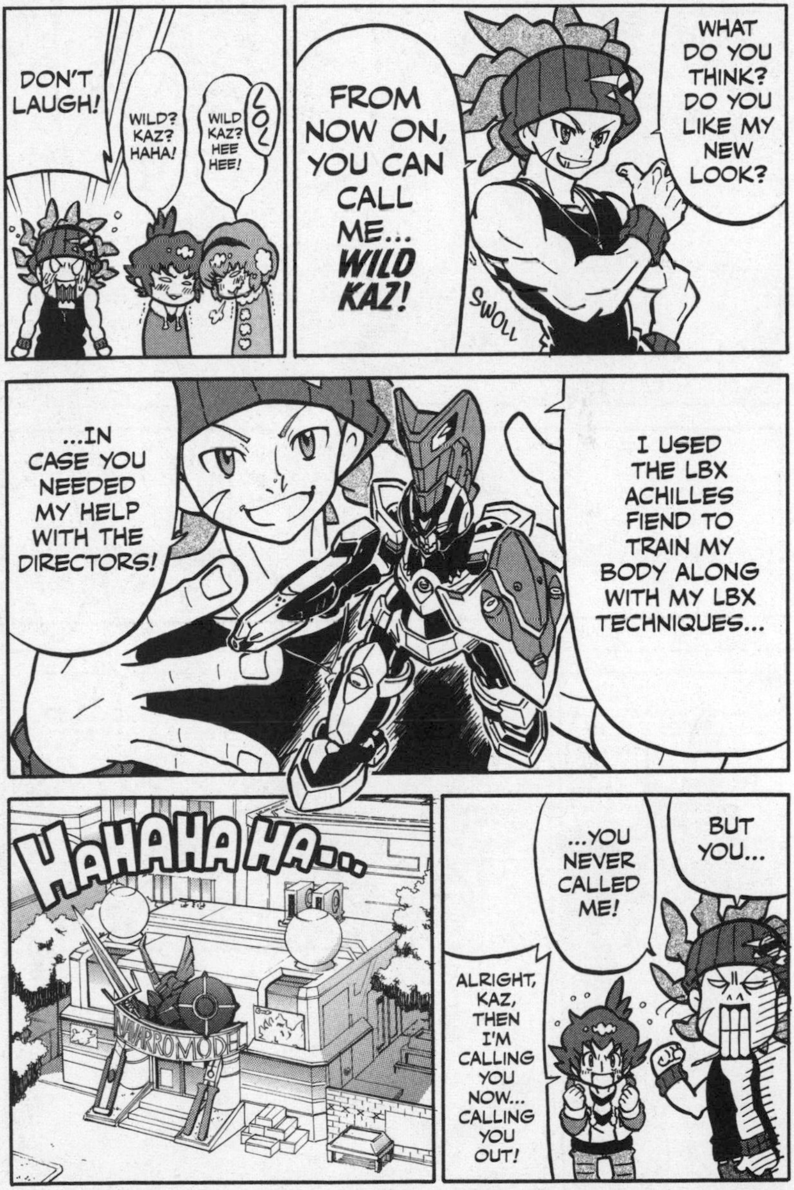
WHAT DO YOU THINK? DO YOU LIKE MY NEW LOOK?
FROM NOW ON, YOU CAN CALL ME... WILD KAZ!
SWOLL
LOL
WILD KAZ? HEE HEE!
WILD? KAZ? HAHA!
DON'T LAUGH!
I USED THE LBX ACHILLES FIEND TO TRAIN MY BODY ALONG WITH MY LBX TECHNIQUES...
...IN CASE YOU NEEDED MY HELP WITH THE DIRECTORS!
BUT YOU...
...YOU NEVER CALLED ME!
ALRIGHT, KAZ, THEN I'M CALLING YOU NOW... CALLING YOU OUT!
HAHAHAHA HA...
NAVARRO MODE

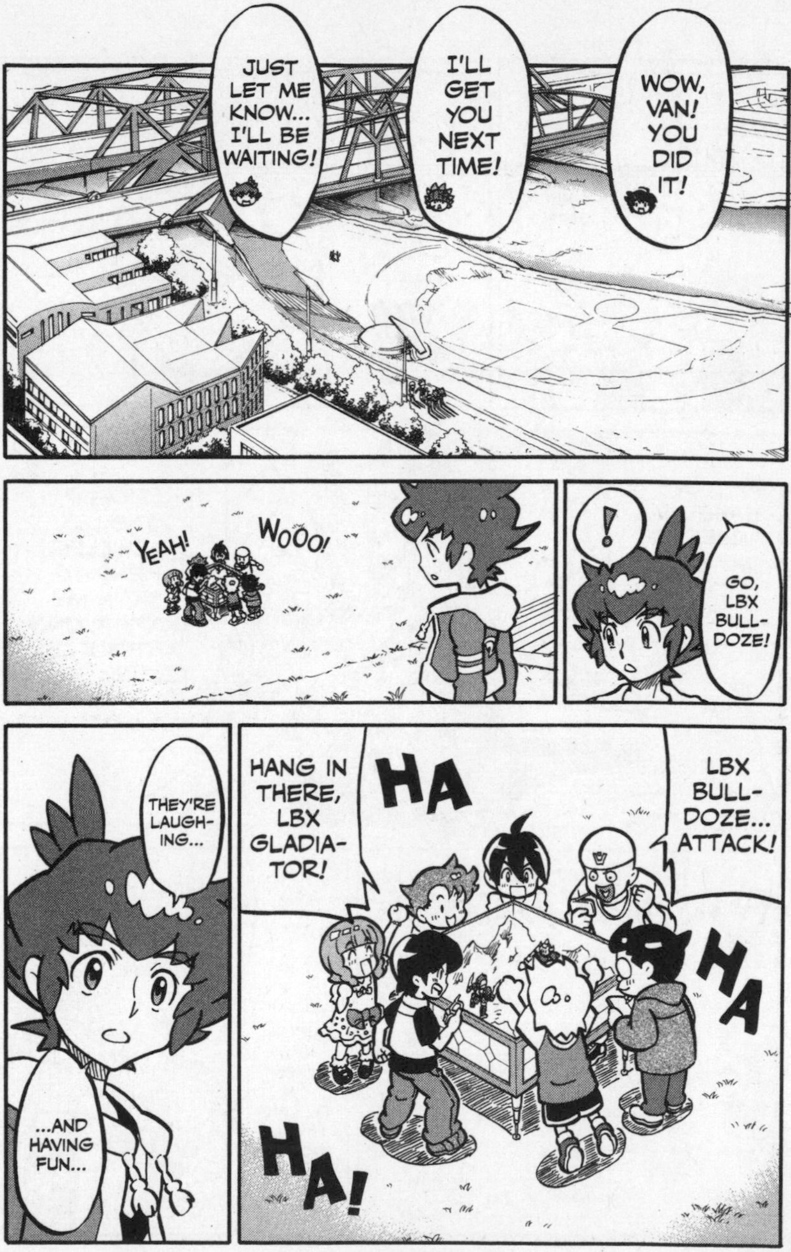
WOW, VAN! YOU DID IT!
I'LL GET YOU NEXT TIME!
JUST LET ME KNOW... I'LL BE WAITING!
!
GO, LBX BULL-DOZE!
WOOO!
YEAH!
LBX BULL-DOZE... ATTACK!
HANG IN THERE, LBX GLADIA-TOR!
HA
HA
HA
HA!
THEY'RE LAUGH-ING...
...AND HAVING FUN...

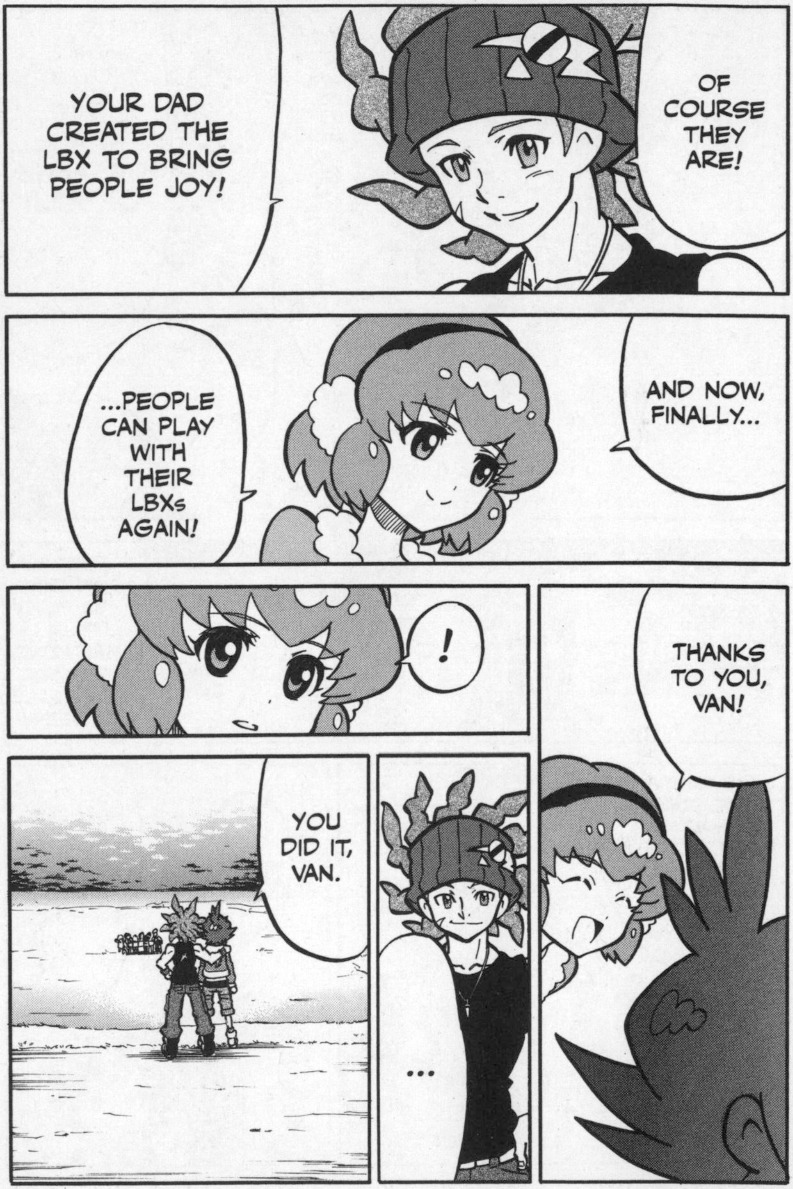
OF COURSE THEY ARE!
YOUR DAD CREATED THE LBX TO BRING PEOPLE JOY!
AND NOW, FINALLY...
...PEOPLE CAN PLAY WITH THEIR LBXs AGAIN!
THANKS TO YOU, VAN!
!
...
YOU DID IT, VAN.

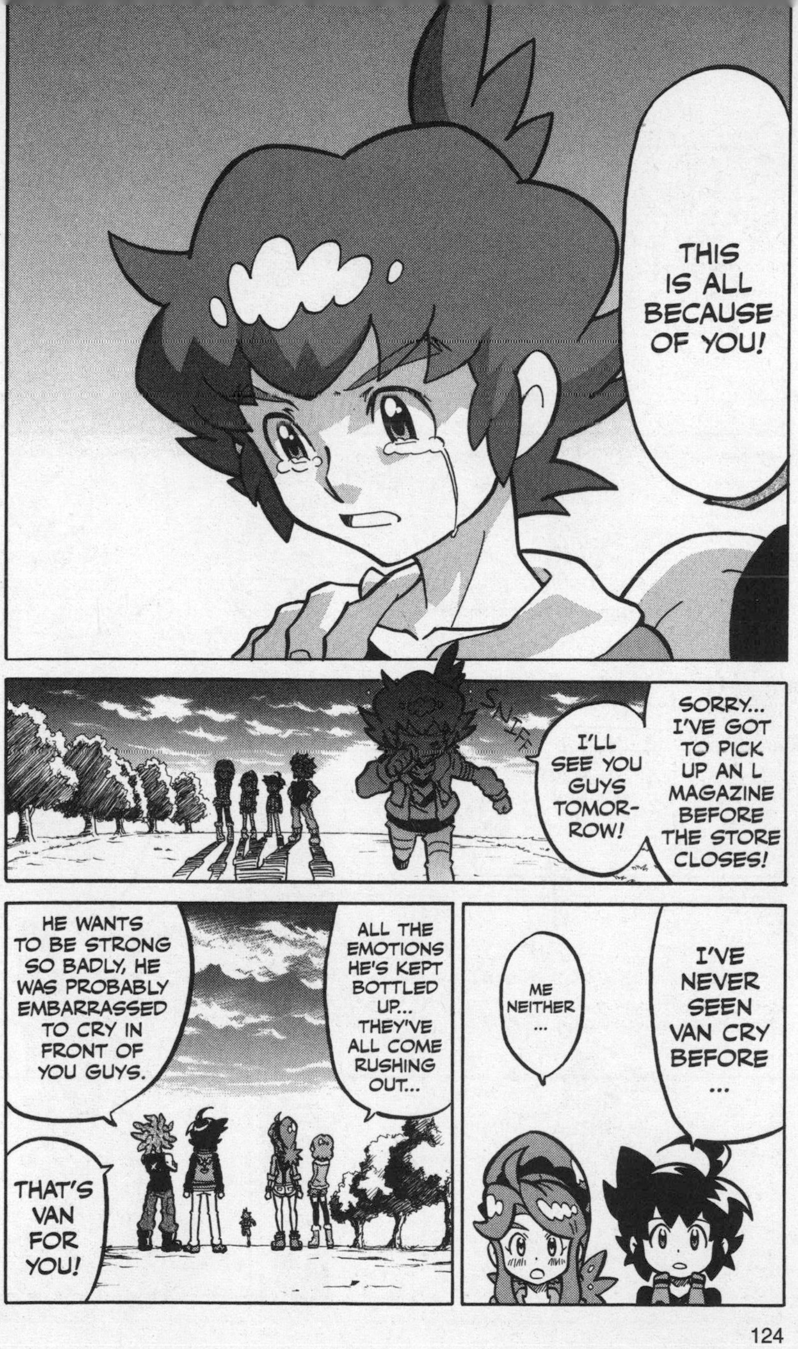
THIS IS ALL BECAUSE OF YOU!
SORRY... I'VE GOT TO PICK UP AN L MAGAZINE BEFORE THE STORE CLOSES!
I'LL SEE YOU GUYS TOMOR-ROW!
SNIFF
I'VE NEVER SEEN VAN CRY BEFORE ...
ME NEITHER ...
ALL THE EMOTIONS HE'S KEPT BOTTLED UP... THEY'VE ALL COME RUSHING OUT...
HE WANTS TO BE STRONG SO BADLY, HE WAS PROBABLY EMBARRASSED TO CRY IN FRONT OF YOU GUYS.
THAT'S VAN FOR YOU!

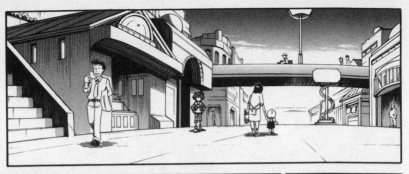

EVERYONE IN TOWN IS SMILING AGAIN.
THE DIRECTORS ARE GONE...
....AND THE WORLD IS AT PEACE!
SHWOOO...
HEY... LOOK!
MURMR
WHAT IS IT?!
MURMR
?
WH-WHAT...?!

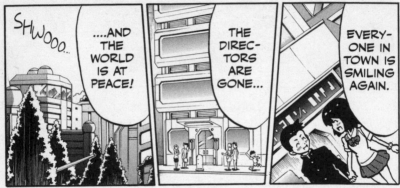

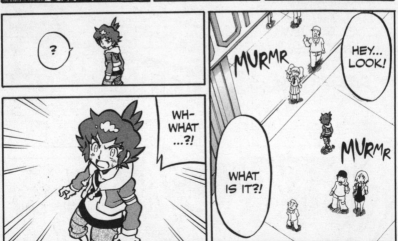

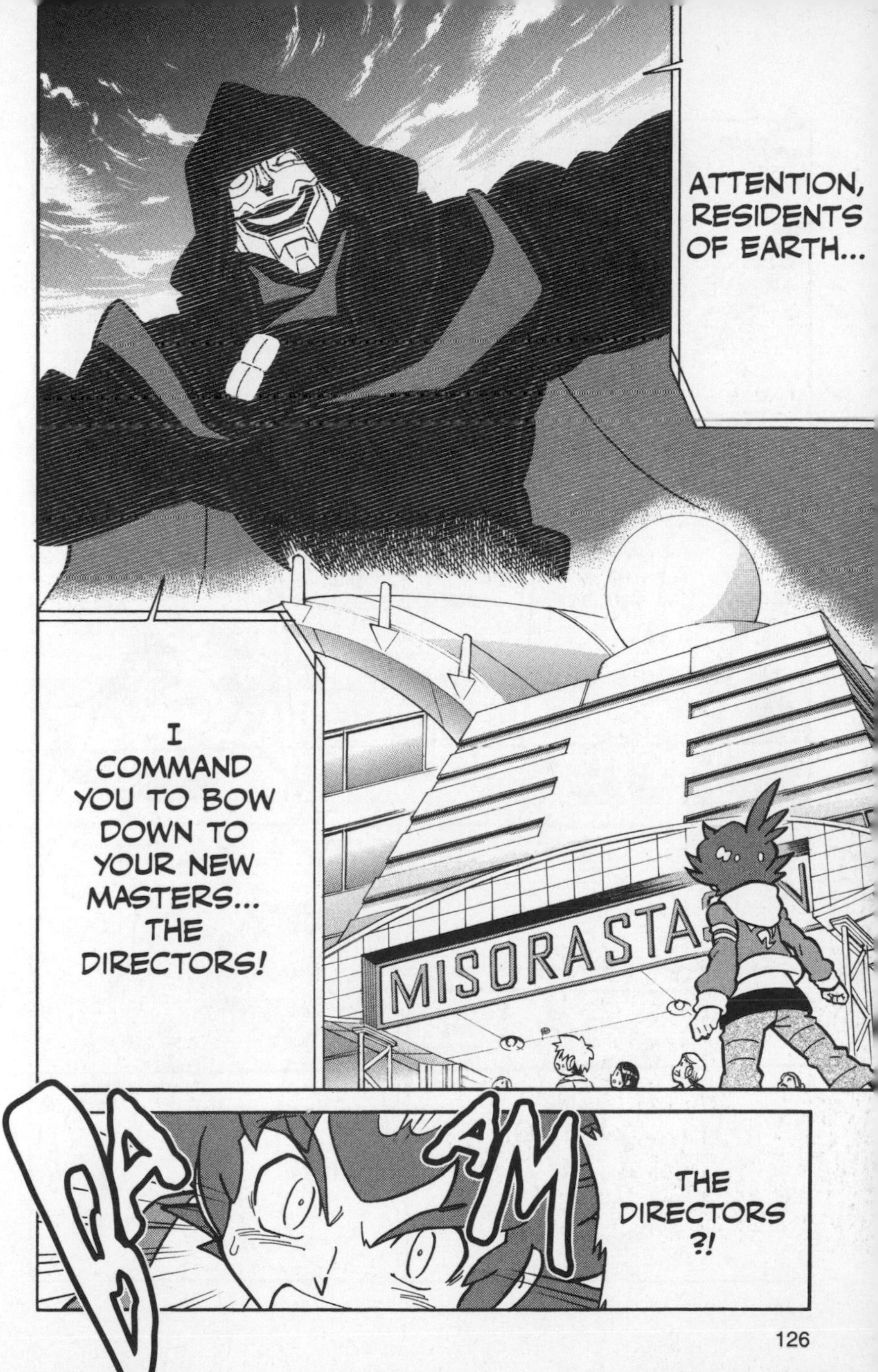
ATTENTION, RESIDENTS OF EARTH...
I COMMAND YOU TO BOW DOWN TO YOUR NEW MASTERS... THE DIRECTORS!
MISORA STA
THE DIRECTORS ?!
BAM

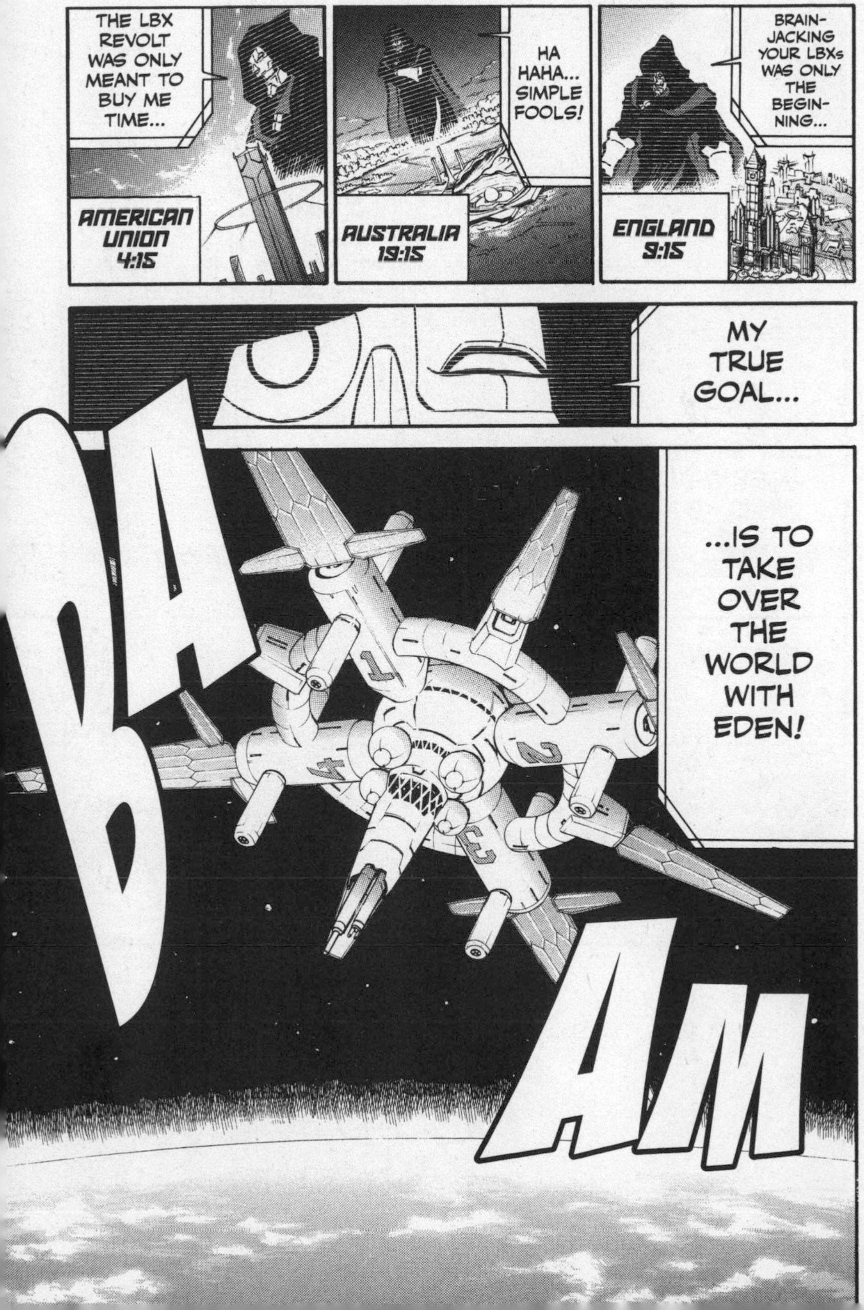
BRAIN-JACKING YOUR LBXs WAS ONLY THE BEGINNING...
ENGLAND 9:15
HA HAHA... SIMPLE FOOLS!
AUSTRALIA 19:15
THE LBX REVOLT WAS ONLY MEANT TO BUY ME TIME...
AMERICAN UNION 4:15
MY TRUE GOAL...
...IS TO TAKE OVER THE WORLD WITH EDEN!
BAAM

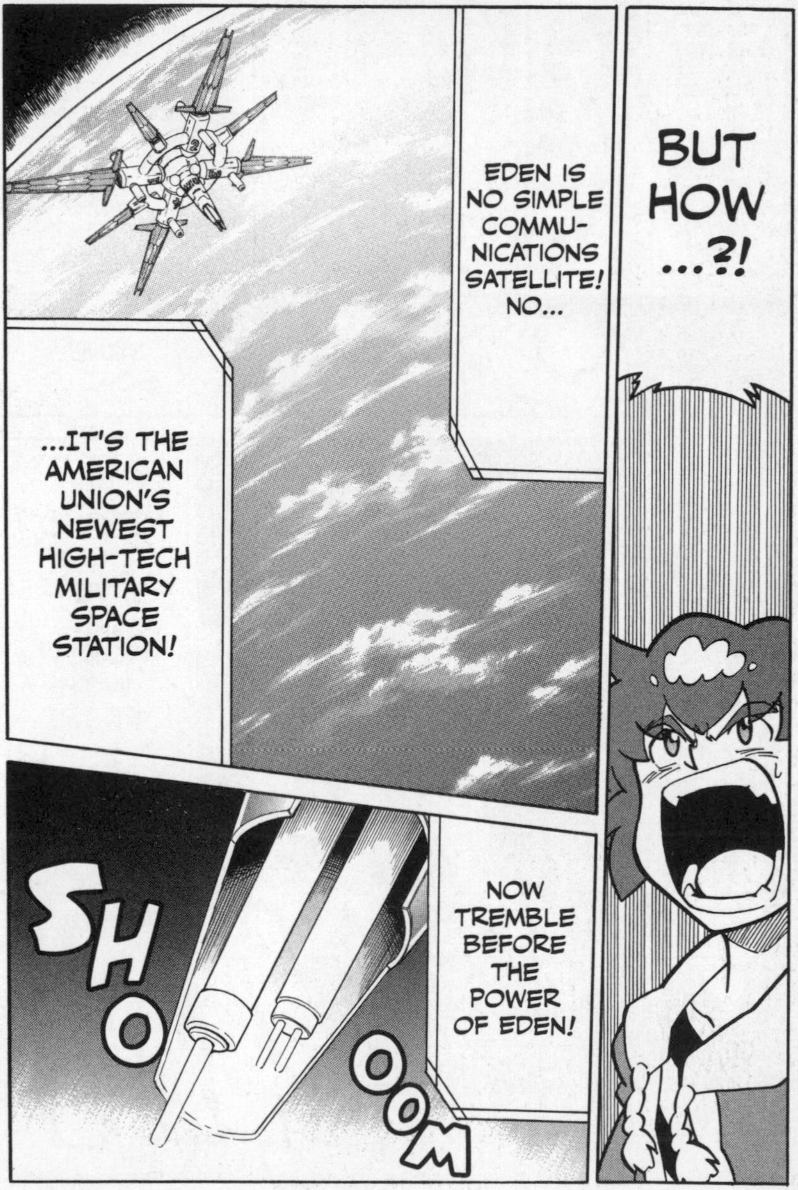
BUT HOW ...?!
EDEN IS NO SIMPLE COMMUNICATIONS SATELLITE! NO...
...IT'S THE AMERICAN UNION'S NEWEST HIGH-TECH MILITARY SPACE STATION!
NOW TREMBLE BEFORE THE POWER OF EDEN!
SHOOOOM

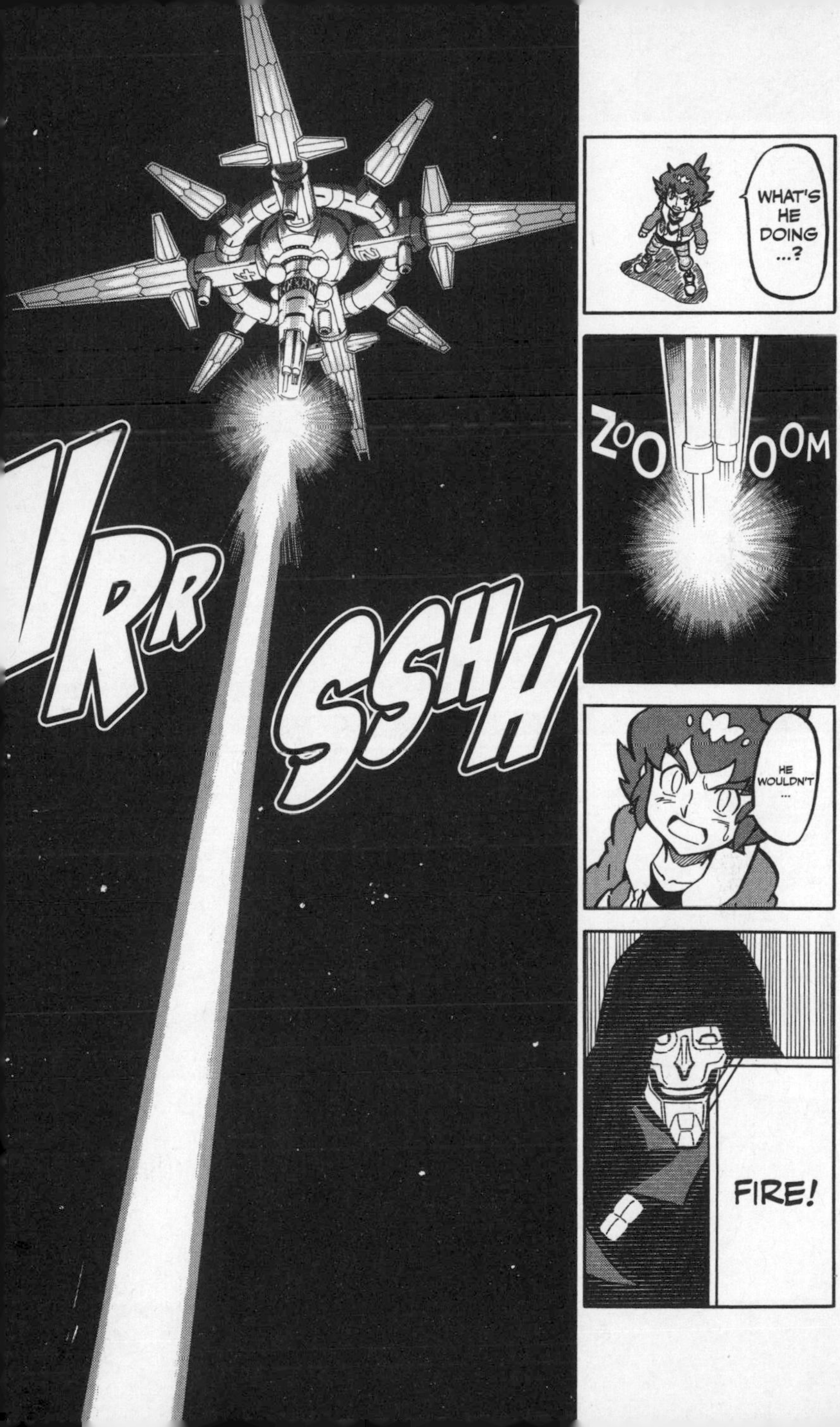
WHAT'S HE DOING ...?
ZOOOOOM
HE WOULDN'T ...
FIRE!
RR
SSHH

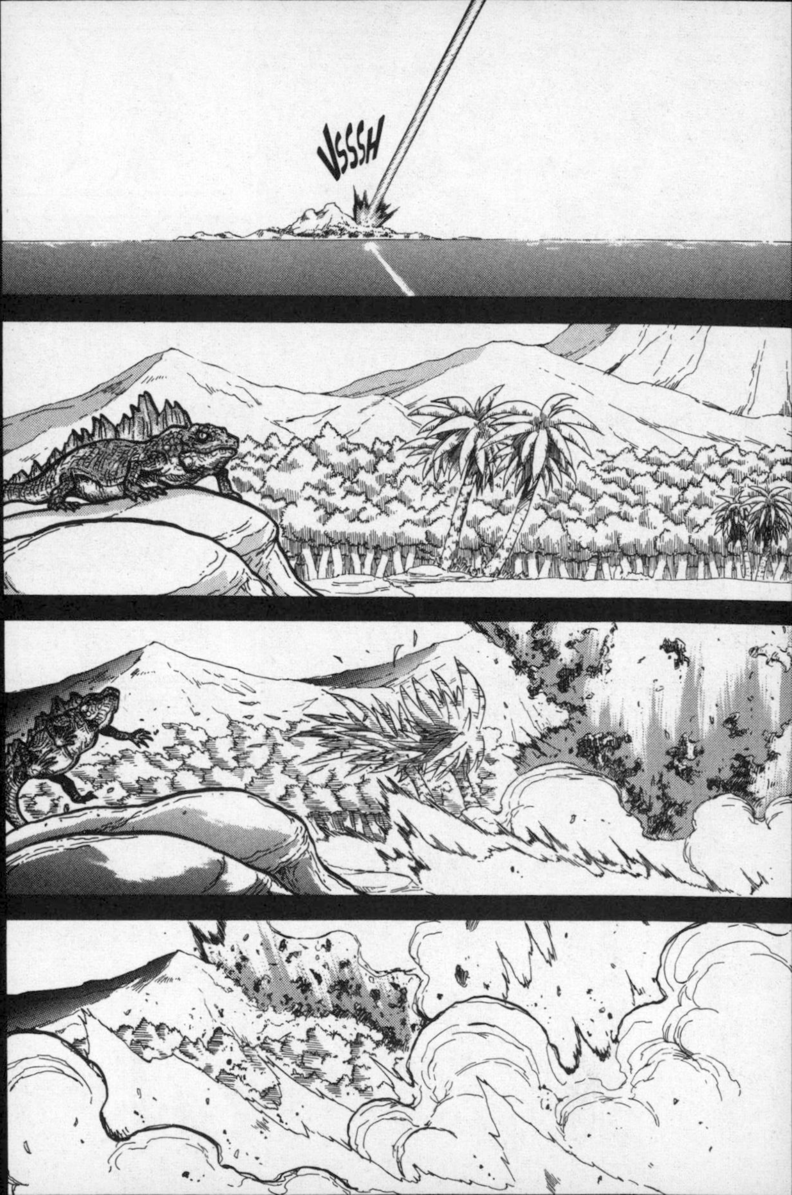
VSSSH

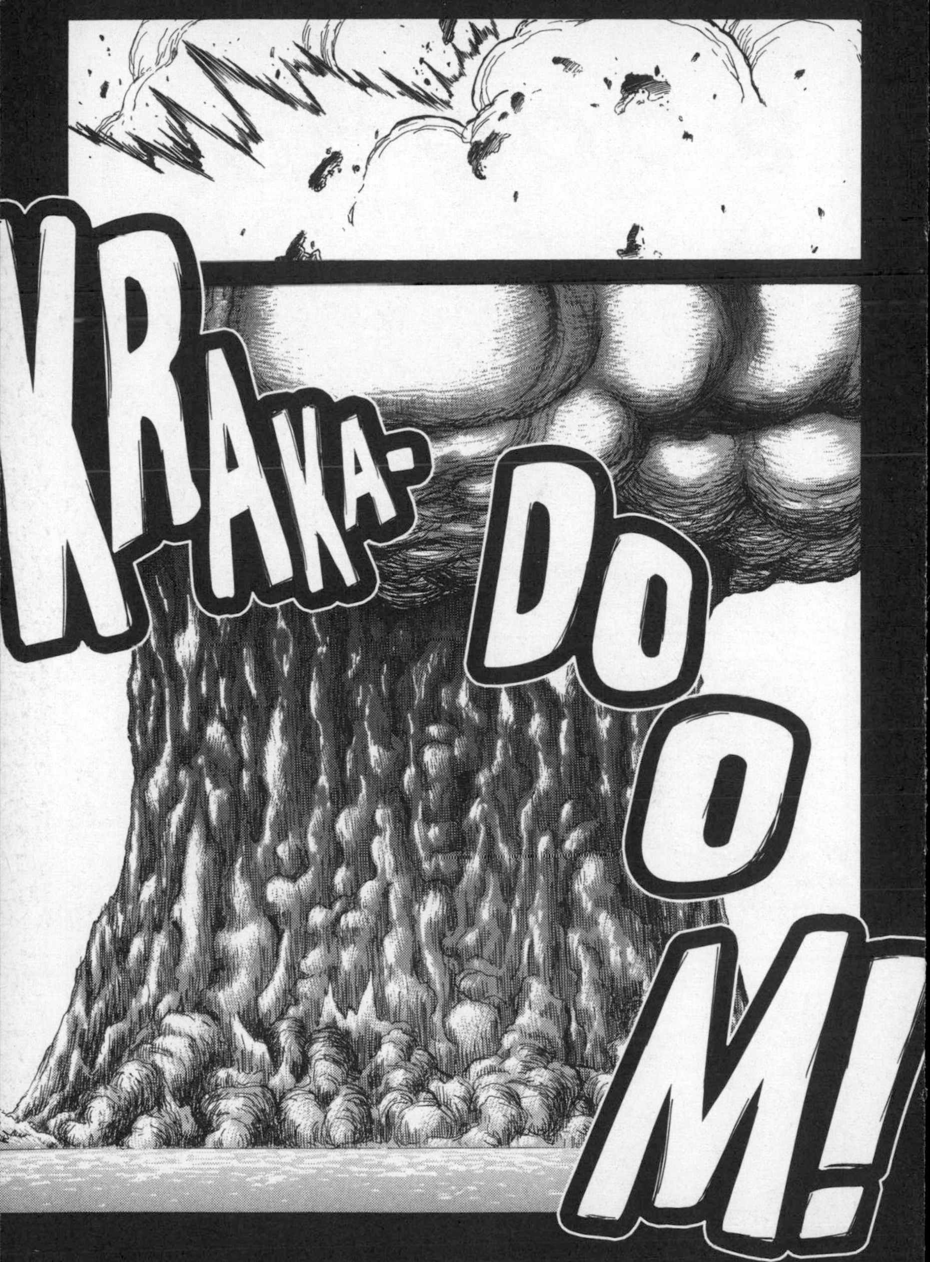
KRAKA-DOOM!

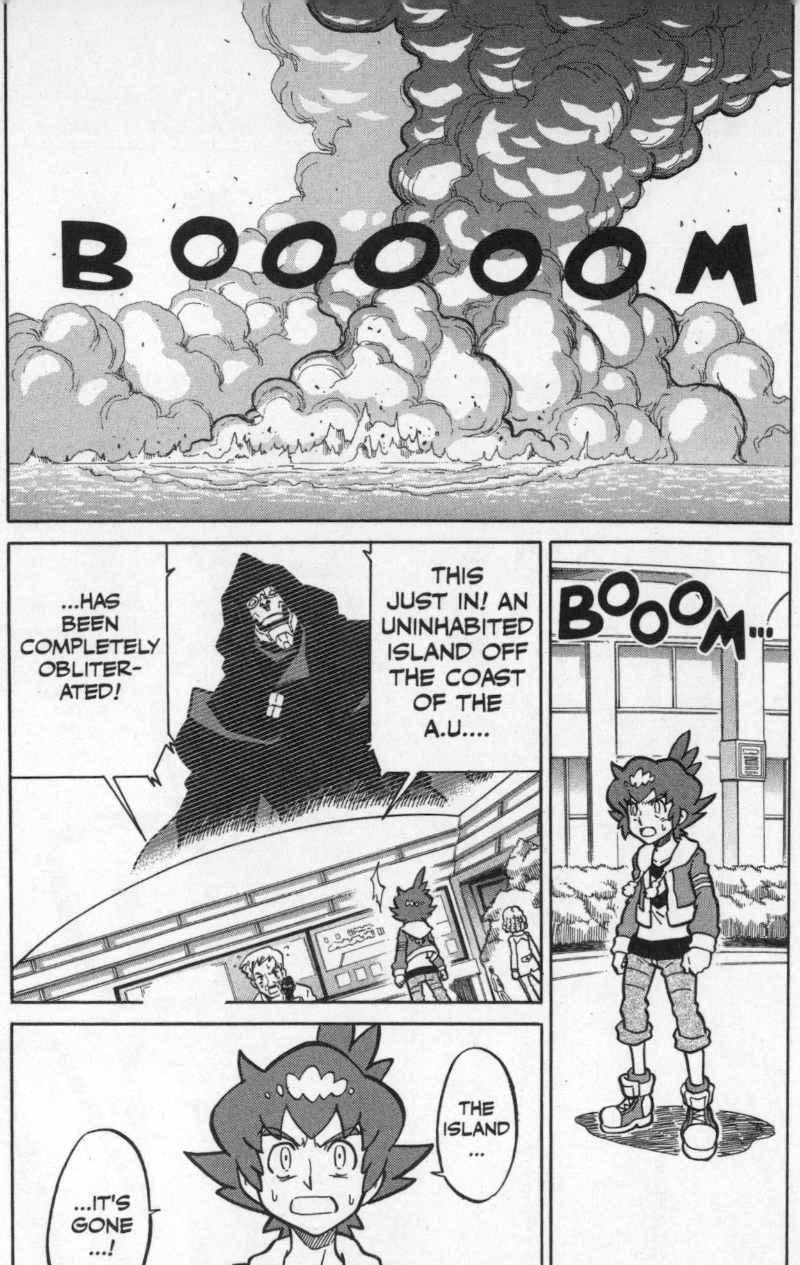
BOOOOOM
BOOOM...
THIS JUST IN! AN UNINHABITED ISLAND OFF THE COAST OF THE A.U....
...HAS BEEN COMPLETELY OBLITERATED!
THE ISLAND...
...IT'S GONE...!

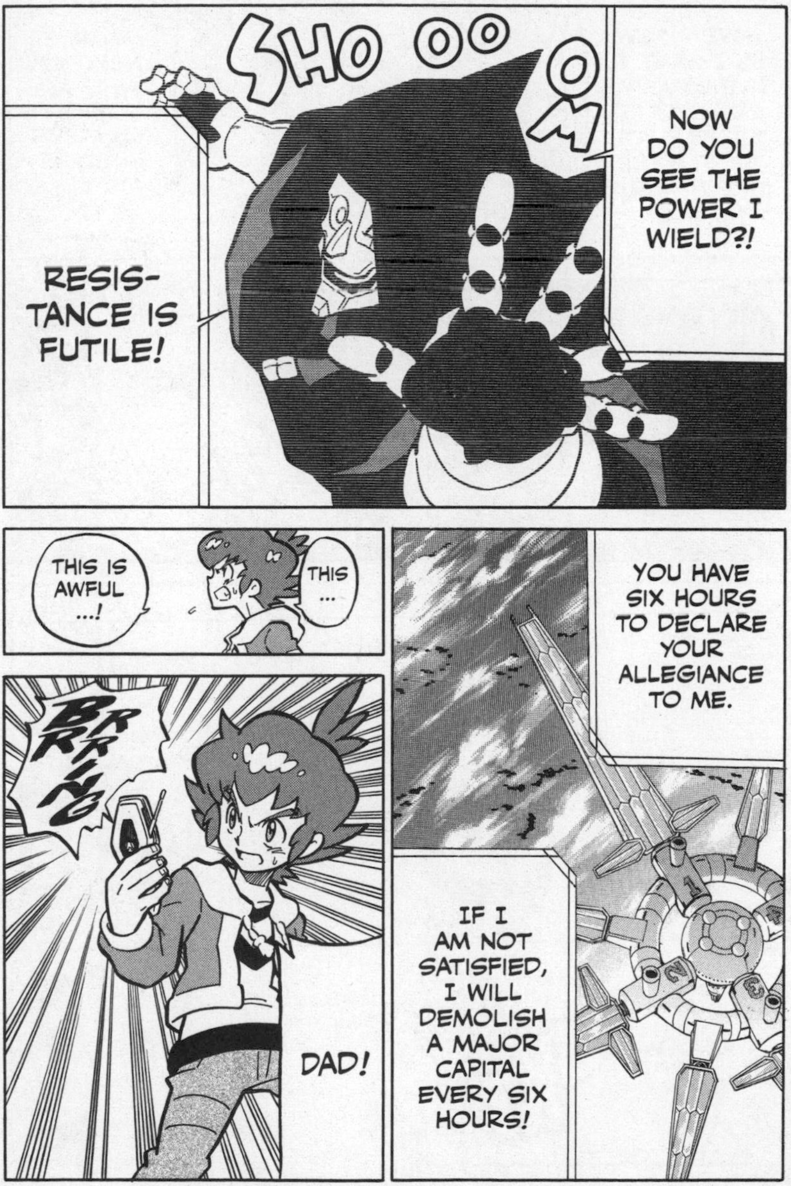
SHOOOOM
NOW DO YOU SEE THE POWER I WIELD?!
RESISTANCE IS FUTILE!
YOU HAVE SIX HOURS TO DECLARE YOUR ALLEGIANCE TO ME.
IF I AM NOT SATISFIED, I WILL DEMOLISH A MAJOR CAPITAL EVERY SIX HOURS!
THIS ...
THIS IS AWFUL ...!
BRRRING
DAD!

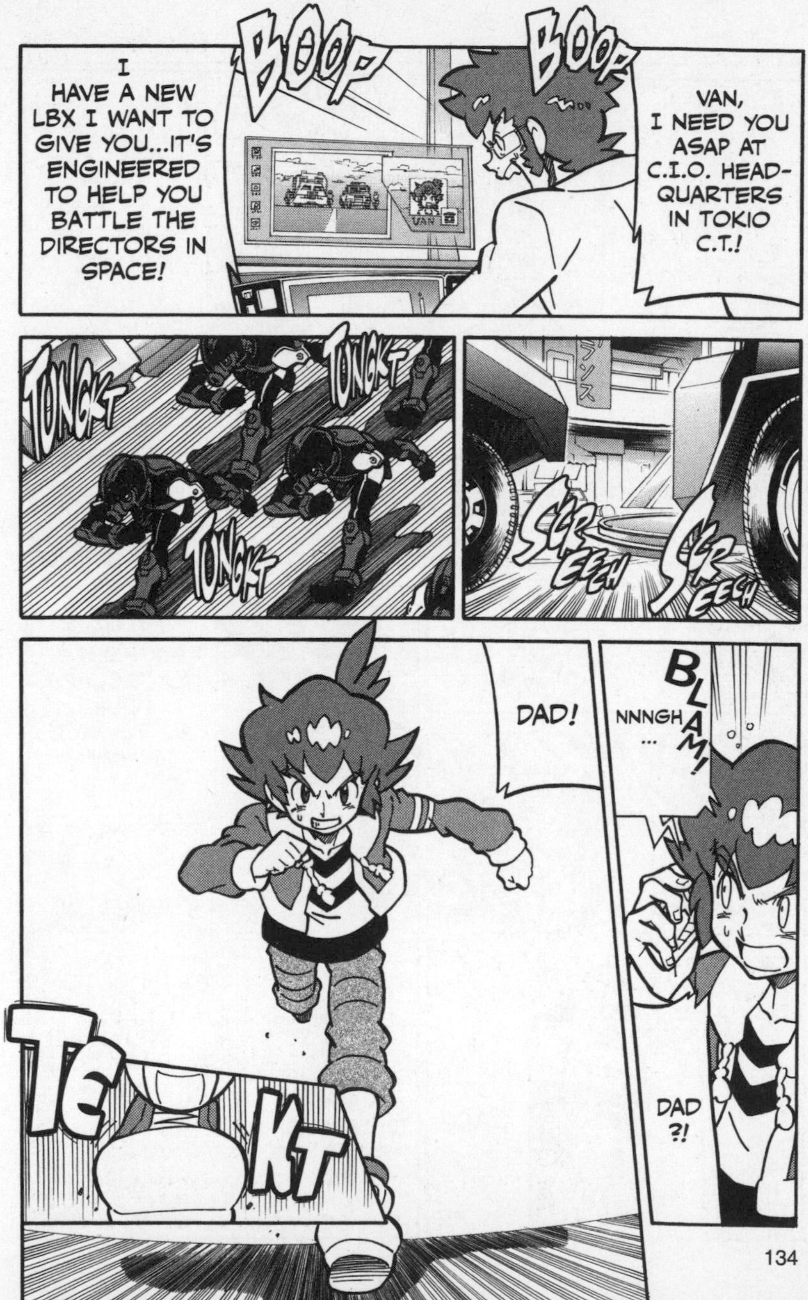
BOOP
VAN, I NEED YOU ASAP AT C.I.O. HEAD-QUARTERS IN TOKIO C.T.!
BOOP
I HAVE A NEW LBX I WANT TO GIVE YOU...IT'S ENGINEERED TO HELP YOU BATTLE THE DIRECTORS IN SPACE!
SCREEECH
SCREEECH
TONCKT
TONCKT
TONCKT
BLAM!
NNNGH ...
DAD?!
DAD!
TE KT

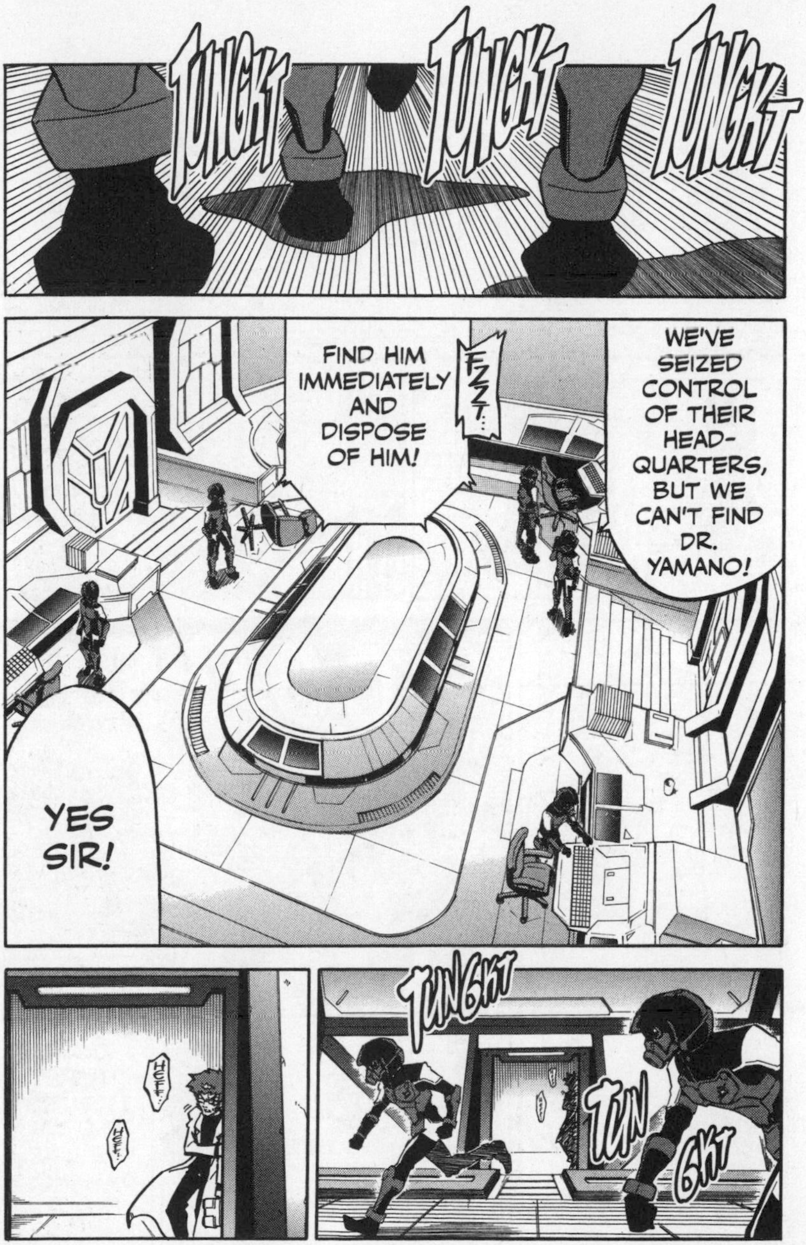
TUNGKT
TUNGKT
TUNGKT
WE'VE SEIZED CONTROL OF THEIR HEAD-QUARTERS, BUT WE CAN'T FIND DR. YAMANO!
FIND HIM IMMEDIATELY AND DISPOSE OF HIM!
FZZT...
YES SIR!
TUNGKT
TUN GKT
HEFF...
HEFF...

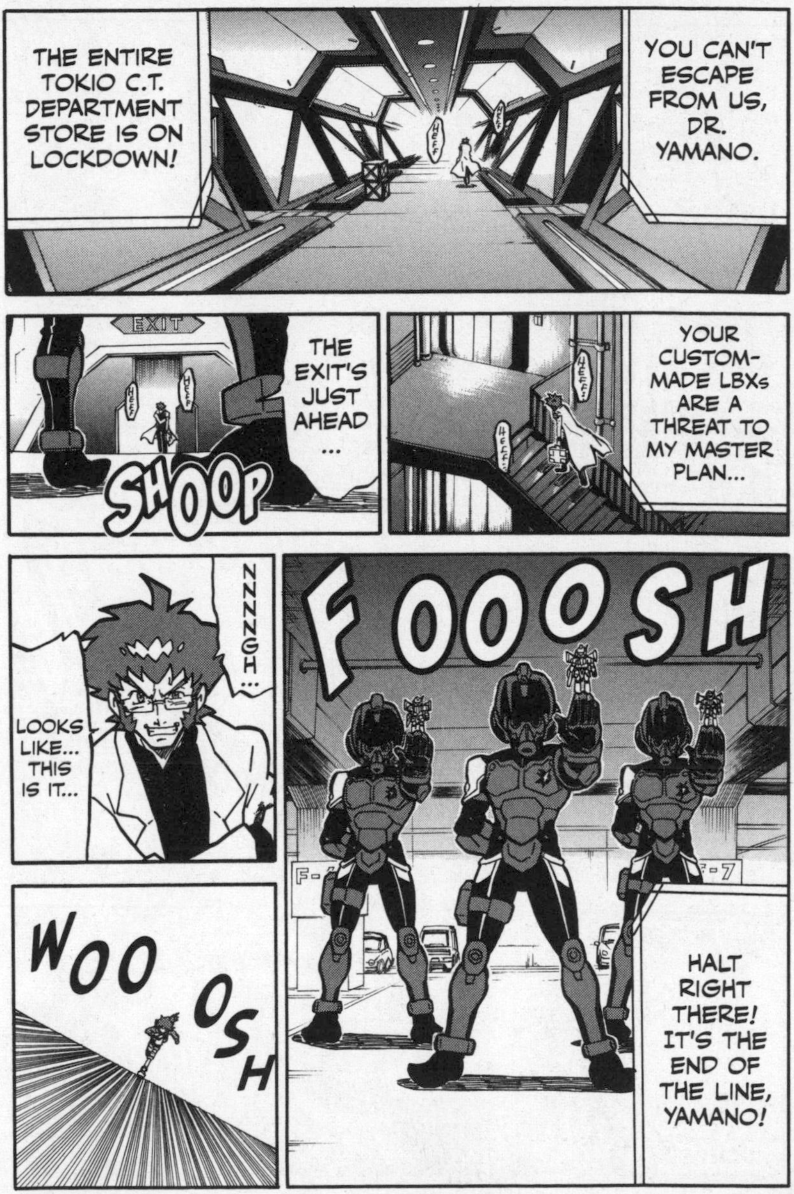
YOU CAN'T ESCAPE FROM US, DR. YAMANO.
HEFF
HEFF
THE ENTIRE TOKIO C.T. DEPARTMENT STORE IS ON LOCKDOWN!
YOUR CUSTOM-MADE LBXs ARE A THREAT TO MY MASTER PLAN...
HEFF
HEFF
THE EXIT'S JUST AHEAD...
EXIT
HEFF
HEFF
SHOOP
FOOOSH
HALT RIGHT THERE! IT'S THE END OF THE LINE, YAMANO!
NNNNGH...
LOOKS LIKE... THIS IS IT...
WOOOSH

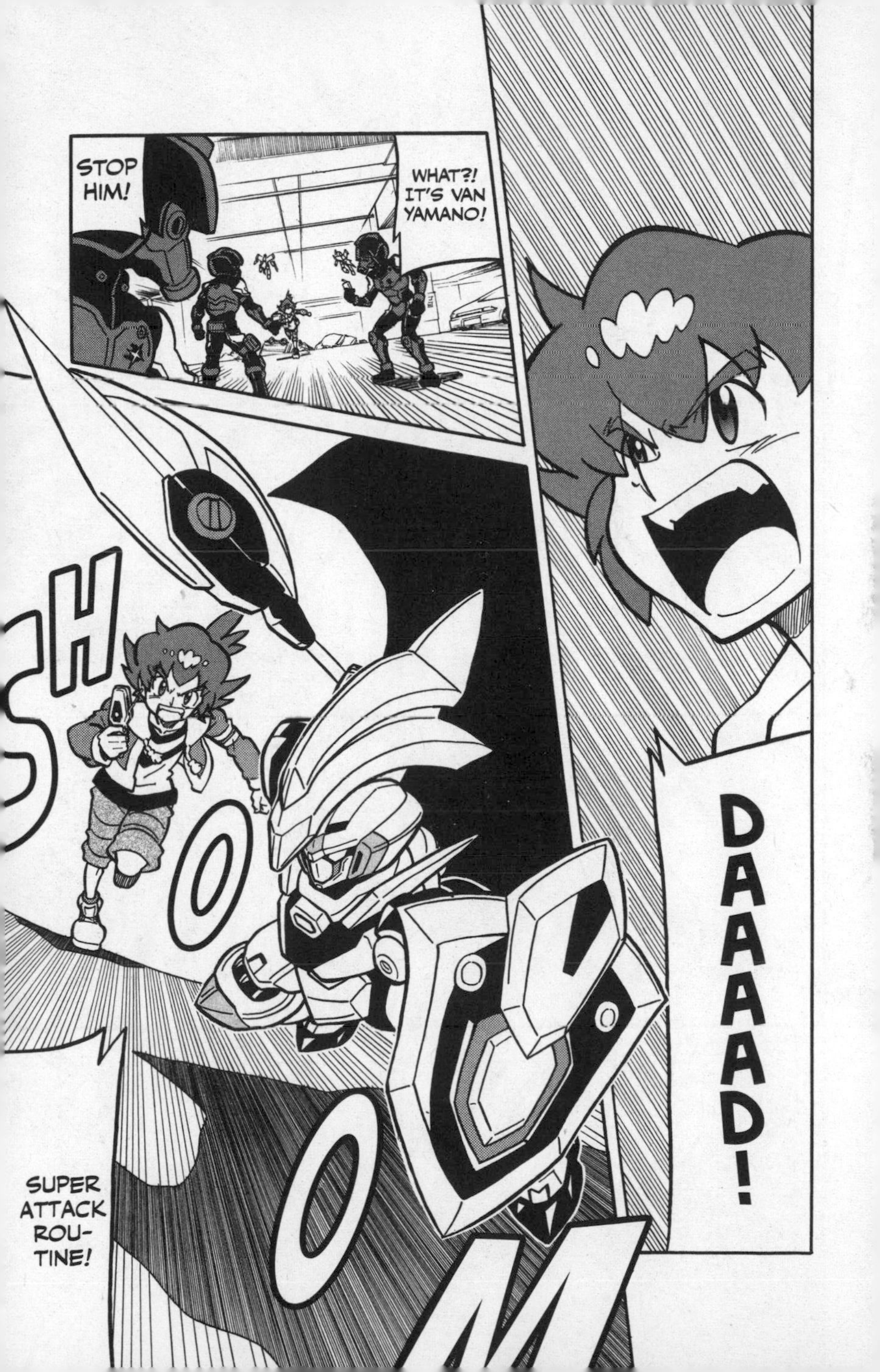
DAAAAD!
WHAT?! IT'S VAN YAMANO!
STOP HIM!
SHOOOM
SUPER ATTACK ROUTINE!

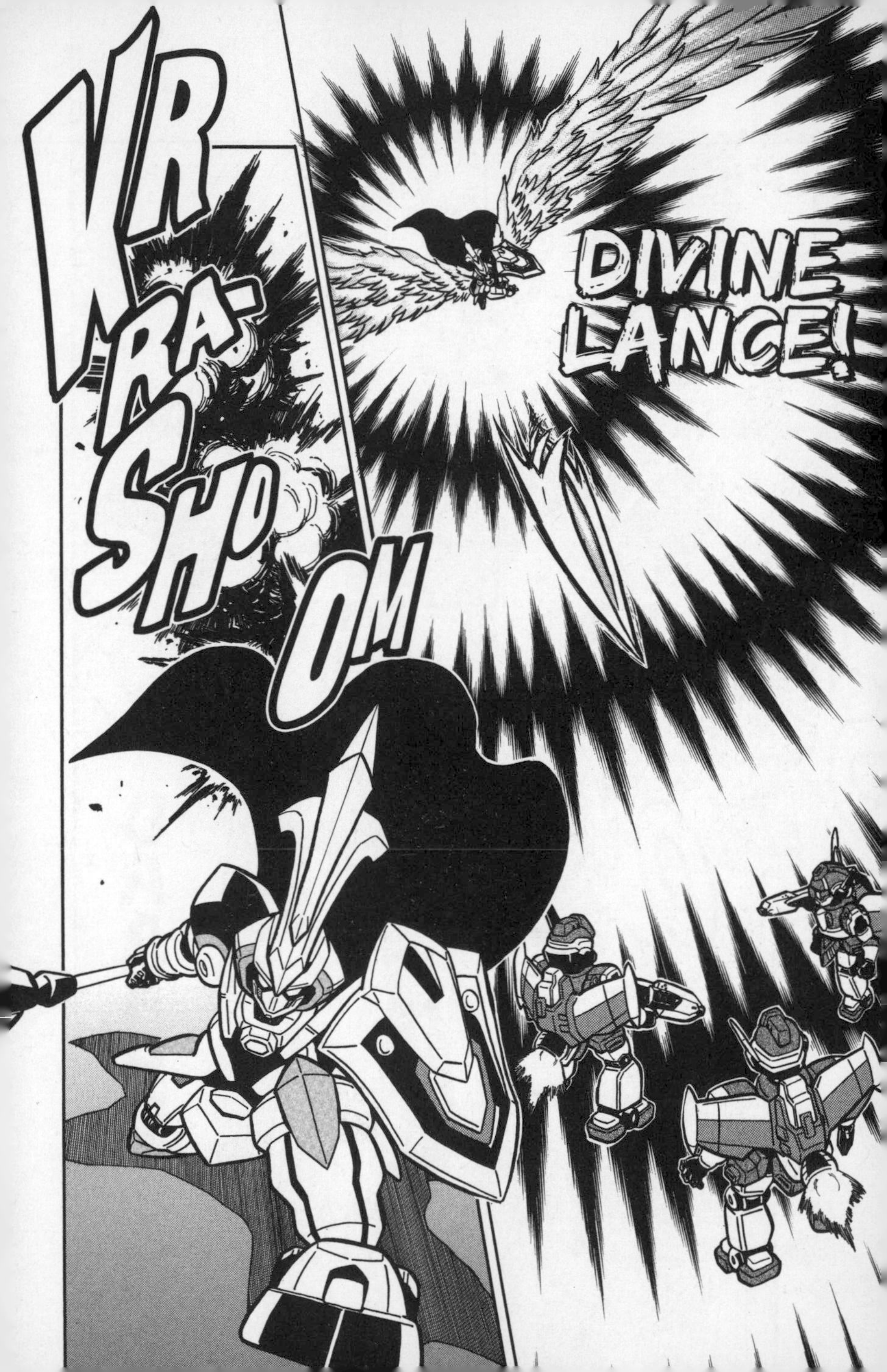
DIVINE LANCE!
VRRA-SHOOM

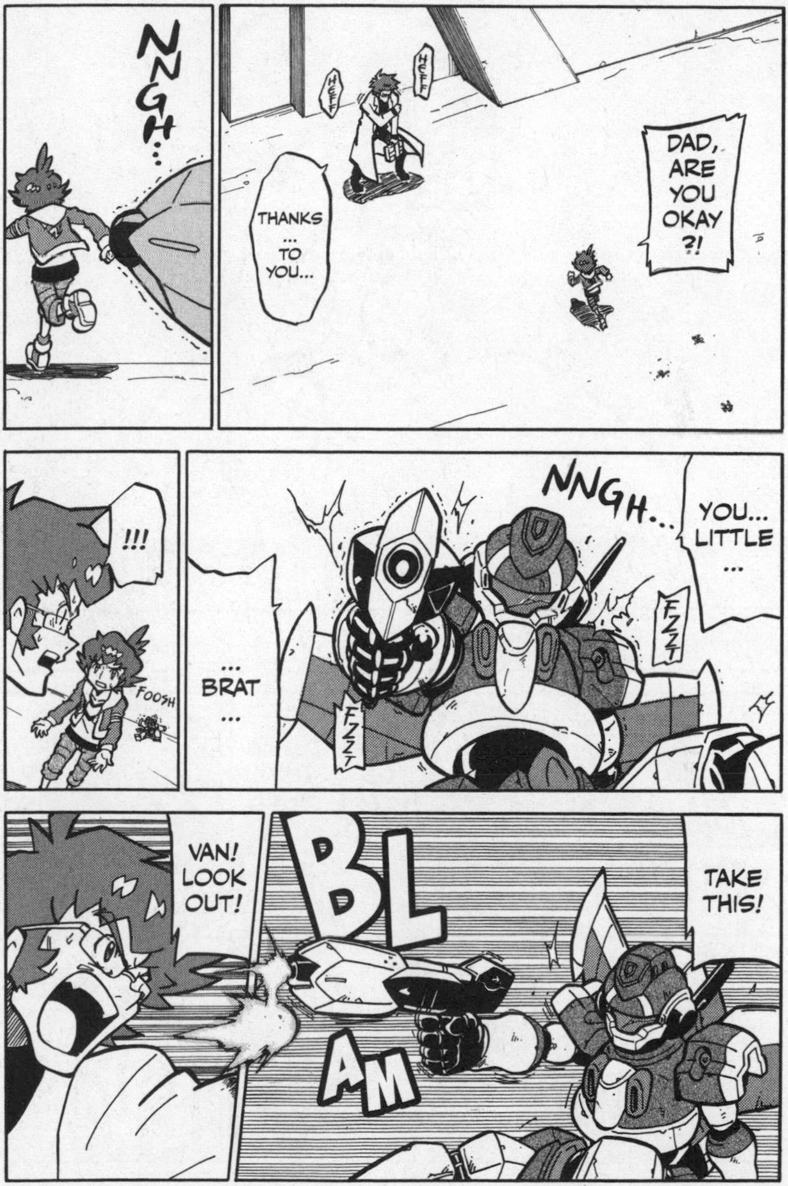
HEFF
HEFF
DAD, ARE YOU OKAY?!
THANKS ... TO YOU...
NNGH...
YOU... LITTLE ...
NNGH...
FZZT
... BRAT ...
FZZT
!!!
FOOSH
TAKE THIS!
BLAM
VAN! LOOK OUT!

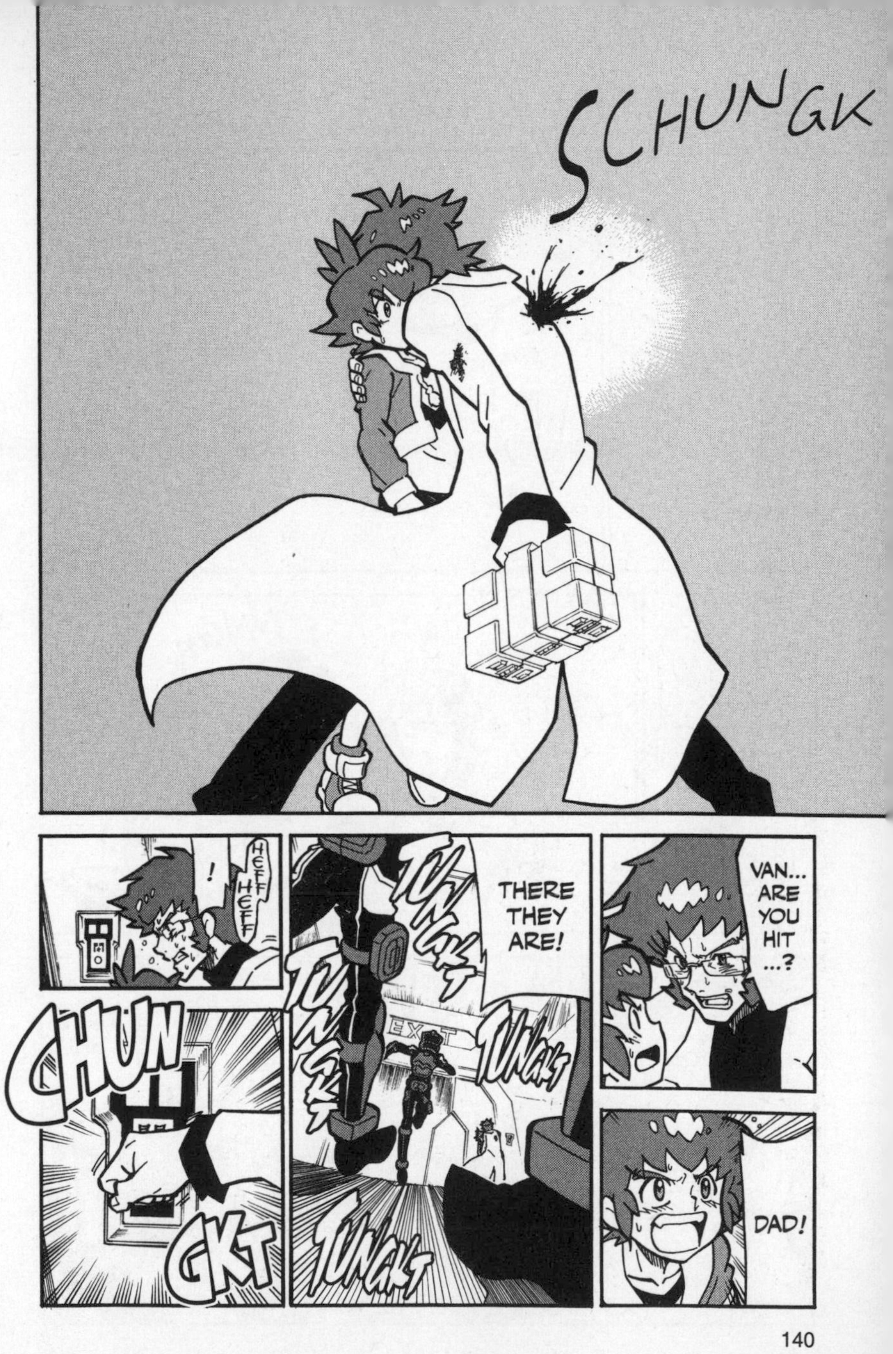
SCHUNGK
VAN... ARE YOU HIT ...?
DAD!
THERE THEY ARE!
TUNGKT
TUNGKT
TUNGKT
TUNGKT
!
HEFF HEFF
CHUN GKT

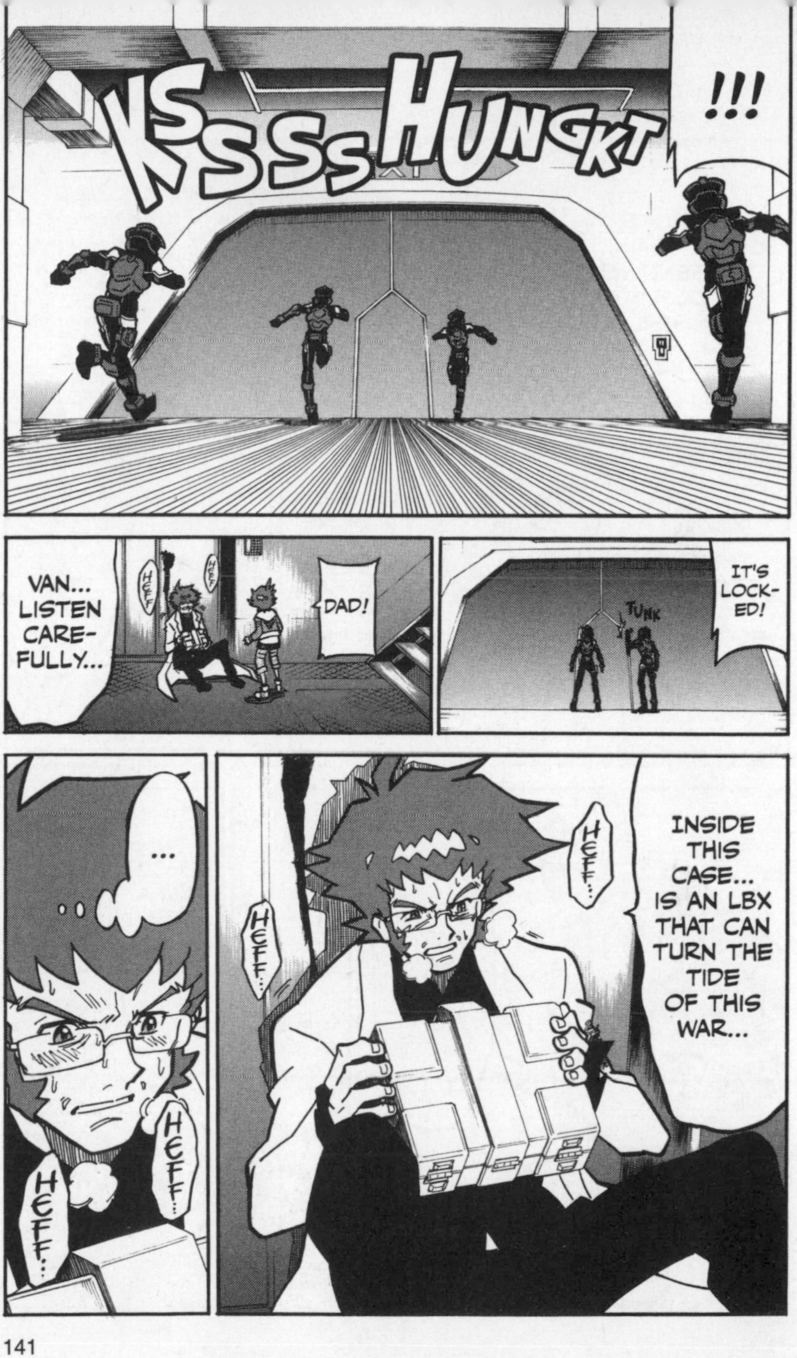
KSSSSHUNGKT
!!!
IT'S LOCKED!
TUNK
DAD!
HEFF
HEFF
VAN... LISTEN CAREFULLY...
INSIDE THIS CASE... IS AN LBX THAT CAN TURN THE TIDE OF THIS WAR...
HEFF...
HEFF...
...
HEFF...
HEFF...

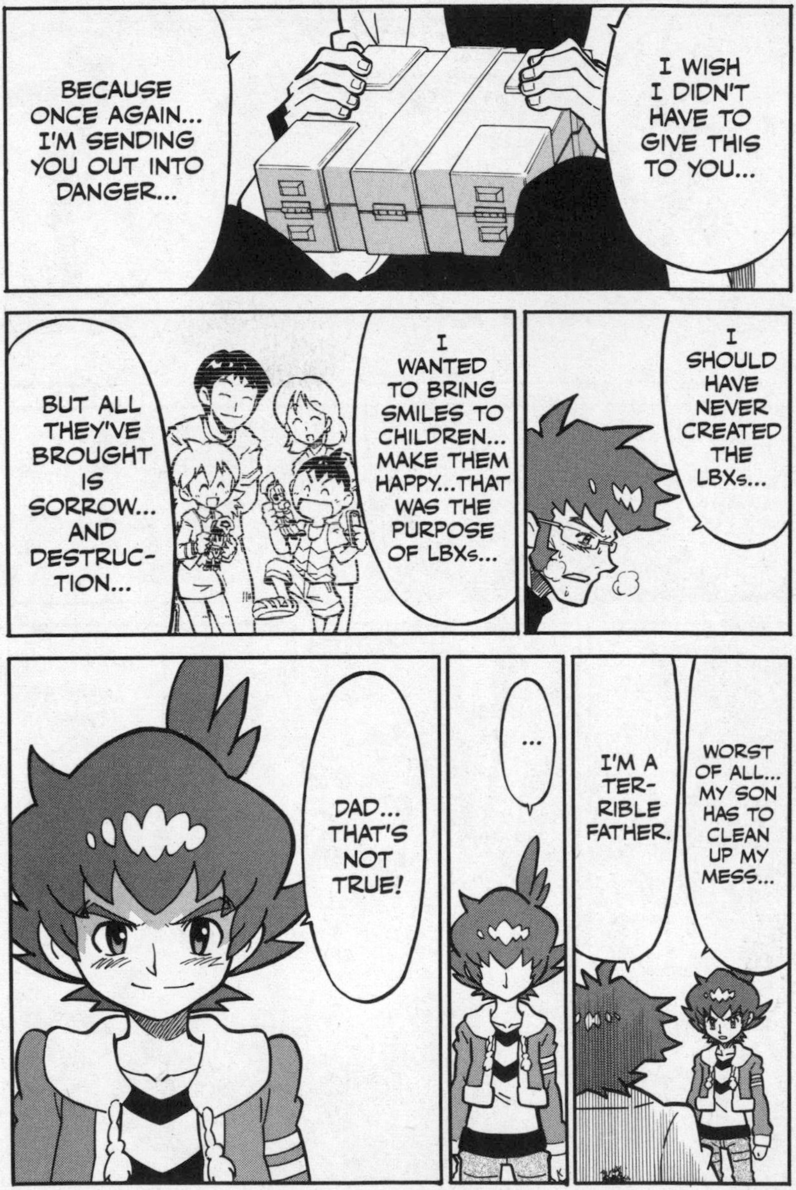
I WISH I DIDN'T HAVE TO GIVE THIS TO YOU...
BECAUSE ONCE AGAIN... I'M SENDING YOU OUT INTO DANGER...
I SHOULD HAVE NEVER CREATED THE LBXs...
I WANTED TO BRING SMILES TO CHILDREN... MAKE THEM HAPPY...THAT WAS THE PURPOSE OF LBXs...
BUT ALL THEY'VE BROUGHT IS SORROW... AND DESTRUC-TION...
WORST OF ALL... MY SON HAS TO CLEAN UP MY MESS...
I'M A TER-RIBLE FATHER.
...
DAD... THAT'S NOT TRUE!

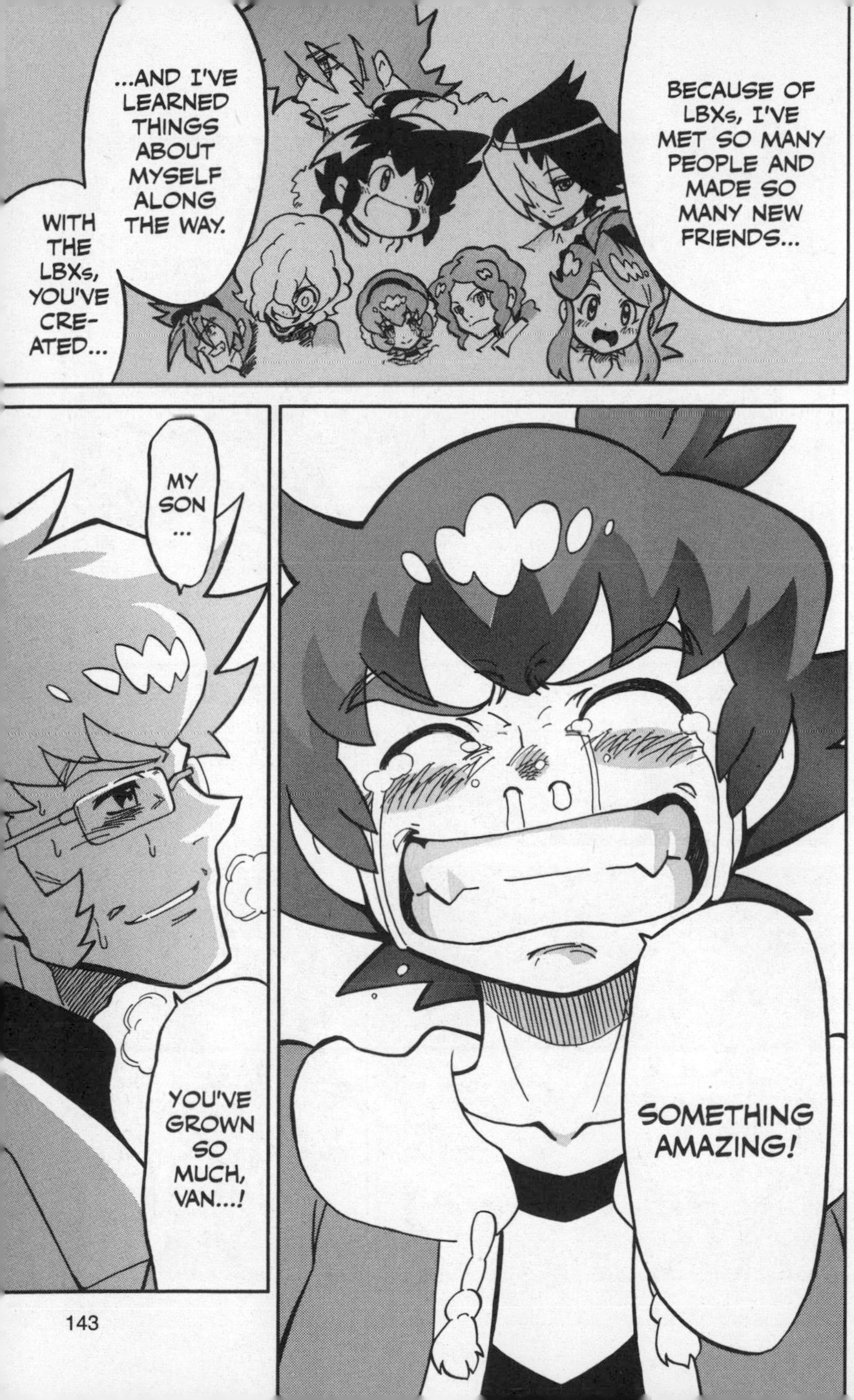
BECAUSE OF LBXs, I'VE MET SO MANY PEOPLE AND MADE SO MANY NEW FRIENDS...
...AND I'VE LEARNED THINGS ABOUT MYSELF ALONG THE WAY.
WITH THE LBXs, YOU'VE CRE-ATED...
SOMETHING AMAZING!
MY SON ...
YOU'VE GROWN SO MUCH, VAN...!

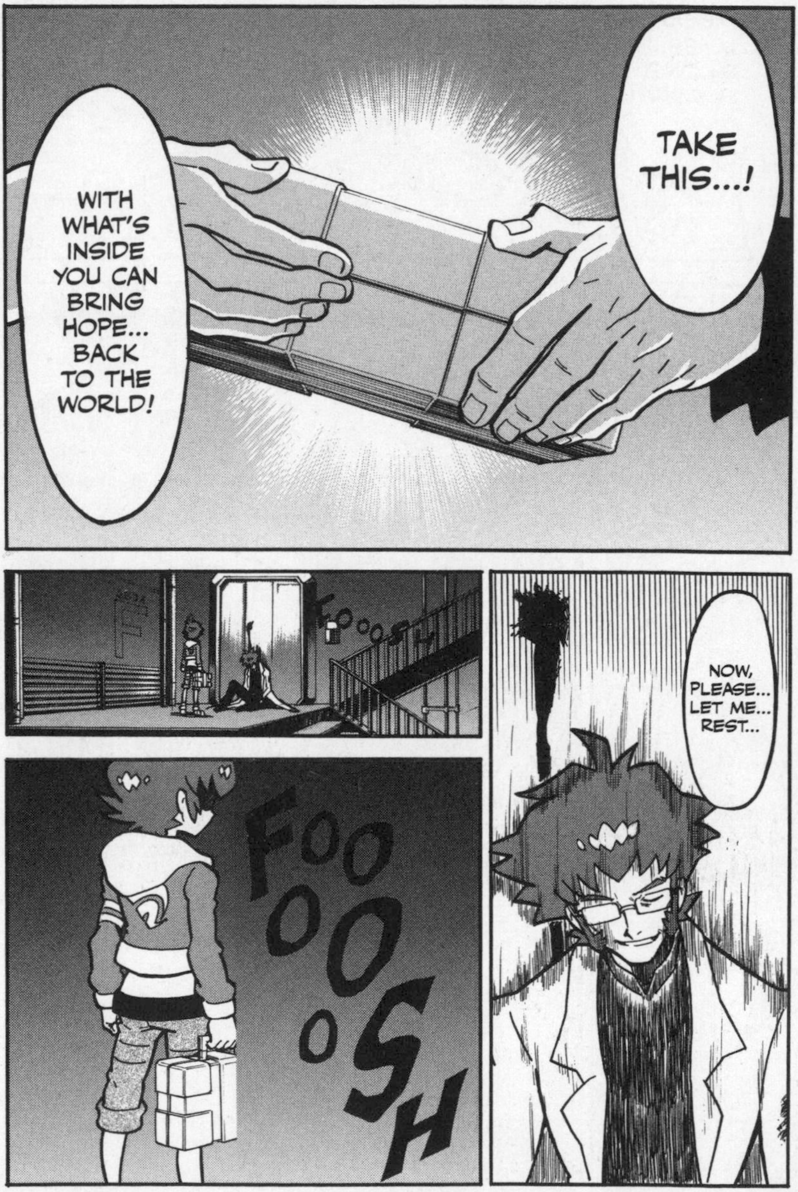
TAKE THIS...!
WITH WHAT'S INSIDE YOU CAN BRING HOPE... BACK TO THE WORLD!
NOW, PLEASE... LET ME... REST...
FOOOSH
FOOOOOSH

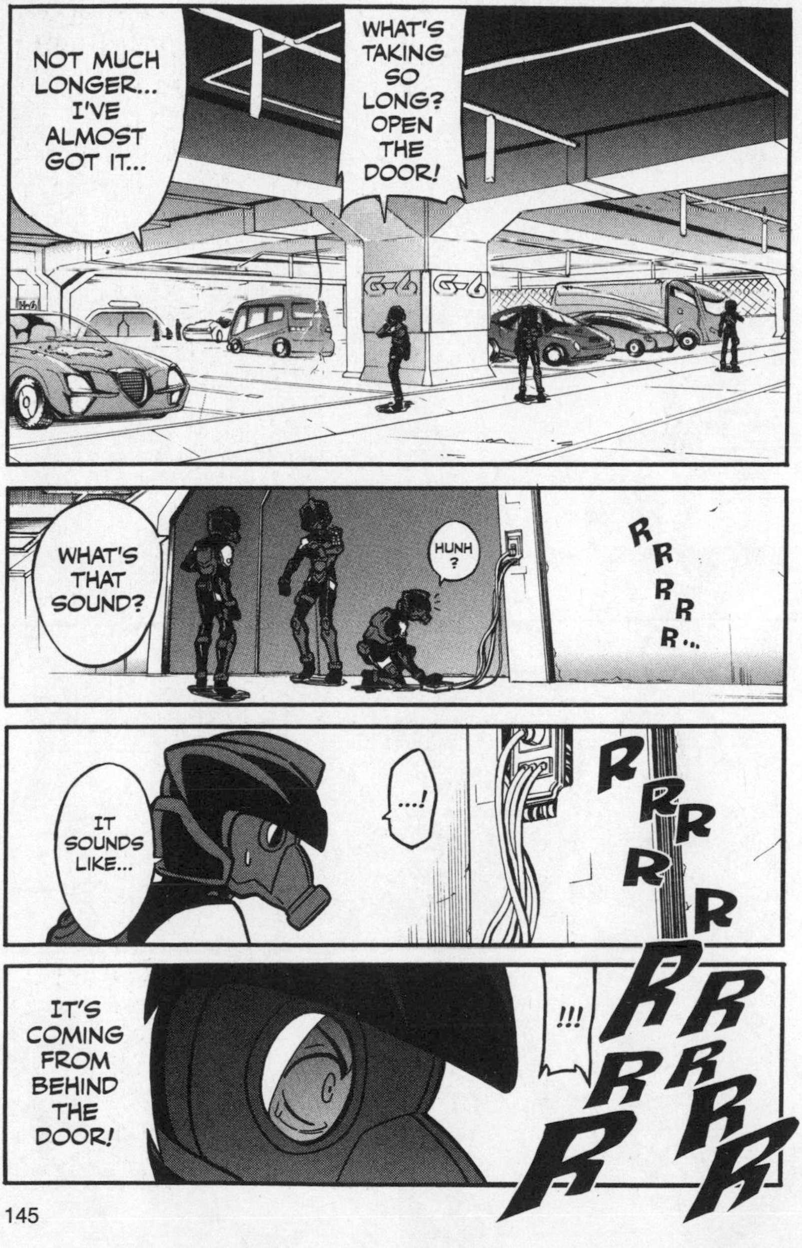
WHAT'S TAKING SO LONG? OPEN THE DOOR!
NOT MUCH LONGER... I'VE ALMOST GOT IT...
RRRRR...
HUNH?
WHAT'S THAT SOUND?
RRRRRR
...!
IT SOUNDS LIKE...
RRRRRRRR
!!!
IT'S COMING FROM BEHIND THE DOOR!

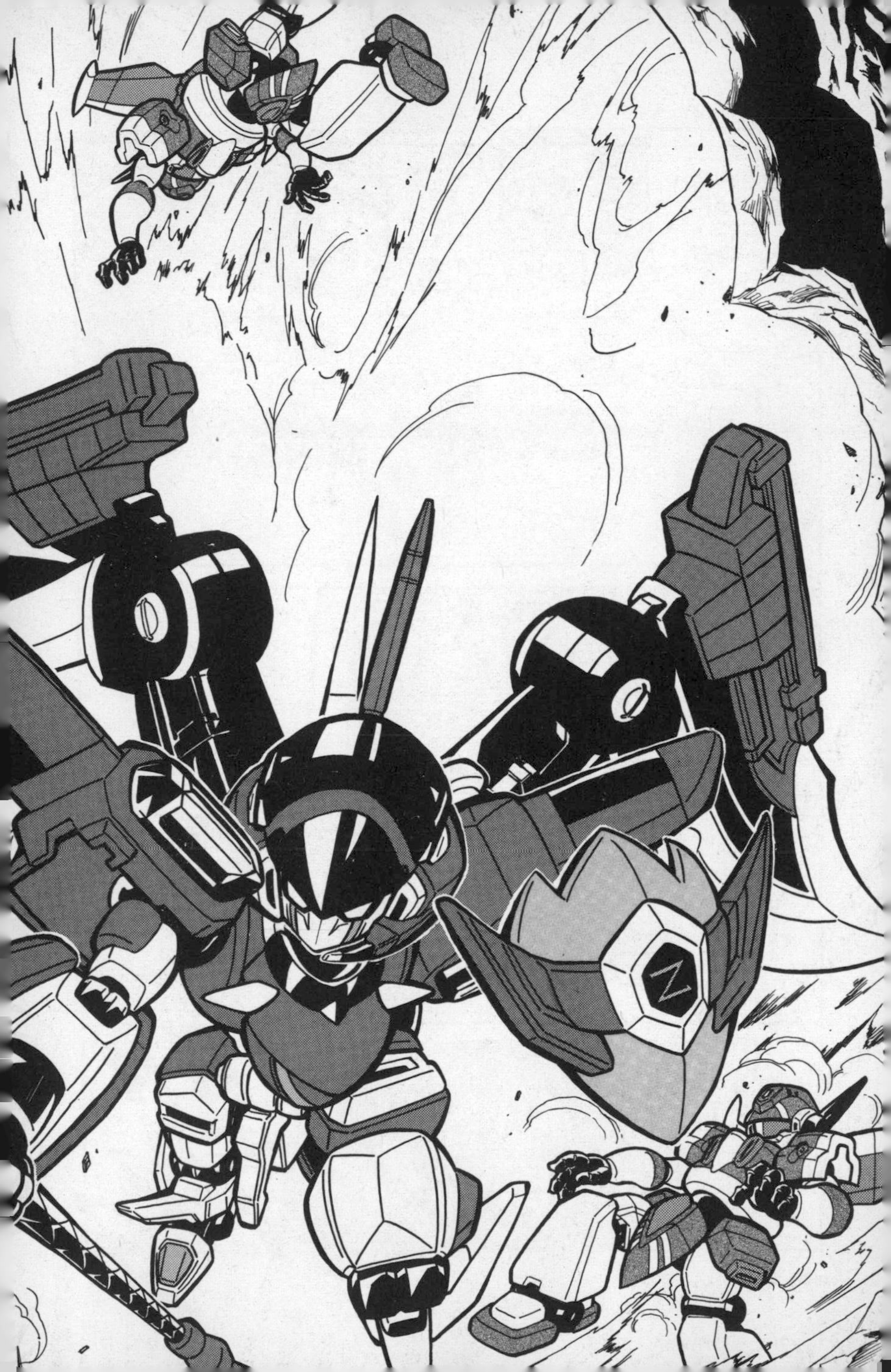

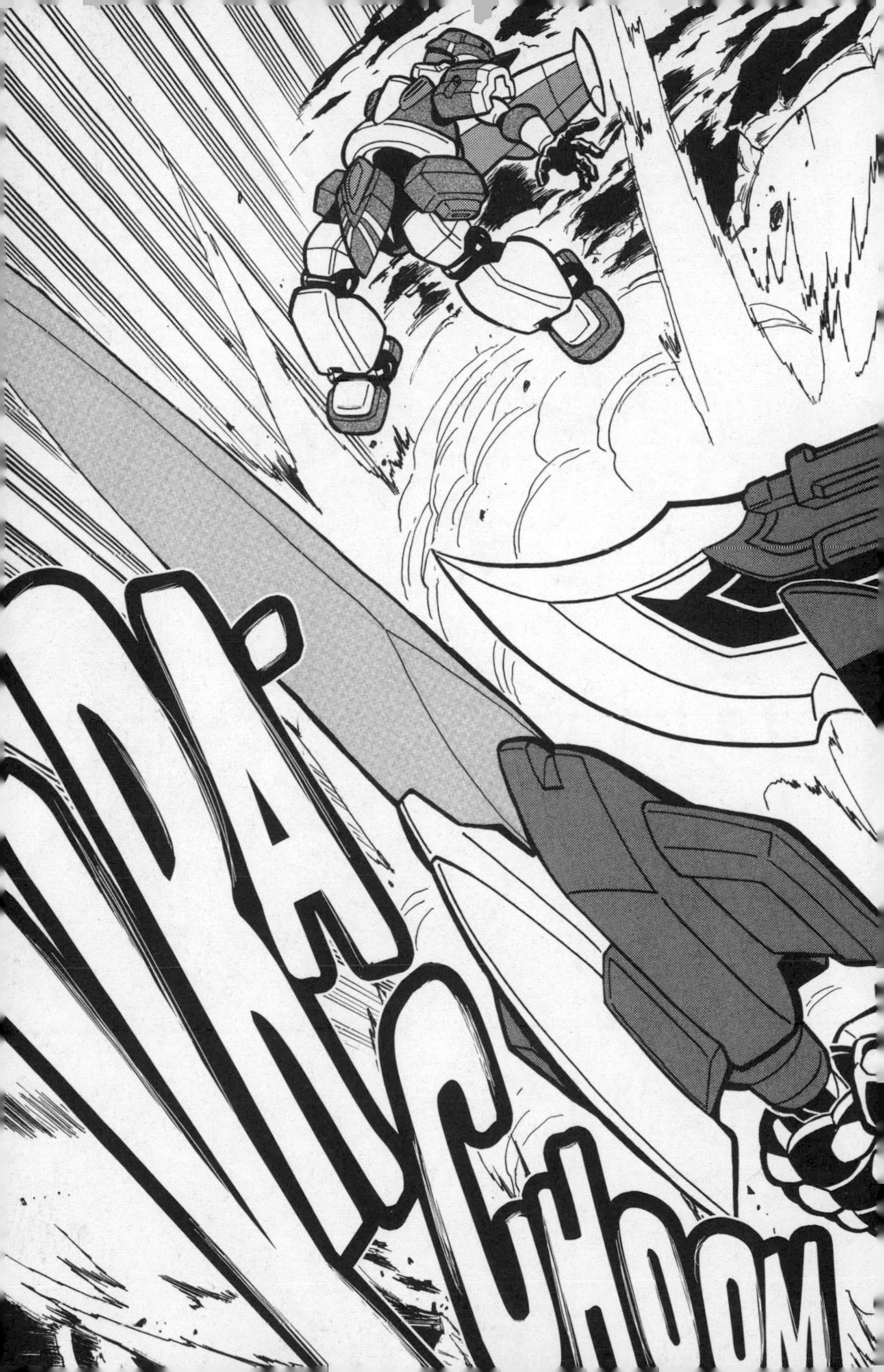
CHOOM

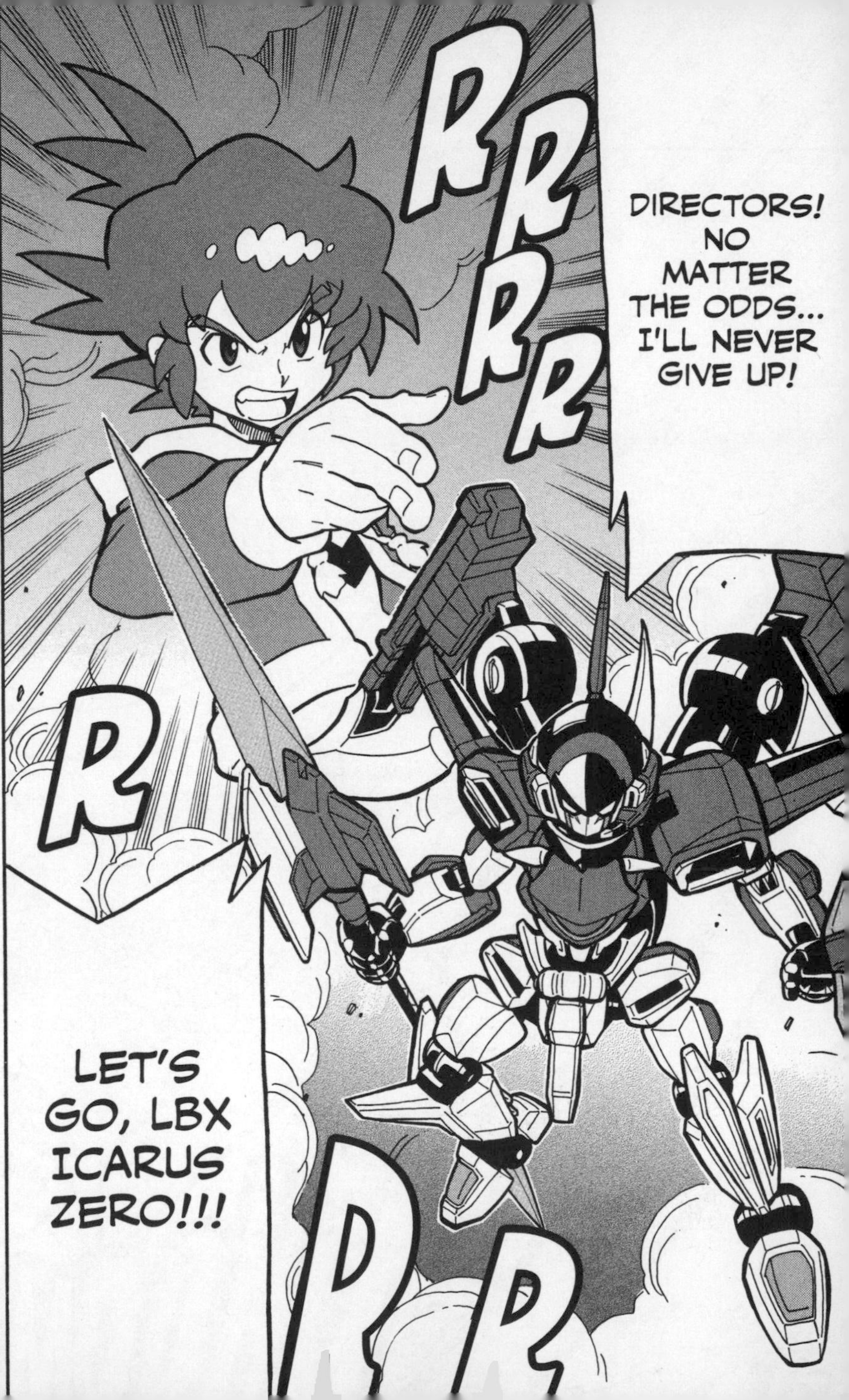
DIRECTORS! NO MATTER THE ODDS... I'LL NEVER GIVE UP!
RRRRR
R
LET'S GO, LBX ICARUS ZERO!!!
RR

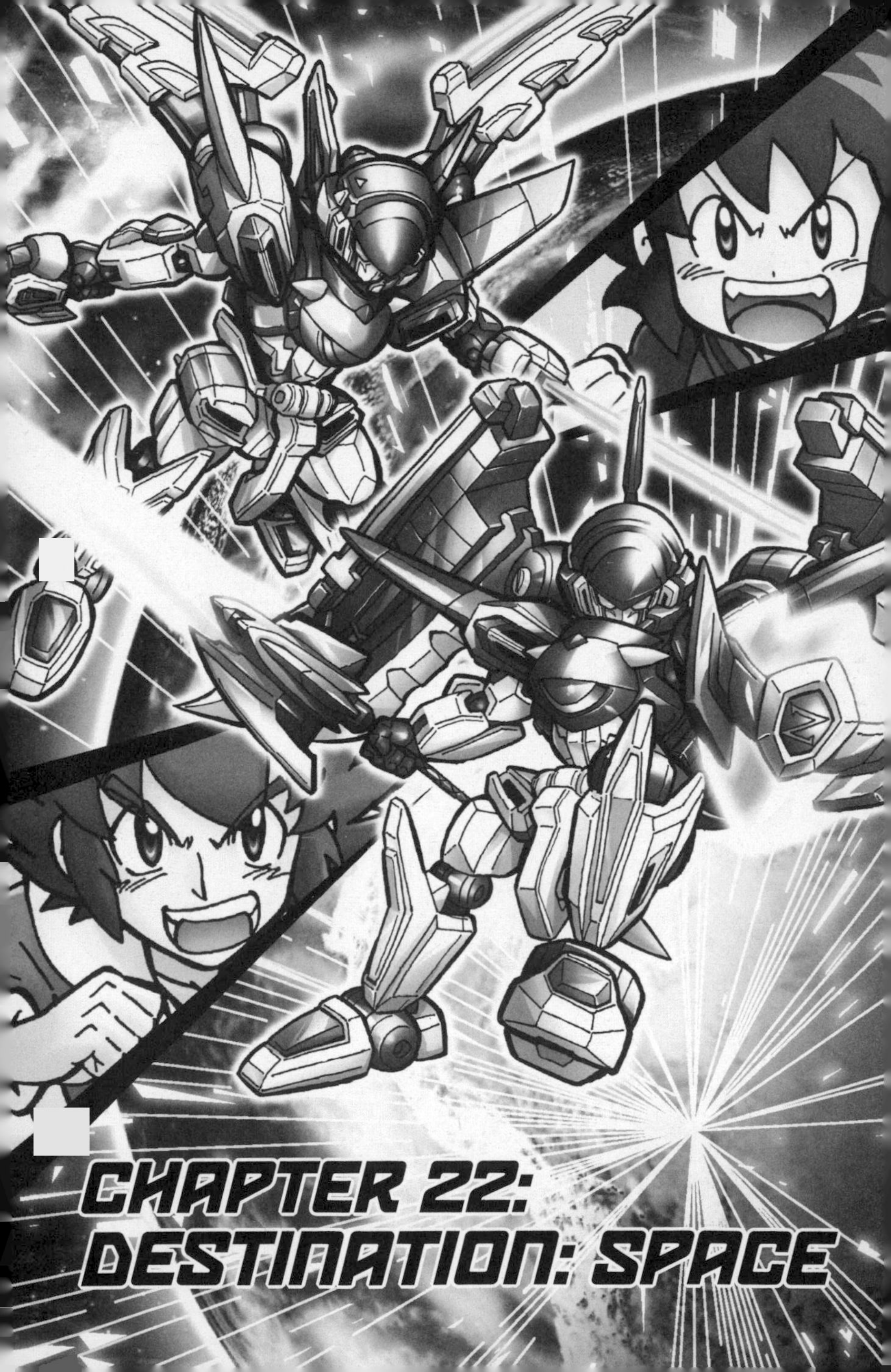
CHAPTER 22:
DESTINATION: SPACE

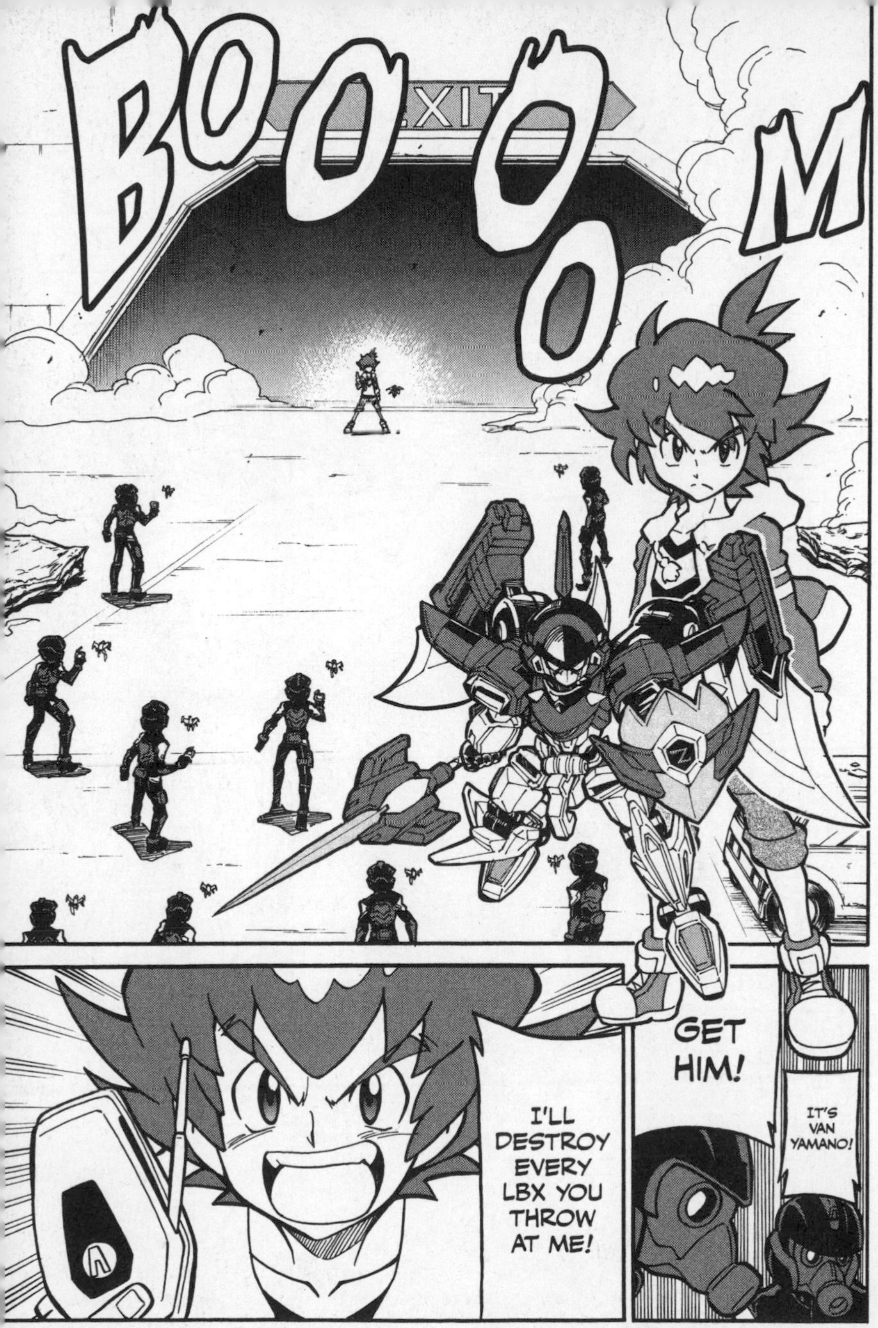
BOOOOOM
EXIT
IT'S VAN YAMANO!
GET HIM!
I'LL DESTROY EVERY LBX YOU THROW AT ME!

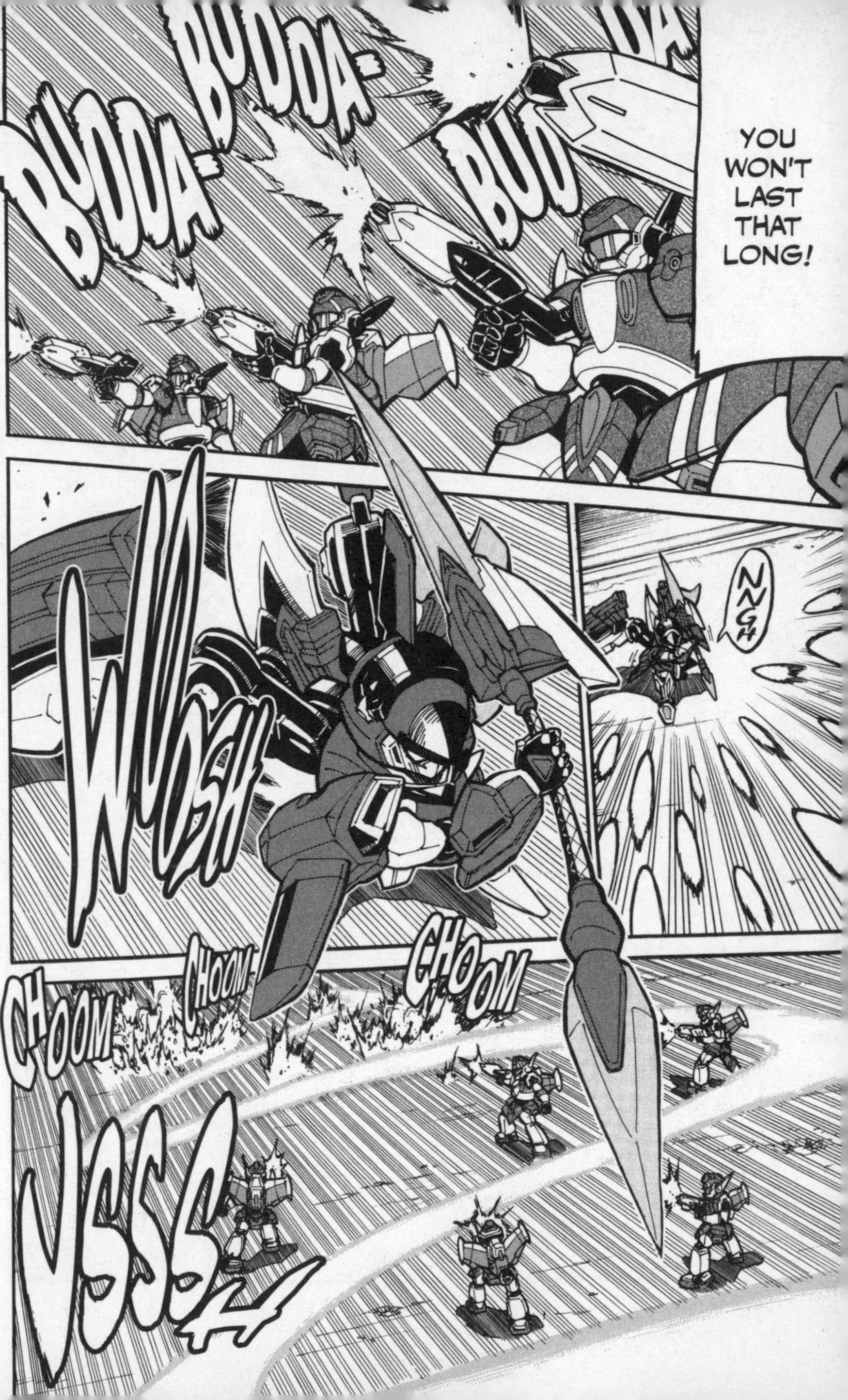
YOU WON'T LAST THAT LONG!
BUDDA-BUDDA-BUDDA-BUD
NNGH
WHOOSH
CHOOM
CHOOM
CHOOM
VSSSH

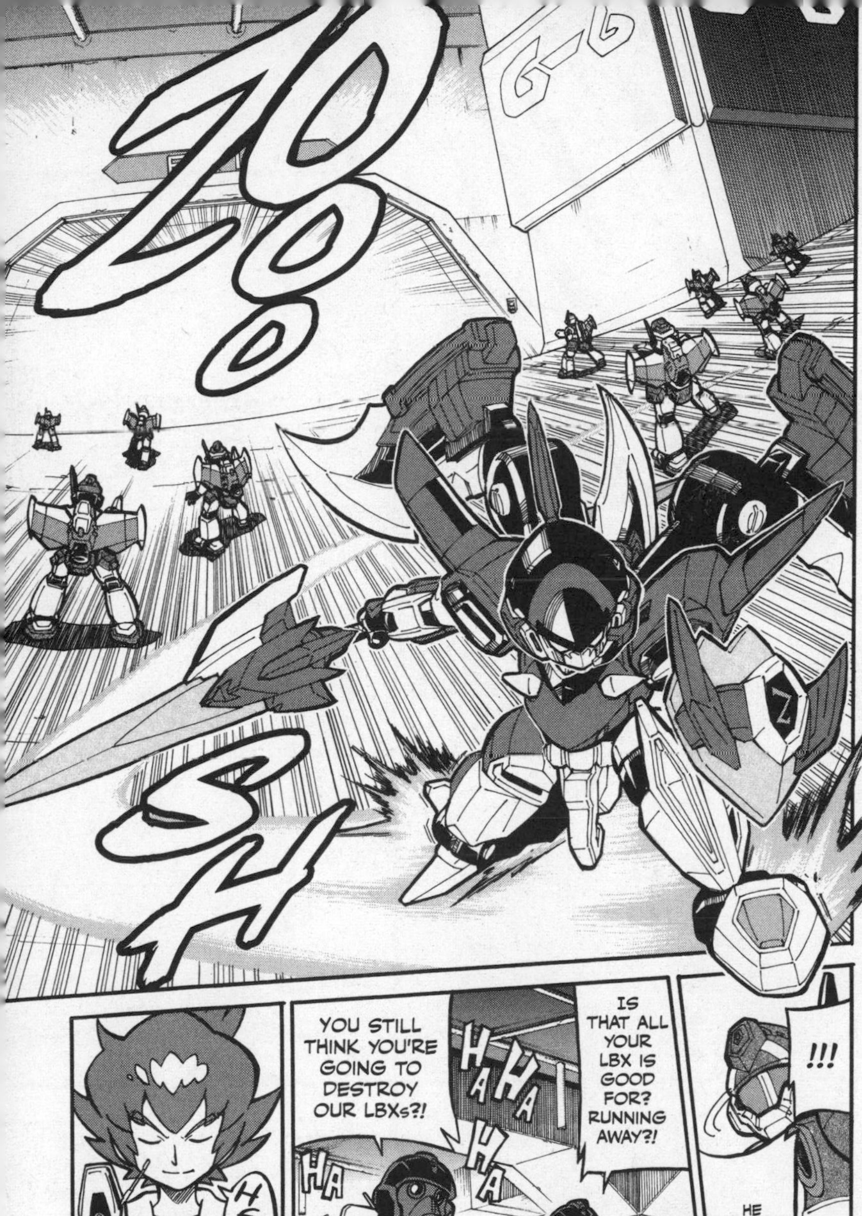
!!!
HE DODGED OUR ATTACKS!
IS THAT ALL YOUR LBX IS GOOD FOR? RUNNING AWAY?!
YOU STILL THINK YOU'RE GOING TO DESTROY OUR LBXs?!
HEH...

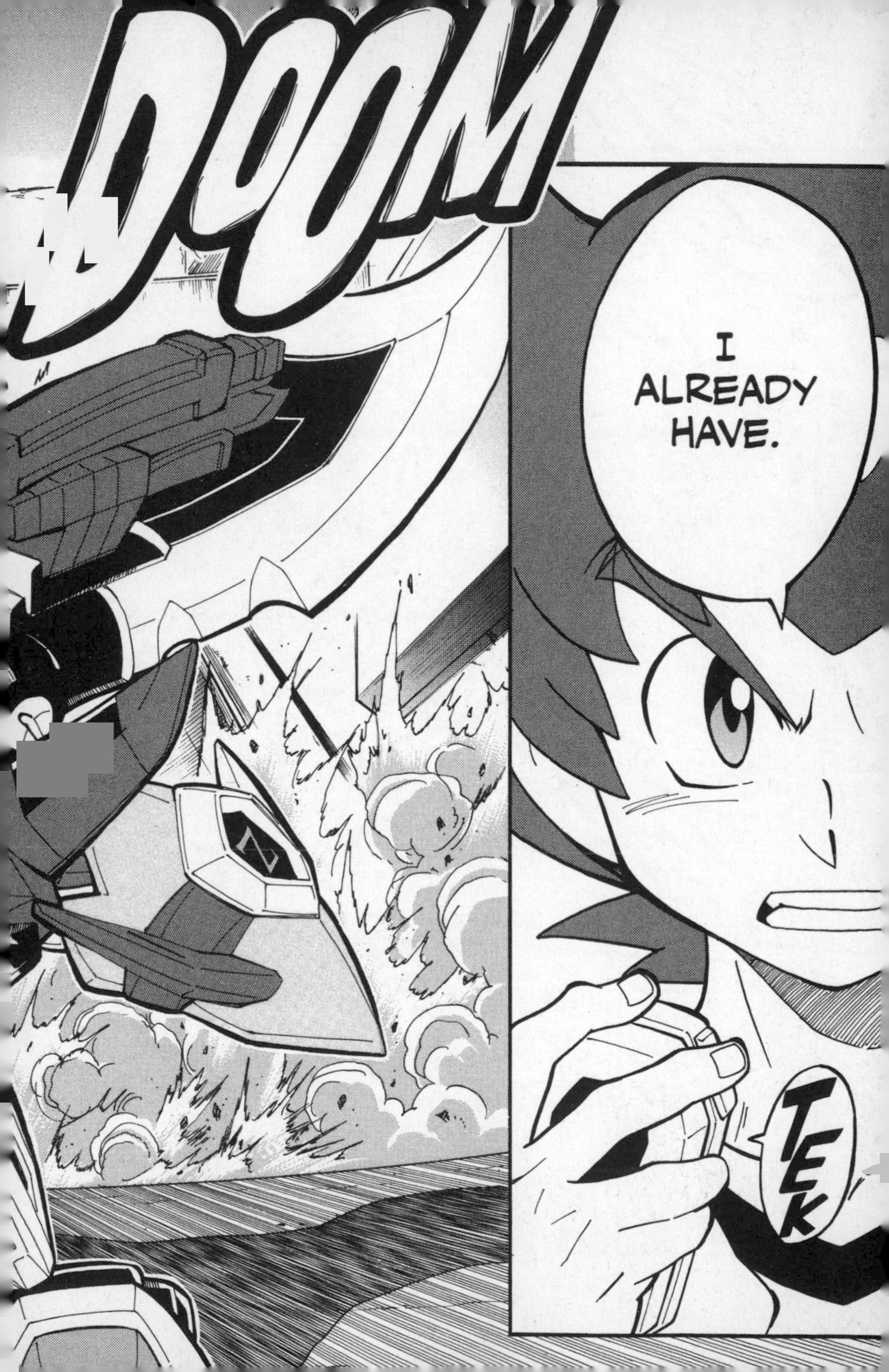
I ALREADY HAVE.
TEK
DOOM

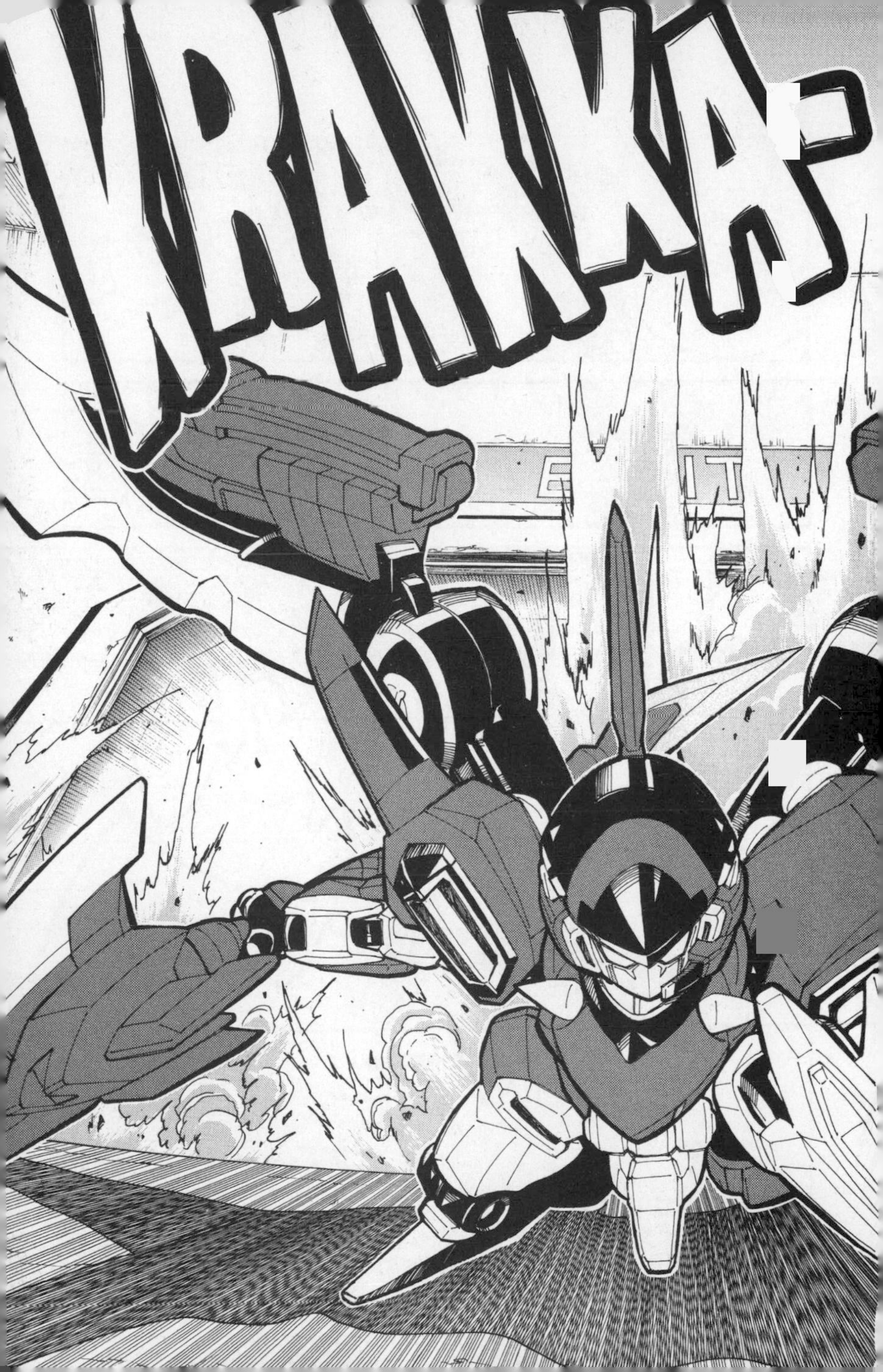

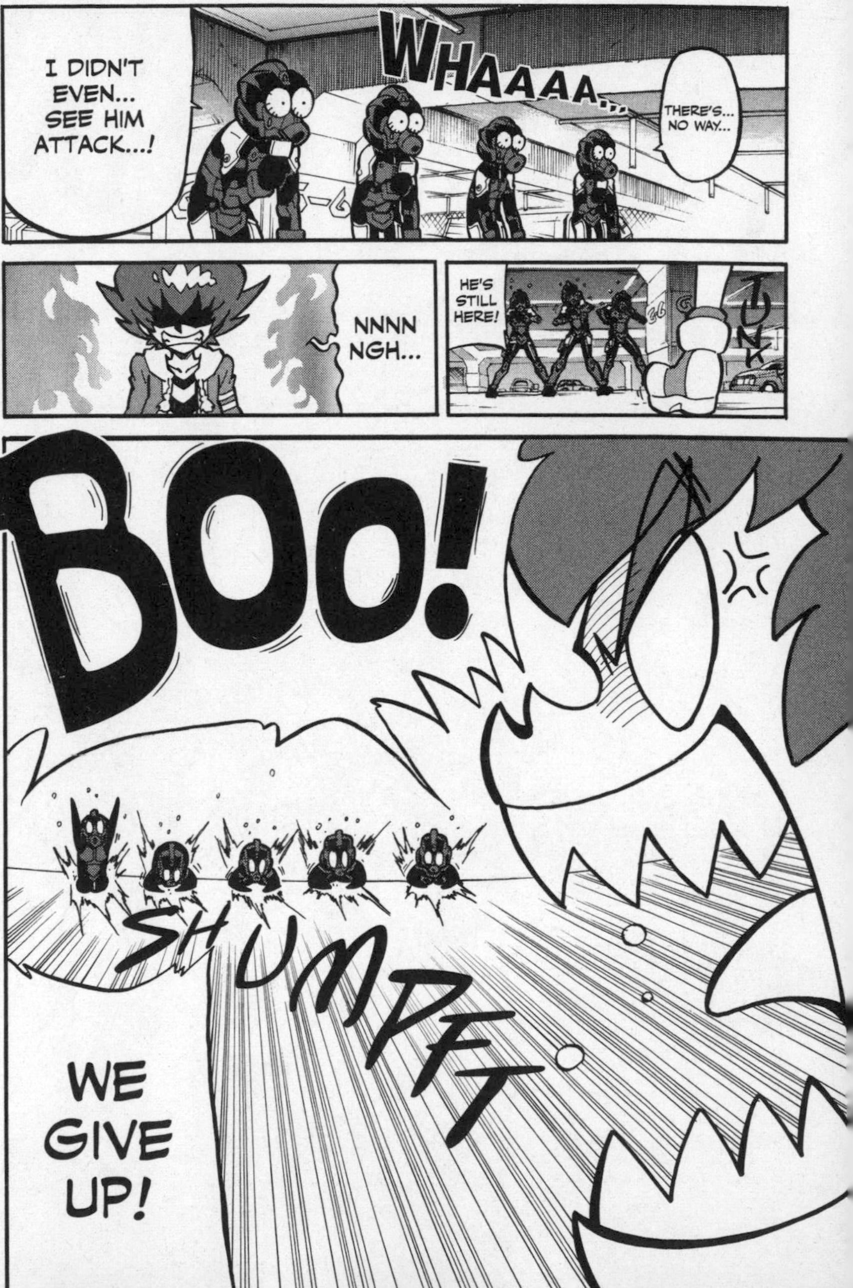
THERE'S... NO WAY...
WHAAAAA...
I DIDN'T EVEN... SEE HIM ATTACK...!
TUNK
HE'S STILL HERE!
NNNN NGH...
BOO!
SHUMPFT
WE GIVE UP!

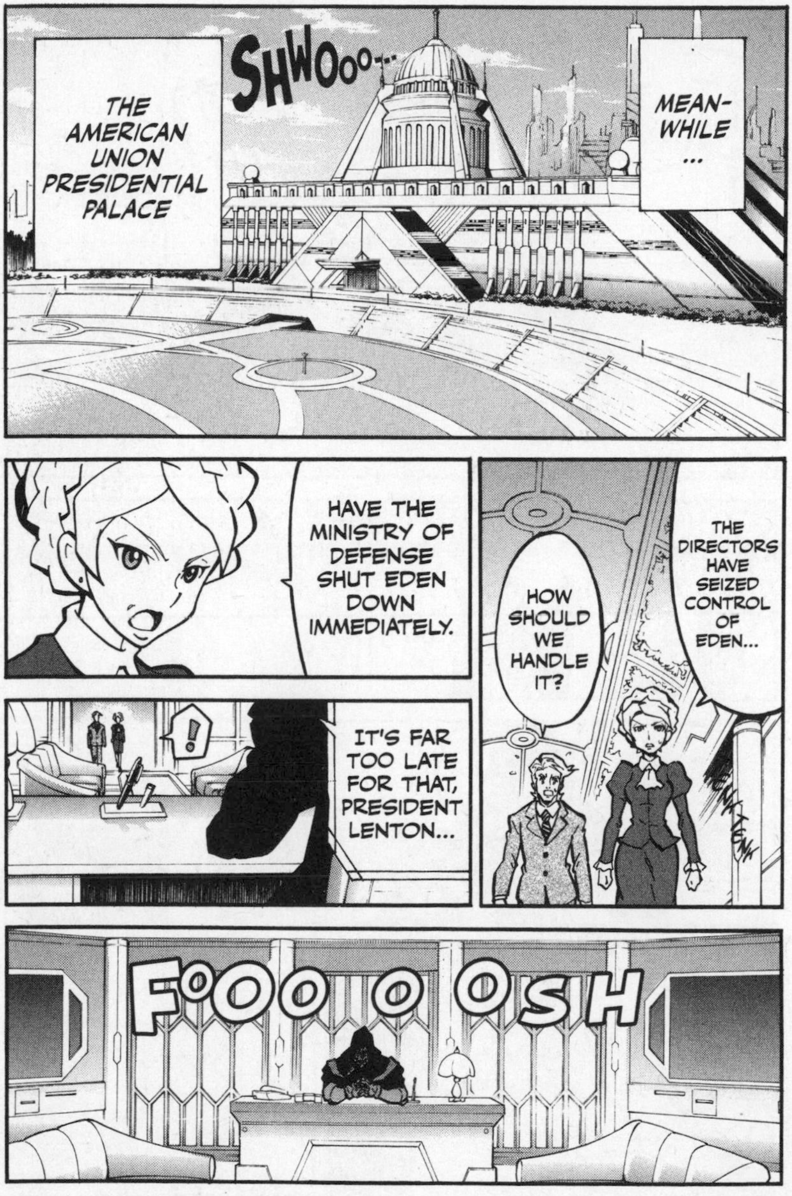
MEAN-WHILE ...
SHWOOO...
THE AMERICAN UNION PRESIDENTIAL PALACE
THE DIRECTORS HAVE SEIZED CONTROL OF EDEN...
HOW SHOULD WE HANDLE IT?
TENK TENK
HAVE THE MINISTRY OF DEFENSE SHUT EDEN DOWN IMMEDIATELY.
IT'S FAR TOO LATE FOR THAT, PRESIDENT LENTON...
!
FOOOOOSH

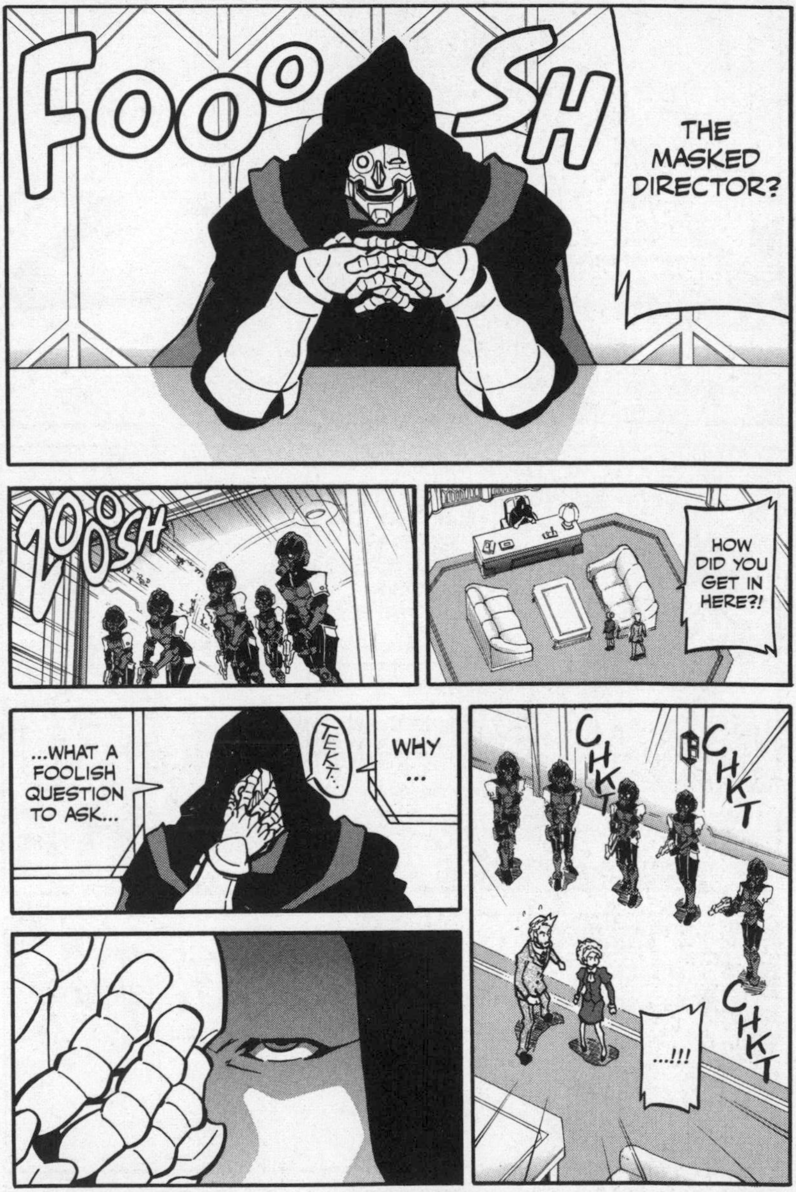
FOOOSH
THE MASKED DIRECTOR?
HOW DID YOU GET IN HERE?!
ZOOOSH
CHKT
CHKT
CHKT
...!!!
WHY ...
TEKT...
...WHAT A FOOLISH QUESTION TO ASK...

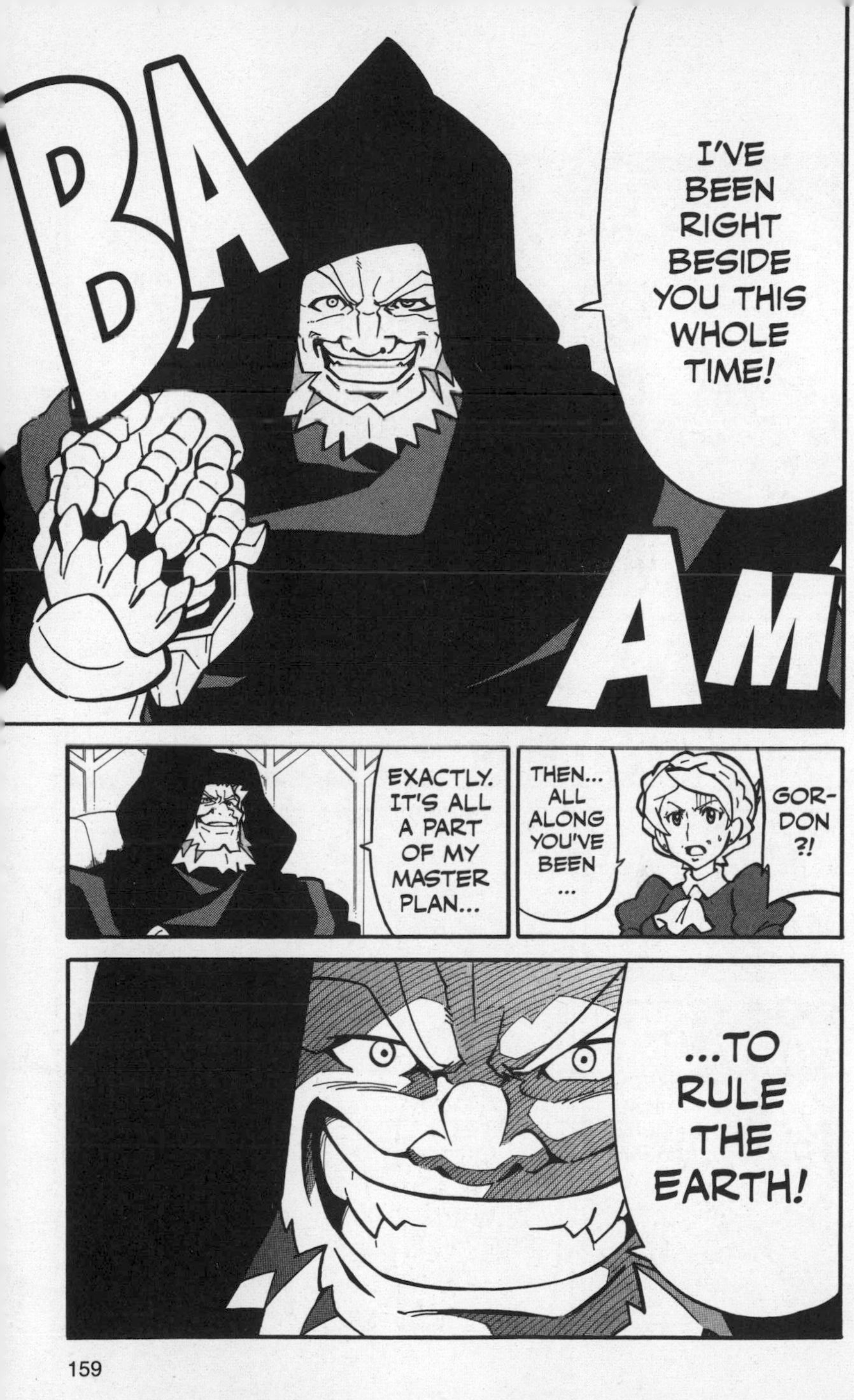
BAAM
I'VE BEEN RIGHT BESIDE YOU THIS WHOLE TIME!
GOR-DON ?!
THEN... ALL ALONG YOU'VE BEEN ...
EXACTLY. IT'S ALL A PART OF MY MASTER PLAN...
...TO RULE THE EARTH!

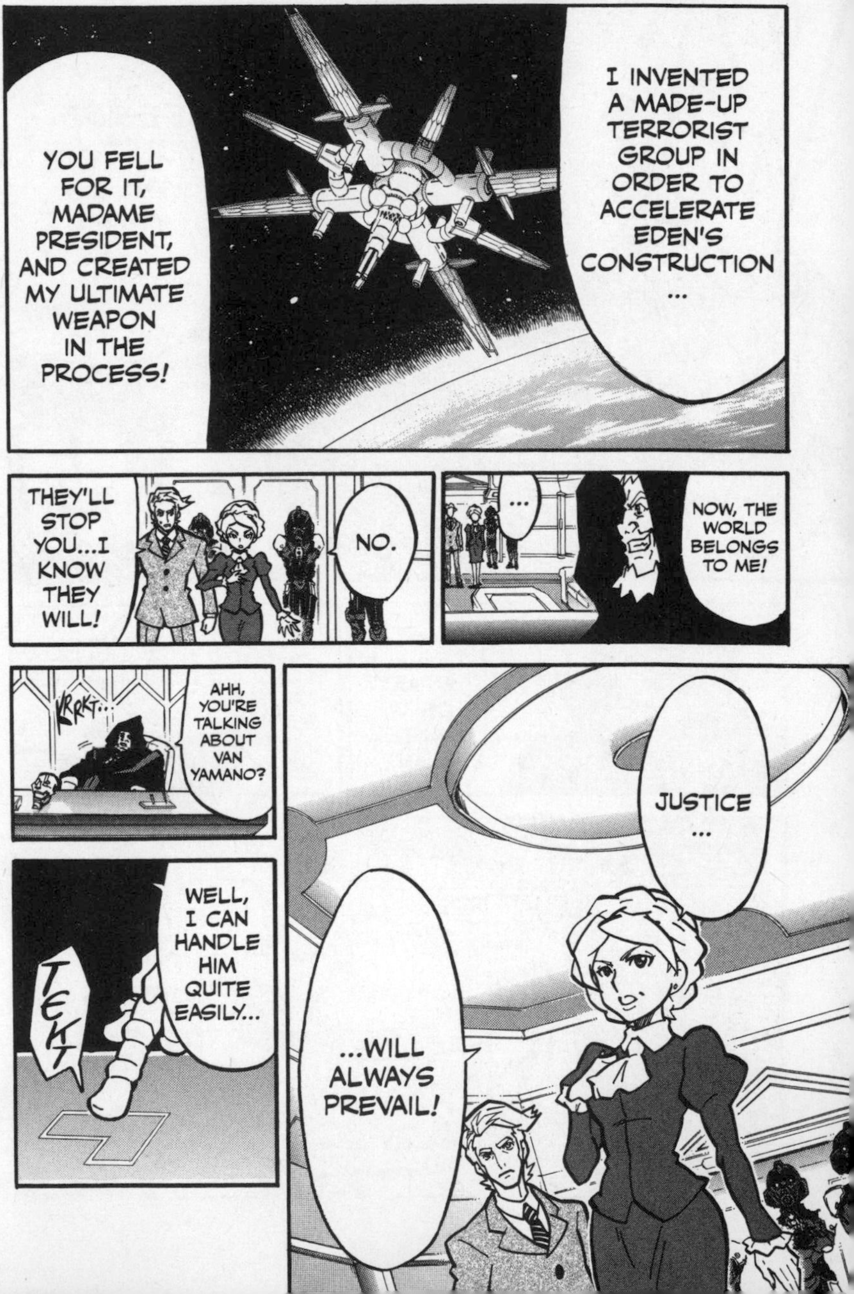
I INVENTED A MADE-UP TERRORIST GROUP IN ORDER TO ACCELERATE EDEN'S CONSTRUCTION ...
YOU FELL FOR IT, MADAME PRESIDENT, AND CREATED MY ULTIMATE WEAPON IN THE PROCESS!
...
NOW, THE WORLD BELONGS TO ME!
NO.
THEY'LL STOP YOU...I KNOW THEY WILL!
JUSTICE ...
...WILL ALWAYS PREVAIL!
KRRKT...
AHH, YOU'RE TALKING ABOUT VAN YAMANO?
TEKT
WELL, I CAN HANDLE HIM QUITE EASILY...

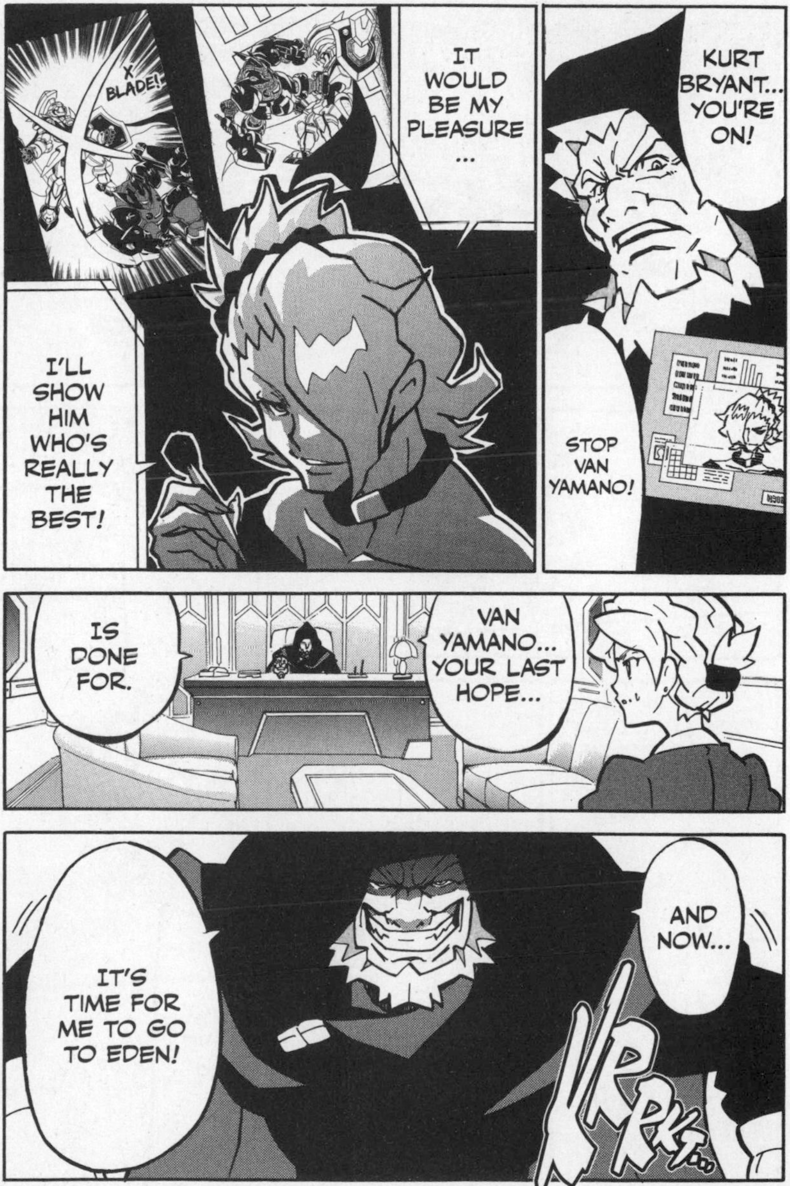
KURT BRYANT... YOU'RE ON!
STOP VAN YAMANO!
IT WOULD BE MY PLEASURE...
X BLADE!
I'LL SHOW HIM WHO'S REALLY THE BEST!
VAN YAMANO... YOUR LAST HOPE...
IS DONE FOR.
AND NOW...
IT'S TIME FOR ME TO GO TO EDEN!

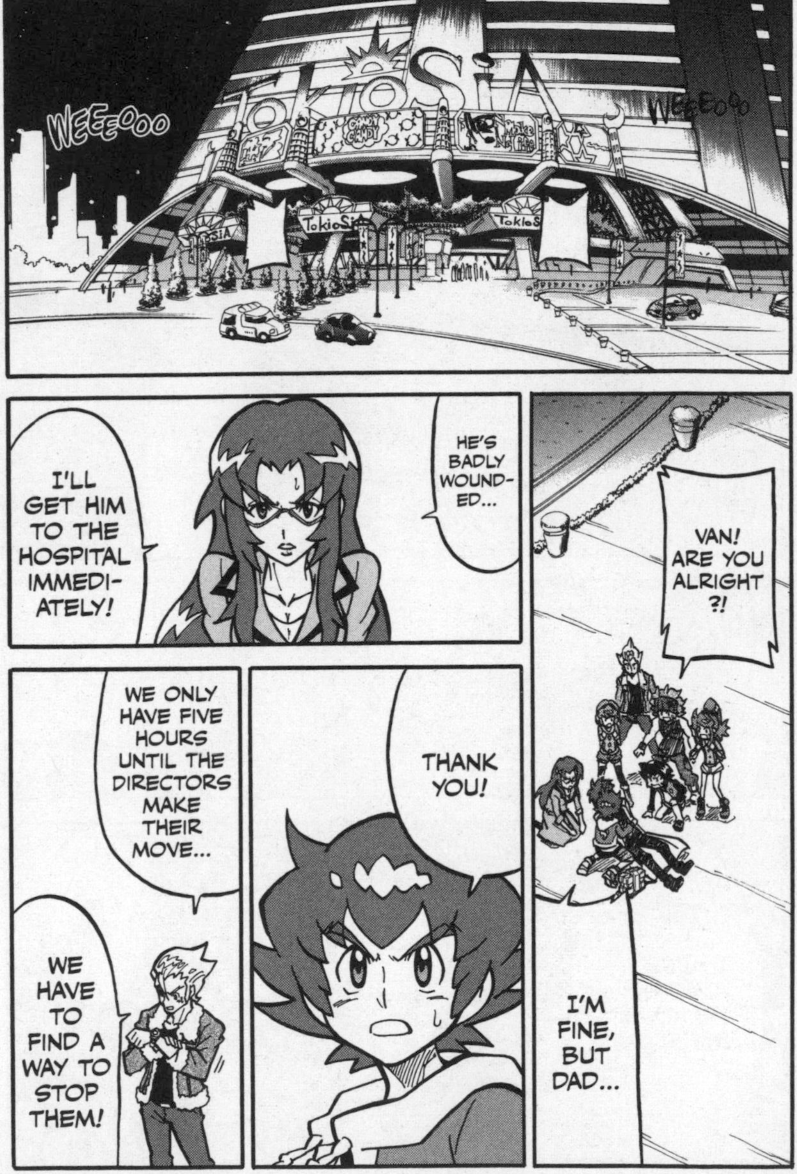
WEEEOOO
WEEEOOO
VAN! ARE YOU ALRIGHT?!
I'M FINE, BUT DAD...
HE'S BADLY WOUND-ED...
I'LL GET HIM TO THE HOSPITAL IMMEDI-ATELY!
THANK YOU!
WE ONLY HAVE FIVE HOURS UNTIL THE DIRECTORS MAKE THEIR MOVE...
WE HAVE TO FIND A WAY TO STOP THEM!

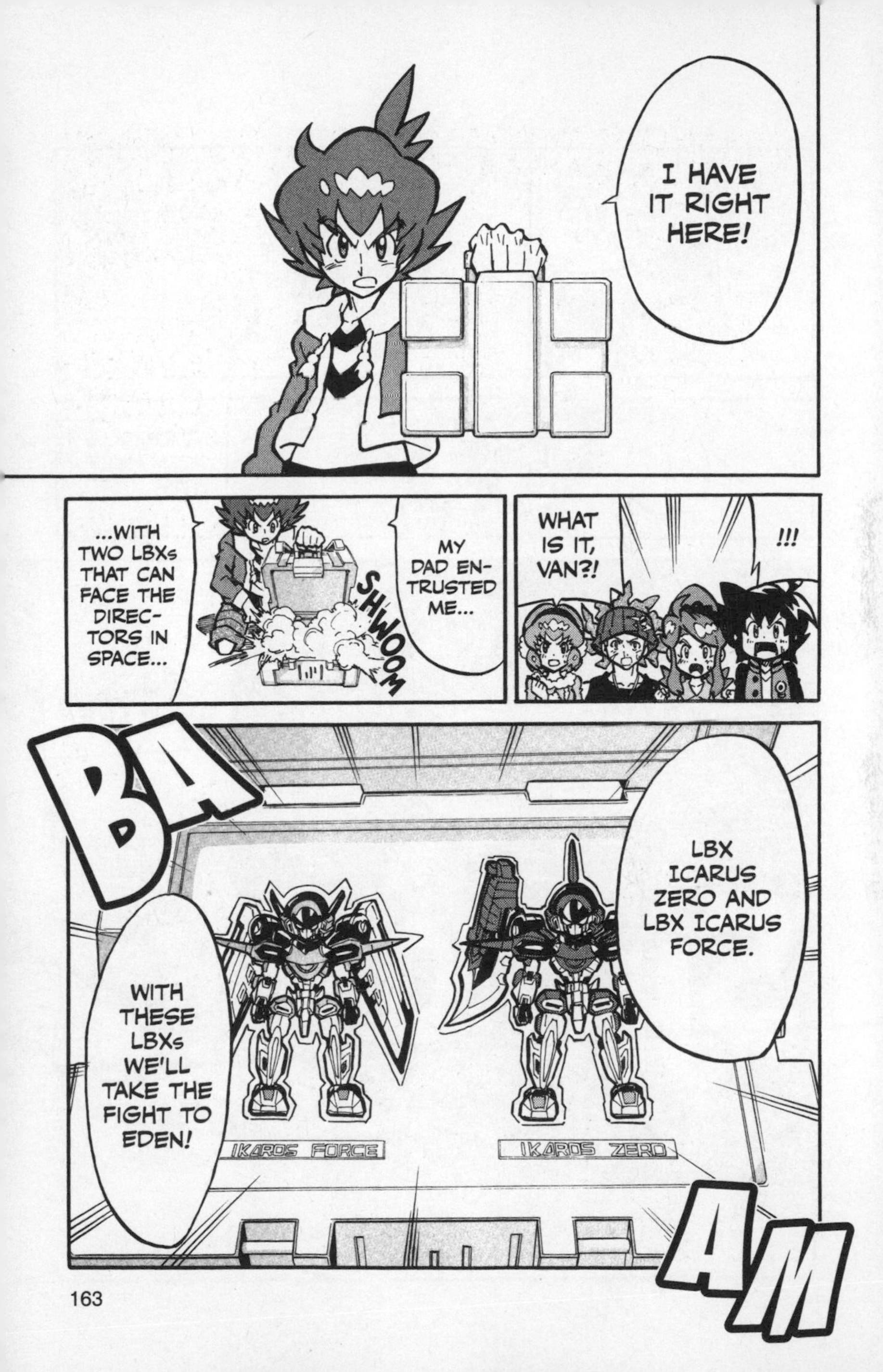
I HAVE IT RIGHT HERE!
!!!
WHAT IS IT, VAN?!
MY DAD EN-TRUSTED ME...
SHWOOM
...WITH TWO LBXs THAT CAN FACE THE DIREC-TORS IN SPACE...
BA
LBX ICARUS ZERO AND LBX ICARUS FORCE.
WITH THESE LBXs WE'LL TAKE THE FIGHT TO EDEN!
IKAROS ZERO
IKAROS FORCE
AM

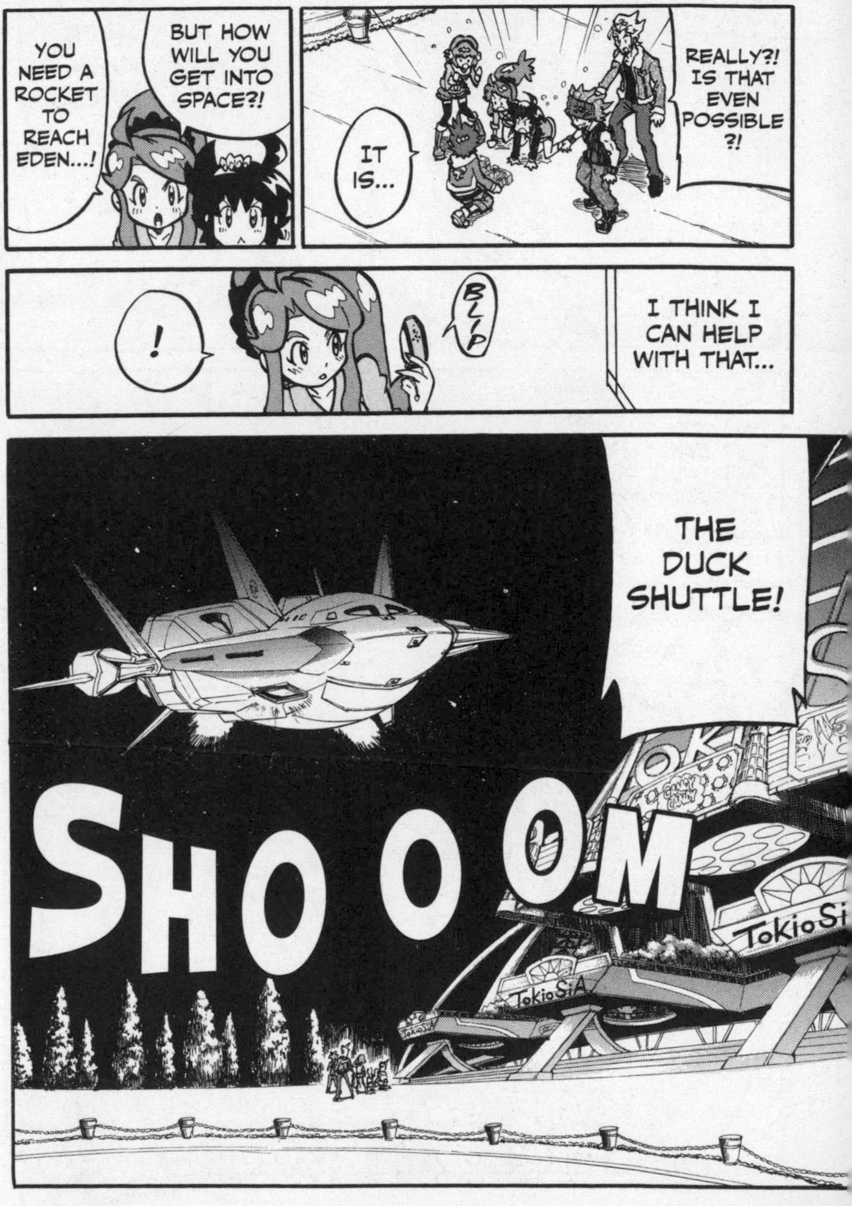
REALLY?! IS THAT EVEN POSSIBLE?!
IT IS...
BUT HOW WILL YOU GET INTO SPACE?!
YOU NEED A ROCKET TO REACH EDEN...!
I THINK I CAN HELP WITH THAT...
BLIP
!
THE DUCK SHUTTLE!
SHOOOM
TokioSiA

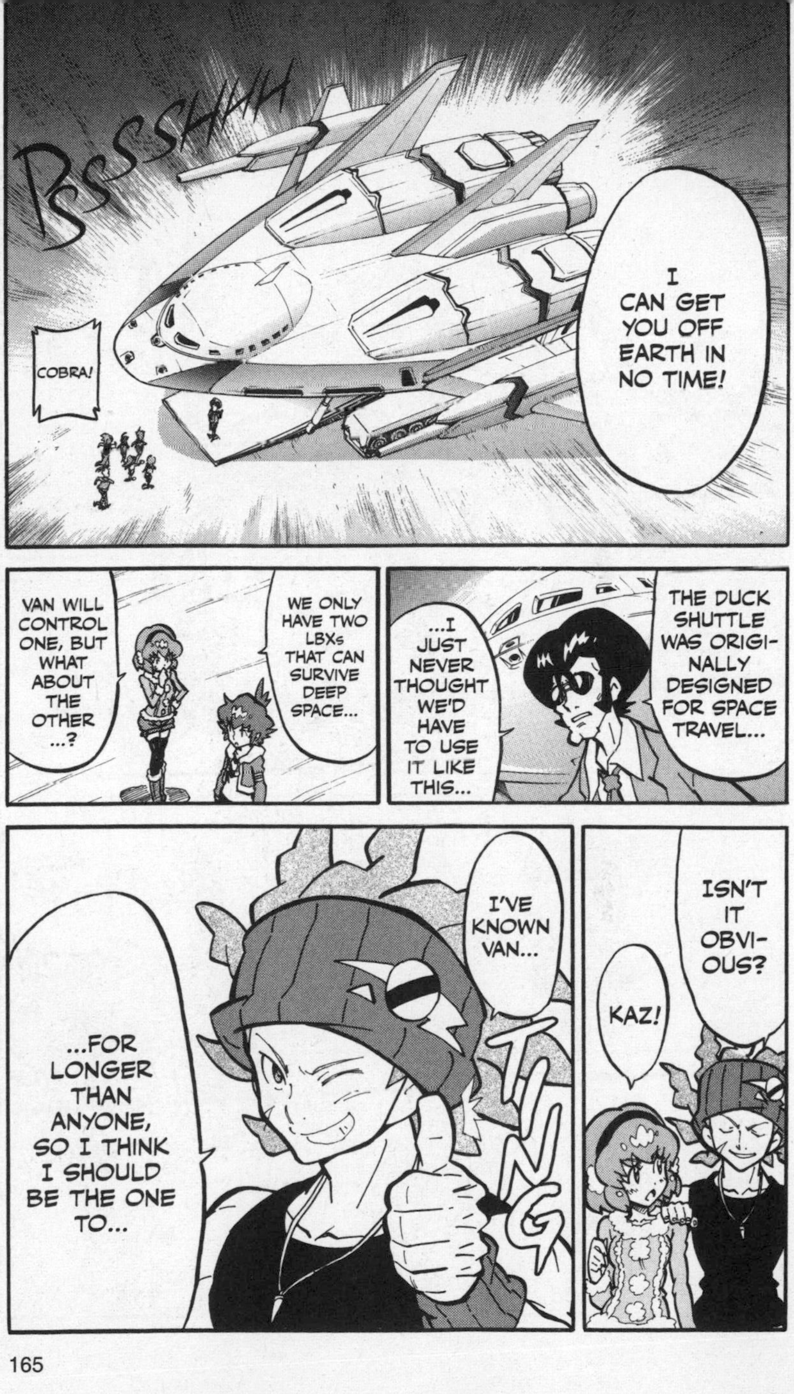
I CAN GET YOU OFF EARTH IN NO TIME!
PSSSSHHH
COBRA!
THE DUCK SHUTTLE WAS ORIGI-NALLY DESIGNED FOR SPACE TRAVEL...
...I JUST NEVER THOUGHT WE'D HAVE TO USE IT LIKE THIS...
WE ONLY HAVE TWO LBXs THAT CAN SURVIVE DEEP SPACE...
VAN WILL CONTROL ONE, BUT WHAT ABOUT THE OTHER ...?
ISN'T IT OBVI-OUS?
KAZ!
I'VE KNOWN VAN...
TING
...FOR LONGER THAN ANYONE, SO I THINK I SHOULD BE THE ONE TO...

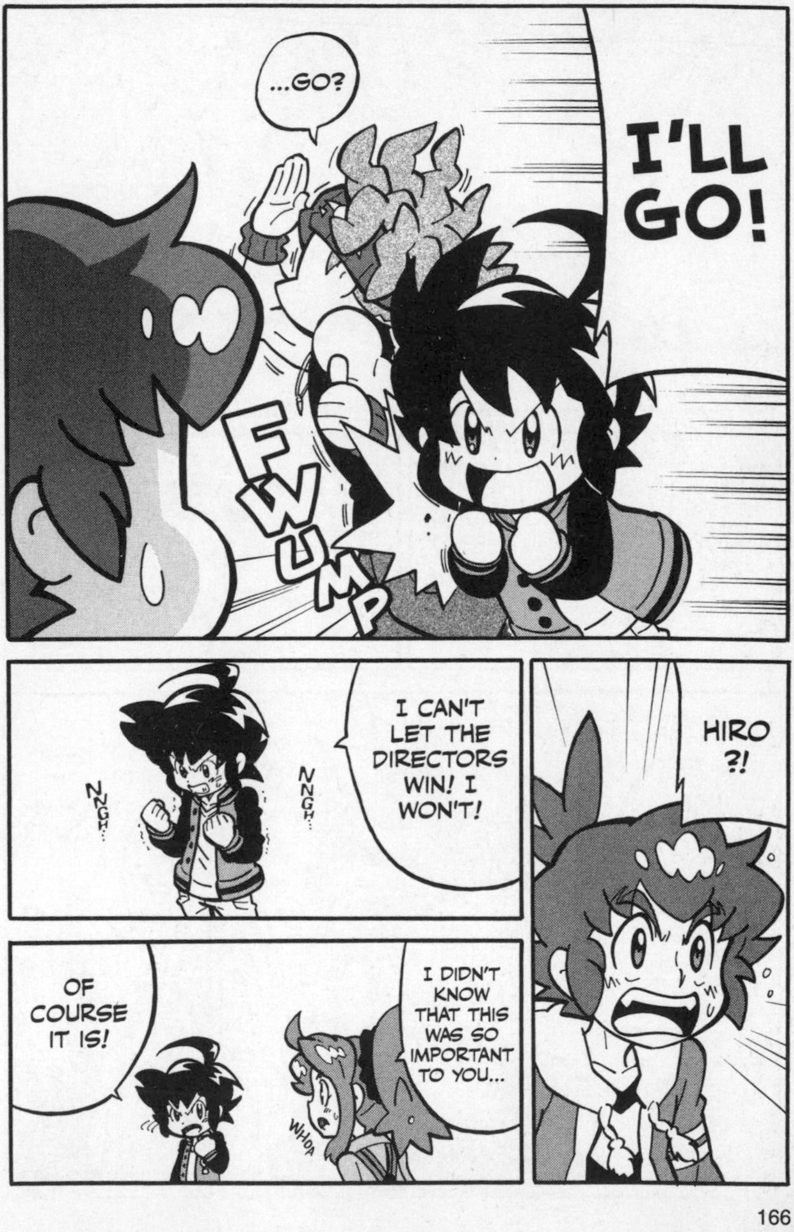
I'LL GO!
...GO?
FWUMP
HIRO ?!
I CAN'T LET THE DIRECTORS WIN! I WON'T!
NNGH...
NNGH...
I DIDN'T KNOW THAT THIS WAS SO IMPORTANT TO YOU...
WHOA
OF COURSE IT IS!

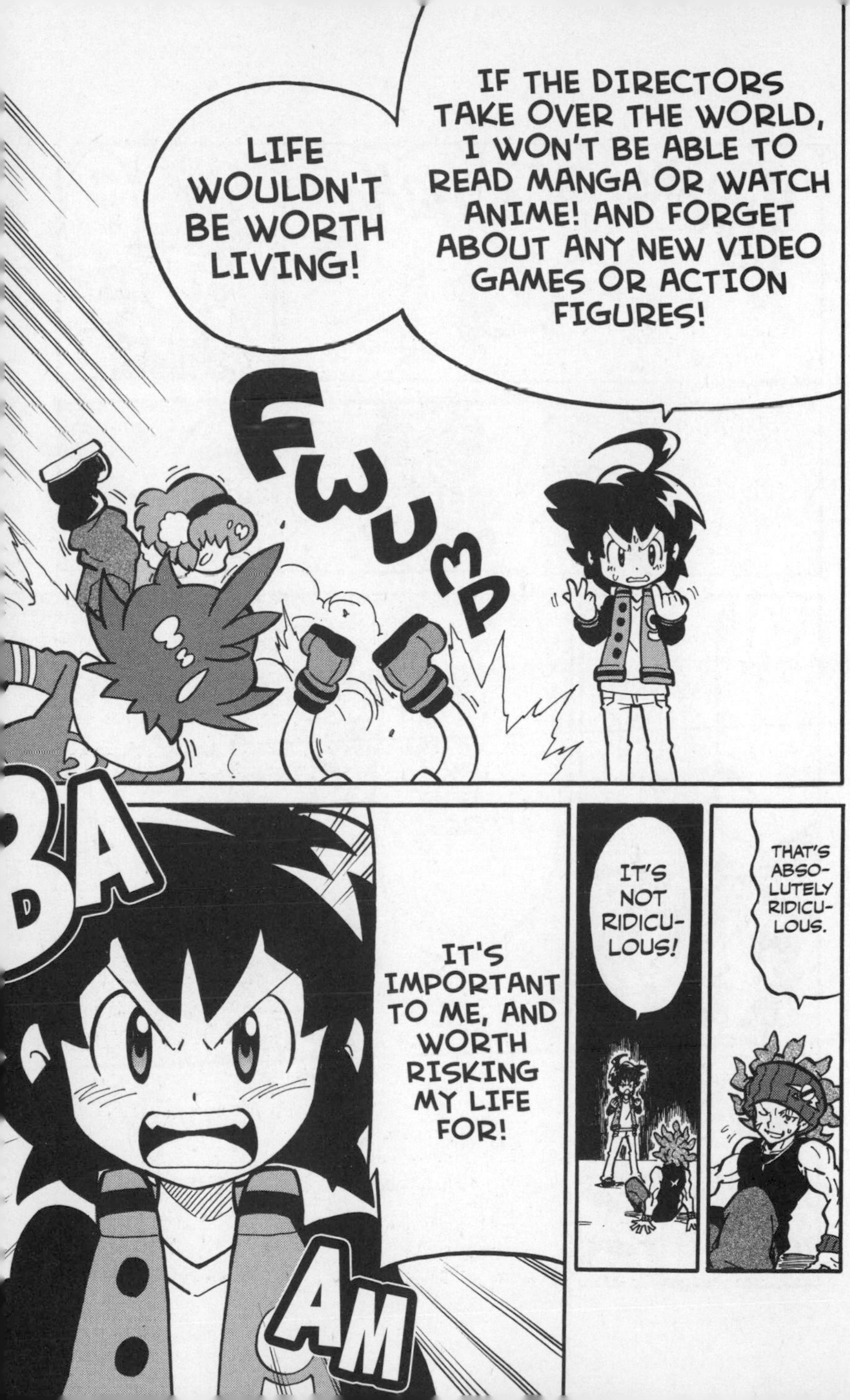
IF THE DIRECTORS TAKE OVER THE WORLD, I WON'T BE ABLE TO READ MANGA OR WATCH ANIME! AND FORGET ABOUT ANY NEW VIDEO GAMES OR ACTION FIGURES!
LIFE WOULDN'T BE WORTH LIVING!
FWUMP
THAT'S ABSO-LUTELY RIDICU-LOUS.
IT'S NOT RIDICU-LOUS!
IT'S IMPORTANT TO ME, AND WORTH RISKING MY LIFE FOR!
BAAM

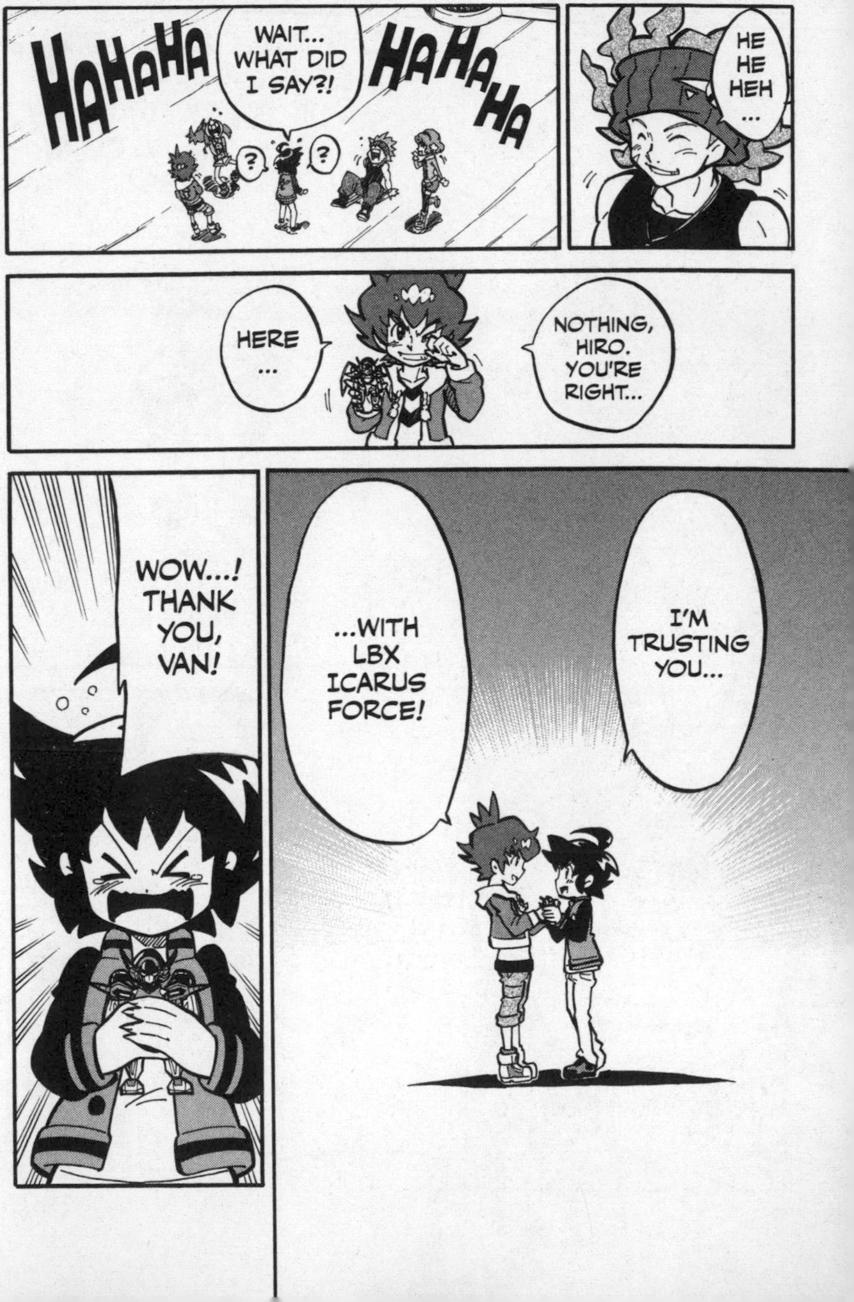
HE HE HEH ...
HAHAHA
WAIT... WHAT DID I SAY?!
HAHAHA
?
?
NOTHING, HIRO. YOU'RE RIGHT...
HERE ...
I'M TRUSTING YOU...
...WITH LBX ICARUS FORCE!
WOW...! THANK YOU, VAN!

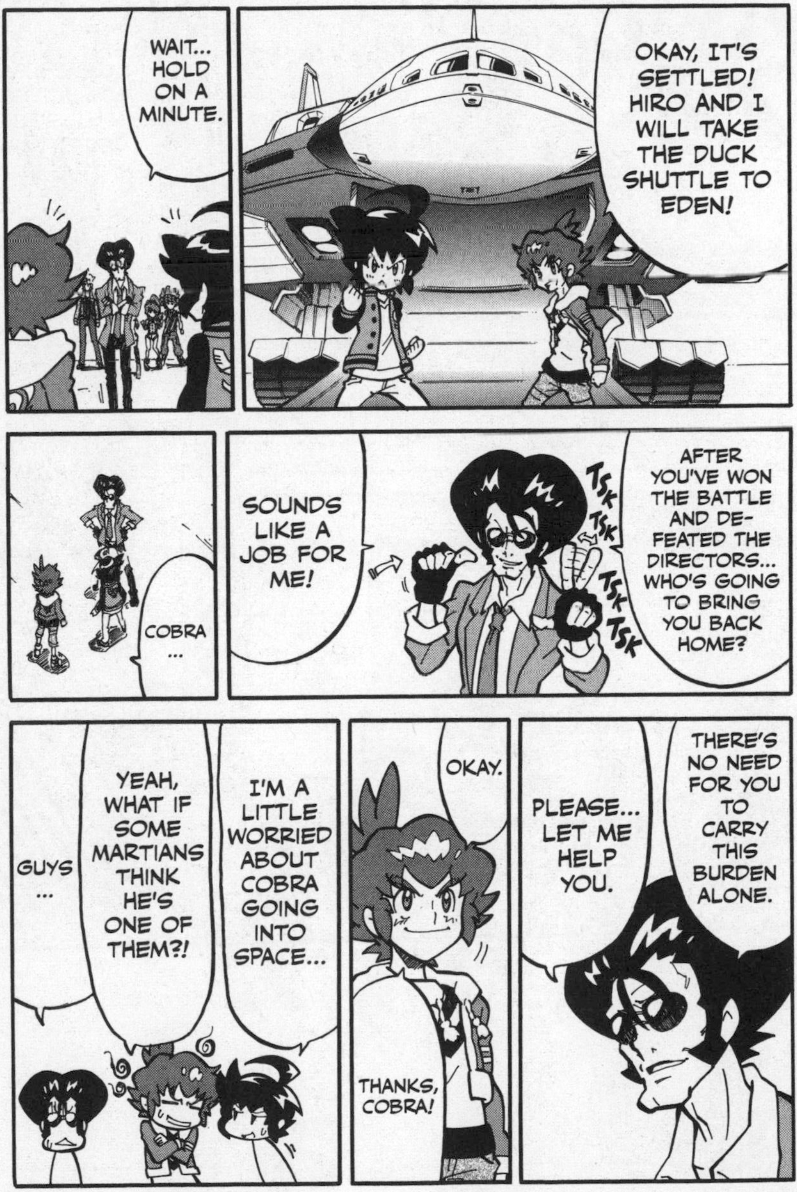
OKAY, IT'S SETTLED! HIRO AND I WILL TAKE THE DUCK SHUTTLE TO EDEN!
WAIT... HOLD ON A MINUTE.
AFTER YOU'VE WON THE BATTLE AND DE-FEATED THE DIRECTORS... WHO'S GOING TO BRING YOU BACK HOME?
TSK TSK TSK TSK
SOUNDS LIKE A JOB FOR ME!
COBRA ...
THERE'S NO NEED FOR YOU TO CARRY THIS BURDEN ALONE.
PLEASE... LET ME HELP YOU.
OKAY.
THANKS, COBRA!
I'M A LITTLE WORRIED ABOUT COBRA GOING INTO SPACE...
YEAH, WHAT IF SOME MARTIANS THINK HE'S ONE OF THEM?!
GUYS ...

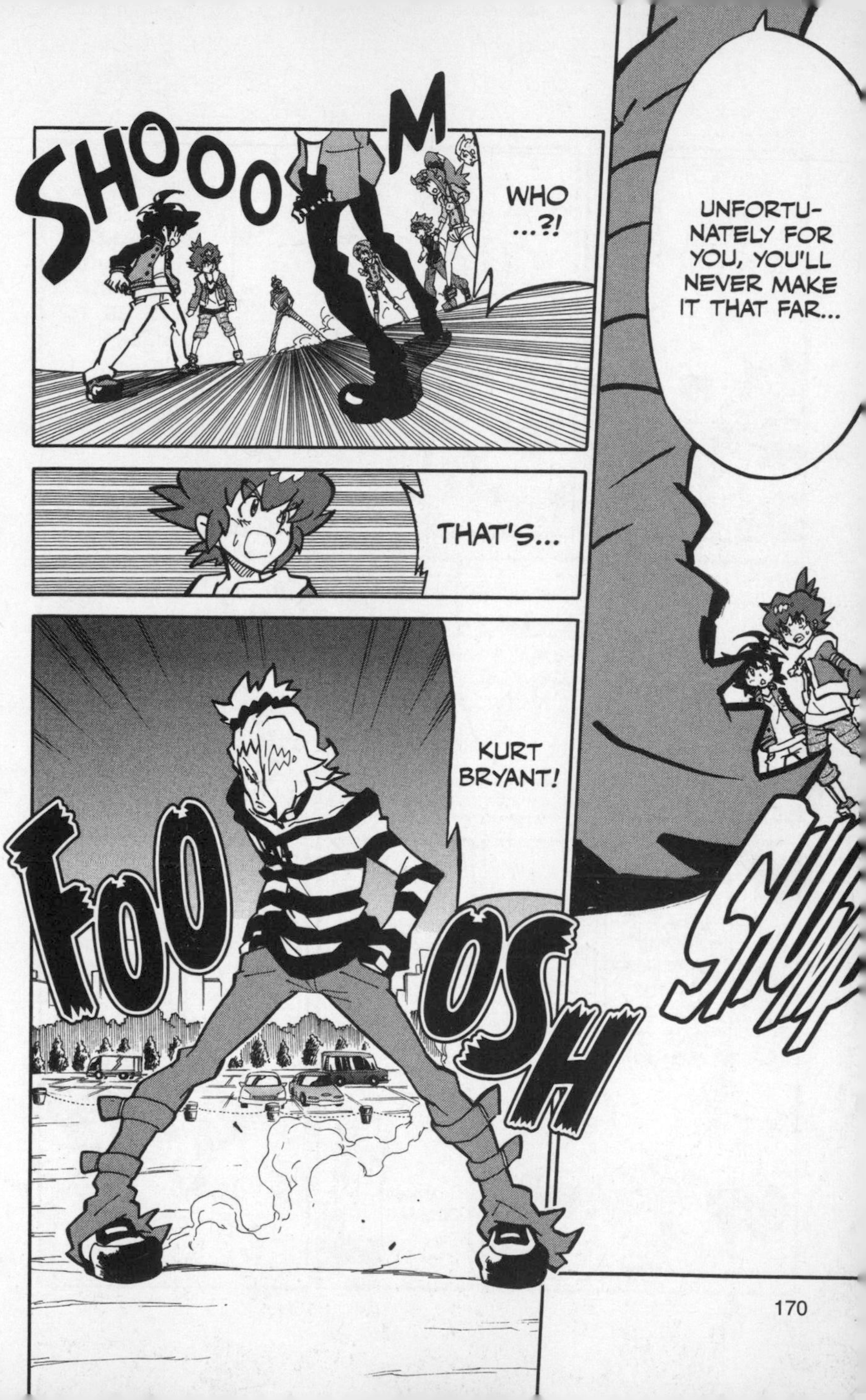
UNFORTU-NATELY FOR YOU, YOU'LL NEVER MAKE IT THAT FAR...
SHOOOM
WHO ...?!
THAT'S...
KURT BRYANT!
FOOOSH

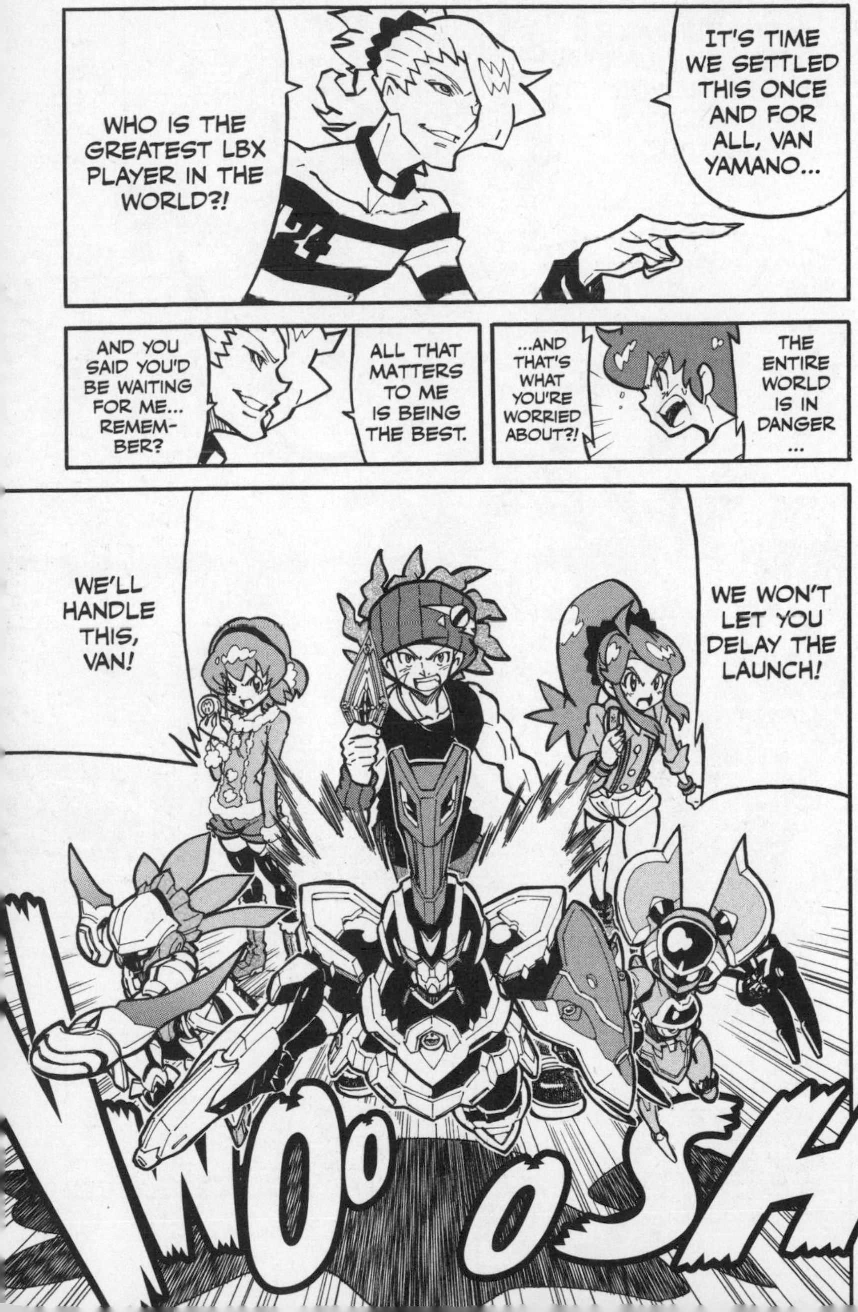
IT'S TIME WE SETTLED THIS ONCE AND FOR ALL, VAN YAMANO...
WHO IS THE GREATEST LBX PLAYER IN THE WORLD?!
THE ENTIRE WORLD IS IN DANGER...
...AND THAT'S WHAT YOU'RE WORRIED ABOUT?!
ALL THAT MATTERS TO ME IS BEING THE BEST.
AND YOU SAID YOU'D BE WAITING FOR ME... REMEMBER?
WE WON'T LET YOU DELAY THE LAUNCH!
WE'LL HANDLE THIS, VAN!
WHOOOSH

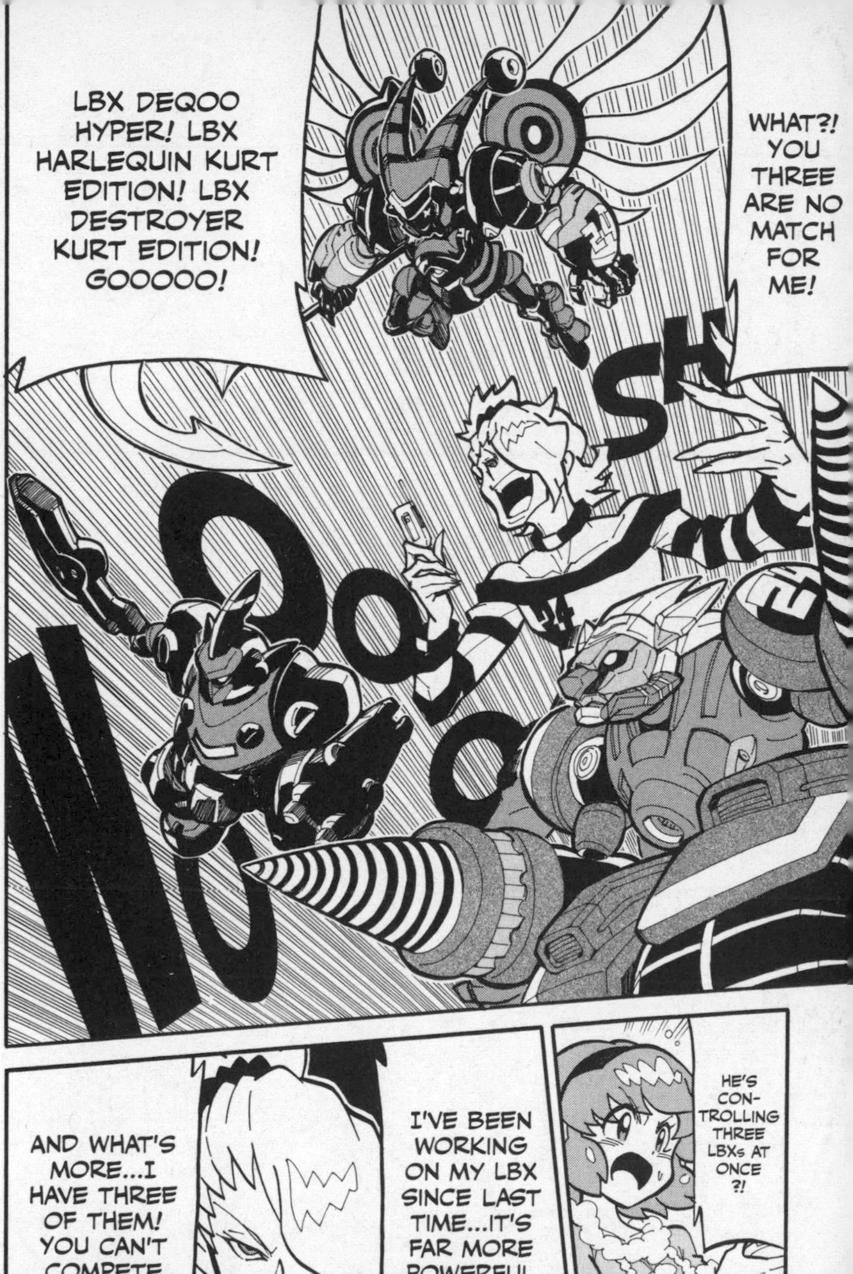
WHAT?! YOU THREE ARE NO MATCH FOR ME!
LBX DEQOO HYPER! LBX HARLEQUIN KURT EDITION! LBX DESTROYER KURT EDITION! GOOOOO!
WOOOOSH
HE'S CON-TROLLING THREE LBXs AT ONCE?!
I'VE BEEN WORKING ON MY LBX SINCE LAST TIME...IT'S FAR MORE POWERFUL THAN EVEN LBX ELYSIAN!
AND WHAT'S MORE...I HAVE THREE OF THEM! YOU CAN'T COMPETE AGAINST MY FLAWLESS TECHNIQUE!

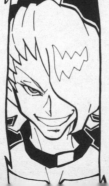

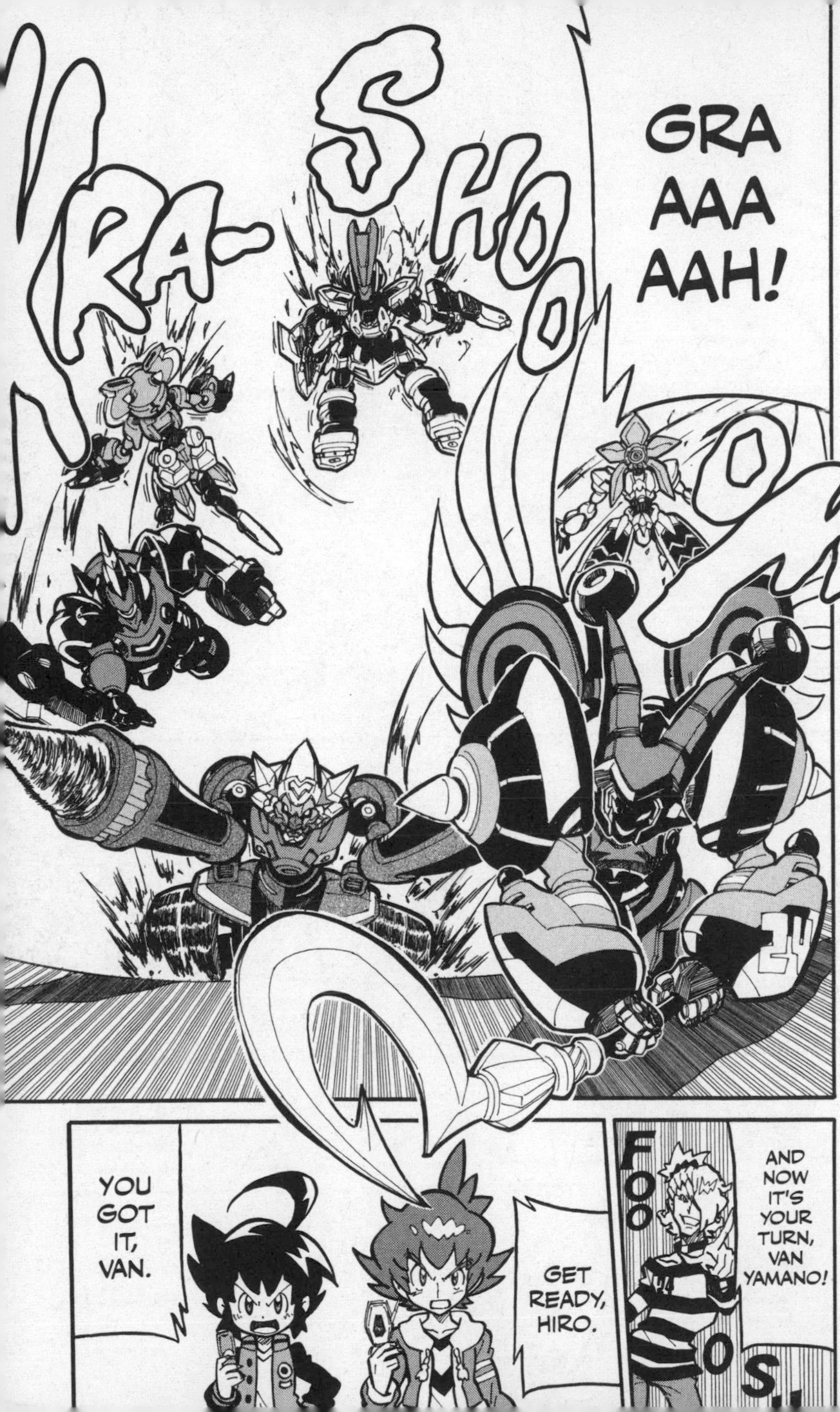
GRA AAA AAH!
KRA-SHOOOOM
AND NOW IT'S YOUR TURN, VAN YAMANO!
FOOOS...
GET READY, HIRO.
YOU GOT IT, VAN.

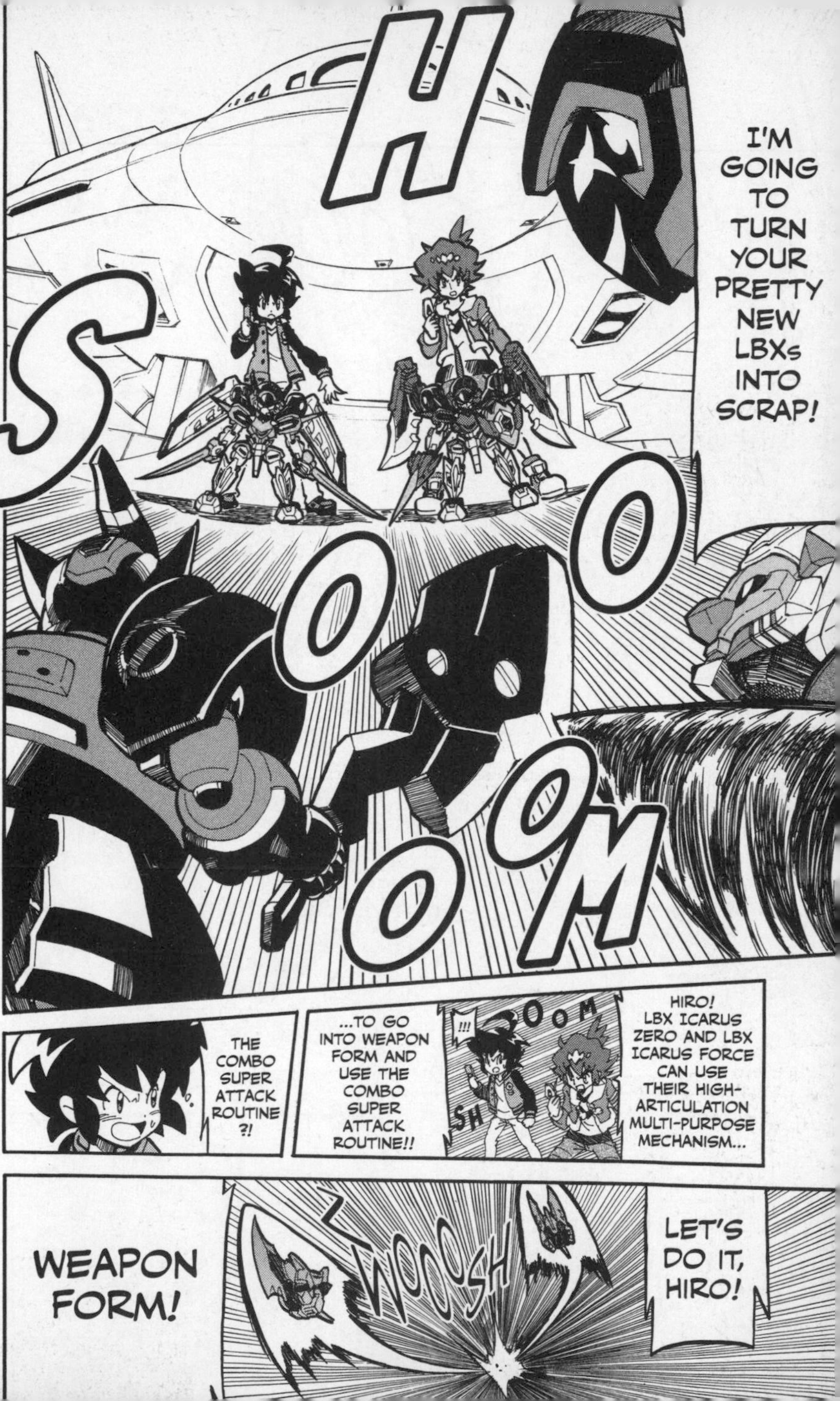
I'M GOING TO TURN YOUR PRETTY NEW LBXs INTO SCRAP!
SHOOOOOM
HIRO! LBX ICARUS ZERO AND LBX ICARUS FORCE CAN USE THEIR HIGH-ARTICULATION MULTI-PURPOSE MECHANISM...
!!!
BOOM
SH
...TO GO INTO WEAPON FORM AND USE THE COMBO SUPER ATTACK ROUTINE!!
THE COMBO SUPER ATTACK ROUTINE ?!
LET'S DO IT, HIRO!
WOOOSH
WEAPON FORM!

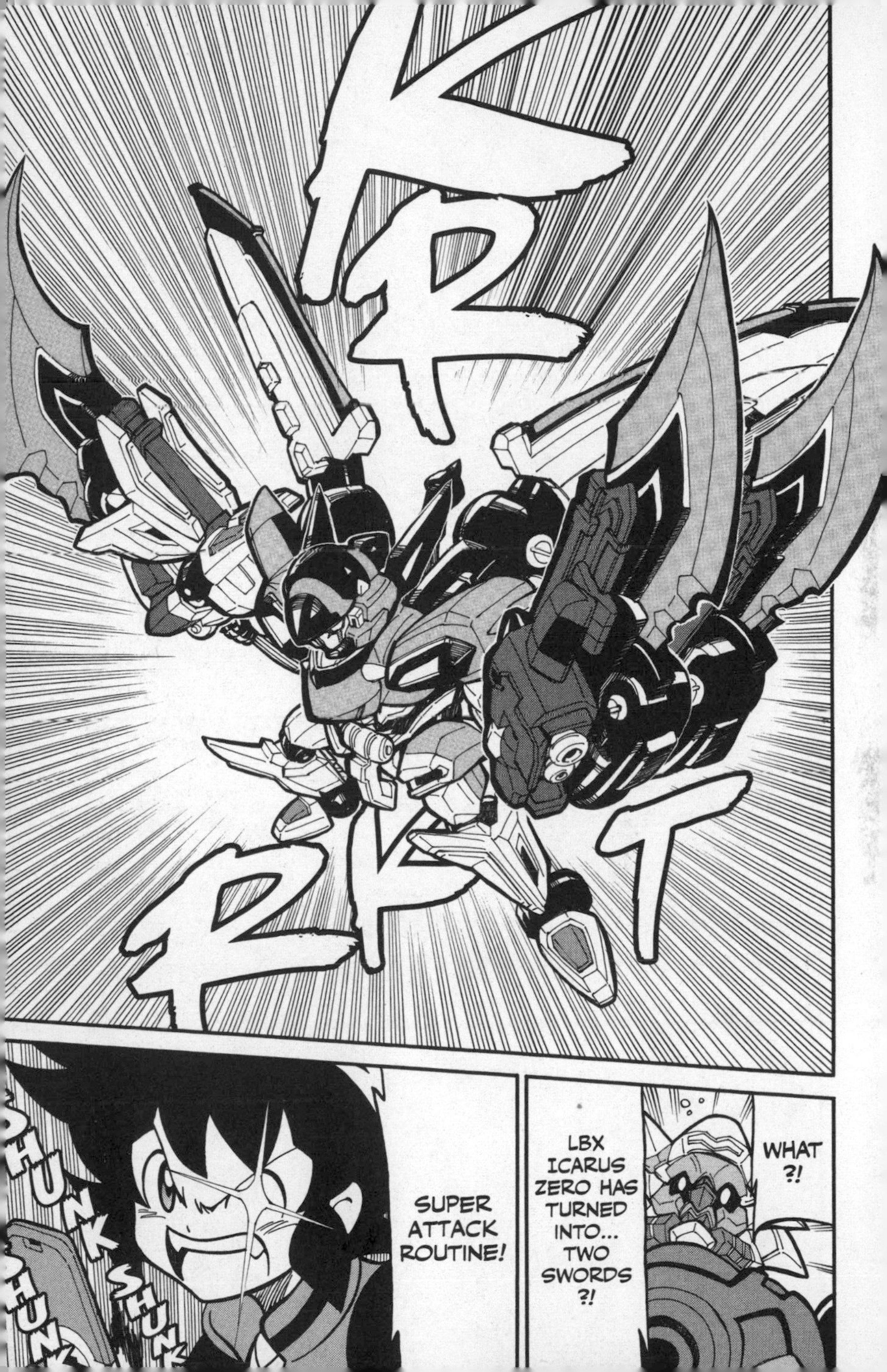
WHAT?!
LBX ICARUS ZERO HAS TURNED INTO... TWO SWORDS?!
SUPER ATTACK ROUTINE!
SHUNK
SHUNK

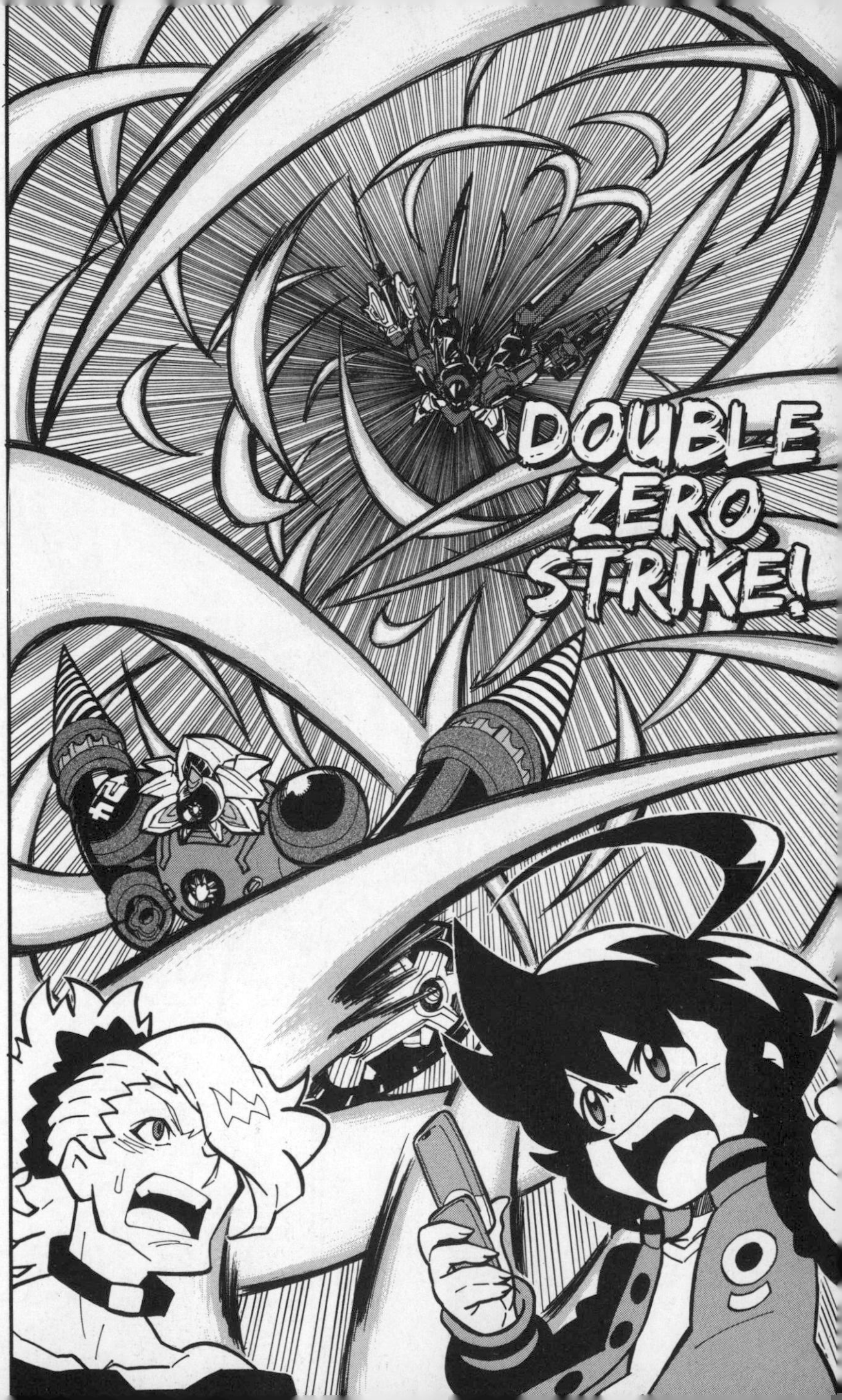
DOUBLE ZERO STRIKE!

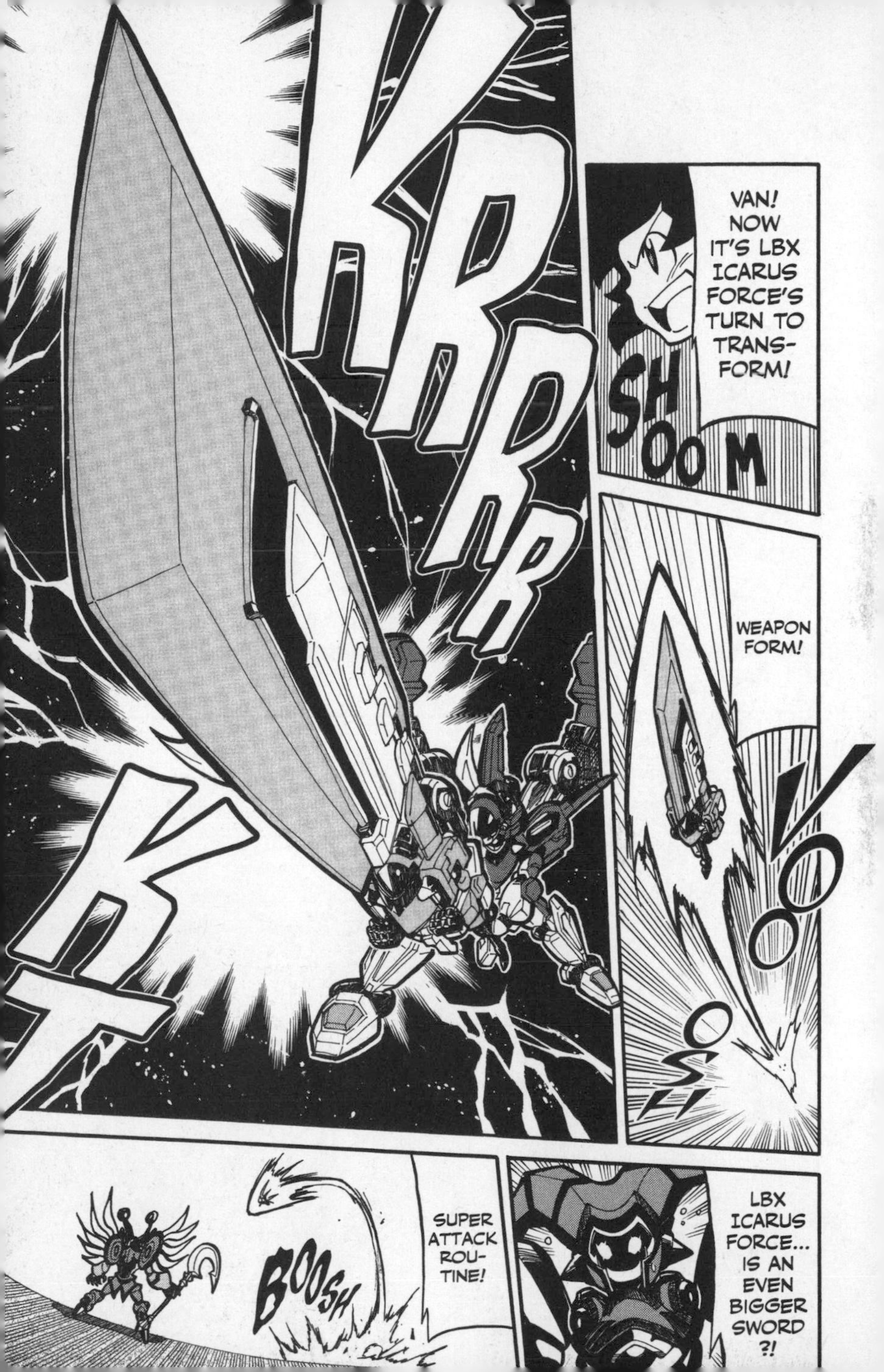
VAN! NOW IT'S LBX ICARUS FORCE'S TURN TO TRANS-FORM!
SHOOOM
WEAPON FORM!
VOOO
KRRRR
LBX ICARUS FORCE... IS AN EVEN BIGGER SWORD ?!
SUPER ATTACK ROU-TINE!
BOOSH

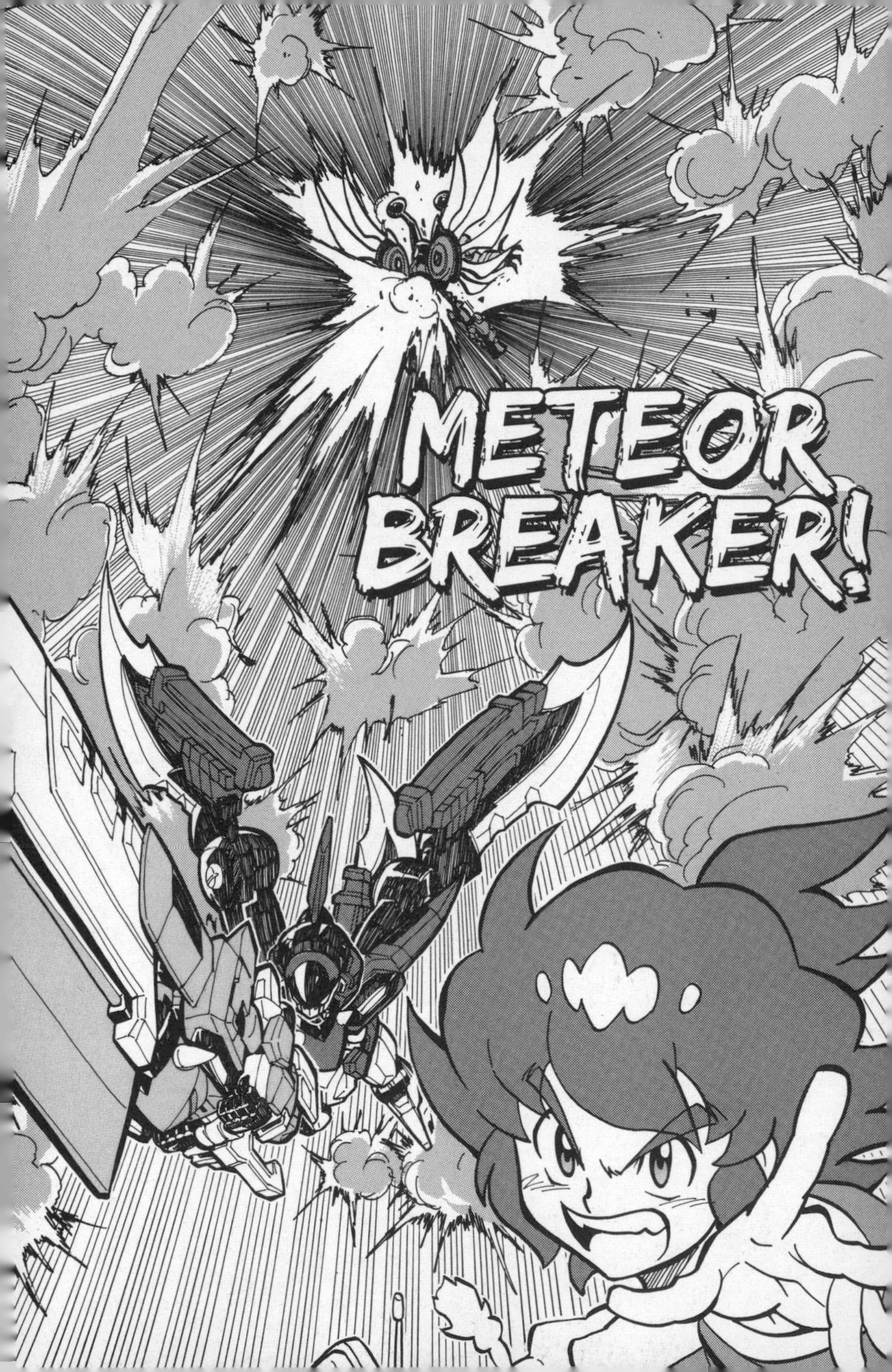
METEOR BREAKER!

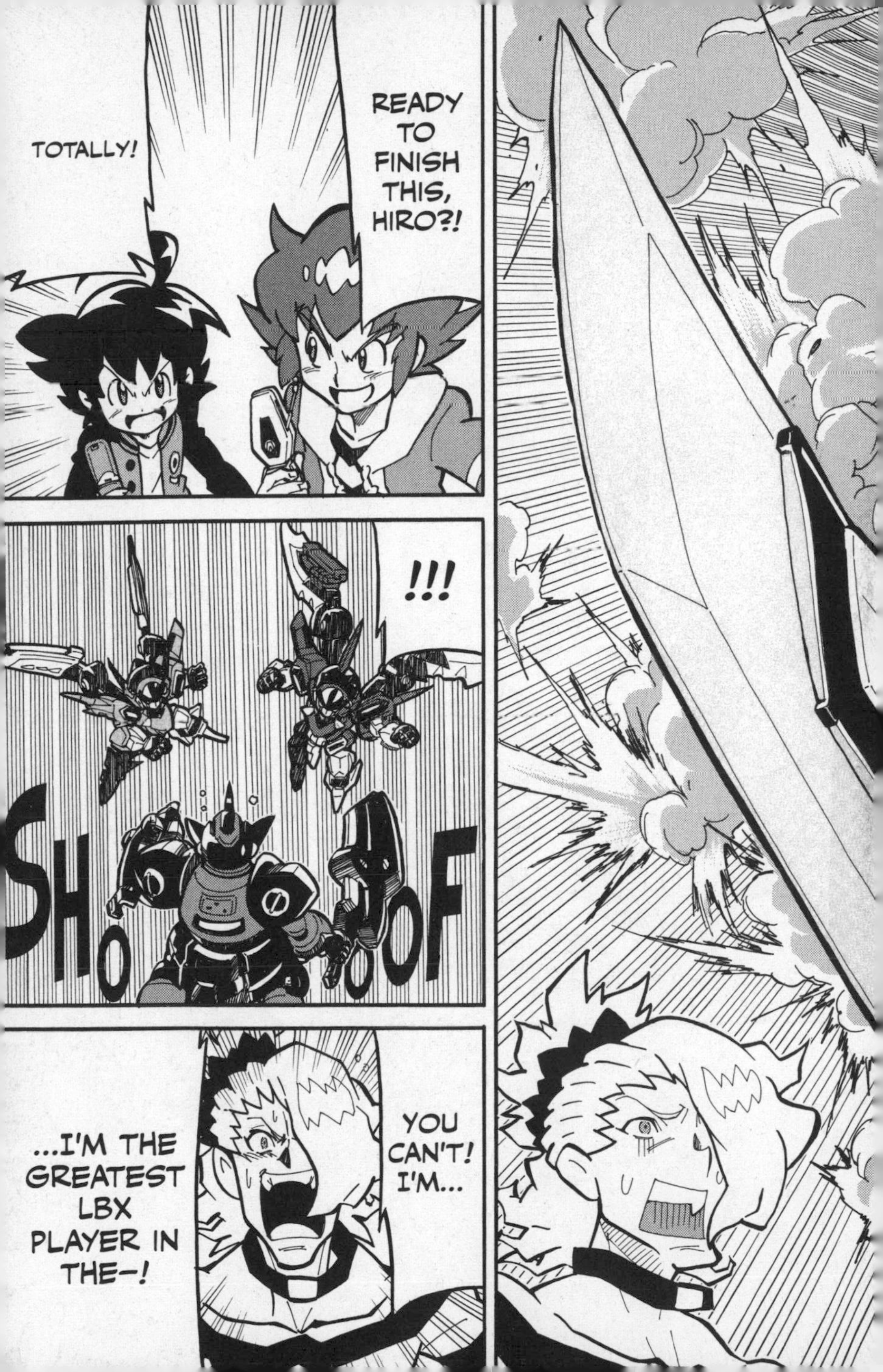
READY TO FINISH THIS, HIRO?!
TOTALLY!
!!!
SHOOOF
YOU CAN'T! I'M...
...I'M THE GREATEST LBX PLAYER IN THE-!

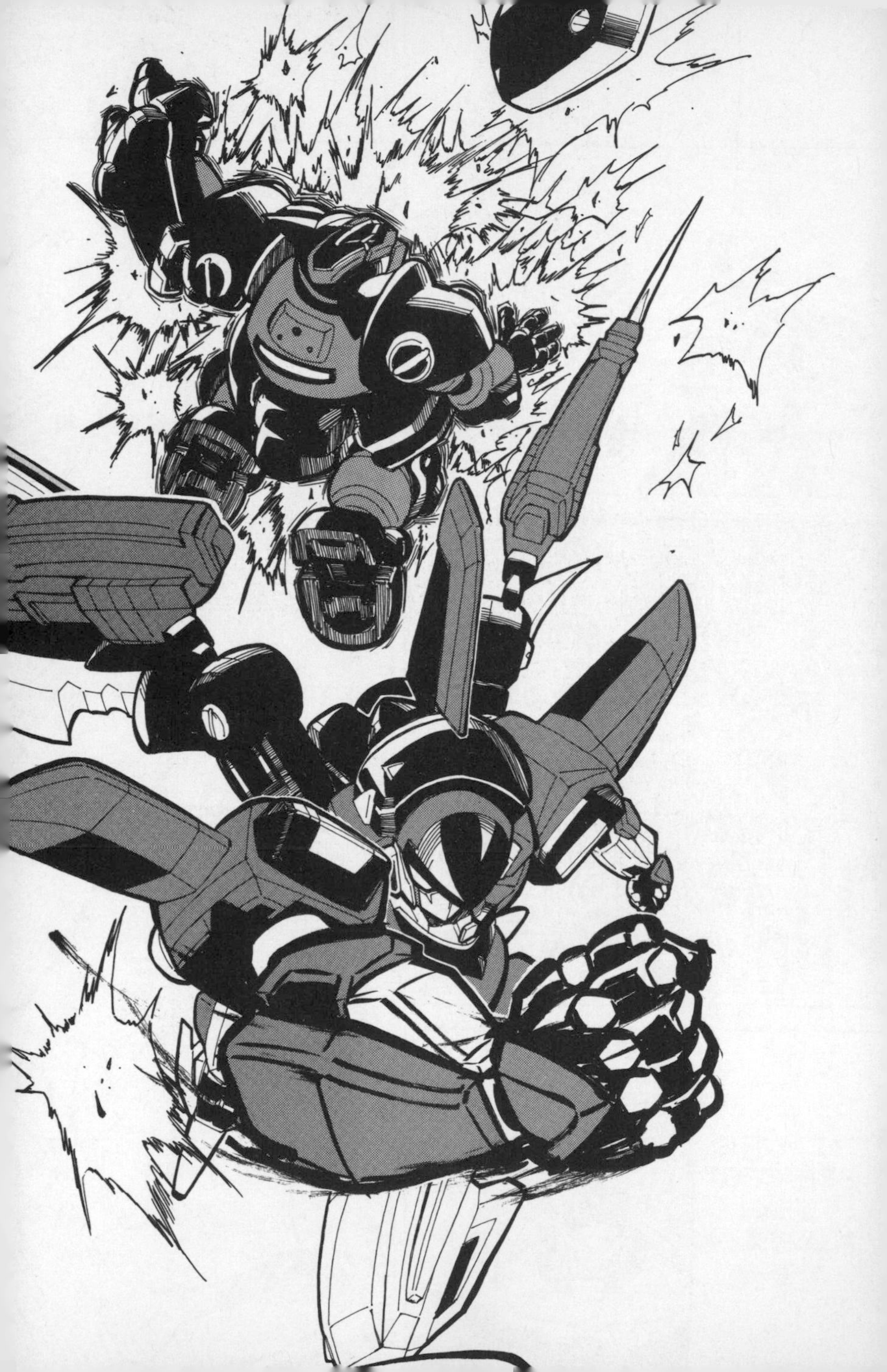

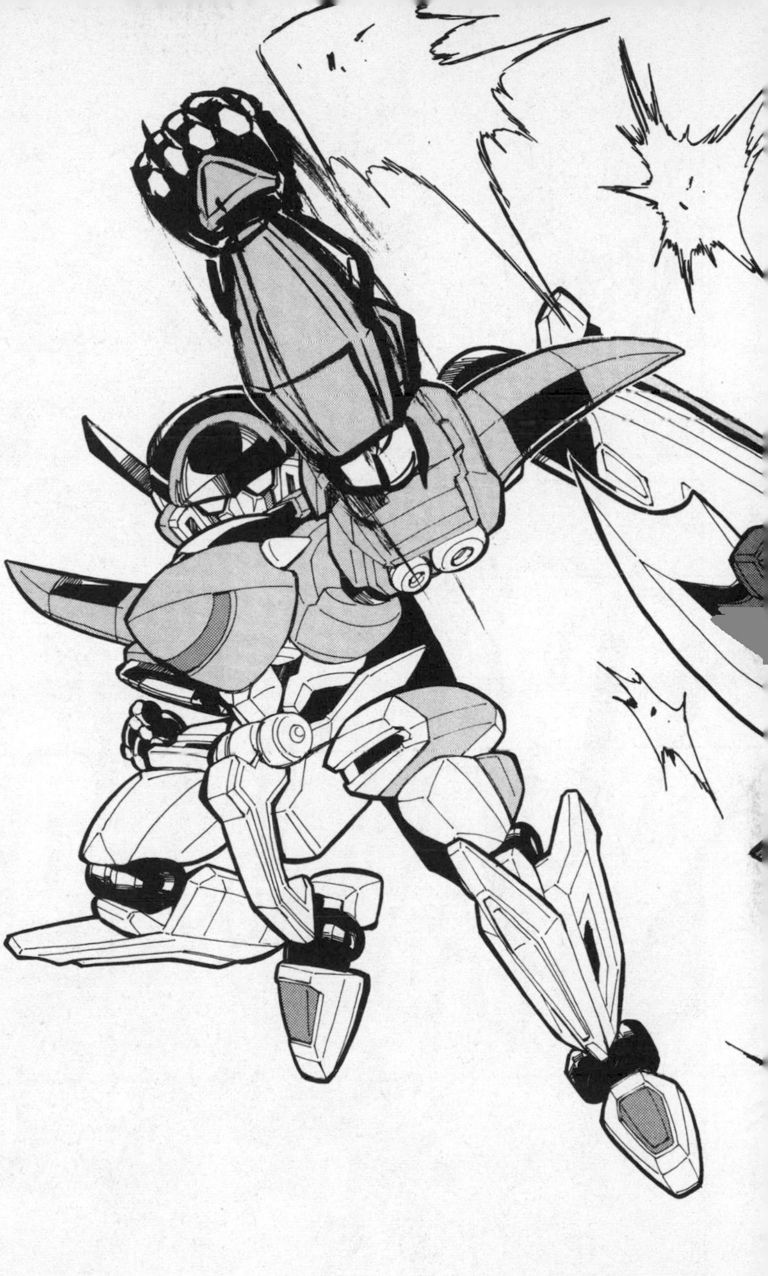

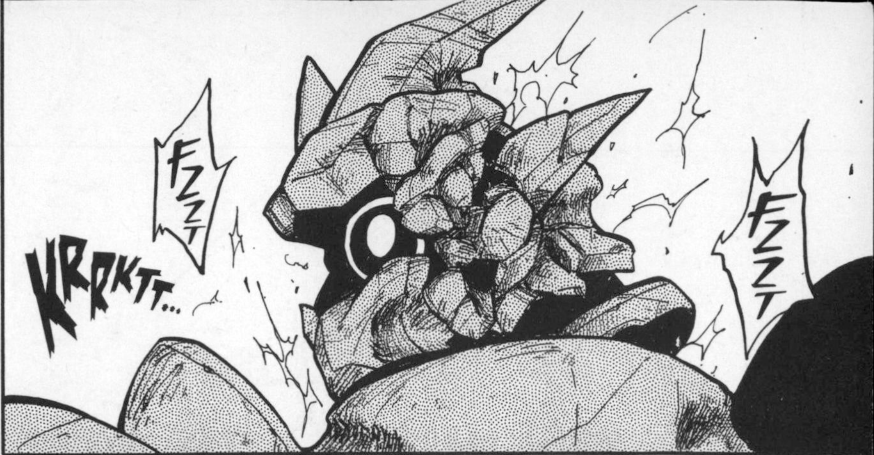
FZZZT
FZZZT
KRRKTT...
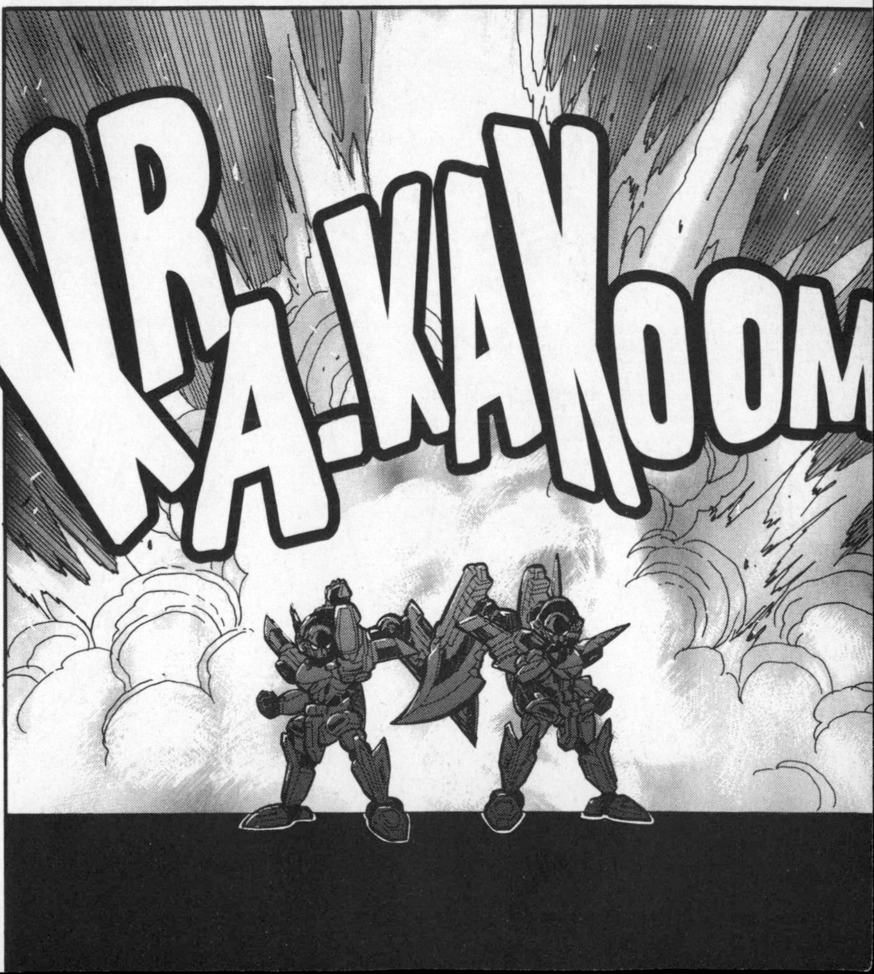
VRA-KAKOOM

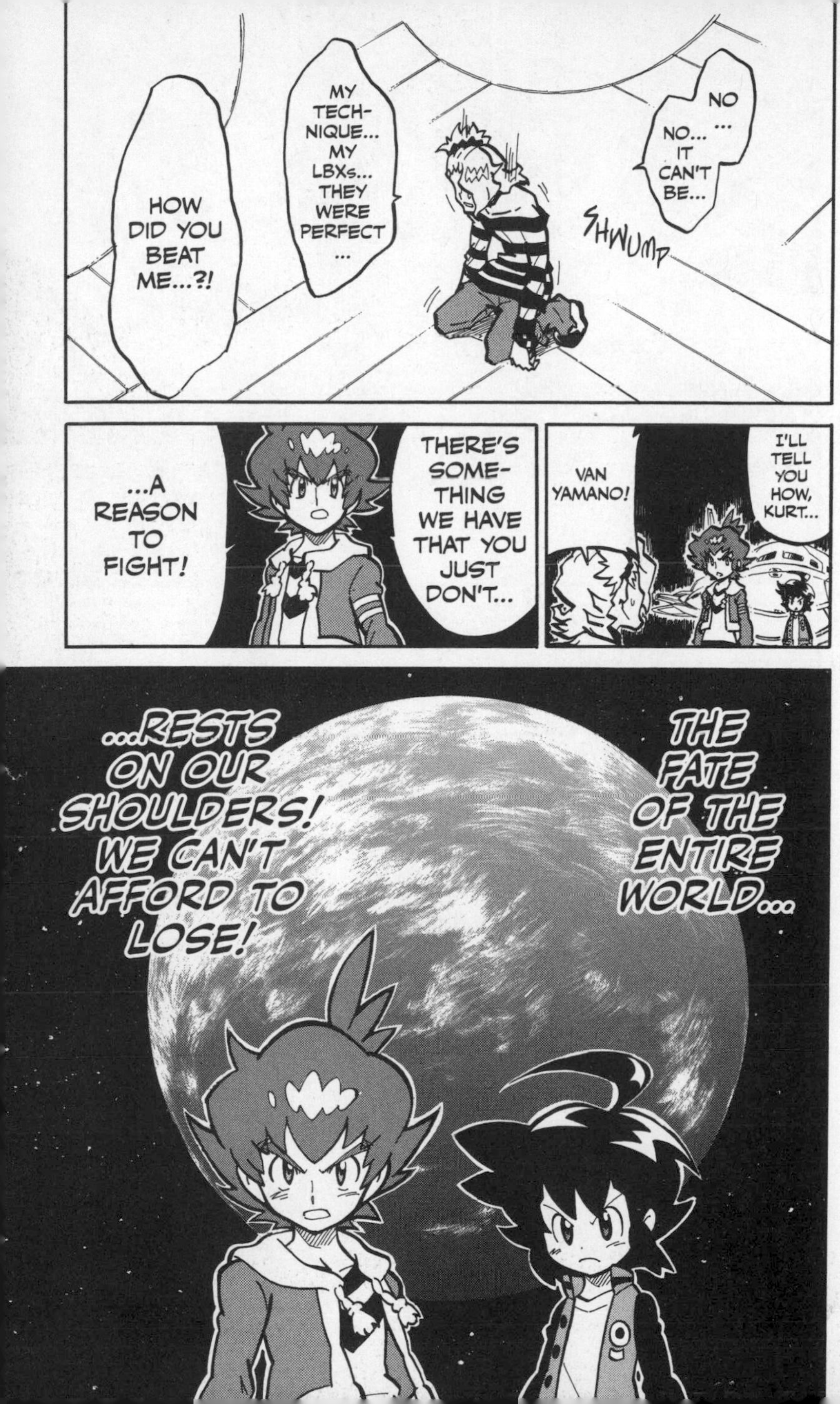
NO... NO... IT CAN'T BE...
SHWUMP
MY TECHNIQUE... MY LBXs... THEY WERE PERFECT...
HOW DID YOU BEAT ME...?!
I'LL TELL YOU HOW, KURT...
VAN YAMANO!
THERE'S SOMETHING WE HAVE THAT YOU JUST DON'T...
...A REASON TO FIGHT!
THE FATE OF THE ENTIRE WORLD...
...RESTS ON OUR SHOULDERS! WE CAN'T AFFORD TO LOSE!

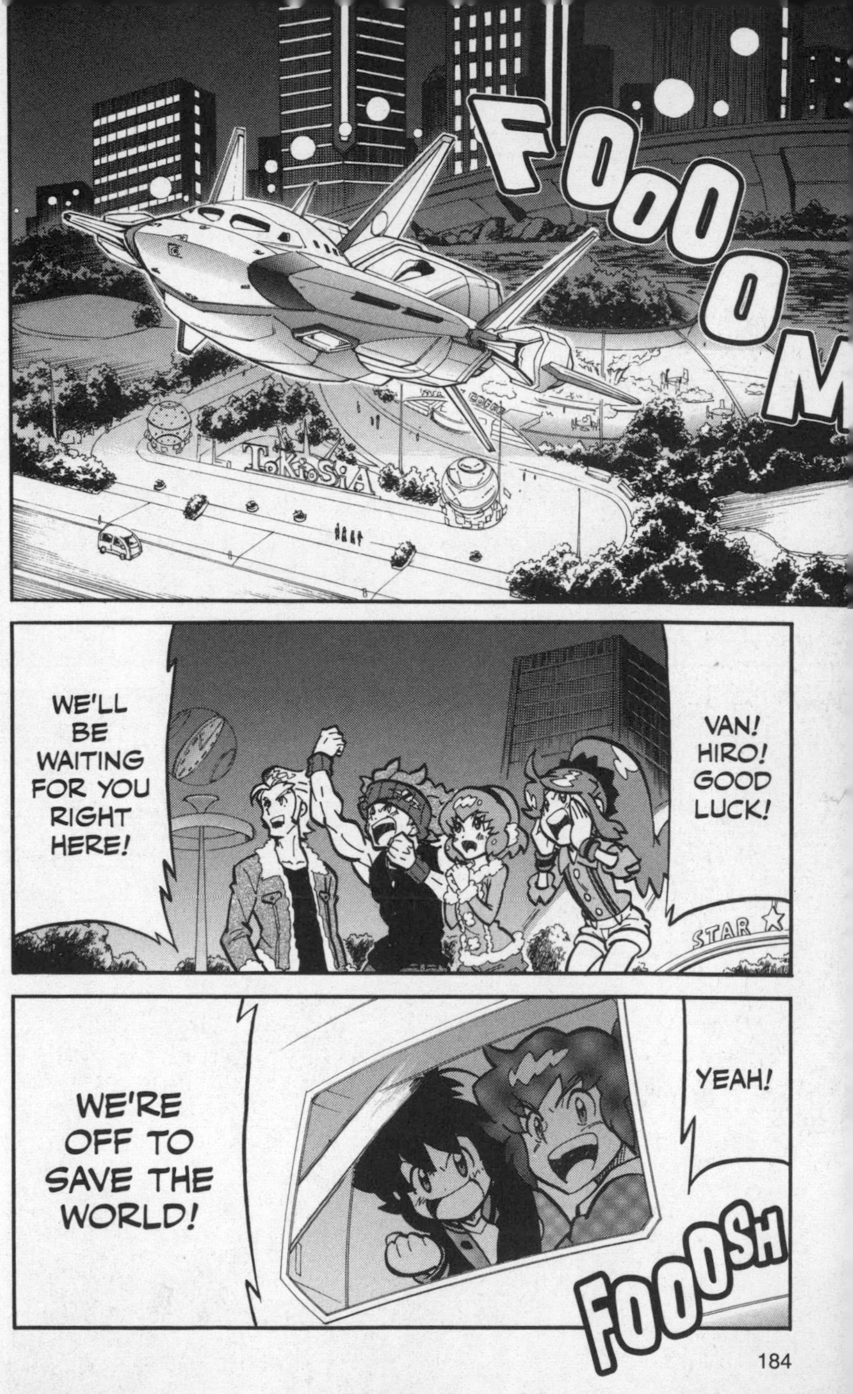
FOOOOOM
TOKIOSIA
VAN! HIRO! GOOD LUCK!
WE'LL BE WAITING FOR YOU RIGHT HERE!
STAR
YEAH!
WE'RE OFF TO SAVE THE WORLD!
FOOOSH

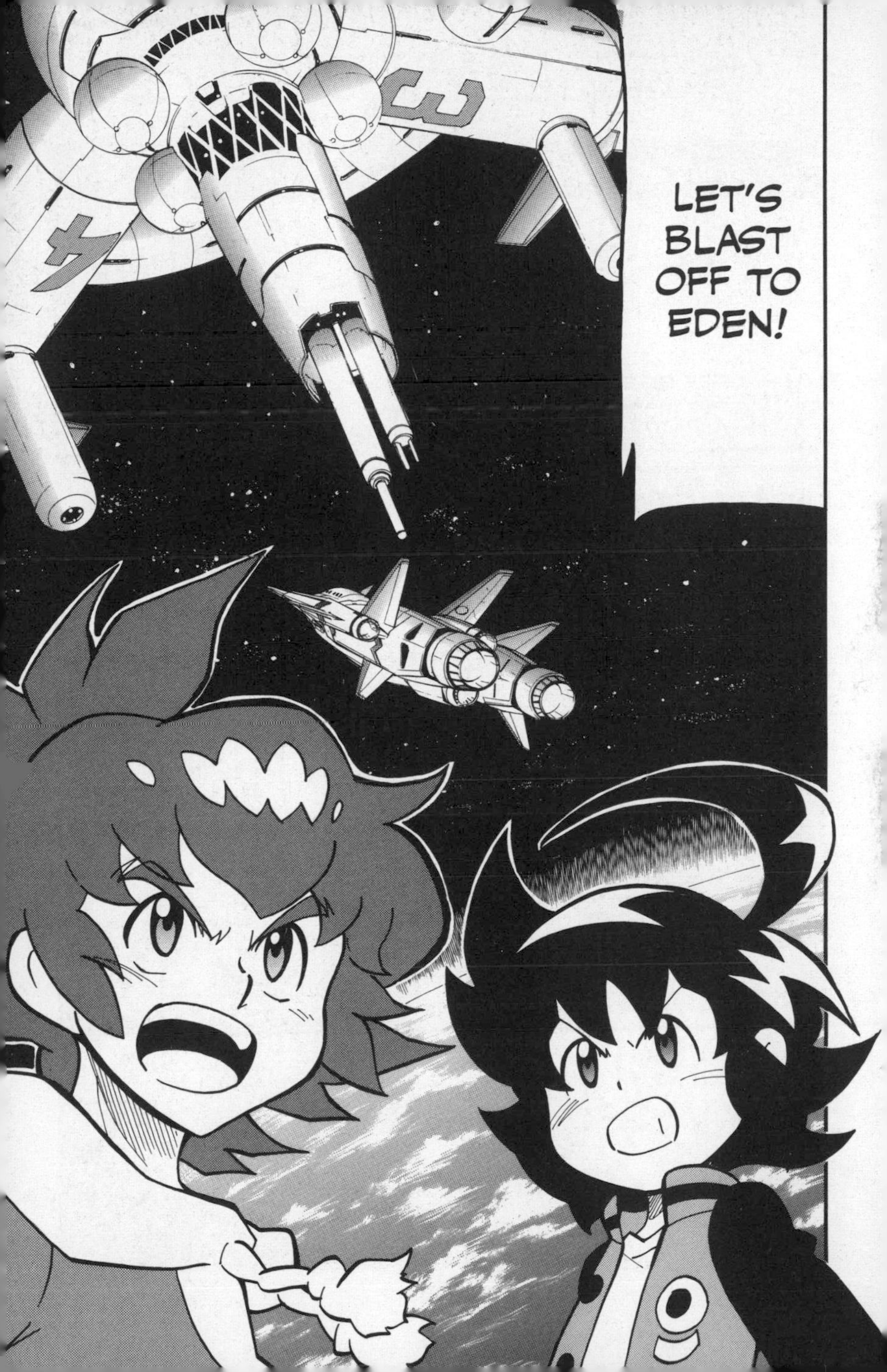
LET'S BLAST OFF TO EDEN!

EXTRA BONUS FUNNIES

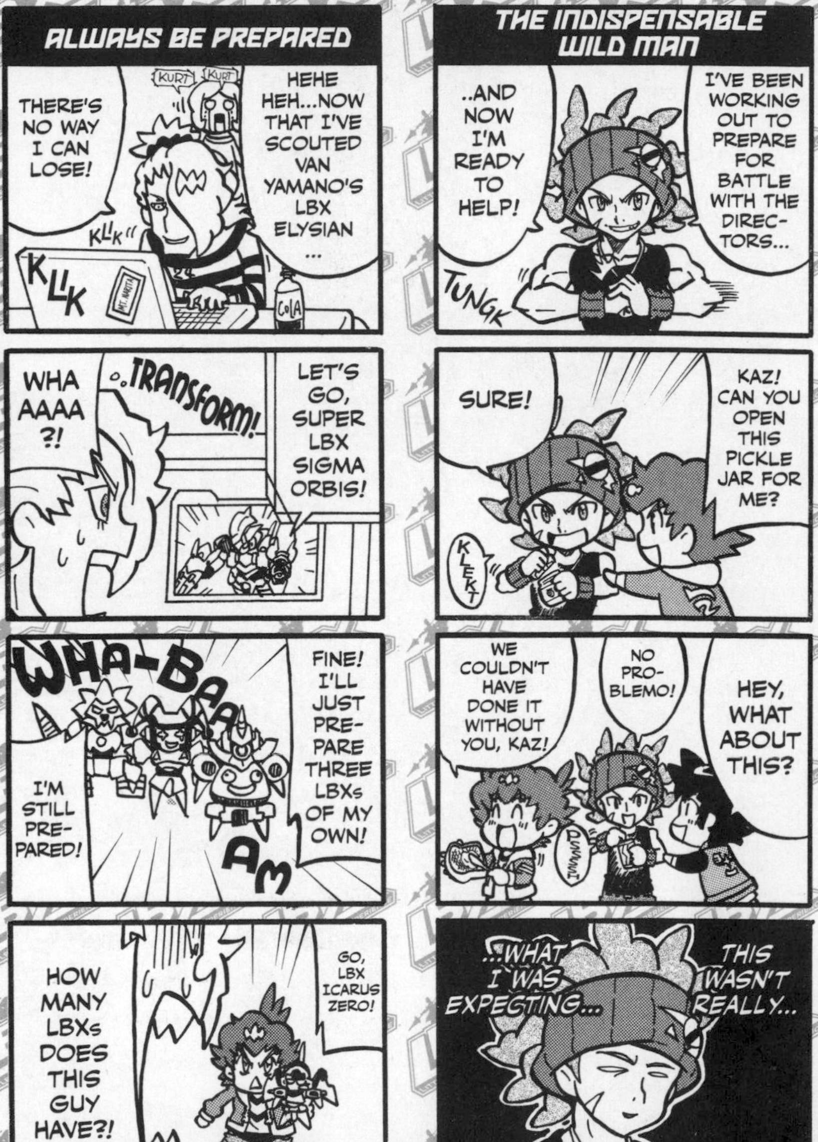
THE INDISPENSABLE WILD MAN
I'VE BEEN WORKING OUT TO PREPARE FOR BATTLE WITH THE DIRECTORS...
..AND NOW I'M READY TO HELP!
TUNGK
KAZ! CAN YOU OPEN THIS PICKLE JAR FOR ME?
SURE!
KLEKT
HEY, WHAT ABOUT THIS?
NO PRO-BLEMO!
WE COULDN'T HAVE DONE IT WITHOUT YOU, KAZ!
THIS WASN'T REALLY...
...WHAT I WAS EXPECTING...
ALWAYS BE PREPARED
KURT
KURT
HEHE HEH...NOW THAT I'VE SCOUTED VAN YAMANO'S LBX ELYSIAN ...
THERE'S NO WAY I CAN LOSE!
KLIK
KLIK
MT. NARITA
COLA
LET'S GO, SUPER LBX SIGMA ORBIS!
...TRANSFORM!
WHA AAAA ?!
FINE! I'LL JUST PRE-PARE THREE LBXs OF MY OWN!
WHA-BAAAAM
I'M STILL PRE-PARED!
GO, LBX ICARUS ZERO!
HOW MANY LBXs DOES THIS GUY HAVE?!

THE THREAT OF THE DIRECTORS IS GROWING EVER SO LARGE! YOU MUSTN'T LET THEM TAKE OVER THE WORLD! VAN! HIRO! STOP THE DESPAIR WITH YOUR **NEW LBX, ICARUS ZERO** AND **ICARUS FORCE**!! NOW, BATTLE START!!!

◆ Hideaki Fujii ◆

Hideaki Fujii was born on December 12, 1977, in Miyazaki Prefecture. He made his debut in 2000 with *Shin Megami Tensei: Devil Children* (*Monthly Comic BomBom*). His signature works include *Battle Spirits: Breakthrough Boy Bashin* and many others. Blood type A.

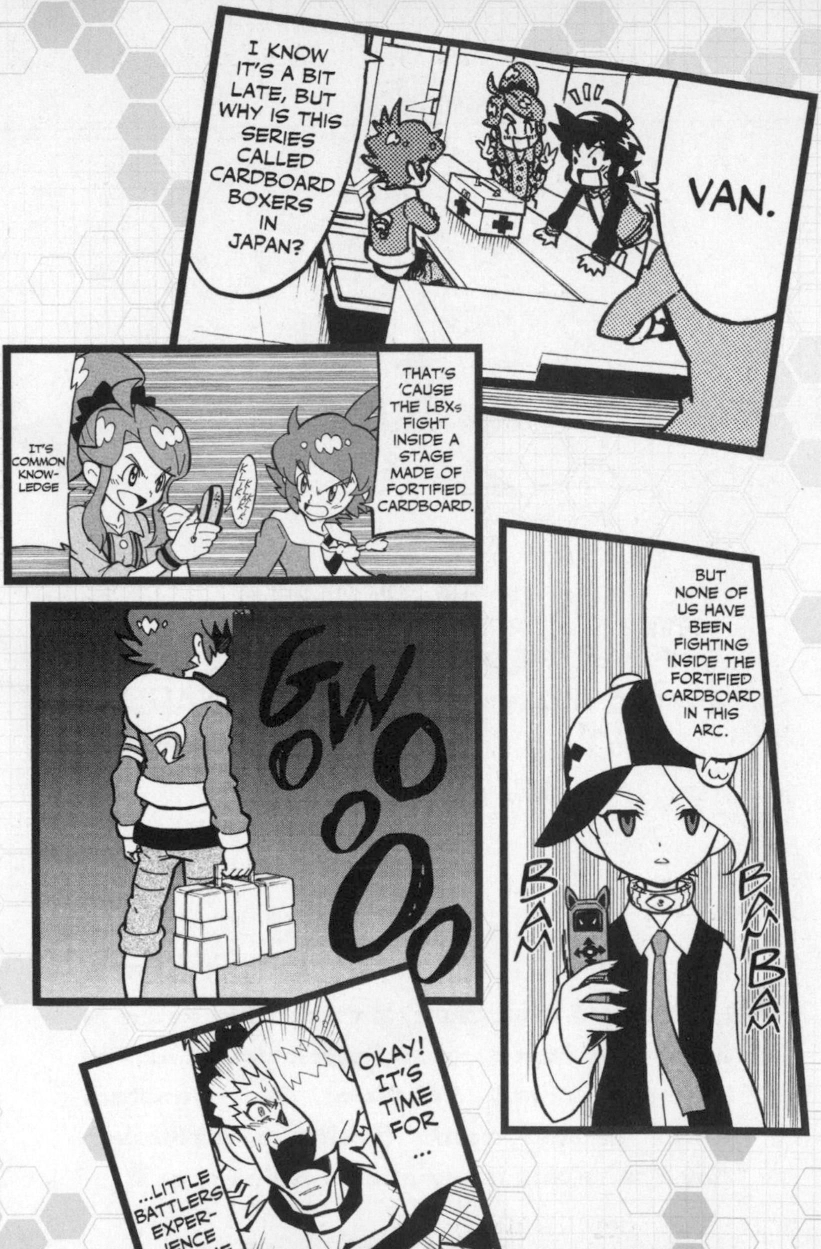
VAN.
I KNOW IT'S A BIT LATE, BUT WHY IS THIS SERIES CALLED CARDBOARD BOXERS IN JAPAN?
THAT'S 'CAUSE THE LBXs FIGHT INSIDE A STAGE MADE OF FORTIFIED CARDBOARD.
KLAK KLAK
IT'S COMMON KNOW-LEDGE
BUT NONE OF US HAVE BEEN FIGHTING INSIDE THE FORTIFIED CARDBOARD IN THIS ARC.
BAM
BAM BAM
GWOOOOOO
OKAY! IT'S TIME FOR...
...LITTLE BATTLERS EXPER-IENCE VOLUME 5 TO START!!!

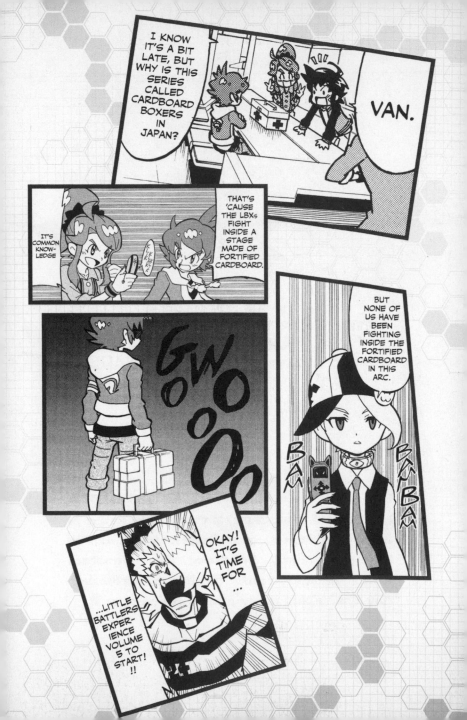